HEA

His Town.
Her God.
Let the Battle Begin.

# A LADY IN DEFIANCE

## ROMANCE IN THE ROCKIES: BOOK ONE

# *A Lady in Defiance*
## *Romance in the Rockies*
## *Book One*
# By Heather Frey Blanton
# Published by
# Rivulet Publishing
# Print Edition

Copyright 2012-2014

Heather Blanton

*A man's heart deviseth his way:
but the LORD directeth his steps.
Proverb 16:9*

# _Foreword—_

They say truth is stranger than fiction. I prefer to say that truth is more miraculous. What we as authors can make up in our own heads doesn't compare to what the greatest writer of all can do. Take for example the story that inspires my character of Hannah:

In the early 70's my family used to drive up from Florida to camp in the mountains. In the summer of '73, we discovered a beautiful, sleepy, small town in Western North Carolina. My sister also discovered a boy there; her soul mate, really, but who would have believed that? The following summer we moved from Florida to this town and, not long after, my sister Suzy announced she was pregnant . . . at the tender age of 15.

I cannot repeat the things my mother said to my sister. Sadly, while my sister forgave her years later, I don't think my mother ever forgave herself. Certainly, my father and most of the locals weren't much kinder. Florida trash. Floozy. Slut...you name it, they said it. I can still hear my mom's high-pitched, screechy voice as she screamed hysterically at Suzy.

My sister was pushed by both families to have an abortion and she agreed. How could she refuse? After all, it was pretty clear this would "ruin her life," and there was "no future for an unwed mother," especially since she would "never claw her way out of poverty." With prophecies like that, abortion was a godsend. In the doctor's office, however, Suzy changed her mind and said she couldn't go through with it. The phone rang and it was the father of the child; he didn't want Suzy to go through with it, either, but he still wouldn't marry her.

Suzy went, instead, to a half-way house in Alexandria, Virginia to have the baby and give him up for adoption. A month before she was due to deliver, the father of the baby finally stood up to his father and told him he loved Suzy and was going to Virginia to get her. Suzy told me years later that this boy had asked her to marry him much earlier . . . on their first date! They were simply meant to be.

The two teenagers were married and God's plan unfolded for their lives. She and her husband gave their hearts to the Lord and went on to have two more children. Suzy matured into a mighty, spirit-filled woman of God, finished her GED, earned a degree as an R.N., and became a licensed minister in the Church of God, all while raising children and helping her husband farm. She was a popular speaker at women's conferences, went on mission trips and also worked as a Hospice nurse for over two years. During that time, Suzy led many people to the Lord, literally some from their death beds.

No one who met my sister was immune to her infectious smile, vivacious personality, gentle faith, and graceful ways. The love of Christ literally shined from this woman like a beacon on a hill.

When breast cancer claimed Suzy in 1999, over 800 people attended her funeral. In a town that twenty-five years earlier had spurned her, affection poured out. The funeral was standing-room only; former patients wrote good-byes in the local newspaper; people we hadn't seen in years called with condolences. And the "unwanted" baby that was almost aborted grew into a man who now pastors a church in that same small town.

Suzy is not only the inspiration behind my character of Hannah, but her story is the reason I know God can take the most grim, hopeless situation and show us the beauty in it. Profound, miraculous happy endings are possible when we "let go and let God."

If you are the mother of a pregnant teenage daughter, I pray you will think before you speak and then speak with love. If you are the daughter, please don't abort that baby. Give God a chance to do what he does best—bring beauty from ashes. He loves you; he loves that child you're carrying. Trust Him to work it out.

~~~

# _Prologue—_

Naomi anxiously watched her husband from her seat in the wagon. John leaned forward in the saddle. Stroking Sampson's neck, he assessed the narrow road before them. Little more than a rutted mule trail, it sliced unevenly across a steep, treeless, mountainside. The high bank along the left battled to hold back crumbling, jagged rocks while the right side of the road stalked the edge of a stark, breath-taking cliff. The edge plummeted several hundred feet to the ground below and then rolled into a wide, yawning valley surrounded by towering, snow-tipped mountains.

Truly a magnificent view, but the cliff sent an icy fear slithering up Naomi's spine. The road was barely wide enough for a wagon; the wheels would be mere inches away from...nothing. What would they do if something went wrong? There was no room for maneuvering. She knew by John's hesitation that he was thinking the same thing.

He turned and looked back at Naomi and her sisters perched together on the Conestoga, a deep V etching his brow. She tried a brave smile but realized she was choking the reins so tightly her nails were gouging into her palms. Perhaps reading her true feelings, John quickly traded the worried expression for a mischievous smirk.

"You're not scared are you, Wild Cat? After all," grinning devilishly, he tilted his hat back and shot her a cocky wink, "you're a better driver than most men I know."

While she appreciated his attempt to encourage her, today his playful banter couldn't ease her mind. She _really_ didn't want to make this crossing, but decided to keep her fears to herself so as not to alarm Rebecca and Hannah. By the looks of them, clutching each other's hands and staring at the ledge with wide eyes, they were scared enough already.

"Would you rather I take the wagon across?" John asked more seriously as a breeze rustled through his shaggy blonde hair.

She bit her lip and pondered the request. Most likely everything would be fine. It was only five hundred yards or so. Surely they could make it across without any trouble. She gazed out at the valley and caught sight of a lone hawk drifting on the wind, peaceful and content. She took it as a good sign. "No, I can do this. I'm sure it'll be fine."

She finished the sentence with a glance at her sisters, needing their confirmation.

Rebecca nodded. "As long as we don't look down."

Apprehension glittered in her eyes. Hannah nodded, though her gaze didn't leave the cliff.

Naomi circled her shoulders to loosen the stress and relaxed her grip on the reins. "It's not *looking* down that worries me," she muttered.

"Everything'll be fine, ladies," John promised turning back to the road ahead. "Slow and steady." He prodded Sampson and called over his shoulder, "Keep the reins slack and the wagon smack in the center of the road." He and the horse ambled forward, carefully pacing the mules behind them. After several slow, tense yards, John fell into an easy rhythm with the sway of Sampson's body and Naomi breathed a little easier, too. Yes, this wasn't so bad.

Cautiously letting go of her fear, she swung her eyes again to the majestic view beside them. Jagged, white-tipped mountains clawed the cloudless, azure sky; slender Ponderosa pines and perfectly reflective alpine lakes dotted the rolling green hills below. A distant river of shimmering, blue water snaked its way through the valley's heart. Above them, the hawk dipped and spiraled on the breeze, frolicking in the glorious playground.

Naomi savored the gentle July sun on her shoulders and thought, with a little satisfaction, how folks back in North Carolina were already basking in intense heat and humidity. She for one was happy to be cradled in these high mountains and wondered if they might find a campsite near that river tonight. The possibility of a bath was positively intoxicating.

More than happy to let such trivial thoughts draw her away from thinking about that ledge, Naomi absently noted

7

the small rock outcropping ahead but paid it no mind. It wasn't intrusive enough to alter John's or the wagon's path. Instead, she appraised her sisters out of the corner of her eye and appreciated how the journey had agreed with them.

Neither of the three much cared for bonnets and, as a result, they all had a little too much sun on their faces, especially their noses. Hannah's hair, like her own, had turned the color of wheat in late summer and even Rebecca's dark hair flashed hints of caramel. The ladies back in Cary would have been scandalized by their earthy appearance, worn calico dresses and lean bodies carved by three months on the trail—lean, except for the slight rounding of Hannah's stomach, that is.

Dirty faces and all, they weren't very pretty right now and Naomi couldn't have cared less. She was done worrying about what scandalized who. California was their chance to leave all that behind.

A clean slate was especially important for Hannah. No one there would know the *son* of a rich banker had led her on, lied to her, promised her the moon and then left her alone with a child on the way. No one had to know the *rich banker* had offered Hannah money to leave town and never contact his son. Of course, she hadn't accepted, but the handwriting was on the wall. Their lives in Cary were over. John's brother Matthew had been inviting them out to California for years. Unanimously, they had agreed to go west.

And what about Rebecca? Widowed seven years now, Naomi could see a change blossoming in her older sister. She held her head higher than she had in a long time and her shoulders were no longer slumped as if she was carrying a weight. Rebecca was done, too. Done with grieving, done with paying penance for having survived a fire that took her husband and her daughter. Done with living in the past. They were all ready to discover some new horizons. Hannah's scandal had at least brought that about and Naomi was grateful for small favors.

She almost sighed in contentment. She loved an adventure and as long as she had that man up there on the horse, she would be fine. John was her rock, her oak, her everything. With him, she would cross a continent and not think twice about it. She wished she could be in the saddle with him, his arms, the size of small trees, wrapped securely around her. Oh, how safe and wonderful she had always felt with him.

A rumble of thunder drew her eyes to the west end of the valley where a mass of black clouds were carving their way through the jagged peaks. Even that made her smile. She could curl up beside John in the tent tonight, listen to the rain, trace that wide jaw and those broad shoulders, and kiss that silly grin right off his face. Warm. Dry. Safe. Yes, indeed, she was filled with all kinds of hope for their future.

Apparently John's thoughts had drifted as well. Interrupting her musings, he hollered back to the girls, "That must be the Animas River down there. My map says it isn't far from here. How do y'all feel about trout for our dining pleasure this eve—"

Sampson didn't see the rattler sunning on the outcropping until it was inches from his head. Startled out of its slumber, the snake coiled and struck out angrily. The thirteen-hundred pound horse neighed, jerking his head away from the fangs with a mammoth movement of muscle. John, nearly flung out of the saddle by the unexpected reaction, clawed for the saddle horn and tried to hang on with his legs.

At the horse's commotion, the mules snorted and jolted the wagon backwards. Rebecca and Hannah squealed in fear. Naomi tightened her grip on the reins and fought for control of her own spooked animals, yelling, "Whoa, boys! Whoa!"

Busy wrestling her team, she could only focus on the battle up ahead in snatches. Sampson attempted to bolt, but, clawing his way back into the saddle, John grabbed the left rein and yanked Sampson's head around, trying to get the panicked animal to walk in tight circles. The snake rattled in fury again, throwing Sampson into another round of pawing, prancing, snorting terror.

"Easy, Sampson," John commanded. "Easy…"

But fear in prey animals is as contagious as a cold.

9

Mindless panic gripped the mules. Naomi seesawed back and forth with the reins as the pair tossed their heads, whinnied in panic and side-stepped, rolling the wagon away from the hysterical horse but toward the ledge. One wheel went over and the wagon lurched, tilting hard and then sliding further back. Gasping, Hannah and Rebecca clung to the seat and each other with white-knuckled grips.

"Oh, my Lord!" Hannah screamed. "We're slipping!"

"Hold on, Hannah," Rebecca croaked. "Hold on!"

Gritting her teeth and praying, Naomi jammed her foot firmly on the brake as she struggled with her team. "Whoa! Whoa!" she raged at the mules, sweat breaking out on her lip as she yanked on the reins. Frantic to get the team moving forward, she released the brake and snapped the reins. "Yaaah, get on now!"

Rock and sand made a grating noise as the wagon slid again, and tilted at a sharper angle, but the mules obeyed the snap and tried pulling.

"Jump," Naomi commanded her sisters but they didn't move. She couldn't worry about them, too, and their foolish hesitation incensed her. She yelled again, this time with fury in her voice, "Jump!"

Hannah and Rebecca flinched at her tone then leaped from the wagon as it bucked again. The mules couldn't get that back wheel up over the ledge. In front of them, John abruptly gave up trying to calm Sampson. He sprang from the saddle and raced toward Naomi's team. The mules, seeing Sampson rear and then run in the opposite direction, made an attempt to follow.

"Stay on'em, Naomi!" John shouted, fear lacing his voice—his tone frightened Naomi even more than the cliff. She obediently whipped the reins again as he grabbed a mule's halter and whistled the plowing command to *pull*.

The mules strained forward again, then backed up a step. Naomi quickly slammed her foot down on the brake to stop the backwards motion, snapped the reins and urged them forward, releasing the brake when she felt some traction. Working the lever was exhausting but she was determined not to lose the wagon without a fight. Suddenly more gravel gave way beneath the back wheel; the wagon bucked and jumped as gravity and the mules fought it out. Naomi heard Rebecca and Hannah shriek.

"Get off a there, Naomi!" John yelled. "Just jump!"

"Not yet," she cried, meeting his gaze. They couldn't lose everything. "Not yet!"

Not wasting time to argue, John cut the air with another whistle, this one much louder and longer. Naomi slapped the reins again as John pulled on the mule's halter. Sampson came running back at his master's call, eyes wide, nostrils flaring, reins twitching and jumping on the ground like live snakes.

John gathered the reins, tied them quickly to the yoke then grabbed Sampson's halter. "Yah, back," he yelled, coaxing Sampson to pull. Naomi popped the reins hard across the mules' backs, praying to God Sampson would be strong enough to get the wheel back up on the road. The strain was tremendous; the mule's legs quivered with the exertion. "Yah, come on now, mules!" She barked.

John switched from Sampson to the mule closest to the ledge. He yelled, "Gee, Gee," while pushing the mules forward but away from the ledge. The wagon jumped and bucked again as it tried to crown the road. The path was so narrow John had to work with the mules and Sampson mere inches from the ledge. "Almost, Naomi! We're almost there!" Veins bulged in John's neck as he pulled the mule forward.

She felt the tension on the wagon and the mules. Sampson was straining using his massive bulk to pull backwards; his leather reins looked as tight as guitar strings as he tried to bring the team with him. She heard her sisters' voices lifted up in desperate prayer and added her own *Please, God, help us . . .*

At the moment that the rear wheel jumped back up on the road, a cracking, shattering sound exploded from the front of the wagon. In a blur of a motion, the mule closest to the ledge and Sampson broke apart; half the yoke hung from the mule's harness and it swung round like a hammer, catching John in the side of the head.

Naomi saw in an instant the fear in his eyes, that he knew what was coming, and there was no stopping it. He and the mule, loosed so suddenly from the wagon tongue and harness, simply launched like projectiles over the ledge.

John reached for her but before she could even blink, he disappeared over the ledge.

She heard her sisters scream. (Or was that her?) She heard the mule's panicked, desperate braying and then . . . silence.

~~~

## One

Charles McIntyre stared placidly at his cards and stifled a yawn. He had not expected young Isaac Whicker to present such an entertaining challenge. Their little game had started at three and by seven they were still playing, though in a nearly empty saloon. This was the calm before the Saturday night gale.

Absently noting the low rumble of thunder, McIntyre decided it was time to finish the game. He had better things to do. Glancing across the table at his sallow-looking, gangly opponent, he could see the boy swaying and blinking as he fought against the effects of the whiskey. Hunched bleary-eyed over his cards, Whicker had fought surprisingly well to keep from losing his mercantile, but he'd never really stood a chance. McIntyre needed the store back and would have it back if he had to crush Isaac Whicker like a bug to get it.

Ironically, he realized, that wasn't the best way to start this new venture of making Defiance *respectable*, as the railroad gents had termed it. A lawless town would be a trackless town, they warned. Fine. Get a few legitimate businesses running, calm the town down, put a nice hotel where the mercantile is. Then the great American iron horse would come steaming into Defiance, bringing with it opportunity, success and wealth. Not to mention, carrying his gold away to the mint in Denver.

Oh, he knew he could simply bribe the right people, grease the wheels as it were, but he preferred to seek that as a last option. He even had the funds now to build his own railroad, if he desired, but McIntyre liked his money right where it was–in his own pockets. For the time being, he'd decided to take the easy road.

Ending the game with more boredom than ceremony, he laid down his cards. A royal flush. He thought he heard Whicker's breath catch and looked up. The boy had turned impossibly pale and his blond hair suddenly turned dull and lifeless, like that of an eighty-year-old man. The tiniest speck of compassion attempted to make itself known to McIntyre, but he irritably flicked it away, like a greasy crumb on his silk vest.

Scratching his thin, black, and perfectly trimmed beard, he leaned back in his chair. "Unless you can beat that, I own the mercantile."

Whicker shook his head and slowly placed his cards face down on the table. "No," he whispered, "I don't reckon I can."

Satisfied that was an admission of surrender, McIntyre rose to his feet. This game was over and he was ready to spend some time with the intoxicating Rose catnapping in his bed.

"You played a good game, Whicker," he drawled in a deceptively charming Georgia accent. "The best I've had in some time, but you were destined to lose. I'll give you forty-eight hours to clear out. As we agreed, the inventory and gold stake are mine. You may keep all of your personal effects, including the wagon and your horse."

That last was overly generous, but taking a man's horse was just plain mean and McIntyre did not consider himself that callous–although he was quite sure Rose would have something to say about it. That feisty Mexican wench held on to things with the death grip of a mountain lion. Whicker replied only with a lingering blank stare. McIntyre concluded that the boy was neither in a hurry to accept his fate nor leave the saloon.

Unwilling to be held up by the gloom in the air, he reached for the deed sitting forlornly in the middle of the table. "Let yourself out, Whicker, and have a safe trip back to…" Kansas, was it? He waived his hand dismissively. "Wherever you're from." Then he added generously, "You're an enterprising young man. I'm sure you'll be able to start over again."

McIntyre was almost surprised at himself for offering the words of encouragement and raked his hand through his black, wavy hair as if that would clear these dark thoughts.

He supposed it was that accursed Southern upbringing which equated rudeness with horse stealing. In the cold light of reality, though, Whicker was nothing to him but an obstacle. And now an obstacle removed.

Well, nearly. The boy still hadn't moved. Sighing, McIntyre tucked the deed into his breast pocket and headed upstairs to his room. He paused ever-so-briefly at the top of the stairs to again flick away that crumb of compassion. After all, it had been a truly fair game. McIntyre hadn't cheated. He hadn't forced the boy to drink, nor had he forced him to bet the store.

Slapping the rail twice as if dismissing Whicker from his conscience, McIntyre strode across the hall to his room. Imagining a bath and Rose's heady kisses, he turned the brass door knob and entered his room. From below, and barely above the soft thump of rain drops, he heard the boy mutter miserably, "Missouri. Hannibal, Missouri."

But the words were lost. McIntyre eyed the voluptuous Rose seductively draped in his silk sheets and, undoing his tie, closed the door on Whicker.

~~~

In the dream, Naomi sat alone at the campfire waiting for her guest. She tended to the fish in the skillet and kept a watchful eye. Shortly, Jesus joined her. He sat down on the other side of the fire and offered her a tender smile.

"Naomi, do you trust me more than these?" She was surprised to see that Rebecca and Hannah had joined them, too, though they acted unaware of her or Jesus.

"Yes, Lord, you know I trust you."

"Then go where I send you." She put the fork down on the rock next to the fire and looked at him, puzzled by his statement. Again he asked, "Naomi, do you trust me?"

Her brow furrowed. "Yes, Lord, you know I trust you."

"Then go where I send you." She sat back and crossed her legs, puzzled, but sure there was more. Staring at her with dark, intent eyes, Jesus asked again, "Naomi, do you trust me?"

She sighed, frustrated with him. "You know everything; you know my heart. So you should know that I trust you."

"Then go where I send you. There are those around you living in defiance. Take to them the Good News." And then he pleaded softly, "Love them as I do."

"I will go where you send me, Lord." Her heart ached to ask one question of him, though. "But can't you please tell me why you took Jo—"

Jesus put a finger to his lips, cutting off the question. His countenance voice gentle, he replied, "You'll have your answer in time. I have children lost in darkness. Take to them the Light…and don't stand on eighteen."

~~~

Naomi opened her eyes and looked up at the bottom of the wagon. A gray light crept stealthily upon them and she knew it was time to get moving. Slowly, gingerly, she climbed over her sleeping sisters and crawled out from underneath a home she now despised.

A lonely apprehension seized her as she wandered over to the dead fire. As she moved to sit on a fallen tree, she stopped short. Either Rebecca or Hannah had left John's map out, folded to reveal a small section. She picked it up and studied the lines and topographical details. John's accident had happened on what he'd called the Million Dollar Highway, the way most of the gold and silver was taken out of the valley. She let her finger dance over the map as she searched for something, some landmark or town, some hint of what to do next, where to go…

"Defiance…?" She stopped her finger at the town. The name tweaked her memory. "What…?"

The Lord's words leaped to her mind: *There are those around you living in Defiance. Take to them the Good News. Love them as I do.*

She stared at the word. The town was only a few miles due west. She also knew, with a searing dread, that it was their destination. Feeling sick and overwhelmed, she closed her eyes and went back to that dream which was now painfully vivid. She had told Him three times she would go where He sent her.

*Not willingly,* she admitted. *Forgive me, Lord. I go grudgingly, to say the least. With John beside me, I would have gone to Hell and back. I had my heart set on growing old with him. Where didn't matter. Now nothing matters.*

*The truth be told, Lord, I don't like You very much right now.*

The admission broke her heart as much as the loss of her husband. If she didn't have the relationship with God that she had always counted on, then she had nothing. Yet, getting past her anger at this sudden destruction of her dreams was proving nigh unto impossible. She cried over her loss and her smoldering resentment and begged God to help her get past them both.

~~~

# Two

Inside the Iron Horse Saloon, McIntyre drummed his fingers on his desk. The letter did not bring him the news he wanted and he despised not getting what he wanted. He read that one particular line again: "while Defiance is in an excellent location to provide a hub for spur lines up from Animas Forks and Pinkerton Springs, the town's lack of civil organization, or for that matter, civility, distresses us."

The same complaint...again.

So Defiance was a bit on the wild side. He stared out the window of his office at the bustling horde of scruffy miners. These men suffered from the consuming malady of Gold Fever and he was there to nurse them through it with wine, women and song. After all, what more could a man really want?

Possibly a hotel room without a female already in it. A night without the eruption of gunfire. A duly elected mayor. A legally deputized marshal. Law and order. Churches. Schools.

He sighed like a man accepting his fate. Defiance had to be tamed. If he wanted the railroad to come in, he was going to have to get on with it. He heard the front doors squeak and looked up. His office afforded a view of the entire length of the bar and he straightened attentively as a pretty little blonde entered and removed her bonnet. Hands clenched tensely at her waist, her eyes were glued to the nude painting over the bar.

Whoever she was, she had never seen anything like that and he smiled as she turned away. How long had it been since he had seen a woman blush? He couldn't honestly recall. He enjoyed gazing upon her for a moment, taking in the slim, curvaceous figure and that long, golden braid running down her back like Rapunzel's. She was tanned from the sun and her dress showed a fair amount of wear. Still, she was enjoyable to study and it wouldn't take much for his mind to wander. . .

She looked around the rest of the empty saloon and finally her eyes found him. He stood as she approached his office door. "Are you Mr. McIntyre?"

"I am," he agreed in his most charming Southern accent. He skirted his desk and met her in the entrance, momentarily struck by the contrast of ocean green eyes in a beautiful, tanned face. High cheekbones, freckles and a slightly pug nose, she was a fresh-faced, wholesome change from the women currently populating Defiance. And he had picked up on her accent before she had spoken her second word. "A fellow southerner." Extending his hand, he admitted, "Though I can't quite place the accent, Miss..."

"We're from North Carolina and it's *Mrs.* Naomi Miller."

He nodded, accepting her correction. "Mrs. Miller. To what do I owe this distinct pleasure?"

He held on to her hand much too long as he boldly appraised her up and down. Frowning slightly, she pulled her hand away. He grinned at her obvious discomfort, enjoying the sport. He could tell she didn't like him already.

"I was wondering if we might talk a little business?"

"Why certainly." He motioned to one of the green-topped poker tables behind her. "Please have a seat and I'll get us some refreshments. I have everything from whiskey to coffee."

"Coffee?"

He chuckled at the longing in her voice, knowing full well that coffee was always the first supply to run out on the trail. "I'll just be a moment."

Going behind the bar, he caught sight of himself in the mirror and wondered if she admired his wavy, jet black hair, brown eyes and painstakingly trimmed, pencil-thin mustache and beard. Tall, slender and well-dressed in a perfectly tailored dark grey suit, he was a far cry from the war-weary Southern expatriate who had discovered this valley. Or, for that matter, the green lieutenant who had spent four years covered in blood and guts for his beloved Confederacy. He would never live like that again he vowed as he poured the coffee. For further proof, he admired his clean hands and superbly manicured nails.

McIntyre rejoined Naomi, bearing a silver tray dotted with sugar and cream vessels, sterling silver spoons and two delicate china cups filled with steaming coffee. The saloon was a rough and gritty affair reeking of cigar smoke and sour whiskey so this touch of elegance was, he hoped, a pleasant surprise for her. With fluid, confident movements, he set her coffee before her, poured in cream at her nod, and stirred in one spoonful of sugar.

She sipped the coffee and for a fleeting moment was the very picture of contentment, as though she'd forgotten where she was and why she was there. Still, he thought she looked tired; her calico dress had seen better days and her bonnet, resting on the table beside her, was faded and fraying. He assumed she had been traveling for quite some time. It pleased him to offer her this little moment of rest, though he couldn't say why. Probably for the same reason he gave a stray dog a scrap—he still claimed a morsel of unjaded humanity.

"Mrs. Miller, please forgive me for asking," McIntyre began as he prepared his own cup, "but I am not used to doing business with a woman. Might I enquire about your husband?"

She swallowed the coffee and huffed a heavy breath before answering. "My husband. He was killed nearly a week ago on the trail."

McIntyre's brow furrowed deeply more out of disappointment than sympathy. Just another Flower for the Garden. And he had been hoping for something more interesting. "I am very sorry to hear that. However, it happens rather frequently in the west, especially in mining towns. Women are left with so few options under such circumstances." His spoon clinked against this cup as he stirred in sugar. "You are a very beautiful woman, though, Mrs. Miller. I can promise you won't starve. And generally speaking, I believe my Flowers are fairly satisfied with their working conditions. I pay a generous percentage and the rooms are large and comfortable. You also receive all your meals for free—"

Naomi threw up her hand, cutting off the rest of his words. "Stop talking!" McIntyre blinked, feeling a bit like a court jester failing to properly amuse the queen. Hand still up, she acknowledged with firmness, "I can see where that would be an assumption someone in this Godforsaken town could make about a woman, but it was rude, nonetheless, and wrong. Very, very wrong."

Amused by her imperious reaction, but also honestly apologetic, he lowered his head. "I am sorry." He could have easily added, "Your Highness," but bit it back. Leaning back in his chair and crossing his legs, he made no attempt to hide his confusion. "Obviously I misconstrued the reason for your coming here. My assumption was inexcusable."

Naomi's cheeks were positively glowing. "To say the least." Hiding a smile behind his coffee cup, he gave her time to compose herself. "My sisters and my husband and I were on our way to California to join his brother there. Since his death, we've had a rather astonishing change of plans." He could see she was warring with the final statement and waited patiently for her to frame it. "We feel strongly led to stop our journey here in Defiance."

"Led?" He didn't miss the use of the word. "Are you Mormon missionaries?" His voice had sounded vaguely disdainful, though he hadn't meant for it to. God had no time to waste on Defiance and McIntyre was happy to return the favor.

"Not missionaries, so to speak, and not Mormons. We are Christians and we feel that God…Well, we feel he wants us to settle here, at least for a while." He didn't miss the sadness in her eyes or the disapproval in her voice. "Believe me, this place wouldn't be my first choice, but we met a Mr. Whicker as he was leaving town and we learned that his building is vacant."

Whicker's name got his attention and he listened carefully, watching her over the top of his cup.

"In fact," she continued, "he said his building was

originally designed as a hotel though he had used it as a mercantile. That's what got us thinking and why I came to speak with you. My sisters and I were toying with the idea of opening up a hotel and restaurant." She pointed out the window at the flowing street and the crowded boardwalk. "The town at first glance seems busy enough. Could it support such a venture?" He heard hope in her voice, though he wasn't convinced she was hoping for a yes.

But the plan to open a respectable hotel was exactly the reason he had reclaimed Whicker's building in that less-than-fair game of Texas Hold'em. The one flaw in this scheme, though, was the troublesome issue of finding respectable innkeepers. Taking in the lovely Naomi Miller, McIntyre believed the answer had, quite fortuitously, fallen into his lap. This thought triggered an entertaining idea.

He sat up, set his coffee off to the side and started shuffling the deck of cards that was a fixture at every table. "So what you're saying is that you believe God has sent you to Defiance? To open a business? And then what? Will you try to save the town? Convert us all to Jesus?" There was no malice in the questions, just bland curiosity.

Naomi inclined her head to one side and bestowed a haughty look on him. "Forgive me, Mr. McIntyre, but why is the town named Defiance?"

He allowed a well-practiced, but admittedly insincere, smile to creep across his face. "Are you familiar with the writings of Milton, Mrs. Miller? He wrote that it is better to rule in Hell than serve in Heaven."

Her face softened and she nodded slowly. Had he seen a glint of compassion in her eyes, he wondered, uncomfortable with anyone's pity. Nonetheless, he briefly shared his story.

"I came to the San Juan range with a group of fourteen other prospectors just after the war. We broke up into three groups to better scout the valley, but in dividing, one group fell under attack by a superior force of Ute Indians. I watched while men two and three times my age begged God for death as their skin was flayed from their bodies." Goosebumps rose on her skin. "God did not save them; God stood silent while those men suffered and died." He fanned the cards out on the table, gathered them up with practiced skill, and shuffled them again.

"Couple that with all the atrocities I saw during the war and I've pretty much decided that God is about as useful as an absent father." He shrugged, surprised that he had told her so much. "Perhaps the name was my way of shaking my fist at God, daring him to set foot in my town."

Naomi bit her lip as she pondered his tale. "A sort of line in the sand, is it?" Shadows of pain flitted across her face. "I wish I had answers for why God does what he does, allows what he does, but I'm still working on that one myself."

"Oh, I don't mean to make it sound as if I'm angry or to be pitied, Mrs. Miller. I'm truly content." He placed cards on the table with skilled, easy movements as he talked. "Taking God out of the equation frees a man to find his own destiny, make his own way without worrying about divine whimsy . . . There."

Naomi looked down. He had placed two cards in front of each of them; a ten and an eight stared up at her. He was graced with a king and a five.

"The French call this Vingt-Et-Un. We call it Blackjack," he explained. "The object is to get as close to twenty-one as possible without going over. Whoever is the closest wins. If you win, Mrs. Miller, I will give you that building for your hotel. If you lose," he paused. "If you lose, you will run the hotel for me."

Her face paled. "I can't agree to that."

"You're fifteen hundred miles from the Carolinas and still a thousand miles from California. I'd say your options are limited." While the statement was true, he didn't wish to frame things in such a grim light. "I've got fifteen," he said tapping his cards. "You have eighteen. The odds are in your favor."

Naomi eyed him warily. "Why not just sell it to us? Why play a game of cards—" But as the question left her mouth, her expression changed to one of confusion. She looked again at the cards and touched them, as if confirming they were real. "Eighteen?"

Fascinated by the way this day was turning out, he set the deck of cards between them. "I was just wondering if God speaks my language," he answered in truth.

"So you want to hear from him despite your defiance?"

Their eyes locked in an unspoken battle of wills over the assertion. McIntyre suspected this might be the first of many skirmishes with the little princess from the South. The thought amused him and he chuckled good naturedly. "That's not what I meant exactly but you can put it that way if you like. I make my living with cards. *They* speak to me."

"All right," she nodded. "I think you ducked the question, but all right. So all I have to do is get twenty-one?"

"You can stand on eighteen. I would. However, the house is going for another card."

"No, I want another card."

He liked her spirit. "You're feeling lucky today, are you?"

She speared him with a somber gaze. "There's no such thing as luck, Mr. McIntyre. Like it or not, there's only the hand of God."

Her words hung in the air, throwing him off track for a moment. "Perhaps," he muttered. Emotion swirled in her eyes, but he couldn't decipher it.

He recovered quickly, though, shifting in his chair and changing the subject. "Indeed, Mr. Whicker's mercantile was originally designed as a hotel. I built it knowing that the Brunot Treaty would be ratified and this corner of Colorado would explode with settlers." He whistled in amazement. "I didn't count on my geologist finding a sixty-foot thick vein of quartz in my own mine. Silver, gold and even a little copper." He was still unable to comprehend his growing fortune. "Silver took precedence over the innkeeping business so I sold the building."

He absently tapped the deck of cards in the middle of the table and knit his brows together. "I have to admit, the timing of your arrival is, well, strangely opportune as I was pondering this venture again. It's the very reason I helped

Mr. Whicker leave our little community."

"Then why would you want *us* to get the hotel," she asked with an I-don't-trust-you-as-far-as-I-can-throw-you look on her face.

"It has come to my attention that Defiance could be passed up for some opportunities if the town doesn't become more *civilized*." He raised his hands in a gesture of surrender. "I must give up a portion of my kingdom to decency if I want the town to grow. Most likely you'll do a far better job of running a nice place than I would."

Naomi stared intently at McIntyre and he could see the wheels turning behind those stormy green eyes. She was questioning everything about him and this situation. Though he knew, somehow, she would go through with his challenge.

"Maybe that's what this is all about, Mr. McIntyre," she suggested, sounding both wistful and melancholy. "Maybe, now and then, we have to give up a portion of our kingdoms—the things we hold dearest—to find what it is God wants for us."

The thought intrigued him and he decided he was eager to do business with her Ladyship.

She shook her head and heaved a great sigh. "This is absurd. I should inspect the building first, haggle with you over a price, discuss it with my sisters . . . but I think that would defeat the purpose of why I'm here." Inexplicably, he sensed a confession in the statement.

"Well, this shouldn't be an issue since you're going to win," he joked, lightheartedly mocking her faith, "However, if you do lose, I want your word you'll run the hotel for at least two years."

Naomi opened her mouth, to protest he assumed, but thought better of whatever she started to say. Instead, she sagged a bit and offered softly, "I wish I could tell you—"

A million things? If they could sit and talk like two polite people from genteel Southern society, what would she tell him, McIntyre wondered.

Naomi shook her head again as if clearing her thoughts. "Let's just play this hand." He liked the grit he heard in her voice, her determination to face things unflinchingly. Oh, yes, he was quite sure he was going to enjoy having her in Defiance. Pun intended.

Without hesitating, he drew a card for himself and laid it next to the other two. A red queen of hearts gazed coolly back at him. "Dealer busts; if you go over twenty-one, we play another hand." Enjoying the drama, he slowly slid a card off the deck and pushed it to her, face down.

Naomi drummed her fingers for a moment then reached for the card, hesitated, then flipped over a three of spades. "Twenty-one," she whispered sounding incredulous. A slow, sad smile spread across her face. She looked up at McIntyre. He was surprised by the weary expression on her face. "I guess we own a hotel?"

~~~

# Three

For a man who had just lost a card game and a building worth who-knew-how-many-thousands of dollars, Naomi saw not a hint of disappointment in Mr. McIntyre's eyes. Quite the opposite. He looked as jovial as if he had *won* three thousand dollars.

She, on the other hand, was trying desperately to remain calm and collected. The fact that she had just played a hand of cards to determine her and her sisters' destiny was simply incredible. Using a strategy that had only *appeared* to be gambling, God had delivered a soon-to-be hotel and restaurant into her hands. She was clearheaded enough to suspect that the particular method of transfer, though, had been more for Mr. McIntyre's benefit than hers.

As they stood and shook hands, she couldn't help but wonder what plans God had for him. Admittedly, she would enjoy watching the Almighty take this pompous peacock down a peg or two…if she had time to bother with him.

"Mrs. Miller, I do hope you find Defiance to your liking." He covered her hand with his and gazed deeply into her eyes. "And please know that I truly want your hotel to be successful. I hope you won't mind if I'm intimately involved with the details."

She jerked her hand away and scowled at him. "I'm quite sure my sisters and I can manage without your assistance."

"Not in my town." The comment had come through smiling lips, but something in his dark eyes walked a tightrope between menacing and bewitching. It gave Naomi a chill. "But I'll try not to be too much of a nuisance."

Why did she have the feeling she had just made a deal with the devil? What wasn't he telling her?

"Whicker's Mercantile is the third building from the end of town, on this side. You'll find it right where the street bends. I originally was going to call it the Elbow Inn," he shrugged noncommittally, "but I'm sure you'll choose a more refined name. Ten minutes?"

"We'll be waiting."

The end of their conversation was interrupted by a commotion outside. Naomi heard Hannah squeal in fright and both she and Mr. McIntyre bolted for the door. Together, they exploded through the bat wings to find three, mud-encrusted miners playing keep-away with Hannah's bonnet. She and Rebecca sat, clinging to each other, in the wagon and shrilly demanding the return of the hat.

"Gentleman!" Mr. McIntyre's commanding voice stopped the horse play cold. "That will be enough."

A grotesquely fat man with jiggling jowls caught the last pass of the bonnet and pressed it innocently to his grimy chest, as if it belonged to him in the first place. Furious beyond description, Naomi stomped towards the man and shoved him with all the ferociousness she could muster in her small frame. "Get away from my sisters!"

The man's eyes widened in shock at the violence of the attack then a huge grin split his face, revealing rotten, yellowed teeth swimming in tobacco juice. Naomi's stomach threatened to rebel, but her anger overcame it and she snatched the bonnet from his dirty, fat hands.

"Whew, ain't she a spunky one," the man joked, spitting on the ground. "I'll be your first customer, angel."

Before she could respond, Mr. McIntyre stepped between them and put a hand on the fat man's chest. "Be about your business, Sam. These girls are none of your affair." Naomi didn't miss the lowered tone in his voice and the way he scanned the street. The commotion threatened to draw a crowd and apparently Mr. McIntyre did not want that to happen. "You and your boys come back tonight and I'll give you one on the house," he glanced at the other two men, just as grimy as the first. "Now, go on. I'm sure you've got some place to be. Doesn't your shift start soon?"

Grudgingly, the three ambled away muttering something about she-devils while throwing dirty looks over their shoulders. The slowing sea of gawkers picked up speed again, convinced the entertainment had ended. Still, eyes stayed trained on Hannah and Rebecca in the wagon till necks wouldn't twist anymore.

Fighting for calm, Naomi forced her heart to slow, but the anger did not want to surrender. "Are you all right, Hannah?"

Flushed with color, her blue eyes as wide as half-dollars, Hannah nodded weakly. Tucking a wayward gold strand of hair behind her ear, she reached for her bonnet. "They didn't hurt us—"

"But they scared us to death," Rebecca interjected breathlessly.

"I'm very sorry, ladies," Mr. McIntyre apologized from behind Naomi. "Beautiful women are as rare as elephants in Defiance, especially ones who don't work for me."

Naomi spun on him. "Yes, I noticed you cleared that right up." She hoped her sarcasm was palpable, she was so irate with him. "You said the hotel is ours. We don't work for you. We shook hands on it."

"We did," he agreed, fighting a smile. "In this particular instance, I thought it the better part of valor to get them on their way rather than engage in an explanation of your virtue. For the moment, you were under my protection."

Naomi had the urge to smack that arrogant grin off his suave, handsome face, but balled her hands into fists instead.

"I assure you, I will clear up any misunderstandings forthwith," he promised, sounding more amused than contrite. "For now, why don't you ladies proceed to the hotel where we can conduct our business away from all these prying eyes? I'll be there shortly."

Her emotions in a dither, Naomi huffed her disapproval and climbed up into the wagon. Mr. McIntyre retreated inside. For a moment, the three girls sat in silence. Looking as if she wanted to hide under a rock, Rebecca hunched lower in the seat and clutched the reins so tightly her knuckles were white. Hannah brushed the mud off her bonnet and gingerly replaced it on her head. Naomi drummed her fingers on her knees and stared straight ahead. She swallowed, attempting to loosen the tension in her jaw and somehow force herself to think through the fury.

The men populating the street stared brazenly, and several even whistled and made obscene suggestions. She glanced over the swirling sea of faces, searching for some hint of normalcy and civility. They were young and middle-aged, mostly bearded, dirty, and flashing a dangerous glint of the untamed in their eyes. So different from her beloved John.

*Oh, God,* she cried out, *what are you thinking?*

"We have to move, Rebecca," she heard herself order, surprised at the steadiness of her voice. She didn't feel steady. Not one bit. But she had to hold herself together, at least until she was alone.

Rebecca straightened and lifted the reins. "Which way?"

"It's the third building from the end." Naomi pointed ahead of them. "It's right there where the street bends." Rebecca clucked her tongue and the mules obeyed. As the wagon rolled forward, Naomi fumed aloud over the citizens while trying to ignore their bold gazes. "They've the manners of pirates here, and stare like they've never seen women before."

"It's not just the men," Rebecca countered, tugging on the reins to veer away from an on-coming wagon. "We saw three women peeking at us from upstairs at the saloon."

Hannah's eyes widened with a scandalous admission as she scratched at her waist: "I waved at one of them, but she jerked away from the window like I'd fired a gun at her."

Naomi pondered her little sister–she had the beautiful, delicate features of a China doll but was still so naïve considering all that she'd been through. If Mr. McIntyre so much as *looked* at her or Rebecca the wrong way...

Naomi clenched and unclenched her fists, trying to cool down her frustration. What kind of a man was so devoid of a conscience that he could employ women into prostitution as easily as one would hire out a man to chop wood? To think that someone like him was a form of protection for them right now was almost more than she could bear.

~~~

Lighting a cigar, McIntyre stood far enough back from the saloon's windows to study the girls without being seen. He was pleased to discover that the other two sisters were just as handsome as Naomi. However, he considered their planned future a waste of good flesh. Two golden-haired beauties and a dark one would draw in the miners; they always liked fresh meat.

The variety in the sisters' ages was a selling point as well. The youngest, petite and blonde like Naomi, looked to be about sixteen. The one with chestnut hair and more regal, almost Indian-like features, was probably approaching forty. He guessed his feisty new business partner was somewhere in her late twenties.

Alas, they would have to remain unsold and unsoiled. He would put the word out. Women were nearly as valuable as gold and silver in the West, but these three would have to be off limits, at least to the general public. He, of course was a different story. But that could wait for a while, too.

Pulling his watch out of his vest pocket, he chuckled when he thought of Naomi throwing up her hand to stop his offer of employment. No one had talked to him like that in years. And he had even seen her blush. He didn't know women still did that. Yet, she had jumped ol' Sam like a wolverine trying to protect its young. Delicate and genteel but, by Dixie, sassy as a red pepper! Whistling a cheerful tune, McIntyre went back to his office to grab his hat and the keys for the newest residents of Defiance.

~~~

Hannah tried for one last glance up at the window where she had seen the girls but as they pulled away, the wagon's bonnet blocked it. She settled back down in her seat, scratching at her waist, and pondered Defiance. The town terrified her. Even so, she could see past the wanton lust, the drunkenness, the false bravado exhibited so perfectly in their "welcoming committee." Against her better judgment, she looked into the sea of faces and met the bold stares.

Going deeper, she saw emptiness, loneliness, hopelessness. Like their clothes, threadbare and worn, so were their souls.

How could she know that? How could she sense it so perfectly?

Hannah also knew, however, that once word was out about the baby, these people would probably be more vicious than her "friends" back home had been.

. . . Home.

Her memories of Sunday afternoon picnics, summer nights sitting on the front porch with Momma and Daddy, even the sweeter remembrances of Billy, had been shoved to the background because of that one, humiliating night in church. The thought of home now conjured up, in exquisite detail, the shame of confessing her sin before her congregation and the resulting torrential rain of judgment.

*"She is young; she made a mistake."*

*"Young and loose it sounds like!"*

*"She's asking for forgiveness!"*

Hannah squeezed her eyes shut as if that would silence the voices in her head.

*"We can't turn her out! It wouldn't be right."*

*"We certainly cannot have her teaching our children in Sunday school."*

*"This should have never happened in the first place."*

*"We can't be seen as condoning this situation."*

At her lowest point, when she was raw and bleeding from the verbal lashing, God had reminded her that she was not alone nor was she forsaken. She was forgiven. That thought on its own had made it possible for her to walk out of church instead of crawl.

The wagon lurched; Rebecca gasped and Hannah's eyes flew open. A man had leaped up on the step, pulling himself to within inches of Naomi. Spackled with mud and smelling like sweat, rotten food and alcohol, this new troublemaker removed his shoddy brown bowler in a grand, sweeping gesture. Naomi grimaced.

With the slurred Irish accent of a proficient drunkard, he announced, "Ladies, I am Grady O'Banion. Allow me to welcome ye to Defiance."

Naomi recoiled at his breath and scowled menacingly. "We've had enough of this town's welcome. Now, get off our wagon."

The man's drunken countenance changed instantly, darkening to a more threatening expression. "Ye need to learn some manners, missy," he growled, reaching out and grabbing hold of Naomi's wrist.

"Not today and not from you!" Acting on instinct, Naomi slammed her boot into the middle of his breastbone and shoved with a force that astonished Hannah. The man went flying, landing flat on his back and knocking his head against a hitching post with an audible thud. The men nearby who had the chance to witness the encounter roared with laughter. It had happened so fast Rebecca hadn't stopped the mules and the wagon was still moving forward.

"Pick up the pace, sister," Naomi ordered, the color draining from her face.

Rebecca urged the mules into a trot, navigating them around the traffic as Hannah stared at Naomi. She wondered if her feisty, hot-tempered sister was about to get them killed. Eyes round like saucers, Naomi held her hand over her mouth in a what-have-I-done gesture and looked over her shoulder at the man. "What if I killed him?" she whispered. "No, wait . . . He's moving . . . I think."

The distress in Naomi's voice and her rapid breathing released Hannah from her shock. She reached out and took her big sister's hand to show her respect. "If you ever wonder for one second why we need you, Naomi..." Hannah shook her head. "Don't."

"Amen," Rebecca agreed. "They'll think twice before tangling with us again," she cut her eyes over at her younger sister, "with you again."


McIntyre stepped outside the saloon in time to see O'Banion come flying off the wagon and land in the dirt with a breath-stealing "OOF." The sisters' wagon rolled on and McIntyre honestly wondered if they could make the next fifty yards without any further incidents. Sweet Nellie, at least he hoped so. He didn't have the men available to assign a security detail to the belles.

Laughing in spite of the potential trouble, he slipped his hat on and strode down to where the town's most ornery and abrasive citizen lay in the dirt. Covering the troublemaker with his shadow, McIntyre nudged him with the toe of a perfectly polished deer skin boot.

O'Banion looked up, rubbing the back of his head. "Mr. McIntyre, yer new Flowers need a wee bit of trimmin', I'd say."

"They're not Flowers and they're not for sale." He addressed the crowd that was still hanging about. "I won't take it too kindly if they're accosted." A few brows rose at the use of the unfamiliar word. McIntyre rolled his eyes. "I do forget the company I'm keeping." As if speaking to a slow child, he clarified the comment. "Don't touch them. They're not for sale. Pass the word." The crowd was none too happy with the order and disbanded, grumbling at his high-handedness. He waved them off like gnats and went to find his marshal.

~~~

*four*

As the sisters rode the rest of the way down the street, they didn't speak of Grady O'Banion, but Naomi glanced back several times. The crowd filled in around him pretty quickly and she wasn't able to catch sight of him. She was comforted some by the fact that he didn't leap to his feet declaring his desire for revenge, but she was sick over her brazen, thoughtless tussle with the man. What if he'd had a knife or a gun? Rebecca or Hannah could have gotten hurt. Would this O'Banion hold a grudge? Had she humiliated him enough to make him seek retribution?

*Dear Lord, what is the matter with the men in this town?* She cried in anguish. As if she didn't have enough to deal with, now she was seriously considering wearing John's gun on her hip. She realized in her present state of mind that was akin to throwing a match on a powder keg, but no one was going to hurt her sisters.

No one . . . .

Rebecca pulled the wagon to a halt in front of the soon-to-be-hotel. *Their* hotel, Naomi thought. The building, lapped in golden pine siding, featured four large windows across the front of both floors, sizeable French doors at the entrance, and a large balcony on the second story. The slats in the rail were made of crooked, though skillfully placed, peeled branches. Unfortunately, the windows and doors were trimmed in that gaudy red.

Still rustic but far more finished than most of the other structures in Defiance. It defined the town's transition from mining camp to permanent settlement.

The sisters quietly climbed down, trying to draw as little attention as possible to themselves, and took up positions at the windows. Sheltering their eyes, they each peered into the darkness.

Naomi could see empty shelves and, toward the back, a bare counter. An L-shaped set of open tread stairs hugged the wall on the right, a stone fireplace was built into the center of the wall on the left, and a room in the back, which Naomi assumed was Whicker's small apartment, took up most of the rest of the building. Not as wide as the building, though, it left room for a hallway that led to a back door.

Naomi pulled away from the window and considered the passing reflections in the glass. The traffic on this end of the street was noticeably thinner. Perhaps because the buildings off to the immediate left were still under construction. Suited her just fine; maybe this was the quiet part of town. The way her muscles were singing from all this excitement, she was eager for some peace. A little hammering and sawing would be a pleasant respite from the cat calls and lewd comments.

Rebecca cupped her hands around her eyes and peered deeper into the store. "I didn't expect this to happen so fast," she said sounding uncertain. "One moment we're talking about what to do for a living and the next, we own a hotel."

"One that looks to need a complete renovation." Naomi snapped her fingers. "Nothing to it."

"What do you think we ought to do first?" Rebecca asked, ignoring the sarcasm.

Out of the corner of her eye, Naomi noticed Hannah scratching at her waist, something she had been doing more and more of late. Puzzled, and interested in observing, she turned and leaned her shoulder on the window.

"Get the restaurant up and running," Rebecca continued. "Maybe that will only take some minor renovation, but we've got to get tables and groceries from somewhere…"

Hannah was still peering into the building and still scratching. Naomi couldn't take it anymore. Her nerves crawling from stress, she wanted the annoying action stopped. "Hannah, what is the matter with you? Have you got fleas?"

He sister jerked up, embarrassed, and her hand went to her back. "No, I don't have fleas." Her indignation over the question was obvious in her squared shoulders and rigid back.

Abruptly, Rebecca walked over and spun Hannah around so she could see her back. She raised her shirtwaist and revealed that two of the buttons on her little sister's skirt were undone and the skirt still looked to be pinching her waist.

Rebecca hung her head. "Oh, honey. Why didn't you tell us?" She offered both her sisters a resigned smile and tried to stifle a laugh. "Hannah here is bursting out of her clothes."

Hannah whirled away angrily. "It's not funny. It's driving me crazy!"

"Simmer down, simmer down," Naomi urged, fighting a grin. "We're going to have to dig to the bottom of the wagon for that box of pinafores and dresses from Ms. Dawn."

Hannah was not amused. "Well somebody better do something or I'm just going to start sporting around in my pantaloons."

The ridiculous and irrational threat brought a snort out of Rebecca. "Trust me, eventually those won't fit you either."

Hannah opened her mouth, ostensibly to offer another sassy reply, but the sound of boots at the far end of the porch drew their attention. The sisters turned to see Mr. McIntyre approaching with another man, a taller, muscular red-headed gent wearing a badge. As they stomped up the steps, Naomi thought she noticed the slightest limp in Mr. McIntyre's step.

"Ladies," Mr. McIntyre greeted them, taking Hannah's hand first. "I apologize for my rudeness earlier in not doing introductions. I'm Charles McIntyre."

"Well, we were all a little preoccupied at the time," Hannah forgave. "I'm Hannah Frink."

He touched the brim of his hat in greeting, but froze before moving on to Rebecca. "Frink. I've heard that name somewhere." He puzzled over it briefly. Raising an eyebrow, he promised Hannah, "It'll come to me. It's an unusual name."

He turned to Rebecca, reaching for her outstretched hand. She smiled coolly at him. "I'm Rebecca Castleberry."

Naomi knew that voice: polite but reserved; Rebecca

was evaluating this man before she formed an opinion one way or the other.

"A pleasure. This is our town marshal, Wade Hayes."

The young man, his freckled face framed by shoulder-length, shaggy red hair and a beige cowboy hat, winked boldly. "Ladies."

*Should we swoon now?* Naomi wondered. This town positively overflowed with swaggering, arrogant men. A thought that took her directly back to missing John . . . .

Mr. McIntyre fished the key out of his pocket and shoved it in the front door. "Mrs. Miller, after you've had a chance to look around, if you would be so kind as to accompany me to the bank," he flung the door open and ushered the group inside, "we can sign the papers and conclude our business."

She slid past him without meeting his gaze. "That would be fine." The sooner she was done with Mr. McIntyre, the better.

Hands in his pockets, McIntyre leaned against the wall as the sisters strolled around the large, empty room. Attempting to take his mind off their feminine curves, he tried to guess what they might see in this empty room. Could they imagine dining room tables covered with red check table cloths, politely chatting customers, the sound of klinking silverware?

Hugging the far right wall, L-shaped stairs led to the second floor. He could envision the hotel desk sitting right below the landing, a few red velvet chairs and a settee gathered to create a small lobby. At least that was how he imagined it in a few years. To get started, they would have to be satisfied with log benches and mismatched furniture gathered up from everyone in town who owed him money.

"Were you raised by wolves, Mr. McIntyre?" Naomi's haughty tone and impatient glare perplexed him, until he realized she was looking at his hat. Memories of being chastised by his mother bombarded him and he snatched the Stetson off his head. Huffing, Naomi went back to surveying the new real estate.

The group made their way back to the apartment in the rear, but McIntyre caught Naomi considering the marshal, who stood by the front door, arms folded across his chest as if he was standing guard. He was impressed with her awareness of her surroundings, a skill he'd learned to appreciate during the war. The marshal *had* been ordered to keep an eye out for trouble as McIntyre wasn't completely convinced O'Banion was through sulking over his humiliation. McIntyre suspected, though, that if the annoying little Leprechaun tangled with Naomi again, the outcome would be the same.

Naomi stepped into the small back room and McIntyre heard a sigh of disappointment. He joined her in the doorway and as she and her sisters assessed the dirty, dusty little room. Barely larger than a generous parlor, it had one small buck stove anchored against the back wall, a cot shoved up against the far wall, a few cabinets hung entirely too high on the left wall and a dry sink situated underneath them. Pretty much nothing in it was usable for a commercial kitchen.

After the girls spent a few minutes inspecting the apartment, however, he decided it was time to spell out their next steps. Burning daylight was not something he ever did on purpose.

"My architect, Ian Donoghue, has the finished blueprints for the hotel. I'll send him over tomorrow. Feel free to make changes as you see fit." Naomi crossed her arms and tapped her foot. Ignoring the message her stance screamed at him, McIntyre casually rocked on his heels and addressed her sisters. "All the carpenters in town work for me, of course."

"Of course," Naomi echoed under her breath.

"So I'll round up a crew to get the renovations started in here. I'll have them build some tables for the dining room until we can get decent ones from Pueblo or Denver. We'll need to draw up a building plan and create a list of supplies for the restaurant." He turned to Naomi. "I don't have enough in my other store to provide for that, but there is a freight wagon that comes up daily from Silverton and a larger one that comes from Gunnison. I'll get you the names of some reliable grocers, farmers, etc."

He wandered over to the one dirty window in the room and looked out on the backyard. His leg was weary already and, without thinking, he dropped his hand down to rub his thigh as he considered the yard. Whicker had added a small corral and a lean-to, but there was still a roomy hundred feet or so of grass that rolled down to the banks of the La Plata, the local tributary to the Animas River.

"If you don't wish to sell your mules and horse straightaway, you can keep them back there for a while. They're a little footsore but they will sell. Animals are always needed for running the freight wagons—"

"Mr. McIntyre—" Naomi cut him off, stopping his rapid fire assault of details. "Mr. McIntyre," she repeated, softening her voice. "We're not completely helpless and we would like some say in our own plans. No one died and made you God."

He grinned, amused by her grit. Turning to her, he brazenly assayed her curvaceous figure and haughty expression and decided it was time to put her in her place. "I'm the closest thing you've got in Defiance, Your Highness, and I'm only trying to help. We'll get more done if you won't try to be such a royal pain in the a—"

"Mr. McIntyre," Naomi interrupted again. Breathing faster, he wondered if from anger or his appraising eye, she took a step towards him. "Sadly, it is apparent that your help is unavoidable . . . " She let the insult sink in then continued. "But we need a few days to . . . to recover from our trip and gather our thoughts. Can you understand that? Sampson was my husband's horse. He loved that animal. I . . . " She searched for words, "I—we just can't make all these decisions right now." She crossed her arms tightly across her chest, sending a clear message. "We need some time."

He glanced at her sisters, read the bewildered panic in their eyes, and contritely clutched his hands behind his back. "My most sincere apologies, ladies. I'm a man of action. I don't believe in wasting time or opportunities. However, I should learn to be more sensitive. You've been through a lot," his eyes swung back to Naomi, "all of you." She only nodded curtly at his acknowledgement.

He stepped outside to the hallway, quickly noted that Wade was still stationed at the front entrance, and then addressed her again. "We can go to my attorney's office whenever you're ready. I'll tell Wade to bring your wagon around. There's a large stoop just off the back door there," he motioned towards the rear of the building. "I'll also send a man over to assist with your heavier items."

"That's not necessary," Naomi countered.

"Oh, but I insist. That would be the gentlemanly thing to do . . . and I don't often get to be one of those."

"Then if you'll give me a few moments with my sisters, I'll meet you out front." It wasn't a request.

"Very well." In parting, he turned to Hannah and Rebecca. "You needn't fear for your safety in Defiance. What happened with the men today won't happen again. I'll make it clear that you are not to be accosted in any way."

McIntyre sauntered out to the front porch and lit a cheroot. As he pondered his plans and the next steps for his new tenants, he realized he should make the offer of a bed. He had an exceptionally large one in storage on the second floor and they could certainly use it. The thought of telling these proper young ladies what he'd intended to do with that bed made him smile. He was willing to bet such carnal ideas had never entered their pretty little heads.

In spite of the erotic goals for the four-poster, he thought this was a worthwhile sacrifice. He wouldn't guess how many nights it had it been since these girls had slept on an actual mattress. Feeling generous, he gave the marshal instructions for it as the lawman climbed up into the wagon. As McIntyre walked back to tell the sisters, the sound of Rebecca's voice lifted up in prayer stopped him short.

" . . . and Father, we ask that you would give us courage as we face the unknown here in Defiance. Help us to rely on you and trust completely in your plan. We pray especially that you would strengthen Naomi, Father. She has the difficult burden of dealing with grief on top of all the additional challenges of building a new life. But your word promises us that you won't put more on us than we can bear and we all know how strong you've made her. Give her, give all of us, wisdom and discernment as we deal with each new situation . . . "

He turned away and walked back outside, lost in thought. Memories flooded him and he was ten-years-old again. Sweat trickled down his brow and his tie grieved him fiercely. He remembered a preacher, new to Charleston, who had droned on and on in the suffocating August heat about the Savior's great sacrifice.

Even then McIntyre had been disinclined to accept that Jesus could love the whole human race so much He would willingly die for it. But he also remembered his mother beside him on the pew, lost in prayer, seeking the will of a god who loved her.

He cleared his throat. *But apparently no one else,* he mused, thinking over the monstrous acts of violence he had witnessed with his own eyes. God, he had firmly decided years ago, was a crutch for compassionate and genteel women who would never see the things he had seen.

"You all right, boss?" Wade asked from the wagon seat. "Did you eat some bad elk?"

McIntyre waved at him with that practiced air of hauteur. "I'm fine. See to those things I asked you about." Wade nodded and snapped the reins.

Strangely disquieted by the prayer, McIntyre took a puff on the cheroot and wondered if maybe he had made a mistake in letting these women come to his town. The thought was short lived. How much damage could three Bible-toting, prudish Southern belles do in a town this mean? They would be lucky to survive it. He would be lucky to keep them from being kidnapped by randy miners or renegade Utes.

Troubled, he rubbed his neck. Yes, indeed, those were always possibilities. Muttering a curse, he snuffed the barely smoked cheroot under his boot and decided he would make sure Wade kept an eye on the little angels until further notice.

~~~

# ~five

As the Conestoga disappeared around the corner, Naomi stepped outside. McIntyre thought she looked, well, refreshed, or at least more relaxed. That was good, considering what was coming. Maybe she wouldn't reach for a gun when she found out the details of this business deal.

"The marshal has taken your wagon around back. I've asked him to find Emilio to help unload the heavy items."

"Thank you," she replied, less haughtily than he'd expected.

He pointed across the street. "The bank is just over there."

"Well, I'm ready."

As they crossed the street together, McIntyre asked, "When is your sister's baby due?" Naomi's quick stumble and clenched jaw was all he needed to know he was right. He assumed, therefore, he was right about the absent father as well.

"Baby? What baby?" He thought her voice sounded shrill and shaky.

"Come now, Mrs. Miller," he chided as they negotiated street traffic. "You should remember that I have several women in my employ. I notice things about a woman's figure that most men don't."

"What you don't know..." She turned on him as they reached the boardwalk and raked him with an icy stare that would have terrorized a lesser man, "is that not everything in Defiance is your business."

He begged to differ, but didn't say so. He had acquired enough of this woman's animosity and still might have more coming once they were in the attorney's office. Acquiescing only for the moment, he ushered her further down the walk.

"You need to learn the difference between friends and enemies, Your Highness. Perhaps the question was rather

43

impertinent of me, but I was thinking of Hannah's wellbeing. Should she need the services of a doctor or midwife—"

"We don't need anything," Naomi spat.

He took the hint and changed the subject. "Speaking of health, the man you encountered on the street today—"

"*Which* man? The one who took Hannah's bonnet or the drunk who nearly climbed in the wagon with us?"

McIntyre didn't miss the subtle accusatory tone in her voice, as if all the rude behavior in Defiance could be traced back to him.

"Yes, O'Banion. He doesn't bring much to this town, but he does have a lot of friends. In a matter of hours it will be all over Defiance that you're not in my employ and neither are you working girls. If there are any further...*incidents*, I'll see to it that the marshal and his deputies camp on your doorstep."

Naomi peered up at McIntyre with those green eyes that for the first time weren't flashing like a storm over the Rockies. For the sweep of an instant, she unexpectedly lowered the veil of defensiveness and sighed, a deep, melancholy sound.

"Last July we were harvesting corn, planning picnics, eating fried chicken after church. And now..." She trailed off, pain etching itself in her furrowed brow and trembling lips.

He wished for something helpful to say but words eluded him. It had been so long since he had been required to offer even the smallest amount of comfort to another human that he felt incapable of it. Anything he could think to say would only earn him a fierce slap across the face and he preferred to delay that as long as possible.

Trying to move them past this awkward moment, he touched her on the elbow and pointed at the next entrance. Opening the door for her, she entered the bank and several men—employees and customers—acknowledged her with appreciative glances. In turn, they also offered greetings to McIntyre as he and Naomi walked toward the back of the bank. They climbed a set of steps that took them to a door labeled Davis Ferrell, Esq.

Naomi didn't speak as she and Mr. McIntyre climbed the stairs. She did inhale his scent of a musky cologne and apple-sweetened tobacco. Pleasing odors even if the man was less-than-likable.

She felt completely foolish for having dropped her guard that way outside, revealing such personal thoughts to this pirate. She attributed her momentary weakness to simply being overwrought with grief . . . and irritation. It grated on her nerves that he had spotted Hannah's condition right off . . . which brought her back to the statement he had made about women in his employ. How could he act like running a brothel was as respectable as managing a mercantile? Disgusting. Whatever the case, she would work harder to keep her chin up and back squared in front of this rogue.

They reached the door and Mr. McIntyre knocked but did not wait for an answer as he opened it for Naomi. They stepped into a small office and found Mr. Ferrell at his desk. He looked up from his paperwork, casually removing the spectacles from his nose.

Remembering his manners belatedly, he leaped to his feet and reached for Naomi's hand. "Pardon my manners. Mrs. Miller, it's a pleasure to meet you. McIntyre," he acknowledged him with a nod and his clients took the two seats in front of his desk.

A skinny but dapper man wearing a plain, grey suit, he moved with swift, jerky motions. Naomi wondered if he was always like that or if Mr. McIntyre made him nervous. "I've just finished up the transfer of deed for the hotel." He slid a piece of paper over to Naomi and held out his pen. "If you'll write your full name here and here and sign here and here, that will do it."

Naomi took the pen but also took a moment to review the deed. Mr. McIntyre leaned in uncomfortably close to her ear and whispered, "Davis may look and act like Ichabod Crane, but he's quite a gifted attorney."

Frowning, she moved away from his breath ruffling her hair and perused the legal document in her hand. Naomi noticed almost immediately that there was no description of lot size or water rights, only information on the building.

"I—I'm sorry," she sputtered puzzled. "This doesn't seem to be complete. Why is there no mention here of the lot size? And there is a well, isn't there?" she asked, eyeing both men.

"Lot size?" Mr. Ferrell echoed. "I'm not sure I follow. I was under the impression you were getting the building only." He turned to Mr. McIntyre. "You were in a hurry when you stopped by, but I thought I understood it was the building and not the land."

~~~

# Six

"Not the land?" Naomi repeated toward Mr. McIntyre, knowing there were daggers in her eyes.

"Let me explain," he said, pulling a cigar from his breast pocket. "You see, you came and asked to buy the building. You made no mention of the lot. I assumed you didn't need it or want it. This is a common practice here in the west."

Naomi was dumbfounded. Struck completely speechless, but only for a moment. The glowing ember of anger in her gut caught fire. Her voice dropped to a deceptive calm as she addressed the attorney. "So we own the building, but not the land on which it sits. Is that right?"

"Yes," Mr. Ferrell answered simply.

She cut her eyes over to Mr. McIntyre. "Why would anyone buy a building and not the land? And why didn't you tell me you were separating the two?" She was furious, but mostly with herself for being so stupid.

"Buying the building without the land keeps things affordable and allows land owners to collect rent. I don't want rent, however. Just think of us as partners in the hotel business."

Naomi jumped up so suddenly, she nearly flipped her chair over. Fuming, she stomped away from the men as far as the little office would allow, all of about six feet. Looking out the window, she couldn't have cared less about the low afternoon sun reaching to kiss the distant shimmering mountains. She could've kicked herself a hundred times for getting in this mess and now she would have to explain it to her sisters. How could she have been so stupid?!

*Think, think, think,* she told herself angrily, determined to hold back tears or die trying. *Protect yourself. Lord, help me . . .*

She spun back around. "You are a scoundrel, Mr. McIntyre, but I have learned my lesson. You want to own everything in this town, don't you?" He dropped his eyes, but only for an instant. "So this is what I want." Tilting her chin toward Mr. Ferrell, she kept her eyes on Mr. McIntyre. "I want it in writing that Mr. McIntyre cannot in anyway restrict us from the well. Also, I want monthly payments that will buy the lot in the space of one year. I'll give you $100 for it."

Mr. McIntyre snorted at the offer, but sobered quickly under her burning gaze. He studied her hard but Naomi didn't wilt or redden under the scrutiny this time. If anything, she straightened up more defiantly.

"All right, let's deal." He took a match off Ferrell's desk, struck it on his boot heel and lit the cigar. "The lot is a good acre and this is a boomtown," he told her between puffs. "I'll take one thousand dollars."

"Back home you'd be hung for asking a penny over two hundred."

"Let's say we split the difference." He blew a smoke ring, watched it float over their heads while he thought, and then countered with, "Four hundred."

"And the water rights," she demanded.

"And the water rights."

This time they shook on the deal. Naomi couldn't help but notice how fine and smooth his hands were, not big and calloused like John's. Funny how hands could speak volumes about a man. She wondered when he had last done some actual physical labor or did he have a "man" for everything?

"It'll take me a few minutes to write that up," Mr. Ferrel reminded them, peering over his spectacles. The crease in his brow said he hoped they might take their obvious differences outside.

"We'll wait," Naomi assured him through clenched teeth. Mr. Ferrell sought out Mr. McIntyre for the final answer.

He shrugged. "It's fine, Davis. I'm in no hurry."

"All right then." The attorney sighed and pulled out a fresh sheet of parchment paper. Mr. McIntyre tapped his cigar on the ashtray then took his smoke to the window. Naomi settled back into her seat and stared into the top of Mr. Ferrell's balding head.

"Mrs. Miller, I believe you and your sisters have arrived at an exciting time in Defiance's life." Mr. McIntyre spoke in a conciliatory tone. "Our little town is growing. More people are coming every day. Businesses are expanding. A sixty-foot thick vein of quartz runs underneath our feet. They'll be digging silver and gold out of the ground for another century."

She did not respond to his speech, but he kept going anyway.

"We've already got two stages coming in every week. I'm courting the railroad as well. Yes, sir, in the not-too-distant future, Defiance could rival Denver. We have the common goal of seeing your hotel and restaurant succeed. I hope you believe that."

She cut him a disdainful glance. "You're not a complicated man, Mr. McIntyre. You will help us as long as it benefits you. I believe that."

"Then we understand each other."

"Oh, completely." She turned her eyes back to Ferrell and focused again on his last few remaining hairs. She wondered if he'd pulled them out because of his business dealings with Mr. McIntyre. It would be entirely understandable.


McIntyre considered how Naomi spoke down to him, as if he were an annoying flea, but once they were passed this paperwork, he was quite sure he could win her over. Granted, she was probably the kind of woman who could hold a grudge for a month of Sundays, but his magnetism, money and power were relentless persuaders. He had charmed feistier women onto their backs and this arrogant, self-righteous little belle would be no different.

On the way back to the hotel, McIntyre made a few more polite attempts to settle their little misunderstanding, but Naomi was having none of it. A stubborn woman, he knew she would use this as an excuse to keep him at arm's length. He thought about reminding her of her Christian duty to forgive trespasses, but decided to stay away from that subject matter.

Finally, at the door, he made one more attempt at putting them on some kind of speaking terms. In his experience with Naomi thus far, there was only one thing that got her talking…anger.

"Look, Your Ladyship, there's no reason to be upset with me. This mix-up was not intentional. You assumed the land was part of the deal. I assumed you knew what you were doing."

"My name is not Your Ladyship!" She snapped. "Or Princess. It's Naomi." She shook her head for correction. "I mean *Mrs. Miller* to you. And *you* were the one who knew exactly what you were doing. But that was the first and last time you will take advantage of us, Mr. McIntyre."

Naomi pointed an accusing finger at him for emphasis as her temper flared. "You're a scoundrel and a snake. I won't make the mistake of trusting you again."

He couldn't help but grin. "Now you're getting it. That's the only way to do business in Defiance, much less with me."

Naomi's brow arched. Rolling her eyes, she grabbed the doorknob and spoke without meeting his gaze again. "I see. Now, for the next few days at least, could you leave us alone to settle in?"

He understood the reasons for her request and decided to offer some mercy. He had other enterprises that certainly needed his attention as well. Needling this little princess wasn't making him any money, even if it was grand entertainment. Emilio and Ian could keep him apprised of things here.

"As you wish, Mrs. Miller." He tipped his hat and started off for the Iron Horse, but stopped abruptly. "Oh, by the way…" He waited for Naomi to look at him. "I've left you and your sisters a gift upstairs." He flashed his most winning, most rakish smile at her. "Perhaps you'll think of me when you use it."

~~~~

When Naomi entered the hotel, she heard a commotion upstairs: voices and what sounded like furniture scraping across the floor. She called out to her sisters and they answered excitedly.

"We're up here, Naomi!"

"Come see what Mr. McIntyre has given us."

Was this the gift he'd mentioned? Tired of the emotional rollercoaster he caused her, she trudged up the stairs and turned the corner of the rail to discover her sisters and an underfed, young Mexican boy assembling a massive pencil post bed. Lying next to it was a gigantic mattress, factory made and apparently stuffed with something other than cotton rags or corn shucks.

*He hoped she'd think of him every time she used it?* The audacity and lewdness of the comment shocked Naomi. Had the man no decency whatsoever to say such things to a widow? She was utterly appalled.

Eager to forget Mr. McIntyre, she surveyed the vast, open space of the upstairs floor which was intermittently broken up by the sparse, unfinished skeletons of walls and one stone fireplace. The area was warm and dry, though, and would sport a real bed in a few minutes. It was enticing, Naomi admitted grudgingly. Maybe she would actually sleep tonight.

When Hannah looked up and saw Naomi, she dropped the bed rail she was holding and ran to her sister. "You must see this," she sang joyfully, leading Naomi over to the mattress. "Lie down on it." She pulled Naomi down to the mattress and forced her to recline on it. "Isn't it wonderful?" Hannah flopped down beside her, giggling.

Naomi had to agree it was far more comfortable than the ground underneath a wagon and even beat their cloth tick mattress back home. She closed her eyes and tried to lose herself in the relatively soft bedding, the way it supported and comforted her. Then there was the image of Mr. McIntyre and she sat bolt upright.

She hadn't slept well since John's death and the stress of it was beginning to show. The nights were hideously long.

She dreaded the darkness, the silence, the loneliness of them. Would this bed be a magic carpet to Dreamland? Would she sleep through the night without waking and reaching for John? Tempted, she lay back on the mattress again and gave into the experience.

"Naomi, this is Emilio." Rebecca spoke from the other side of the almost complete bed, tightening a screw in the headboard. "Emilio, this is my sister Naomi."

Naomi and Hannah both sat up. Just a gawky teenager, about the same age as Hannah, he dipped his chin and grinned sheepishly. "*Hola, Senora.*"

"We just couldn't help ourselves," Rebecca rushed on. "When the marshal told us about the bed, we came right up and started putting it together. I can't wait to sleep in it."

Naomi stood up and pulled a folded piece of paper from her waistband. "I don't know if we own the bed, but we own this hotel." She walked over and set the deed on the dusty windowsill. She decided not to share the story of why they didn't own the land upon which the hotel sat. That could wait.

She turned back to Hannah. "Why don't you and I start unloading the wagon and let them finish here? But don't worry, Rebecca, we'll save the heavy stuff until y'all come down." Naomi turned to Emilio. "Thank you for your help. We appreciate it."

The boy bobbed his head like an excited bird. "*De nada.*"

As Hannah and Naomi marched down the stairs, Naomi was curious about the boy and how he had come to live in Defiance. "Does Emilio speak any English?"

"A fair amount from what I could tell." Hannah answered. "He seems to get by—"

A knock at the front door as they reached the landing stopped their progress. They could see the shadow of a man through the frosted glass of the French doors.

Hannah quirked an eyebrow nervously. "Our first guest?"

*Not likely,* Naomi thought, headed for the door. Wishing

she had her gun on her hip, she opened it to discover the marshal fanning himself with a book. He greeted her with a cocky tip of his hat. "Ma'am. Mr. McIntyre asked that I drop this by to you." He handed her a Montgomery Ward catalog.

"Oh," Naomi gasped. She was as pleased to see it as Hannah, who squealed with delight and took it off her hands. "Thank you, Marshal," Naomi quipped, unable to hide a grin over her sister's enthusiasm. Some normalcy in this new life was comforting and Hannah did love to shop, even if she couldn't buy. "I'm surprised. Are we able to get Montgomery Ward to ship here?"

"Ma'am, there's a sayin' in mining towns: if you've got money, men and mules, you've got the world. There's a saloon over in Eureka that sports a real chandelier, come all the way from London, England around the horn to San Francisco to here. Not one crystal was broke." He smiled as if remembering the grandeur of the light. "The saloon over in Animas Forks has an I-talian sculpture of a naked lady— oh, I do apologize, Ma'am."

"Thank you, Marshal. You've made your point." She appreciated the apology. Obviously it wouldn't have fazed Mr. McIntyre a bit to share such lewd information. "But why is it that all the finer items go to the saloons?"

The marshal shrugged. "I reckon 'cuz the saloon owners are the only folks plannin' on stayin'. Most folks are just passin' through, lookin' for that big strike."

Naomi chewed her lip, pondering the violent, unwashed, ill-mannered population of Defiance. As if reading her mind, the marshal added, "Also, Ma'am, I just wanted to remind you that if you've any errands to run, it would be best to get them done before dark. After that, you might be mistaken for . . ."

"I understand. We were going to try to make it to the general store before it closes. Do you know what time that would be?"

"Yes'm, six o'clock." He pulled a watch from his vest pocket and flipped the lid open. "It's right now 4:30."

"Thank you again, Marshal," she told him, slowly

closing the door.

Marshal Hayes tipped his hat, grinned broadly and departed.

~~~

Rose clenched her jaw and wished for a rock to the throw. From the window in McIntyre's room, she had a commanding view of Main Street and her heart burned with jealousy. He had let the little *gringas* in the mercantile, then had escorted the skinny, golden one to the bank.

Rose would not stand for another woman near her man; her plans were too delicate to be upset. This town was hers; Mac was hers. She would simply have to teach these invaders their place.

In an attempt to keep McIntyre in his, Rose lit a candle and set it on his dresser. Reaching between her breasts, she pulled out a small leather pouch. Working it open, she tapped a tiny amount of the brown powder over the candle. It fizzed and sparkled, then released a heavy, sweet scent into the room.

She smiled, confident in her powers and her potions. The scent would relax McIntyre's mind and make her suggestions more enticing to him. Satisfied she had used the right amount, she returned the pouch to her hiding place.

It was a powerful mixture of herbs and prayers. One pinch in the candle eased the mind and the muscles. But a slightly larger amount in a glass of whiskey made a man willing to disclose the value of his claim or even how much gold dust he had in his pockets.

The mood set, Rose reached into a small box of cosmetics she kept on his dresser. She touched up her lipstick, deepening the red of her lips, and sketched a heavy line of coal around her dark, chocolate eyes. Surveying her image in the full length mirror, she untied her silk robe and pushed her corset higher to lift her generous bosom.

Turning from side to side, Rose admired her curvaceous lines. She liked the way her dark skin glowed against the pink silk undergarments and her eyes flashed a dangerous, consuming fire. She didn't really need the powder, she knew, but the voices encouraged her to trust them for more and more of their knowledge. She was desperate to gain all that she could. Pleased with the image in the mirror, she pulled a jet black curl from behind her neck and draped it between her breasts like an arrow pointing to naughty pleasures. Rose was hungry for more than knowledge tonight.

A soft tap at the door made her step away from the mirror and slide her robe seductively off one shoulder. Her mood turned dark when little Daisy peaked around the door.

"I thought you were Mac," Rose complained as the girl let herself in the room.

Daisy's eyes widened. "No, he's still downstairs talking with the man from the stagecoach. He sent me up here to get his mail."

Rose knew she scared the girl. She grinned with cruel pleasure as Daisy nervously searched his desk for the letters. *Daisy* was the perfect flower name for this wisp of a girl. She was small, delicate, and pale just like a wild daisy. And from what the customers told her, Daisy had all the passion of a dried flower.

Not like Rose.

She liked the power her long, tall, buxomly body gave her over men. Even McIntyre was weak-kneed around her at times, with or without the powder. Consequently, she could pick and choose her customers; Daisy had to take whatever nasty, drunken miner came her way.

"Tell the Flowers I'm expecting Pete Waters tonight." Daisy nodded obediently as she continued rifling through McIntyre's desk. Pete owned a profitable claim and was a big tipper. Better yet, he always bathed before visiting her. The girls knew better than to distract him from Rose...or there would be Hell to pay. The thought of tormenting her fellow soiled doves with a headless rat in one bed or the other brought a smile to Rose's face.

"Daisy," McIntyre called irritably from downstairs. "Hurry up, girl."

"Got them, Mr. McIntyre!" She scurried out the door with the mail in her hand.

Delighted with her power, Rose stretched herself out on McIntyre's sofa. After nearly two years here, they had established a comfortable routine before heading downstairs to work. He would be up in just a moment, a snifter of whisky in his hand. She would massage his shoulders, then they would move to the bed and make love, the only passion for her since anyone after that was merely a customer, and then they would sleep for a while. At least, *he* would sleep.

Rose would stay awake, whispering dark prayers over him, prayers passed down from Mayan mothers to their daughters for centuries. When she uttered the words of her ancestors, she could hear their voices, and they would tell her things. Show her things. Someday, Defiance, McIntyre and all he owned would be hers. The voices had promised her–

McIntyre entered the room, glanced at Rose, then went to his desk and sat down. Her brow furrowed with uncertainty. She had seen a flash of something in his eyes she didn't like. Had it been boredom? Disappointment? Something else? Deciding to overcome it, she got to her feet and glided over to him. As he studied the liquor inventory, she rubbed his shoulders, reaching deep into the muscles, opening his mind to the scent in the air.

"Tell me about the *gringa* women," she purred in a silky Latin accent. He was more tense than usual. "Do they upset you? Your muscles are like guitar strings."

He slapped his pencil down. "They do not upset me."

Afraid of losing the moment, she moved to a fresh set of muscles, kneading them, caressing them. Slowly, the tension turned to liquid and drained away. He leaned back in his chair, inhaled deeply and let her work her magic.

"They are sisters," he murmured. "The middle one, I think, she lost her husband back on the trail. The other two aren't married."

"Did you offer them jobs? I saw them here earlier."

"Women like that don't work in saloons." He rolled

56

his head around, loosening the tense muscles. "Bible-toters we call them. They think God told them to settle here in Defiance, so I gave them Whicker's building. The town needs decent women."

"Decent," Rose scoffed. "They sound crazy. And any woman, desperate enough, would work here for you, my love," she whispered, snaking her hands across his chest. Rose knew her dark skin, dangerous eyes and unabashed passion was a wonderful diversion. She owned McIntyre, body and mind. That was enough, for now.

~~~

## Seven

The day was fading quickly and Rebecca and Naomi were running out of time to make a trip to the mercantile. They insisted this would be the time for Hannah to get some rest while they ran the errand and summarily put her to bed. Emilio had insisted on walking with them to the general store, telling them that if they didn't need his help, he would go on home. Secretly, Rebecca was glad for the escort, even though she figured the stringy teenager wouldn't exactly intimidate a determined miner. She was afraid of this town but wanted to be able to live in it without being bullied by it.

She and Naomi kept their heads down, bonnets hiding their faces and hurried through the crowd. A few men called to them, some whistled, a handful even followed from a distance, but no one attempted to stop them. Rebecca could hear the whispers, though, as if the men were debating the repercussions of approaching them.

"Naomi, we didn't finish unloading the wagon, but I'm afraid something's missing." Rebecca's tone was mysterious and Naomi obligingly slowed her pace. Rebecca leaned towards her sister and lowered her voice. "I didn't see the box with the pinafores, dresses, and baby clothes in it."

Naomi's brow shot up. "I thought you said you packed it."

"I said I'd tend to it, but it was too heavy. I asked Hannah to ask John to load it…I think we left it behind."

Naomi shook her head. "If we forgot that, we've got a problem on our hands. You know I can't sew very well."

Rebecca chuckled. "I can, little sister. It will be all right." She sighed wearily. "It's just an inconvenience, not the end of the world, but there were some really precious things in that box."

As they discussed their plans without mentioning Hannah's condition, Marshal Hayes materialized out of nowhere. With a cocky tip of his hat, he fell into step beside

Naomi and Rebecca. "Afternoon, ladies. Allow me to escort you on your errand." He nodded at Emilio. "I think you could do with a bit more size to your bodyguard."

Naomi responded to the marshal's request with ingrained politeness. "Oh, that's not necessary, Marshal."

"Or is it?" Rebecca half-argued, jabbing her sister in the ribs.

The marshal lowered his hat over his eyes to block the low afternoon sun and looked over at Naomi. "There's talk of a rematch between you and O'Banion, but this time in the Pit. Does that answer your question?"

"The Pit?" Naomi asked.

"In a minin' town, men'll fight just about anything and pay to see it. Drunk enough, I could see 'em cartin' you off to our little arena. Which is one of the reasons Mr. McIntyre asked me to keep an eye on you and your sisters. By and by, the men'll get used to you being here and come to understand you're not," he lowered his voice, "loose women."

By and by? And just how long would that be, Rebecca wondered.

Her question was cut short by a bloodcurdling scream from somewhere in front of them. Abruptly they were confronted by an unmoving wall of plaid and leather-covered backs. The men were fascinated by some commotion on the street, but Naomi and Rebecca couldn't see a thing. The shriek was instantly followed by another, yet this was a different voice. Rebecca realized the screams were coming from women, but they were filled with rage not fear.

"Fight!" A man yelled gleefully, and the cry galvanized the witnesses. As if the crowd was one body, it surged to the edge of the boardwalk, sandwiching Naomi and Rebecca between smelly, cheering men practically quivering with excitement.

The marshal muttered, "Uh, oh," and pressed his way through the spectators, emerging onto the front row. Through the shifting bodies, Rebecca caught a flash of red and blue silk and what she guessed were gyrating ostrich feathers. She heard several slaps accompanied by astonishingly skilled swearing, grunts and screams akin to animal sounds. She'd never heard women carry-on so and kept thinking it couldn't be what it sounded like.

Curious, she, Naomi and Emilio wiggled their way to the front as well and beheld an eye-gouging, hair-pulling, fingernail-breaking cat fight that would have rivaled mountain lions battling to the death. Two women, both barely dressed, circled each other warily. Blue and pink silk dresses hung in shreds from their bodies, feathers poked wildly from disheveled red and blond hair, blood dribbled from noses and mouths. Everyone within sight of this hellish battle was frozen to the spot. The women lunged at each other and a raucous cheer went up from the crowd as nails sank into flesh.

Trying to work her hands around the blonde's throat, the redhead, fire blazing in her eyes, called the girl an unholy name, and demanded her money. "That's my fifty dollars and I'll get it out of you if I have to rip off your arms, you bi–"

The blonde halted the vile word by slapping the woman's face so hard Rebecca was sure the sound could be heard at the other end of town. The girl then made an attempt to run, but the redhead grabbed a handful of hair and pulled her right back into the fight.

Rebecca, appalled by the barbarous display, was sure the marshal would put an end to it any second. However, when she glanced over at him, he was grinning and shadow boxing with exuberance. Furious, and for once reacting faster than Naomi, she reached over and grabbed his arm. "Why aren't you doing something? Stop this before someone gets hurt."

"Ah, that's just Diamond Lil and one of her girls. She don't usually hurt'em too bad. It'll be over in another minute."

Naomi blinked, as if snapping herself out of a fight-induced hypnosis, and shoved the marshal toward the street. "Do something or we will."

He withstood the shove, holding his ground, but Naomi scowled and shoved again. "I doubt Mr. McIntyre would appreciate it if we became embroiled in that."

That was enough to plant doubt in the marshal's mind as he stumbled off the boardwalk. Frowning his disapproval, he scanned the crowd. "Come on, Corky." He plucked a short, pudgy man from the front lines. "Help me break this up." Corky scratched his head as he pondered the request, but then shrugged and followed the marshal into the street.

The women were on the ground now, rolling about like entwined, murderous snakes. The marshal grabbed the redhead, apparently Diamond Lil, and pulled her, kicking and screaming, off the little blond. Corky grabbed the girl on the ground and helped her to her feet. Scratched and bleeding, she stared defiantly at the wild cat in the marshal's arms.

"All right, Lil!" He pinned the woman's arms to her side and hugged her tightly, picking her up off the ground. She fought harder and screamed louder. He squeezed harder, to the point, Rebecca guessed, her breathing was constricted. That did the trick and the fight went out of the woman. A disappointed roar shot up from the crowd, but the men quickly started drifting away.

The marshal relaxed his grip ever so slightly. "Now, Lil, you and what's-her-name go on back to Tent Town. Keep your trouble over there. You know Mr. McIntyre doesn't like this kind of stuff spillin' out here in front of God and everybody."

The two women singed the air with their hateful stares, but after an instant, Lil shrugged herself loose from the marshal. "Fine, we'll take care of this like ladies." No one missed the dripping sarcasm, including the marshal.

"Corky, see to it they get back to the Broken Spoke in one piece."

The man brightened and released his delicate hold on his prisoner. "Fine with me. I needed a drink anyway." He eyed the angry women and shrugged. "I reckon I can get'em there in one piece. Maybe."

And just like that, things were back to what passed for normal in Defiance. Naomi looked at Rebecca and shook her head. "They're nothing but a bunch of animals here."

Rebecca couldn't argue with that and shot Emilio an accusing stare. "Is it like this all the time?"

Pulling his shoulders up, the boy nodded sheepishly. "Ees Defiance."

Leaping up on the boardwalk, the marshal rejoined them, wearing a pleased expression. "Happy, ladies?"

"No, Marshal, we're not," Rebecca's sharp tone startled him and the marshal inched back. "Do you have no respect whatsoever for the badge you're wearing?" As Marshal Hayes' face fell, a righteous indignation surfaced in Rebecca's heart and she decided to let it square her shoulders. It had been a long time since she'd been passionate about anything. Standing to her full, impressive height, she took a step toward the marshal, coming almost eye-to-eye with him. "You're not doing your job. That star on your chest is not a piece of jewelry. If you have any honor at all, then you know it's a *responsibility*." Turmoil filled the marshal's eyes. He started to speak, but bit it back and only shook his head. Rebecca nodded. "I see."

"No. No, you don't," the marshal argued. A kind of regret softened the younger man's features. "I'm no Wyatt Earp. Defiance has doubled in size since I put this here badge on. There are eight saloons now and a mine that runs twenty-four hours a day. If I tried to settle this town down on my own, I'd be dead before the next shift change."

Rebecca understood the young man was trying to tell her he was not a hero, but he was in over his head. She sympathized with that feeling and lowered her chin, letting some of the steam out of her anger. Reaching for Naomi, who was staring at her as though she'd transformed into some other species, Rebecca pulled her wide-eyed sister away from the humbled marshal. "Let's finish our errands before the next show."

The sisters gave one last glance to the retreating saloon girls who, though separated by an alert Corky, were still eyeing each other warily. Disgusted, Rebecca shook her head. What in the world was the matter with these people?

Was there some beacon that called all the worst elements of society into this valley? Or did Defiance itself corrupt its citizens?

Rebecca was beginning to see why Naomi had so little hope for the town. Women fighting in the streets like rabid dogs. Men cheering it on as if it were a boxing match. She could barely believe it. Still, it had felt almost *liberating* to react to something. Rebecca couldn't remember the last time she had stood up to anybody about anything and that no doubt explained why Naomi was staring at her.

The marshal and Emilio in tow, the sisters marched across the street to the Boot and Co. general store. Rebecca noted that someone had added beneath the name in fresher paint and smaller letters, *Charles McIntyre – Owner*. Two frightfully rotund Indian women sat out front with baskets of colorful, fresh berries for sale. The sisters longingly eyed the blueberries as they passed by and Rebecca knew they would have to purchase some.

Once in the store, she and Naomi looked around and were shocked by the variety of items. To their delight, the general store, though little more than a large log cabin, carried an abundant supply of fresh fruits and vegetables, canned goods, hardware, and smoked meats.

Naomi raised a brow at the marshal, clearly impressed by the little emporium. "Money, men and mules?"

The marshal nodded. "Money, men and mules." Folding his arms over his chest, he puffed up like a rooster, possibly pleased that his town had somehow been elevated in their eyes. "Defiance might be a rowdy hole-in-the wall, but we do like our supplies."

~~~

Hannah was still sleeping when the Rebecca and Naomi returned. Anxious about disturbing her, Naomi suggested they cook dinner outside over a fire one last time. The marshal excused himself, citing important duties, and Emilio started to slink away as well, but the girls weren't about to let him go without showing their appreciation for his help.

"Emilio, you must eat dinner with us," Rebecca coaxed, taking a box of groceries from him and setting them on the kitchen floor. "We'd love to have you stay if you don't have a better offer."

Naomi could see that the boy was waffling and pushed him over the edge. "We insist. If you wouldn't care to chop a few pieces of firewood, I'll get some rocks to ring a pit."

"Ok," he acquiesced, bobbing his head. "Eef you're sure ees OK?"

The warm smiles of his hostesses pretty much answered that question. Rebecca stayed inside to put some things away and check on Hannah while Naomi and Emilio hunted around for the ax. Whicker had left a fairly impressive pile of unsplit logs, but Naomi knew just from Southern winters, it wouldn't be enough.

Once their new helper was on task, she appraised the backyard. The former tenant had also slapped up a small corral and a rickety lean-to, both of which she had initially categorized as an eyesore. Now she was grateful for them.

The chickens, in cages tucked under the lean-to, squawked and clucked when they saw her, eager for some corn. Sampson and the mules trotted over to the fence, neighing expectantly for their evening meal. She let her eyes roam back to the wagon, sitting alone and unhitched. It plucked a string of sadness in her.

Fighting a melancholy mood that threatened to drown her, she meandered down to the stream and enjoyed the warmth of the sun balanced precariously on the ridge of the distant mountains. The mountains glowed a radiant purple in the retreating light and the disappearing sun colored the snowy peaks a pale shade of orange. The peaceful landscape gave her spirit rest. In spite of everything that had brought them here, everything they'd seen, she couldn't help but feel these mountains ministered to her soul. If only John could be sitting here with her now...


Night had descended by the time they were all sitting down

to supper. Naomi had gone to the extra work of choosing unsplit logs to drag up and set around the fire as seats. She couldn't believe after months of camping, that she still had a desire to experience these mountains by starlight. Cool and clear, summer nights in the Rockies suited her perfectly. She didn't care if she ever sweated through the suffocating humidity of the South again.

They ate hungrily—especially Emilio—and the girls couldn't help but notice. Hannah slowly swirled a biscuit around in her gravy as she studied him. "Emilio, do you have family in town?"

"*Si*," he nodded, popping a piece of ham in to his mouth. "My seester ees here too."

"Oh, that's nice. What does she do?"

He stopped chewing abruptly, then slowly shrugged and swallowed. "She work for Meester McIntyre, too."

They knew enough by his reaction not to follow that line of questioning, but Naomi couldn't help but wonder why he was so hungry. "Where do the two of you stay? Who cooks for you?"

"I have a cot in the back room at the Iron Horse and Rose has a nice room upstairs. She bring me food from Martha's Kitchen or sometimes leftovers when she cooks for Meester McIntyre."

Naomi had noticed Martha's Kitchen on their way in. It was a dirty, slapped-together, open-air "restaurant" just a few buildings up the street. Men ate on long tables out in front of it while a woman walked around with a pot dropping unappetizing mush onto the customers' plates. No wonder the child was half-starved. And he slept in the back of a saloon. Pitiful.

"I don't mean to pry, Emilio," Rebecca pressed, "but where are your parents?"

He rested his plate on his knobby knees and thought for a moment. "Banditos burn our farm and shoot my parents when I was small." He shrugged. "I don't remember Mama and Papa. The men who burned us out made us go with them. We lived with them for a long time. I don't know, maybe *cinco*—um, five or six years. Then one night, Rose and I leave." He greedily scraped up some rice and cleaned his plate, satisfaction evident in the shadows on his face. "We find Defiance, about, I theenk two years ago."

Rebecca pursed her lips thoughtfully for a second. "What is it that you do for Meester—er, I mean, *Mr*. McIntyre?" Naomi and Hannah grinned at the slip. The boy's thick accent was infectious and endearing.

"Whatever he saze. Today, he say, help the seesters. Do what they say."

Rebecca nodded. "Well, Emilio, we hope that he lets you come back tomorrow. You've truly been an invaluable help, but please know there is always room for you at our table whether you work for us or not. Will you come to supper again sometime?"

Lowering his head, Emilio looked down and scratched his knee through holey trousers. Naomi could see he was struggling with the invitation and the unexpected friendship behind it. She was rather surprised herself by her enjoyment of his company, but he was such a sweet, unassuming boy. And he had been a tremendous help. She thought he was as out of place in Defiance as the three of them.

"We hope you'll come back to our table lots of times," Hannah invited between bites. "It's good to have a friend in this town."

Tugging nervously at his collar, Emilio rose to his feet. "Eef I say to Meester McIntyre that you need more help, this would be true, yes?"

"Oh, yes," the sisters chorused.

"You've been more help than we can tell you." Rebecca excitedly waved her cup in the air for emphasis. "Truly you have."

The boy nodded resolutely. "Then I tell Meester McIntyre that." Quickly, he turned, set his plate on his seat and disappeared into the darkness, apparently taking a back trail to the saloon.

The boy's abrupt departure puzzled the girls. Listening for his footsteps to fade, the three sat quietly around the fire, but their silence stretched on. Staring up at the stars, Naomi assumed they were all speculating about the future. Or perhaps knowing that they had a warm bed to sleep in made it easier to dawdle outside beneath this stunning canopy.

She had an urge to talk about the day, the boorish men, the fighting prostitutes, but decided not to bring up any of it. So emotionally fragile, she worried any talk about their current circumstances might break down her defenses. She needed to be alone before she thought any more about that.

Eventually, as they sat there, they became aware of the rising volume of noise in the town. Naomi had assumed with darkness Defiance would settle down a bit; but if anything, it was more rowdy. Listening to their fire pop and hiss, they could also clearly hear a raucous, non-stop piano belting out half-recognizable tunes down at the Iron Horse Saloon, accompanied by drunken laughter, raised voices, and the shrill giggles of tipsy women. From the street, the jangle of wagons and clip-clop of horses were punctuated by yelling, cursing and the thud of fists on flesh. Sounds they had heard throughout the day, but now they seemed twice as loud and a hundred times more frightening.

Hannah looked off in the distance, her eyes wide and round. "It's noisy isn't it? Will they do this all night long? Be so rowdy?"

Naomi poked the fire and followed the sparks up as they swirled towards heaven. She suspected the party was just getting started. Fear and loathing in her voice, she whispered, "I wouldn't be a bit surprised."

~~~

# Eight

As Rose grabbed a clean glass from the bar, she caught sight of Emilio slipping in for the evening. Moving fast and sure like a little mouse, he shot through the bat wing doors of the saloon and snaked his way around crowded tables back to the storage room. She flexed her fingers restlessly.

*Stupid brat*, she thought. He hadn't even tried to find her. Well, that just meant she didn't have to waste time being nice. He knew what happened when he disobeyed her.

Forgetting the customer waiting on the glass, she sauntered behind the bar and grabbed a plate covered with a white hand towel. Pushing past Brannagh, the bartender and only man in town who seemed actually bored by Rose, she marched towards her brother's room.

"Emilio," she snapped, bursting through the door. "Wake up you lazy rat." Irritably, she snatched the blanket off him and threw it on the floor. "Get up," she ordered again, setting the plate down on a barrel and lighting the small lamp on the wall. Reluctantly, Emilio sat up and stared at her with weary acceptance.

She settled on a stool across from his cot and spoke slowly, to let him soak up her anger. "I told you to find me before you went to bed. Tell me about the *gringas*."

He ran his hands through his black hair, showing his frustration with her bossiness, which only made Rose smile. "I don't know. They seem very nice. What ees it you want to know?"

She sighed and glanced around for something to throw at him. "*Stupido*," she growled, clenching her fists. "I want to know more. I told you to find out anything you could. Where do they come from? Why are there no men with them? Why are they in the old general store?"

"They come from some place called North Carolina but were on their way to California. The skinny one, *Senora*

68

Naomi, her husband died on the trail. I don't think there are any men with them. They're going to turn the store into a cantina—no, a, um," he snapped his fingers. "A Restaurant. A restaurant and a hotel. That's all I know. But they want me to help again *mañana*."

Rose fiddled with the little gold crucifix at her neck. Were these pale-faced *gringas* trouble or just a small bump in the road? Maybe the answer to that was up to McIntyre. Just how close would he get to them? Best not to take chances. "Surely it wouldn't be too difficult to get them to continue on their way to California," she purred. "They just need to understand how inhospitable Defiance can be."

Emilio groaned. "You should leave them alone. They don't want any trouble."

Rose grabbed her brother's jaw and shoved him back down into his cot, her soul burning with hate. Gouging her fingers into the soft flesh of his cheeks, she hissed, "Did I ask for your opinion? Tell me something like that again and I'll gut you like a pig. I take care of you. You do as *I* say."

Giving him one last, vicious squeeze, she stood up and straightened her gown. "Sleep tight." Chin in the air, Rose spun and opened the door into the light and smoke.

~~~

Pouring his friend a drink, McIntyre walked the whiskey over to Ian then returned to his closet to finish dressing. As he buttoned up a blue silk vest and reached for a tie, he noticed Ian was unusually quiet. He wasn't speaking, but the thud, thud, thud of his cane on the carpet spoke volumes.

"Something on your mind this evening, Ian?"

The cane stopped and he heard Ian shift in the chair. "I was giving thought to the young ladies ye were telling me about." McIntyre smiled at his last word which sounded like *a boot.*

Stepping in front of a full length mirror, McIntyre started to work on his tie, but he couldn't miss the worry in his friend's reflection. "And what were you wondering?"

"How is it ye can be so sure they're they'll run a decent place? Ye dunna anything about them."

McIntyre grinned as he pulled his string tie into a symmetrical bow and straightened it. "Naomi Miller is the kind of woman who would die before ever lowering herself to debauchery. If I know one thing, Ian," he turned to his friend, "I know women. I can't say they're pure as the driven snow, since the youngest one is with child and I strongly doubt she's married, but they are..." He thought for a moment then came up with, "decent, at least by our standards."

"Ye asked me to help ye run our mine and plan a town." Ian sighed and rose to his feet as McIntyre donned his hat. "I can map out ventilation shafts, lay out city streets, even plan a sewer system, but I canna bring in schools and churches and decent folks to attend them. Ye must start contacting respectable businesses for investment in the area." Ian paused and ran a hand along his graying beard. "And ye must treat decent folks well once they arrive. Holding the land back from those decent girls wasna a good start."

McIntyre raised his brow. Ian rarely chided him about his morals, even though McIntyre sensed he often wanted to. "Well, I did agree to sell her the lot and at a ridiculously reduced rate. Does that make you feel any better?"

"Some...maybe."

Ian sounded doubtful and McIntyre thought the man looked a little older tonight, as if fifty was weighing on him.

"I know I told ye that I'd stay through the winter," Ian continued, "but as it stands, now, I'll be leaving at the end of September, or whenever the restaurant is complete. I am an old man and this free-for-all is not to my liking."

McIntyre shoved his right hand into his pocket and ruminated on the announcement for a moment. "That pushes some of our plans back to the spring. And are you sure you trust me with your half of the profits from the mine? No one else would."

Ian slapped his friend on the back and tapped his chest with the handle of his cane—an ornately carved silver wolf's head. A hint of humor glimmered in his hazel eyes. "No one else saved ye from being shanghaied to China. I know I have yer eternal gratitude."

The reminder drew McIntyre to a halt. The events would never be clear, thanks to the drug in his beer, but he recalled a dark alley, the vague understanding that he was being taken where he did not want to go, feeble protests... and the flash of a silver wolf's head.

If Ian hadn't happened by at that precise moment, McIntyre knew he could well be swabbing the deck of a leaky freighter right now. The thought made him shudder and he rolled his shoulders in an attempt to exorcise the memory. "I would say *eternal* is an understatement of Biblical proportions, my friend."

~~~~

Naomi sat by the fire for a long while after her sisters retired, staring into the glowing, orange embers as if hypnotized by them. Her mind mercifully blank, she circled high above her grief like a hawk soaring through an empty sky. She simply wanted to float and let the wind take her where it would. Sampson whinnied in the darkness and the sound carried her spirit home.

She saw John riding his favorite mount into their backyard, right up to where she was beating a rug without mercy. He slid down from the saddle then swept her up into a spinning embrace, laughing foolishly, almost deliriously.

"I asked for a piano and God gave us a wagon!"

His laughter was contagious and Naomi couldn't help but join in, albeit with bemused confusion. When he smacked a big, wet, silly kiss on her, she pushed away from him and placed a firm hand on his chest. "Now, hold on a minute, John Robert Miller! What is going on here?"

Laughing with abandon, he pushed past the hand and pulled her back into an air-stealing hug, spinning her around again as if she weighed no more than an arm load of cornstalks. Struggling to bring his giggles under control, he

71

looked her in the eye and reported gleefully, "If I had tried, I probably wouldn't have been able to find a long-haul wagon for sale within a hundred miles of here, and James Maynard has one right down the road.

"A freight wagon?" Naomi still did not see the reason for his euphoria.

"A Conestoga. The best wagon ever made for hauling a family, not just freight. I was worried it might take days if not weeks to modify our farm wagon and I don't think Page will give us that kind of time. This wagon eliminates all the delays. It's a sign, woman. A sign. I asked God to drop a piano on me so I'd know we were doing the right thing. We've made the right decision to sell out and go to California. I know it now, just as surely as I know my own name."

He hugged her hard again and this time she allowed herself to melt to him. His excitement was so childlike, it gave Naomi a great deal of pleasure to see him this happy. But it worried her, as well.

"John, have you been so unhappy here," she asked against his shoulder.

"No, no." He held her tighter. "I've been truly content here with you, Naomi. If you said right now that you didn't want to go, for whatever reason, then that would be that. We'd try to stick it out here with Hannah. It's just that the West beckons to me. There's a tug I can't deny. If I can take my family with me, then I'll go. That's the only way I'll go."

He kissed the top of her head as she snuggled deeper into his chest. "Wither thou goest, my love," she whispered softly. "Wither thou goest."

She squeezed him again, then stepped back some so she could see his face to tell him about a visitor. "We had a few folks stop by today. You'd be interested in the second guest." He held on to her, obviously not willing to let her go quite yet. "Kate came for a visit."

Stunned, he dropped his arms from around her and moved back. "Kate Page? What in the world did she want?"

"Initially, she wanted us to talk Hannah into accepting

Frank's money to leave town. She pretty much offered any amount it would take. She's afraid that if Hannah doesn't leave, it may be years before Frank let's Billy come home."

"She sounds desperate."

"She is and she's pitiful." Naomi shook her head. "She worships her children, especially Billy. I took pity on her and told her you were going to suggest a selling price for our farms to Frank. If he took it, then she would have Billy home in no time. I suggested she use her spousal influence to talk him into accepting our price."

"What'd she say?"

"She said if Frank didn't take the offer, she would, with her own money."

Brow furrowed, John went and sat down on the back steps. "I wanted to take a bite out of Frank, not his innocent wife." He laced his fingers together and fell into silence. After a moment, he shook his head. "I wanted the high end of fair for our farms and not a penny less, but I reckon I'll be a little more willing to negotiate...."

Smiling, Naomi walked over and joined him on the steps. She leaned back on one elbow and studied him. His mind was racing, she could tell, but for the moment she allowed herself to concentrate on the sprigs of blonde hair poking out from beneath his hat, the dimpled chin, those broad, strong shoulders, and arms that were the size of small trees. She'd known all along he would go to Page with a reasonable price on their farms. Her heart swelled with pride.

He smiled and she knew that he knew she was drinking him in. "Like what you see," he asked huskily.

"Have I ever told you that you are perfect?" She had the desire to curl up in his lap like a contented house cat.

A shot of lightning coursed through her when he turned those lusty hazel eyes in her direction. He slid up alongside her, resting on an elbow as well. Face to face with him, Naomi had to fight to keep from losing her concentration. He kissed her and she reveled in the inviting softness of his lips. It was like a drop of water to a parched man lost in the desert. He encircled her and pulled her on top of him, his mind now distracted with things closer to home.

Hypnotic eyes, filled with desire, lassoed her will as he spoke in a low voice. "Do you know what I'd like to do right now?"

"Well, I sure hope it's chores," Hannah quipped sarcastically from behind them. "Otherwise, I'd better leave."

Naomi and John jumped up as if they'd been shot out of a cannon. Naomi was sure they had never moved so fast as they straightened and tucked their clothing and smoothed down loose hairs. Despite the awkwardness of the moment, Hannah threw back her head and laughed richly, obviously enjoying their embarrassment.

"That's not funny," Naomi scolded. She looked at John and realized she was probably as red-faced as he was. "What are you doing, sneaking up on us like that?"

Hannah shoved her hands onto her hips. "I cleared my throat but neither one of you heard me. Honestly, y'all need a fence if you're going to roll around in your backyard like that."

"We weren't rolling around," John argued, but the laugh escaped his lips before he could finish the sentence. Undeniably caught in the act, he chuckled with resignation. "Well, I believe my work here is done. I'll go take care of Sampson." As he walked by Hannah, he tossed her a mischievous little wink and strode on to the barn, Sampson dutifully following behind.

Hannah pushed past her sister as she climbed the stairs to the back door. "Good grief, Naomi. You two act like you got married yesterday."

Naomi sighed, a dreamy, contented sound. "He's wonderful isn't he? I don't know what I'd do without him."

"Probably more housework." Hannah's sarcastic suggestion was followed by the slam of the screen door.

Naomi laughed aloud at the memory, longing for the contented, easy life they all once shared. Her last words, though, echoed down to her, spoken so easily and yet so prophetically, hitting her with the force of a sledgehammer.

I *don't* know what to do without him.

A cloudburst of self-pity unleashed itself on her. John was dead. Hannah was with child. They were trapped in this horrible town. Mr. McIntyre was the devil in fancy clothes and the citizens conducted themselves with the grace and manners of wolves. She was sick of it...sick of it all.

Naomi knew she should pray . . . knew she should try to square her shoulders and face up to things. Instead, she put her face in her hands and wept with all the force of a bursting dam.

~~~

# Nine

Rebecca worried about Naomi. She wasn't eating enough. She listlessly twirled scrambled eggs around her plate as they discussed writing letters to family and friends. Huddled around the scrubbed-clean kitchen stove, sitting on boxes for seats, they tossed about names. Of course, the obvious choice for the first letter was Matthew, John's brother, but Naomi didn't say his name. Rebecca knew, though, when the time was right, Naomi would handle i—a man's voice calling from out front interrupted their discussion.

"Hellooo in the house," a heavy Scottish brogue queried. "Ladies, are ye decent or shall I come back?"

Rebecca, closest to the door, left her wobbly crate and stepped out into the hallway. Still holding her plate, she looked the man over carefully. "Can we help you?"

He snatched a strange, round cap off his head and crammed it into his hands, where he was already holding a long roll of paper. "Ian Donoghue. I'm the architect Mr. McIntyre told ye about."

He was a tall, older gentleman, nicely dressed, handsome, but with grayish, thinning hair on top and a thickening waist covered by a colorful argyle sweater. "I'll come back if now's no' a good time. It's just that McIntyre asked me to jump right on this."

"I guess now is all right." Rebecca glanced back at Hannah and Naomi to be sure. They agreed readily enough with subtle nods and she motioned toward the kitchen. "We're just having some breakfast. Can I fix you something, Mr. Donoghue?"

He walked quickly back to where she was and took her hand. "Ye are…"

"Rebecca Castleberry." She ushered him into the little room where Hannah and Naomi were rising to their feet to greet their guest. "These are my sisters Naomi Miller and

Hannah Frink."

"No, no. This willna do." His unexpected response drew quizzical looks from the girls. "Emilio," he called over his shoulder. They heard the front door open and the boy came running. "I canna work without a table and chairs. Go to Mr. McIntyre and tell him that *exactly*."

"*Si, Senor!*" The boy practically lunged for the front door.

Ian turned back to the girls and winked. "Tis a true pleasure to meet ye. Now, I've had my breakfast..." His eyes sought Rebecca. "I could, however, do with a wee bit more o' coffee."

Rebecca smiled broadly at him, puzzled that he made her feel so cheerful. "Coming right up." She hurried to the back wall, rummaged through a wooden box sitting next to the stove and came up triumphantly with another cup. As she poured the coffee, Rebecca noticed that Naomi observed Mr. Donoghue with keen interest.

"McIntyre tells me that ye ladies have come all the way from North Carolina—thank ye." He took the cup from Rebecca who couldn't help but linger just a moment, his eyes were so jovial and such a deep shade of blue. "I've only been in America three years and still dunna my geography. It's somewhere in the South, isn't it?"

Rebecca grinned. "Just above Georgia and South Carolina, if that helps. I've never met anyone from Scotland. Your brogue reminds me of the clip-clop of horses on a brick street."

Something akin to astonished delight illuminated Ian's face. "Tha' is the most wonderful description I've ever heard o' my accent. Are ye a writer?"

Rebecca cleared her throat and fought the heat rising to her cheeks.

"Dear sister Rebecca used to work at a newspaper." Naomi stepped up to her sister and hugged her tightly, a move that struck Rebecca as unusually showy. "She is the writer among us."

"How fortunate for ye." Mr. Donoghue's cup was

poised at his lips, yet he hadn't taken his first sip. Instead, he seemed keenly interested in Rebecca.

Uncomfortable with his fascinated scrutiny and Naomi's smothering embrace, Rebecca shoved her hands into her apron pockets. "Well, that's what it reminded me of," she said, gently shrugging off her sister's arm.

Ian cleared his throat. "The difference between the right word and the almost right word is the difference between lightning and the lightning bug. Or so states Mr. Mark Twain. I would believe, Mrs. Castleberry, that ye could describe lightning bolts from God's throne."

Rebecca couldn't stop an awed gasp. "Thank you...do you read much?"

"In Defiance there are three things to occupy a man. Two of them are immoral. Reading is not." The joke worked, evoking a giggle from the sisters.

Handsome *and* clever, Rebecca observed. She was quite amused by him.

Naomi again draped her arm across Rebecca's shoulders. "How did you come to be in America, Mr. Donoghue?"

He sipped his coffee and pondered the answer. "A wandering and restless heart." He stared blankly into his coffee seeing . . . what? Rebecca wondered if he missed the bonnie hills of Scotland and the fields of heather. "I left Sco'land when I was twenty-seven and have never been back." She heard the slightest hint of regret in his voice, but Ian shook his head as if clearing away painful memories. "I'm sorry, I've no desire to be maudlin. I've traveled the world and seen everything from Bangladesh to Bombay, from the Taj Mahal to Buckingham Palace." He punctuated the confession with a wink tossed to Rebecca. "It's been a grand adventure."

His smile, though a little sad, felt like a fresh breeze blowing dust off Rebecca's heart. The sensation took her by surprise and she nodded. "It sounds like it."

To Rebecca's dismay, Naomi chose that moment to abruptly cut between them and take her plate to the dry sink. She set the dishes down with a disturbing clatter and asked, rather loudly Rebecca thought, "How did you wind up in Defiance, Mr. Donoghue? If I'm not being too nosy."

"I met Mac–Mr. McIntyre in San Francisco." Rebecca noted a pause in his story before he continued. "We struck up a conversation in a pub. He is a man with big dreams and he wanted an architect who could envision something o' the American spirit in his town. I am an architect by trade and he thought I was the man for the job. I like Defiance very much and I'll like it even more when it settles down a bit."

"No joshin'!" Hannah joined Naomi and slid her plate into the sink as well. "*Buffalo Gals* is stuck in my head. Is it that noisy every night? I feel like I didn't get any sleep and my back is killing me." Grimacing, she stretched her arms over her head and arched her back in a long cat stretch.

Rebecca watched in horror as the gesture emphasized her quickly rounding stomach. She was positive Ian noticed, but he didn't let on. He sipped his coffee, quickly averting his eyes. Rebecca appreciated his discreetness.

"Well, Mac wants the town to become more respectable and he knows the price will be high. The saloons can't stay open all night and the jail needs to be used for something more than drunks and vagrants. There must be real law, no' just his law. The advantage there to ye ladies is that he truly wants the hotel to succeed."

A banging, scraping noise at the front alerted them that their furniture had arrived. Ian excused himself and returned a moment later with two chairs, his blueprints and his hat shoved under his arms, followed by Emilio who was also toting two chairs, and two men the girls had not seen before carrying a green, felt-topped gaming table.


Moments later, the sisters drew in closer to Ian at the new table, hunching over the plans. He spent the next half hour discussing the fifteen possible rooms and the kitchen layout. Initially, the sisters had thought they wouldn't make any changes to the floor plan, but it was obvious they needed living accommodations, and they agreed it would be good to allow each sister to have her own room. A larger room was assigned to Hannah, without explanation, and Ian didn't ask for one. He sketched quickly on the prints as they talked.

They chatted a while longer about the dining room, for which he had some helpful suggestions about table placement, but everyone was satisfied with the design. The kitchen needed expansion, larger counters, two cook stoves, a window through which to pass food to the dining room, more storage, and a pump inside the building for easy access to water.

Comfortable with their goals, Ian deftly rolled the plans in to a tight wand. "We're to get started on this right away. I dare say, within the next week or so, ye'll think ye're living in a beehive."

Eager for the excitement of the renovation to begin, Rebecca escorted Ian to the door. He chatted comfortably about creating a building plan and the time he would need to make their changes to the blueprints. It struck Rebecca that every time their eyes met, her heart sped up a little and she chided herself for being a foolish old woman.

She opened the door for Ian and squinted up at him as bright morning sunshine streamed into the room. "How long do you think it will be before we can open?"

Ian studied her for an instant then he blinked. "Yes, uh, timing." He rubbed his neck as if he was playing mental catch-up. "I should think ye could be serving meals by September sometime. That depends, of course, on when orders are placed and when items arrive."

Rebecca raised her brows. "That soon. Less than two months."

Ian opened his mouth, held a questioning look in his eyes then changed course. Stepping through the door, he slipped his Balmoral bonnet back on his head and turned again to Rebecca. "I've enjoyed meeting ye and yer sisters immensely, Mrs. Castleberry."

She eyed his hat and noted the embroidered military insignia. "You were in the military?"

"Aye. The Royal Scots, an infantry regiment. I've kept

a fondness for the bonnet."

"I hope we'll get the chance to chat about Scotland sometime." Rebecca nearly bit off her tongue, aghast at her boldness, but she couldn't stop herself. "I've always wanted to see it."

Ian's eyes widened just a bit, then he smiled warmly and the spirit of it glowed in his eyes. Rebecca's heart tripped over itself.

"I would like very much to tell ye about my home. Perhaps at our next meeting I could share some of my favorite books with ye about Sco'land's history?"

"I'd like that." Rebecca thought her voice sounded shaky and kicked herself for it.

They held each other's gaze for a moment longer then he nodded and headed down the walk. Closing the door slowly, Rebecca heard him whistling a lighthearted tune. As she made her way back to the kitchen, head down, lost in thought, she wondered if she had imagined his lingering gazes and attentive conversation. Was it all in her head? She was so old, surely he couldn't—

"My, my, my." Startled by Naomi's voice, Rebecca swung her head up. Her sisters stood in the kitchen's entrance, watching her, arms folded across their chests. Wearing a teasing smirk, Naomi nudged Hannah in the ribs. "I think Rebecca has developed a sudden interest in Scotland." But the smile faded. "And he certainly couldn't take his eyes off you. Pray he has better manners than Mr. McIntyre."

~~~

"Well, that's the last of it." Flushed and a bit sweaty, Naomi dropped a box on the bed and looked around this warehouse space they called their bedroom. After several steady days of unpacking, the second floor, like the kitchen, was now peppered with piles of boxes. Hannah and Rebecca stood amongst a grouping of open trunks and topless boxes. Hands resting on their hips, their disappointment was plain. Naomi patted the container she had just deposited. "This is a box of John's shirts."

The mention of his name dropped a palpable gloom on the three. Desperate not to give in to the pain, Naomi forced herself to cheer up, for her sisters' sakes. "You said it yourself, Rebecca. We'll just have to sew her some clothes."

Hannah's face brightened. "I did find this…" She dug through a trunk and came up with an arm load of powder blue muslin. "I bought this just before Christmas because I wanted to make a few spring dresses out of it." For a moment, her face clouded, perhaps mourning the lost dreams of a future bright with innocence.

Rebecca reached over and brushed the fabric with a loving hand. "I'll make you something nice out of it. You'll be beautiful."

A look passed between the two that Naomi almost envied. Rebecca and Hannah had always shared a special relationship, especially since the death of Rebecca's daughter. Naomi knew she had no one to blame but herself. She'd never been very good at letting her sisters in. She'd always felt the need to *protect* them, like some kind of guard dog.

If she was their rock, then John had been hers. How she had come to give him every inch of her soul, she would never know. Only with him could she comfortably soften and show weakness. And now she was floundering, drowning in uncertainty and grief. Her anger over their current circumstances was a kind of anchor, steadying this swaying, rolling thing she called her life…or so she tried to believe.

Deciding to delve into that at a later time, Naomi dropped her hands to her hips. "I don't recall seeing the sewing kit."

Rebecca gasped and slapped her forehead. "Oh, no, it was with the pinafores and baby clothes. I thought I was being so smart putting it with them in case they needed altering."

Naomi crossed her arms, unhappy with their next step. "You know what that means then."

Hannah hugged her material close. "We have to go

out…down the street…"

Rebecca grimaced. "To the mercantile. Dare we try the journey without the marshal?"

"Yes." Naomi straightened up, refusing to be intimidated by this town. "We can't expect him to be with us every second. It's ten o'clock in the morning. Based on the way this town revels every night, folks here probably sleep till noon." The steady sound of traffic and voices from the street below argued against that, but the volume was less than it would be later in the day. "I wanted to see the buck stove any way. We're going to need some heat up here and that one lonesome fireplace isn't going to do the trick."

~~~

Hannah walked behind Naomi and Rebecca, her eyes roaming all over the town. The street was far less crowded than it had been on their arrival. Still, she was impressed by the busy, but industrious, pace of Defiance this morning. Everyone was doing something in a hurry: driving a wagon at a no-nonsense clip; packing a mule with practiced efficiency; hammering, measuring and sawing with deliberation, or engaging in important, animated conversations. The air positively vibrated with the sounds of squeaking wagons, creaking leather, whinnying horses and boisterous male voices.

The folks who were up at this hour were hitting the day hard and fast. Almost every one of them, though, took time to stare. Two painters above them on a scaffold eyed the girls boldly and one let out a catcall. His partner tagged him forcefully in the gut and apparently lashed him with some stern words. Immediately they went back to slapping paint on the defenseless building.

"At least they seem . . . " Naomi chewed her lip, "more reserved today."

Naomi and Rebecca told Hannah that on their first trip to the mercantile they had been stared at with much more brazenness, until the cat fight, of course. Though today

83

the men deliberately grazed the girls with arms and elbows without so much as an "excuse me," the unbridled bravado was gone and the staring was more surreptitious. Hannah wondered if Mr. McIntyre been true to his word and made it clear they were three women not on the menu in Defiance.

As they strolled along, she decided she didn't feel exactly safe, but at least less threatened. Accepting that as good enough, she looked ahead at the general store, two buildings up on the opposite side of the street. Smiling, she read aloud the sign painted on the store's false front. "Boot & Company. Meat market, storage, groceries, liquors, cigars… Well, I guess that just about sums up the basic necessities, doesn't it."

Rebecca chuckled. "All the comforts of home."

Hannah followed her sisters as they abruptly crossed to the other side of the street. Rebecca let Naomi pull ahead a step so she could whisper to Hannah, "I don't think Naomi wanted to cross over from the saloon–"

Her explanation was interrupted by a deep, silky feminine voice calling out to them. "Welcome to Defiance, girls!"

Raising their hands to block the bright morning light, the sisters looked across the street to the second floor windows of the saloon. Perched in the sills, enjoying their morning coffee, four women stared down at them. Wearing no more than camisoles, petticoats and rouge, they watched the sisters intently, like a pride of lions planning a hunt.

A Negro girl shifted as if to see them better, causing her camisole strap to slide down, exposing a scandalous amount of flesh. "How do you like our town so far?" she called, not bothering to replace the strap.

"Maybe we could get together sometime," the woman sharing the window with her added in a husky, Hispanic voice. "We haven't met for our monthly quilting bee yet."

That was met with rich laughter from the Negro girl, and a red-headed girl sitting in the other window. However, the young woman sitting with the redhead did not laugh. Hannah recognized her as the frail, skinny blonde at whom she had waved the other day. She sat quietly in her window, eyes downcast.

Rebecca smacked Naomi on the arm. "Don't look at them. That's just begging for trouble."

"And Lord knows we don't want any more of that." Naomi's reply carried a steely, sarcastic edge to it that concerned Hannah. Her sister had sounded so cold and defiant.

Apparently desperate to avoid being part of another street spectacle, Rebecca shoved Hannah and Naomi into the store, to the parting tease of, "Let's have tea and crumpets tomorrow. We'll bring the crumpets!"

~~~

*What is a crumpet,* Rose wondered as the dark haired *gringa* quickly shut the door behind her sisters. She didn't really care enough to ask, but Iris told her anyway from her perch in the other window.

"I don't know exactly what a crumpet is, but I had an Englishman a few months back who said he loves'em and they shouldn't be eaten with anything but Darjeeling tea."

Lily, the Negro girl, sitting in the same window with Rose, looked at her Latin co-worker and rolled her eyes. "I keep telling Iris to pay less attention to the customers and just do her job, but she never listens…at least not to us."

"Well, I'm impressed that she could remember the word Darjeeling." Daisy's mousy opinion, offered from the other window, grated on Rose's nerves. The little wretch *always* had something nice to say, whether it was true or not.

Rose heard Iris smack something, probably her thigh, and explode with laughter as bawdy as her fiery red hair. "You are a daisy, Daisy. You always see the silver lining, unlike these other wenches." Iris leaned into the room so Rose could see her mildly disapproving expression.

Rose waved her away, bored with the discussion. The *gringas* had gone into the store. Should she should go get a peek at them? McIntyre had told everyone to leave them alone…but there was no harm in just looking.

~~~

## Ten

A fairly heavy crowd of men in search of a liquid breakfast did not prevent McIntyre from seeing Emilio slip in. He wouldn't have paid him any attention except for the fact that the boy headed upstairs instead of to his own room. Puzzling only a little over Emilio's destination, he went back to adding entries to his ledger, but with an uneasy tickle in the back of his mind. As if by some sixth sense, he looked up a few minutes later to see Emilio come back down and quickly ease his way out the front door.

Irritated, McIntyre bounced the pencil between his fingers. Emilio did his best to avoid Rose. Her temper was like a loaded gun with a hair trigger and the boy was her favorite target. So why would he seek her out…?

When Rose, Lily, Iris and Daisy, mostly dressed, followed close on the boy's heels, he knew something was awry. He dropped his eyes to his ledger again, but listened to the girls whisper as they attempted to leave without drawing attention to themselves. A few of the men in the saloon greeted them; they hushed them up with stern whispers and slipped outside.

Curious now, McIntyre rose and went to his window. Moving the lace curtain aside, he saw Rose and her cleavage-baring entourage march across the street and invade the mercantile. He frowned, wondering what he was missing. Probably nothing, he told himself, returning to his work. He didn't have time to baby-sit everyone in town. He picked up his pencil and started writing again.

~~~

Once in the store, the sisters were pleasantly relieved to find it empty of customers. Rebecca and Hannah wandered over to the sewing section and started perusing buttons and bolts of cloth. Naomi strode to the back of the store to appraise two stoves on display. The proprietor, an astonishingly tall, balding man, who compensated for the lost hair by sporting a huge beard, shoved a pencil into his black apron and hurried over to her. "Because of the crowd, I didn't get a chance to introduce myself when you came in the other day." He stuck out his hand. "I'm Luke Boot. Mr. McIntyre told me to help you ladies get anything you might need."

"I'm Naomi Miller." She shook his hand and nodded towards her sisters, introducing them by name. The girls greeted him from the other side of the store then fell back to studying buttons and a book of patterns.

"I heard you're gonna need several stoves," he told her turning back to the display. "Are you going to put one in every room or just in the suites? One in every room is gonna be a big order."

"Yes, but we haven't made that decision just yet. I'd like one for our sleeping quarters now, such as they are. As soon as I see the final blueprints from Mr. Donoghue, I will place an order. How long will they take to get here?"

"Well," he scratched his head, apparently figuring the ins and outs. "It usually takes about six weeks to get supplies in from San Francisco. Give or take."

She peeked at the tag hanging from the buck stove and gasped over the inflated price. Annoyed, she stepped over to inspect the cooking stove, a beautiful, modern appliance with double ovens, six burners, glossy red paint and white porcelain fixtures on it. It shined like a new penny and Naomi was impressed. "How much for both stoves?"

"Mr. McIntyre told me I was authorized to give you a twenty-five percent discount."

That made the bottom line a bit more palatable, but she promised herself she would make a point of discussing Defiance's cost of living with Mr. McIntyre. "Well, I don't seem to have much choice." She eyed Mr. Boot with a creased brow to emphasize her displeasure at feeling a bit railroaded. "All right, I'd like to get them both—"

The front doors burst open and a suffocating cloud of cheap perfume heralded the arrival of the soiled doves who had been sitting in the windows of the Iron Horse. Everyone in the store gawked as the giggling, swaying girls from the Iron Horse sauntered in. Naomi quickly appraised the brightly dressed, scantily clad, heavily made-up crew then tossed a glance to her sisters. Rebecca and Hannah stood stock still as the inquisitive eyes of the four sirens scanned the store.

Naomi had not appreciated their comments from before, but was not going to let them interrupt her business now. As the tarts spread out through the mercantile like wolves circling their next meal, she pointedly finished with Boot. "As I was saying, I'd like to get both of these along with all the necessary piping and hardware. Do you install?"

Boot was clearly focused on the swell of new females and all the colorful, daringly low-cut silk dresses. Naomi cleared her throat irritably. Boot blinked. "Sorry. Yes, Ma'am, I've got two boys who can deliver them tomorrow and get 'em set up for ya."

"That will be fine."

"Right this way," he motioned, moving toward the counter. "I'll get your total for 'em." She was amazed the man could function, so intent was he on gawking at his voluptuous customers.

Naomi, in turn, sense their stares, especially from the tall, Hispanic one, as she trailed Boot toward the counter. She and her followers had positioned themselves throughout the store, shopping and glancing at merchandise, but they were clearly there to observe Naomi and her sisters. As Boot tallied up and went to the shelves repeatedly to check for hardware, Naomi leaned her hip on the counter and crossed her arms. Casually, she surveyed the store.

A pale, willowy girl wandered the closest to Rebecca and Hannah and was fingering a bolt of lilac-and-daisy cotton that Rebecca and Naomi had noticed on their previous visit. It wasn't hard to miss, specifically because it was only the feminine fabric in the store.

Hannah's eyes brightened. "Isn't that pretty?" Startled, the girl looked up and backed away slightly as Hannah stepped closer. "I love tiny, little flowers like that. Wouldn't it go nice with these buttons?" She showed her the brass buttons she had picked out. "They're a little big, but this store is obviously more focused on clothing the men in Defiance. The pattern book is nothing but men's shirts." She focused a polite but direct stare on the jittery girl. "Do you sew?"

"N-No," the girl stammered, her eyes wide and searching the store over Hannah's shoulder. "At least, not in a long time." Her worried gaze found the Hispanic-looking dove who fired back an ugly glare. Naomi didn't miss the exchange and assumed Hannah didn't either. Clearly, the woman didn't want this girl speaking to strangers.

One of the other saloon girls, in her late twenties with vibrant red hair and wearing a shocking purple dress, sauntered boldly over to where Rebecca was flipping through the pattern book. The girl leaned in to take a gander, brazenly muscling Rebecca out of the way. More than willing to walk away from trouble, Rebecca took Hannah's arm. "Come on. Let's get these and a sewing kit and go start some dresses." Naomi bit her tongue, consciously trying to stay out of Rebecca's business as her sisters walked up to join her.

Approaching the counter, Hannah noticed the jars, dozens of them, filled with bright, colorful candy and her eyes shimmered with wonder. "Oh, Rebecca, look at that: licorice."

Rebecca surveyed the confections. "And peppermint sticks."

In spite of the glares burning holes in the back of their heads, Naomi grinned. "I take it you two would like a little candy?" It had been months since they had even seen candy, much less tasted any. She smiled up at Boot, who was grinning as well, albeit nervously.

The Hispanic gal slithered up just then and draped herself over the tempting sweets. She was wearing a faded yellow gown cut so low Naomi thought her breasts might spill out if the woman breathed wrong. Her hair was twisted up in an elegant style, but she looked cheap and worn. Youth and beauty were fading away, leaving something dark and bitter in their place.

"What about horehound drops," she asked, challenging the sisters with a cool smile. "They're my favorite."

Hannah and Rebecca's own smiles froze. Naomi straightened up and rested one fist on her hip. She made no attempt to hide her disdain for this woman's impertinence and, for an instant, the gal backed up a hair. Naomi wondered if this evil wench was expecting to roll right over them. If she was, then she had another think coming.

Confidence settled back on the woman's face and pointed at herself. "I'm Rose." She motioned to the redhead. "That's Iris . . . and Lily," the Negro girl nodded. "And the frail wildflower over there is Daisy. We make up what the gentlemen in this town call The Garden." Iris and Lily sniggered, apparently over the use of the word *gentlemen*. "And I would advise you not to look down your nose at me like that." Her voice held a venomous warning. "We're the ones who really run this town, not the men. Give us any trouble and we'll run you out."

Naomi immediately thought of hers and John's frustrating meeting with Frank Page just prior to leaving Cary. Shooting off her mouth to the grandfather of Hannah's baby had only made her feel small and foolish. While the burden of her grief and anger were almost more than she could bear, if she lost her temper again, that would only give this trollop what she had come shopping for.

A dozen responses rose to Naomi's lips, but she bit them all back. Her sisters' pleading eyes helped her find the self-control that was so often elusive. *Lord, help me keep my cool.*

Through clenched teeth, she said simply, "We don't want any trouble."

"No, I guess you don't." Rose straightened to her full height, a good head taller than Naomi. "So you were heading to California, huh? Mr. McIntyre thinks you are crazy. He called you Bible-toters. You know this word, yes?" The description caught Naomi off guard and she couldn't help but laugh, as did Hannah and Rebecca. "You think it is funny?"

Despite the tension in the air, the laughter wouldn't leave Naomi's voice. "Yes, actually I do. I guess we are crazy little Bible-toters."

"He said your god told you to come here." Her eyes narrowed. "Does he show you things, too?"

Somehow, Naomi understood exactly what the woman was asking and the laughter died. There was a bottomless darkness in Rose's eyes that sent a chill up her spine. But Naomi also unexpectedly felt a power surge through her and the birth of a steely determination. In an admission that came grudgingly, Naomi told Rose, "I know that God's called us here and nobody other than God is going to run us out."

Fire flickered in Rose's eyes then she shut them as if thinking. Confused, Naomi thought for an instant the woman was about to swoon, but Rose's eyes fluttered open again and she gazed piercingly at Hannah. Appraising Naomi's sister carefully, slowly, from top to bottom, Rose's scrutiny returned abruptly to the girl's barely protruding abdomen. Hannah and Naomi exchanged puzzled looks.

"Well, my, my, the *gringa* baby has a bun in the oven!" Every person in the store sucked in a shocked gasped. Hannah's face turned ash gray as Rose's blood-red lips curved into a sneer. "Where's the papa?"

"He walked out on her." Naomi knew she had offered the explanation too quickly.

Hannah swallowed and raised her chin. "I can speak for myself."

"Really?" Rose took a step closer. "Were you married?"

"Explain to me how that's any of your business," Naomi snarled, inching her way in front of Hannah.

Like a serpent, Rose struck out and grabbed Hannah's left hand. Bringing it to eye level for examination she cried triumphantly, "Ha! No ring, no sign of a ring!" Lips curled back in contempt, she tossed Hannah's hand away as if she were discarding a piece of trash. "At least we're smart enough to get *paid* for lying on our backs."

The last cord holding Naomi's self-control snapped. She opened her mouth to launch an attack on this arrogant, prideful know-it-all that would have blistered her skin, but Rose was faster on the draw.

"You are really something. Come waltzing in here with your oh-so-pious attitudes, acting so saintly." She drew her hands up in front of her in prayer. "Oh, don't touch us. We're so pure and chaste. We say our Hail Marys every morning." She shook her head, sure of her indictment: "You're no different than us."

Jaws clenched and her brain burning, Naomi pushed Hannah aside and stepped in toe-to-toe with Rose. "We're nothing like you—"

"Why Rose, darlin'," Mr. McIntyre called loudly from the doorway. "There you are." He strolled in, casually lighting a cheroot as if nothing in the world was wrong. "There are customers over at the saloon asking after you. Go tend to them…." His words were calm and soft, but edged with a steel bite as he shook the match and tossed it aside. He firmly shouldered a resistant Naomi out of the way and blew a cloud of smoke into Rose's face. "If I wasn't clear, I meant now."

Rose's gaze flicked quickly between him and Naomi, and Naomi saw the fear. With a searing last glance at the both of them, Rose whirled and stomped out of the store as if Mr. McIntyre's words were commandments from God himself. Mr. McIntyre stared at the floor, chewing on the smoldering cheroot and the situation.

His slow, measured breathing told Naomi that things here were not to his liking. Not at all. "Don't cross swords with her, Mrs. Miller." He turned to face her. Concern − for whom or what, she wasn't sure, raged in his eyes. "You will not dissuade Rose with a belligerent voice or the heel of your boot. If you fight with her, you will be fighting for your life . . . and your sisters need you alive. I'm not always going to be just across the street to come to your rescue."

Arrogance and pride pushed Naomi to argue with him. Rebecca quickly placed a restraining hand on her sister's shoulder and begged her with her eyes to let it go. "She'll be careful, Mr. McIntyre," Rebecca promised with a warning look for her sister. "We all will." Mr. McIntyre nodded and marched out the door.

Boot waited for the door to slam shut, and then whistled a relieved tune. "You may never know how much of a favor he did for you, little lady." He sounded as if he had just seen a narrowly averted train wreck. "Rose is mean and she ain't afraid to draw blood. Lots of it."

Naomi didn't really hear. She was still staring out the door. Mr. McIntyre caught Rose on the front steps of the Iron Horse. With a fierce grip on her arm, he shoved her roughly through the bat wing doors into the darkness of the saloon.

Naomi was surprised at herself for wondering if he would hurt her. She didn't wish a beating on anybody, even that particular she-devil, but she was also hoping that Rose would let things pass.

Slowly coming back to the moment, Naomi looked at Rebecca with raised eyebrows and an incredulous shake of her head. Jittery and weak, but trying to calm her nerves, she turned toward Mr. Boot and looked at the ticket on the counter. "Is that the total?"

"Yes, Ma'am. That includes the delivery and installation. I took twenty-five percent off that as well."

"Fine, thank you." She began digging in the little reticule hanging on her wrist to find a small roll of bills. Her hand and her mind wouldn't work together, however, as she kept counting through the bills over and over.

Mercifully, Rebecca reached over to take the purse off her wrist. "I'll count it out."

Naomi let her slip the purse off and stood quietly as her sister paid Boot. Naomi could not believe the viciousness of the woman or, sadly, her own willingness to fight. There had almost been a cat fight in this store that would have made the prostitutes fighting in the street as bland as toddlers in a sandbox. Naomi had to admit Mr. McIntyre's timely arrival probably had averted a disaster. Oh, why was everyone in this horrible town bent on bringing out the worst in her? And why couldn't she stop taking the bait?

While Naomi and Rebecca handled paying for their items, Hannah took the opportunity to walk back to Daisy, who was now flanked by the redhead and the Negro girl. All three were stood quietly, their mouths agape.

"Why does she dislike us so? We couldn't possibly have done anything to her. We haven't been in town long enough to offend anybody."

Daisy straightened up to talk. The fear of Rose that Hannah had seen in her eyes a few minutes ago was gone. "Rose is crazy. She doesn't take to strangers anyway and she's jealous of your sister."

"You're talking too much," Lily, the Negro girl on her left, warned.

Hannah ignored her, eager to pounce on a chance to make a friend and get some information. But because the comment was so shocking, she lowered her voice. "She's jealous of Naomi?! Good grief, why? It's not like she wants her job."

"She's afraid she wants her man," Daisy explained.

"What?!" Hannah was certain she had not heard the answer correctly.

"Rose and Mr. McIntyre sort of have a relationship."

"My sister lost her husband less than a month ago. She doesn't want Mr. McIntyre, or anyone else, right now. And when she does, I doubt it will be someone like him."

Daisy shrugged. "She wants her to keep away from him. That's all I know. Rose doesn't always make sense. I think she's half crazy."

"And she's always looking for a fight," the red-haired girl Iris warned. "Don't let Daisy gentle the situation. Rose is a mean witch—literally. If McIntyre doesn't kill her, you need to watch your backs."

"Now you have said too much," Lily grumbled at both Daisy and Iris. But then it seemed she couldn't keep from adding to the gossip. "McIntyre may be planning to give Rose a good flogging—or worse—but she'll come out of it just as vengeful as ever. And we'd better get our rear ends back to the saloon or he'll come huntin' for us next."

Conceding it was time to go, Iris and Lily filed towards the door, but Daisy hung back. She casually ran her hand over a bolt of fabric and waited for the other two girls to leave before she spoke up. "Is it true, what Rose said about you expecting a baby?"

For some reason, Hannah desperately wanted to be friends with this girl. "Yes, it's all true. Rose was right when she said we're no different. We all make mistakes, even us holier-than-thou-Bible-toters." Daisy managed to give her a fractious smile for the attempt at brevity. As she took a step to leave, Hannah gently grabbed her arm, curious about one thing. "But how did she know?"

Daisy squirmed uneasily, pulling her arm free. "She thinks she's a witch. I think it's mostly Mayan mumbo-jumbo and she just uses it to scare people, but sometimes, she does know things." With that, she abruptly dashed back to work.

~~~

# Eleven

McIntyre practically hurled Rose into his office and slammed the door behind them. Before she could even stand up straight, he was on her again, this time with his hand around her throat. Trying to cut off her air, he shoved her up against the wall and spoke with his face so close to hers their noses touched.

"You seem to have forgotten your place in our arrangement, Rose. I am your employer and you are my employee." He tightened his grip and she clawed at his hand; he could feel her pulse pounding wildly. "None, and I do mean, NONE of my business deals are of any concern to you. You will not speak to those women, you will not look at them. You will cross to the other side of the street if you see them coming. You will not ask Emilio to spy on them and you will cease practicing your voo-doo hoo-doo nonsense in my saloon."

He allowed himself to calm a little and breathe slower, but he didn't loosen his grip. "After the incident with Blossom last fall, I thought you and I were clear on how things are. Apparently I was wrong, so I will clarify one *last* time." He could feel her pulse slowing as the strangle hold took effect and the strength drained from her struggle. Her face swelled and her eyes threatened to roll back in her head. "Cross me again on this and I will send you to work at the Broken Spoke...pray Diamond Lil will have you."

He released her as quickly as he had grabbed her and Rose collapsed to the floor, gasping for air and coughing through, he was sure, a nearly crushed wind pipe. McIntyre straightened his clothes and brushed lint off his shoulders. "Now, get ready for work."

"I'll kill them," she croaked, rising uncertainly to her feet. The hate in her eyes made him wary. "This town is mine. You're mine."

Without hesitating, he stepped in close again and

grabbed her face. He knew he couldn't afford to ever let her think she had the upper hand. "Rose, you are nothing but a crazy working girl to me. In the blink of an eye, I can have you living on the street and tending to customers from the back of a wagon. Hell wouldn't even take you after that." He tried to sear the image into her head with a squeeze of her jaw. "You would do well to stay in my good graces." Sick of her, he shoved her away and reached for the doorknob.

Calmly, he stepped outside and closed the door behind him, leaving Rose to compose herself. The saloon, settling between shift changes, was empty now except for his bartender drying glasses.

McIntyre couldn't believe the violence the wench ignited in him. He had never manhandled a woman before in his life and yet it had happened repeatedly with Rose. Their relationship was a despicable quagmire and he was done with it.

Disgusted with himself, he trudged to the bar. The sensual painting of Eve gazed down on the room and he took a moment to appreciate the serene, languid peace in her eyes. Why couldn't all women be so quiet and willing? Unlike Rose. Unlike Naomi Miller. Wouldn't the fiery little belle just love to know what he had named the portrait? That would probably curl her hair, he speculated with a smirk.

Brannagh, the fifty-ish Irish bouncer he had hired a while back from a tough saloon in San Francisco, nodded at his boss and retrieved a bottle from behind the counter. Old, maybe, McIntyre mused, but still tough as nails and built like an oak. There had been no fights in the Iron Horse since Brannagh had laid down the law. As far as saloons went in mining towns, this was one of the safer ones. He liked to think that hiring Brannagh had been one of his best investments. Apparently hiring Rose was one of the worst.

The burly Irishman poured his boss a short shot and set it before him. "Rose givin' ye trouble . . . again?"

McIntyre fingered the drink. "Let's just say you've done

a far better job, Brannagh, at controlling the drunken patrons in here than I've done handling one crazy, Mexican harlot."

"Ah, ye're Flowers aren't so bad. I've seen worse. Why, I broke up a cat fight one time in Frisco. Worse injuries I ever got. Said I'd never do it again. I got knifed, clawed and kicked in places that still hurt. Men fight like men. Women fight like unchained demons."

McIntyre chuckled and nodded in agreement, but he was struck by the truth behind the statement. He had never laid a hand on any of his girls until he'd hired Rose. Her desire for blood and violence seemed to infect those around her with a brooding malaise, including himself. The realization was disquieting.

Before her arrival, he had never made a habit of usury, running crooked games, watering his whiskey, or encouraging the miners to bet their claims. Before, he had considered himself a mostly respectable man with slightly fluid business ethics. Now, he was more driven and ethics had become a nuisance. When had that happened?

Was he using Rose as an excuse? Surely years of selling whiskey and women, gambling, and associating with questionable persons couldn't have affected him on a basic level. He could hear his mother's sweet, lilting voice reminding him over and over that bad company corrupted good manners.

His eyes traveled over to his closed office door and he pondered the woman on the other side. He could argue that his lack of self-control added more fuel to an already out-of-control fire. Rose seemed to gain strength from these ugly encounters; they hardened her resolve to . . . what? Become the Queen of Defiance?

More like the Queen of the Damned, he thought sourly as he pushed the shot of whiskey away.

~~~

Daisy hid behind the curtain in her room and peered through the lace at the sisters down on the street. She liked the youngest one; she had talked to her in such a friendly way. Was it possible she didn't know exactly what Daisy did for a living? Maybe she didn't understand about working at the saloon—no, Daisy stopped that train of thought. Nobody was that naïve.

Still, she had gone out of her way to make small talk about the buttons and Daisy had not sensed any condescension in her attitude. She had told her the truth about the baby, too. Could it be the girl was just friendly?

Iris burst into the room from behind her and bounced over to the other window to see what had Daisy's interest. The women slogged down the boardwalk, heads down, shoulders bent, obviously less than chipper after their run-in with Rose. The redhead giggled in a bratty way and tapped the glass.

Wearily, Daisy looked over at her. Iris already clutched a bottle of whiskey. It was her ritual for preparing for the night's work. "What's so funny?" Daisy asked sounding as tired as she felt.

"I was just thinking, we'll have to get some rotten vegetables and practice our aim the next time they come to the store."

Daisy was surprised at the anger the comment sparked in her. "Why do you want to say things like that, Iris? Those girls haven't done anything to you."

Iris arched her eyebrows, but the surprise quickly changed to a sneer. "They ain't done nothin' *for* me either."

"Oh, just go on back to your room. I don't want any company right now."

Iris flung a nervous glance to the door then backed up to the window, clutching her drink. "Well, I kinda wanted to stay in here for a bit." Daisy understood. There was safety in numbers. None of them knew what mood Rose might be in when she emerged from Mr. McIntyre's office.

Iris had left the door open and the lack of privacy made Daisy feel vulnerable. Thinking she would shut it against anymore unwanted visitors, she ambled towards it. Lily squeaked through just as she was closing it, slipping in quickly and quietly, with a nervous glance over her shoulder.

"I listened for a second," the black girl whispered in a conspiratorial tone. "I think he must've been chokin' her 'cause I couldn't make out anything she said."

They all shared uneasy fleeting looks with each other and Daisy wondered what new hell Rose would unleash on them when she recovered.

~~~

The sisters trudged down the street in silence. With all these people staring at her, intentionally jostling her, Naomi felt as if she was holding on to her emotional control by a single, fraying thread. Her sisters' silence only added to the burden. She had started out so well. She could have avoided a fight with Rose, if Rose had stayed focused on Naomi. But when the vile wretch had gone after Hannah, if not for Mr. McIntyre's timely interference, blood, hair, fingernails and shreds of clothing would have flown. It hadn't happened, but it would have.

Sick of this town and her own uncontrollable temper, Naomi didn't think she could feel any more like a failure. Why couldn't she learn patience and wisdom? Why couldn't she walk away like Rebecca had?

Naomi glanced over at her sisters who were trudging doggedly alongside her. Their faces said they were as lost in thought as she.

"Well, that was something," Rebecca mused, perhaps feeling Naomi's gaze. "Rose is a rather thorny flower, to say the least." She patted Naomi on the back. "I thought you did well, Naomi, holding your tongue like you did."

The observation made Naomi feel worse and she snorted in disgust. "The only thing I did was get saved from myself by Mr. McIntyre, of all people."

Hannah peered over her shoulder at the saloon and searched the windows. "How did she know about the baby? I'm sure it was more than a lucky guess."

Naomi rolled that around in her head, but didn't have

101

an answer. Rebecca didn't offer a comment, either. Hannah fiddled distractedly with an escapee from her braid, working to tuck it back in its home while she thought. "I saw something in her eyes. She's not right in the head and I think it's more than just crazy."

"I'm the crazy one," Naomi admitted, deeply ashamed of her behavior. "She lit such a fire under me I could've knocked her into next Tuesday."

Rebecca nodded her head emphatically. "That's exactly what she was counting on, I think. If she scared you she won, if you fought her she won."

"Well, she didn't scare me." It wasn't a boast; merely a statement of fact.

Rebecca gave a frustrated sigh. "I know and that's what worries me. She *should* have scared you. I think Hannah's right. There's something evil in her eyes. You heard what Mr. McIntyre said."

Hannah huffed out a breath, dropping her hands protectively to her stomach. "Another minute of that stare and *I* would have run screaming out the door."

Frustrated beyond reason, Naomi shoved her hands heavenwards. "What are we doing here?" she asked loudly enough to cause the men to stare, for different reasons this time. "We don't belong here. To call us fish out of water is like calling President Grant a tea-totaler!"

Rebecca shushed her, forcing Naomi's arms back down to her side. "I know, I know, but try to remember that we're here—"

"Here for a reason," Naomi sang with flagrant sarcasm, wondering what possible reason God could have for stripping her of her one true love and her sanity.

Hannah tossed her braid over her shoulder and eyed her sister disapprovingly. "If he didn't think we could do it, he wouldn't have sent us. Take that girl Daisy. What if we're the only Believers in her life who are ever willing to share with her. What if God sent us here"—she motioned to the town surrounding them—"went to all this trouble—just to help one person? Wouldn't he do that?"

Naomi rubbed her temple, feeling the stirrings of a headache. "He might," she muttered, humbled by Hannah's ever-maturing faith and compassion. "Surely, though, there has to be more at stake here than just one soul."

But, in her opinion, God certainly could have chosen better vessels, at least as far as she was concerned. Naomi wasn't exactly an eager missionary. She only wanted to hold John again, hear him tell her he loved her, but she would not hear his voice again this side of Heaven. Feeling broken and defeated by Defiance, Naomi walked the rest of the way in silence.

~~~

# Twelve

Naomi tried to shake off her melancholy mood as she stepped out on the back stoop to check on Emilio. In the midst of raising the ax over his head, she waited for him to finish the swing. He split a piece of wood with impressive skill and let the pieces fall to the ground. Leaving the ax lodged in the block, he loaded the two pieces in the crook of his arm then stopped to wipe his forehead.

When he saw Naomi, she was surprised by the flood of relief that swept across his gaunt face. "*Senora* Naomi," he breathed. He took an excited step towards her and blinked. "Everything ees OK? *Si?*"

Naomi was puzzled by his strangely exuberant inquiry, but smiled a greeting. "Yes, everything's fine. I was wondering, Emilio, we're having two stoves delivered tomorrow. Do you think Mr. McIntyre will allow you to help us again?"

The expression on his face sobered and his shoulders sagged. "I don't know. Mr. McIntyre ees not so happy with me..." Then he sighed. "Did my seester give you much problems in the store?"

Naomi couldn't track the path of the question at first then she sucked in a breath. "You had said your sister's name was Rose. I can't believe I didn't realize . . . " She cocked her head to one side. "And you were there?"

He nodded meekly. "Outside, watching. I'm sorry if she did anything to you. I told her I didn't want to tell things on you, that she should leave you alone but..." he looked heavenward as if he couldn't bear Naomi's gaze. "I don't know." He shook his head. "I don't know what ees the matter with her."

Feeling a little betrayed, Naomi gazed past the boy, across the backyard and the stream, to the mountains, and into the past. But it did no good to dwell there. She didn't have control over her life; Emilio didn't have any control over that monster he called a sister.

Glad to let some compassion crowd out her grief, at least for the moment, she shrugged. "We'd still like you to stay for dinner…if you will."

Naomi trudged up the stairs but stopped a few steps from the top to enjoy a show, peering at her sisters through the slats in the banister. Hannah had draped her fabric around herself and was parading about the room like a queen as Rebecca laid sewing items out on the bed. Naomi felt, and probably looked, awfully crestfallen, wondering if there was such a thing as honor or truth in Defiance. But as her little sister whirled around in what would be a new dress with a loose, comfortable fit, Naomi cheered up considerably.

Hannah's joy had always been infectious.

Smiling, Naomi dropped her elbows on the banister and rested her chin on her hands. "Well, that makes the encounter with the she-devils well worth it. You'll be beautiful and comfortable."

"Oh, it will feeeel so much better," Hannah sang with delight. "I can't wait to get a few finished."

Naomi started to offer a compliment on Rebecca's seamstress skills, but decided her older sister looked too distracted. With an intent, somber expression, Rebecca pulled straight pins from a new box and carefully stuck them into the pin cushion on her wrist.

Naomi would have been willing to bet she was imagining Hannah's future here. No dress, even one tailored to fit a horse, would hide the situation forever.

Hannah stopped spinning and eyed her sisters with suspicion. "My, you both have the most serious looks on your faces."

Naomi scratched her nose thoughtfully then changed positions from peering over the banister to taking the last few steps up to their level. Leaning back on the rail, she folded her arms and shared her stunning news. "That she-devil Rose is Emilio's sister. He's been spying on us." Her sisters' jaws dropped. "I think he only did it because if he didn't, she'd strangle him. So I asked him to stay for dinner anyway."

Rebecca took a few steps back and plopped down on the bed. "Spying? What could he tell her? It's not like we're hiding anything."

"That's exactly why I invited him. We don't have anything to hide. At least not after the melodrama in the general store."

Hannah started wringing the material in her hands as if it were a wet wash rag. "What if Rose is as mean to Emilio as she is to everyone else? "That girl Daisy told me she practices witchcraft. But she said she uses it mostly to scare people."

Rebecca's head shot up at that news. "She certainly has a flare for the dramatic. I could see where she would flaunt something like that for the effect of it, whether she believes it or not. Oh, poor Emilio," she lamented, shoulders drooping. "He probably witnesses the most unimaginable things in that saloon." Rebecca's lip trembled and she flung an almost accusatory glance at Naomi. "The poor darling. Of course you should have invited him to dinner."

Naomi pulled back a bit at her sister's emphatic reaction. "Well, it's not that I didn't think we should invi—"

"Do you suppose she beats him?" Hannah interrupted. Mindful of the items on the bed, she dropped down beside Rebecca, eyes reflecting the horror of the possibilities.

Rebecca shook her head. "It wouldn't surprise me." She sat up straighter and stuck out her chin. "We'll just have to tell Mr. McIntyre the boy's become indispensable to us."

Hannah excitedly clutched her hands over her heart. "Yes, maybe we could hire him away. He doesn't need to work there. I'm sure we need him more than Mr. McIntyre does."

Naomi rubbed her arms and simply listened as her sisters cut her out of the conversation and eagerly devised a scheme to save Emilio from his bleak and dreary existence. She had been so sure there would not be one soul in this town worth caring about, and then they had met a young orphaned Mexican boy. His dark eyes reminded her of melted chocolate and his sad life did make her want to take him under their roof.

As Rebecca and Hannah bantered ideas back and forth on how to do just that, Naomi considered Rose and what she would think of her little brother making friends with crazy, Christian, Bible-toters. She suspected she wouldn't like it—not one little boiling-cauldron bit.

~~~

McIntyre knocked on the inn's door, but when no one responded, he and Ian let themselves in. For a fleeting, heavenly moment the two turned up their noses and enjoyed the heady smell of truly good home-cooking. Biscuits. Roast. Potatoes. McIntyre's stomach growled enthusiastically. They also heeded the sound of female chatter and giggles and the clatter of dishes as they prepared the meal.

Simple, innocent sounds. By all accounts, the men in Defiance were keeping their distance now and the sisters were settling in nicely. That fact pleased him, though he couldn't say why.

"Aye, that's pleasant." Ian grinned as a wistful contentment settled on his face. "The sound of girlish laughter. Reminds me o' my sisters back in Sco'land."

McIntyre marveled over the fact that women still spoke to each other with such cheerfulness and kindness. He had an irksome suspicion that being around soiled doves for nearly two decades was making him more unsuitable for genteel company than he had imagined. Pushing away such irrelevant thoughts, he called out to announce their arrival. "Mrs. Miller, ladies…"

The noise in the kitchen ceased abruptly and Naomi stepped out from the apartment, wiping her hands on a towel. McIntyre did not miss the lightning flash from cheerfulness for Ian to disdain for him. She flashed a wide smile. "Mr. Donoghue." The smiled faded. "Mr. McIntyre. What can we do for you gentlemen?"

Eagerly, Ian waved his completed blueprints and walked forward, leaving McIntyre trailing. He was not accustomed to bringing up the rear and made a note not to let it happen again. "I've finished the plans, and Mr. McIntyre and I have some things we'd like to discuss with ye, if no' is a good time. If we're interruptin' din–"

"Have you eaten?" A gracious, if not slightly cool, smile returned to her face. Neither of them had and their hesitation in responding answered her question. "Come join us and we can talk over dinner."

The two men entered the crowded little apartment and absorbed its warm smells and warmer atmosphere. McIntyre was stunned to find Emilio setting a tray of hot cornbread on the felt-topped gaming table and raised his brow. "I didn't know you cooked, Emilio."

The boy nodded awkwardly then stepped away from the table waiting for something else to do. The other girls greeted the two new guests with bright smiles, but Rebecca's melted away with a gasp. "Chairs, we don't have enough chairs...We can use the small flower barrel." She pointed at the barrel against the wall behind Ian. He immediately lifted it up and placed it at the table. "And there's a crate..." Hand on her hip, Rebecca looked around the room which was a jumble of stacked boxes. She found an empty one and handed it to Emilio.

They pulled the makeshift seating together and everyone sat down. McIntyre took the opposite side of the table from Naomi and Ian squeezed between him and Rebecca. Hannah and Emilio were off to McIntyre's right.

The irony of eating a simple, wholesome meal around a piece of furniture that normally supported some pretty weighty sins wasn't lost on him. As he pondered the vice and corruption that had no doubt occurred here, the sisters locked hands to pray. Rebecca reached to her right and took Ian's hand. Awkwardly, Emilio accepted Hannah's hand. Then, looking as if he would rather crawl under the table, the boy hesitantly extended his other hand to McIntyre. McIntyre found himself caught between Emilio's outstretched hand and Ian's and felt as awkward as a prostitute in church. Grinning hugely, obviously enjoying his friend's distress, Ian grabbed McIntyre's hand and motioned for him to take Emilio's.

His discomfort was not lost on a waiting Naomi. "We'd like to say the blessing." She nodded towards Emilio's hand. "I don't think he'll bite you."

Feeling foolish and all too equal with Emilio, a mere boy who slept on a cot in the back of his saloon, McIntyre grudgingly did as he was bid. Together, the group bowed their heads and waited.

Rebecca offered the blessing. "Father, thank you for being the Savior to all men and thank you for the precious blood Jesus willingly spilt on the cross. Thank you for the meal we're enjoying tonight, as well as the special fellowship with our new neighbors and friends and we just ask that you would bless this meal. In your Son's name we pray. Amen."

McIntyre released the hands a little too quickly and grabbed his napkin off the table as the food started circulating. Eager to find familiar footing in this uncomfortable situation, he jumped right into business. "We stopped by, Mrs. Miller to discuss with you and your sisters—"

"First," Ian waved his hand over the table. "We've to thank our lovely hostesses for this enchantin' meal." He eyed Rebecca. "I canna remember the last time food smelled this good. I'll live on the beauty of the aroma, even if it tastes like sawdust." He winked at her and grinned. "Though I doubt tha'll be the case."

Trying to hold back her own grin, she passed him the mashed potatoes. "Well, we are planning on opening a restaurant. At least one of us had better be able to cook."

"We already know which one of us can't." The good-natured jab from Hannah extracted a giggle from her and Rebecca, but Naomi's face hardened.

"I can at least make good biscuits," Naomi argued weakly. Clearly displeased they were discussing her lack of culinary talents, Naomi took a lazy bite of cornbread.

Momentarily, a look of ecstasy flooded her face. "Oh, but this cornbread is heavenly, Emilio." She waved the piece in the air and spoke with an unlady-like mouthful. "Mr. McIntyre, you've been very generous letting Emilio spend so much time helping us, but now that we know he's handy in the kitchen—"

"Yes, it's *quite* clear there are several good cooks present." His overly loud comment laced with irritation brought the activity at the table to a standstill. He felt the urge to apologize for his brusqueness, but fought it. "Their talents, however, will go to waste if we do not tend to the business of getting this restaurant open."

Naomi swallowed. "What's the matter, Mr. McIntyre? Afraid you might lose a few dollars if we dally over supper and actually *enjoy* the meal?"

McIntyre appraised her, noting the shimmering golden braid, unflinching wide eyes, squared shoulders and tanned skin that glowed against her starched white shirt. Sassy, opinionated, beautiful, and an absolute joy to tease. He smiled. "Your Ladyship, the *only* thing I am afraid of is losing money."

Naomi's lips tightened into a thin line and her eyes narrowed, but she didn't pursue the verbal battle. Certain he was the winner of their little exchange, McIntyre cleared his throat and moved on. "Mr. Donoghue and I have finished the blueprints for both the restaurant and the hotel. We have a crew coming in tomorrow to start the renovations. Here," he pulled some papers out of his vest pocket and unfolded them, "is a project list. The second page is the estimated cost to complete it." He passed it down to Naomi.

She went straight to the back page and took in the bottom line with raised eyebrows, then scanned both pages more carefully. With her disapproval evident, she handed the paper to Rebecca. "Mr. McIntyre, your labor costs are entirely unreasonable. Why is everything in Defiance so high?"

"It's a matter o' supply and demand." Ian's answer sounded rushed to McIntyre, as if he was trying to avoid more fireworks. Yet, lighting a fire under Naomi was entertaining sport and he intended to continue. She was far more attractive flustered and frustrated than she was as a grieving widow.

McIntyre laced his fingers over his plate. "Most of the men in this town want to look for gold and a lot of them find it one way or the other. The more gold comes out of the ground, the higher the prices of everything climb."

The answer apparently didn't wash with Naomi. "I purchased two stoves last week that cost us almost twice what we would have paid in Cary. Profit is one thing, but blind greed is another."

"Greed is often in the eye of the beholder, Mrs. Miller. Defiance doesn't sit on a flat, easy plain with railroad tracks all around. We are in a difficult and remote location. That adds significantly to our freight costs. Not to mention, the men who do the carpentry work around here leave the gold fields to take on jobs for royalty such as yourself. In their minds, they're giving up a possible strike to make a day's wages. They just want their time to be well spent."

"Do these men work for you?" The tilt of her head told him she already knew the answer.

McIntyre sliced off a piece of roast, but did not take his eyes off her. "You can hire my men and I'll see to it that the job is done right, or you can piecemeal the work, putting together carpenters with an unknown amount of skill, expertise and work ethic and see what you get. Don't let your pride make you foolish, Your Ladyship."

He could see neither option appealed to her, but would she have the wisdom to let his crew do the work? He enjoyed watching her squirm under the subtle, pleading looks from Rebecca and Hannah. They begged her to choose the devil they knew as opposed to ones they didn't.

Naomi nodded in reluctant compliance. "Very well then, Mr. McIntyre." He had the distinct feeling she would say the name Lucifer with more warmth. "But what about supplies," she asked. "Items we can't get from Montgomery Ward, such as groceries?"

McIntyre glanced over at Emilio. He was uncomfortable discussing the details in front of the boy and sensed he was uncomfortable being there. As McIntyre was pondering a way to excuse Emilio, the boy practically inhaled his last bite then asked if there was anything else he could do before he left.

McIntyre waved his hand. "I think they're done with you for the evening."

Rebecca leaned forward. "Thank you again for letting us occupy so much of his time. Emilio truly has been a Godsend…and, as usual, we certainly could use him again tomorrow." She leveled eyes filled with hope on McIntyre.

He, for some reason wasn't exactly pleased with the way the sisters were all but adopting the boy, but his usefulness to them was undeniable. He would have to continue to trust that Emilio would keep his yap shut around Rose, as they had discussed. He dipped his head. "That would be fine." As Emilio stood up to depart, McIntyre snagged his sleeve and spoke softly. "I'm sure Rose is not hearing any of this." Emilio simply shook his head and left.

When she heard the front door shut, Naomi followed up on that subject. "Speaking of Rose, why was she so bent on picking a fight with us? We don't even know her."

"You rarely need to know someone, Mrs. Miller, to assume they are your enemy." McIntyre shrugged, knowing there was no way to explain Rose to a woman like Naomi. "Rose is territorial and she had incorrectly assumed you had crossed into her *domain*, if you will. I have since clarified her boundaries."

"Again," huffed Ian, but he clenched his jaw too late as the complaint escaped.

The girls waited for an explanation. McIntyre's first thought was to change the subject back to the hotel, but perhaps if they knew what Rose was really like, they would be less inclined to dally with her…as Naomi had clearly thought to do. Having these girls cut up—or worse—would serve no purpose and only complicate matters.

"Last summer I added a new Flower to my garden." He

preferred using that euphemism for such delicate company. "However, Rose got it into her head that Black-eyed Suzy was attempting to steal my affections." McIntyre reached for his water and raised it to his lips. "After a few cross words, Rose stabbed her in the neck." He tossed back a sip, and in the sudden stillness, the sound of the water going down his throat was deafening.

Hannah clutched her throat. "Is she all right?"

"She did not die and I sent her back to Denver, costing me a lost investment of $700."

This time he knew the hush was brought on by the insensitivity of his summation. Perhaps McIntyre had been a little too crude, but he was what he was and he was not here to impress these girls.

While her sisters, and even Ian, looked shocked at the callousness of his remark, Naomi merely stared at him with irritated disdain. Her eyes told him that she not only *expected* such insensitive comments, but that they defined the core of who and what he was. She had him pegged as a worthless heathen and nothing short of a miracle would elevate him to something better.

He shook off the unexpected irritation her opinion caused him and decided to find the humor in vexing her. It was a game. How far could he push her before he turned on his charm and reeled her back in? Childish, he admitted, but he suspected the conquest would be so well worth the effort.

He set his cup down softly. "I apologize for the crassness of my remark, ladies, but the Garden is after all, a business. It's not wise to become attached to my Flowers."

Naomi bounced her fork in her hand as she made no attempt to hide her contempt. "Is that why you've given them the names of plants rather than people? So you don't have to deal with their humanity...or your sinfulness?"

That ignited a real spark of annoyance. He was not going to engage in a conversation about sin. For reasons he couldn't explain, he never delved into his spirituality and certainly would not do so now. "Perhaps someday, Your Majesty, I will be inclined to listen to a sermon, but this is not that day."

Their eyes warred as he thought about reminding her of her Pharisee-like arrogance. He would not let her, or anybody else–but *especially* not her–preach to him about the way he lived his life.

Ian cleared his throat to break the tension. "Mrs. Miller, I think it goes without sayin' that McIntyre lives by a different book than ye, namely a ledger." He cast a reproving glance to his friend. "Politics and business do make strange bedfellows." He scanned the sisters' faces. "Perhaps if we just stuck to business, *hotel* business."

When no one responded, McIntyre finally took his eyes off Naomi. He was more than willing to get back to the important conversation but having her look down her nose at him like that was, well, a difficult pill to swallow. No, he wasn't a missionary feeding the homeless and adopting orphans, but Her Holiness wasn't perfect either. Clearly, she was far from it. He decided he was indeed going to enjoy showing her just how human she was.

Saving all that for another day, he went back to *his* salvation: business. "I expect the hotel renovations will take approximately three months or so. However, if we go ahead and order the kitchen and dining room items immediately, Ian and I are in agreement that you can have the restaurant open perhaps by the end of September."

The discussion of things to do, orders that could be sent by telegraph, cost of the project, and a million little deadlines and details kept them talking until well after ten. Though the conversation was at times as strained as government negotiations with the Ute Indians (at least between himself and Naomi), business was accomplished.

There was something else going on at the table as well. McIntyre didn't miss the subtle but friendly glances between Rebecca and Ian during the evening. Or the way their conversation stuttered if their elbows happen to brush. His first reaction led him to wonder how such an alliance might impact the business. Since there was nothing he could do about it at the moment, he opted to let it play out on its own. At least for now.

When Hannah nodded off at the table, everyone concluded it was time to end the meeting. They would pick back up in the morning. Ian warned the girls that the carpenters would arrive with the sun. He and McIntyre then thanked their hostesses for the meal, telling them they would let themselves out.

As the two men grabbed their hats from the counter out front, Ian shook his head in disgust. "Mac, I say this in the spirit of friendship. Ye need polishing. Ye've the manners of a goot."

"A what?"

"A goot."

McIntyre frowned, wishing his friend would learn to speak English. Ian sighed in frustration. "The farm animal–"

McIntyre yanked his hat down. "Never mind. I understand your point."

Scowling, he stepped into the cool night air and regarded the busy, flowing street for a moment. Use to the frenzied sounds of laughter, horses hooves and jangling hardware, he turned inward and wondered why he had this malaise of sorts.

His emotions bordered on irritation and something else he couldn't put his finger on. Naomi was a frosty, but entertaining, handful. The bustle of Defiance reminded him, though, that he may have more to worry about than playing cat-and-mouse with Her Highness. Three beautiful, respectable women were an explosive ingredient in a town that was a powder keg anyway.

He hadn't counted on keeping randy miners and hostile prostitutes away from the sisters, while butting heads with Naomi in an honest attempt to help build their business. He had his own matters to manage, including a mine with over a hundred employees. Now he had to keep an eye on Ian and Rebecca, too, to make sure any relationship developing there was in *his* best interest.

Frankly, manners were the least of his concerns.

~~~

Naomi dried the last plate and set it in the rack next to the sink. The pan of dishwater needed to be dumped, but it could wait till morning. She had finished cleaning the kitchen alone after insisting that Rebecca and Hannah retire. Wisely, they had left her alone.

The events of the last several days, much less the last few weeks, weighed on her like boat anchors. She needed time alone and knew she wouldn't sleep anyway . . . again. The infernal beating of that out-of-tune piano every night was enough to make her scream. Now someone had added a tortuous harmonica.

Trying hard to shake off the frustration and sadness, Naomi grabbed a quilt they had packed dishes in, wrapped it around herself and headed down to her spot by the stream. Sitting down on a large piece of driftwood near the water's edge, she gazed up at the richly glittering night tapestry. She could stare at the infinite weaving of twinkling lights, shooting stars and ancient constellations for hours. In the vast grandeur of the Colorado sky she could lose herself. The beauty of it was the only thing *right* with this place.

She had come here every night since stumbling into Defiance. In her heart she wanted to pray, but the grief was still too fresh, her anger too blinding. Instead, she had just floated away into the velvety, twinkling heavens or drifted off with the gurgling sound of the stream. She felt God approved; her spirit was weary and sometimes all a parent needed to do was hold his child. Words could come later.

Tonight, however, there was no peace in the works of His hand. She was angry. She was grieving. She was tired of holding it all back. And, finally, she was ready to pray.

"I am failing you so badly, Father. My relationship with you is in shambles and this is the last place on earth you should have sent me."

Naomi sat still then for a long time considering things, seeing the faces of Grady O'Banion, those two harlots on the street, the Flowers from The Iron Horse; not to mention, Rose, and Mr. McIntyre. Their ugly attitudes in her mind were representative of the whole town.

"I don't like these people, God, and I don't have compassion for any of them." She was whining, but at least she was praying. "I know you want me to care, but they've all *chosen* their lives here. They choose to wallow in whiskey. They choose to debase themselves and barter in flesh. Then so be it," she fussed dismissively. "Your own Word says that a man reaps what he sows."

She felt a sting in her conscience. Naomi knew with that last statement, she had overstepped her bounds in this discussion. He hadn't sent her here to tell them about justice. God was offering the gift of grace to Defiance. Who was she to decide whether the gift was delivered?

"I'm sorry. I'm sorry," she cried, hiding her face in her hands. "I need John here. He softened my rough edges. Corrected me with a gentle heart. If John was here, he could have helped me see them as lost souls, not just prideful, arrogant sinners blinded by their own rebelliousness."

Slowly, though, a faint light of understanding dawned in her heart with those last words. She peered through her fingers at the water shimmering in the moonlight. "That—that wasn't his job, though, was it?"

Emilio popped into her mind. She hadn't expected to find anyone in this town worthy of her compassion and now she and her sisters had practically adopted the waif. Then she thought of Daisy. How had she come to be here? What was her story?

What had turned Rose's heart to pure hate? Had she ever thought once about a god who loves her? Could Mr. McIntyre ever come to understand the sacrifice Christ made and why?

Hate, anger, self-loathing, greed, all things that grew in this town like weeds. Yet God's redeeming love was here, too, and someone had to tell them. John wasn't here to do it for her. Rebecca and Hannah couldn't do it alone.

In her dream, God had asked her to take them the light. "But we're so unprepared, Father. At least I am." She sniffled and wiped her nose with the back of her hand. "Rebecca and Hannah are miles ahead of me in their faith.

117

They're full of compassion. I'm full of grief and anger… at the people of Defiance…at you." She pulled the blanket tighter and thought about her losses. "I feel like I'm nothing without John. But I know I'm nothing without you." Naomi continued to stare at the stream for a time, no thoughts, no words, no more arguments. The rushing water filled the silence and she waited.

*Look at my cross,* the Lord whispered. *You can see it now. John no longer stands between us. Look with your own eyes and your own heart and see that I gave my life even for these.*

That revelation grew in her heart and, like a burning sun, overtook the darkness of her grief. "I did let John stand between us, didn't I?" Her chin quivered and her throat tightened as she thought of how desperately she wanted him back. "You've broken my heart, Lord."

Naomi mourned, her heart full of memories of her beloved. As if she was lifting the weight of the world, she stood and looked up at the black sky dusted with diamonds. Eyes shining with tears, she opened her arms in surrender. "You took the one thing that mattered most to me in this world. Please help me to accept it and do what you've sent me here to do." She collapsed to her knees, sobbing. "Break me…here am I, Lord, use me. Help me love you again. Help me love these people if that's what you want."

McIntyre stumbled across Naomi and quickly hid behind the branches of a small pine. She sat and stared up at the stars, agony on her face. He knew he should go, but he couldn't pull himself away. Then she spoke. She talked and wept as if God was standing right beside her…and what she said, she was so candid, speaking her heart, holding nothing back from him. It made the Almighty seem almost . . . real.

He had taken his midnight walk thinking the sound of the water would clear his head and show him how to handle the women and the town. *This* was far more than he had gambled on. He actually felt a pang of guilt, knowing she would be horrified to realize he was listening. Yet, he couldn't move, couldn't *stop* listening. He watched transfixed as she wrestled with God, spoke to him boldly. She was intimate with him and painfully vulnerable.

And then, most amazingly of all, she begged him to break her...so that she could have compassion on this town of sinners and reprobates. Dumbfounded by her prayer, he stepped back, staggered over the rocky ground and turned away. He was confused and a little alarmed by the emotions warring within him. What had he just seen? Why was his heart racing?

He rested against a boulder to find his mental footing on that foundation of serene rebellion and self-gratification. He re-visited the atrocities he had witnessed, the barbaric violence, the blood, the destruction. His life was fine, built as it was around himself and his desires. God was a nuisance, a crutch, a disinterested father.

Yet, his heart wouldn't harden. Perplexed, he discovered that he felt different somehow, but couldn't put words to it. It was deeper than words were allowed to go. Off-balance, and irate at being so, he shook the confusion off his shoulders and decided to do what any man would do with unwanted emotions: drown them with rye whiskey and a willing woman.

~~~

# Thirteen

If August had a sound, Naomi would always associate the one of '77 with the continual whack of hammers or the melodic rhythm of hand saws. Daily, the carpenters showed up at the hotel with the sun and worked till it had set behind the mountains. Constant, but mercifully brief, meetings with Mr. McIntyre and Ian kept the inn's progress on track.

Naomi noted and appreciated that Mr. McIntyre seemed pre-occupied in her presence and a trifle less arrogant. She assumed he was busy with other projects, and didn't mind one bit that their conversations had become less of a battle. She had caught him staring at her a time or two, but in an odd way, as if she had two heads. As long as it made him keep his distance, she didn't need to know the why of it.

In rapid fire succession, telegrams went out daily, items were ordered, and the girls spent almost as much time studying the Montgomery Ward catalog as they did the Bible. Eager to stay busy, they also pitched in on the construction, hauling out debris, painting, fetching nails, whatever the crew and Ian needed. But Naomi and Rebecca made sure Hannah handled the lighter duties.

When they realized with surprise that the month of August had all but disappeared, more than just the hotel had dramatically transformed. Even loose fitting dresses were unable to hide something happening at Hannah's midsection.

Naomi, worried about more trouble for her little sister, asked Hannah to cut down significantly on her trips outside the inn. The questioning looks were turning into bold, knowing stares and gossip had begun following them down the boardwalk – gossip that cast doubt on the sisters' "decent" reputations. Even the men working on the hotel discussed her in hushed whispers and with sideways glances. In light of things, Hannah had acquiesced.

~~~~

Taking a breath, Daisy hugged her two large packages tighter and managed an awkward knock on the hotel's back door. She heard Hannah yell, "I'll see who it is," followed by the muffled patter of steps. Hannah flung open the door. "Daisy!"

Rebecca and Naomi, sweeping up sawdust out front, straightened and froze their brooms. They didn't look as happy as Hannah to see her, but they didn't look offended, either. Daisy was satisfied with that.

"Oh, here let me help." Hannah took one of the cumbersome packages from Daisy. "Please, come in." She turned away, acting as if she fully expected Daisy to follow. Given no choice, she entered and trailed Hannah into the kitchen, feeling wary, like a rabbit expecting to hear baying dogs any second. The renovation in here was nearly complete and a huge rough-hewn, farm style table graced the middle of the kitchen, complete with benches and a chair at each end. Hannah set her package down and turned to take the other from Daisy. "Thank you for bringing this. Is it from Mr. McIntyre?"

Daisy shook her head, setting the package on the table. "Oh, no. I–I had some clothes I thought you might could use." Hannah frowned, confused. Daisy pointed at Hannah's abdomen. "What are you, about seven months or so now? I had a bunch of clothes left over . . . and there's a few things in there for the baby, too."

Naomi and Rebecca peeked into the kitchen, eyes wide with curiosity, but Daisy didn't sense any offense in their expressions.

"Look what she brought me." Hannah tapped on one package. "Clothes. Clothes for my *special* time and even some baby things."

Her sisters sucked in a simultaneous breath. Leaning on the door frame, Naomi shoved her hands into her apron. "Daisy, how kind of you. You don't know how badly Hannah needs those. Can we pay you for them?"

"Oh, no." Daisy waved her hand, moving towards the sisters and the exit they were blocking. "I just don't need them anymore."

Sure she was coming close to wearing out her welcome, Daisy turned a bit, as if to squeeze by Naomi and Rebecca. Better to take off now than stay too long and risk saying something about her profession. But Naomi and Rebecca gently crowded her, acting as if they only wanted to get into the kitchen and see the clothes.

Rebecca placed a gentle hand on her shoulder. "Daisy, won't you stay and have some coffee with us while we see what you've brought our sister?"

Hannah stepped over and grabbed Daisy's hand. "Oh, please stay. It'll be like Christmas. I haven't had any new clothes in, well, since Christmas, I guess."

Naomi motioned towards the benches. "We would really love for you to stay . . . if you can?"

Daisy was profoundly impressed by what seemed a sincere desire for her company. It had been so long since she had been amongst friends. Not that they were, but she liked them immensely; felt drawn to them, in fact.

Hannah might be expecting out of wedlock but it was plain as the nose on Daisy's face that these weren't the same kind of women as those that flowered in Mr. McIntyre's Garden. She had told the other girls that when they gossiped about the sisters, but they didn't care to listen to Daisy.

Curious, and desperately lonely for the innocence of simple friendship, she gave them the smallest nod. The girls showered her with laughter and smiles as Naomi put on a pot of coffee. While Hannah opened the packages and they all oohed and aahed over the new clothes, Daisy slowly let out bits and pieces of her story.

She was a Kansas girl who married her childhood sweetheart. For a while they owned their own small, struggling cattle ranch but he wasn't much of a businessman. Word of gold nuggets jumping out of the ground drew them to Colorado, from one lonely mining town to the next. Defiance, they had decided, would be the make-it or break-it town.

When Hannah draped a blue gingham jumper over

herself to model, Daisy told them how she had come to work for Mr. McIntyre. "We'd only been here a month when Dan found his first gold nugget. He was so proud and so sure he was on the edge of a huge strike." Daisy nervously fidgeted with her fingers, a bad habit she'd had since childhood. "Word got out, though, and two days later someone shot him dead on his way to the Assayer's office."

An awkward, but empathetic, silence filled the room. Compassion in her eyes, Naomi patted Daisy's hand. "I'm sorry for your loss. I know what that's like."

Daisy nodded, having heard the rumor of *her* husband's death. "Claim jumpers took our claim, burned our tent. I guess the stress of everything…" She shrugged, resigned to the way the story had turned out. "I lost the baby. After that, nothing much mattered. Mr. McIntyre gave me a roof over my head…" she finished, expecting the haughty glances that were coming, the quick excuses they would invent to send her out.

Instead, Hannah sat down and took Daisy's hand. "Daisy, would you tell us your real name?"

Blinking, she whispered, "Mollie."

Hannah shook Daisy's limp hand. "We're proud to know you, Mollie."

It was a watershed moment in Daisy's life. She felt liked and wanted and maybe even accepted here. She didn't know how that could be, but she wanted to come back, would come back, soon . . . if they would let her.

Naomi looked up at the clock hanging above the sparkling red and white cook stove. "Mollie, would you like to eat dinner with us? It's nothing special but we hear it's better than what the Kitchen is slinging out."

Daisy laughed, a wonderful, clear, light-hearted laugh that still held the ring of innocence. "Emilio says he's gained five pounds eating dinner with you all…" but the mirth quickly faded. "Lily and I are working the floor this evening," she paused almost imperceptibly here then added, "Mr. McIntyre doesn't like it if we're even one minute late on Fridays or Saturdays." The pained looks on their faces told Daisy they understood. She rose and the sisters with her. "Thank you for the coffee."

Hannah touched Daisy lightly on the elbow. "Can you come back tomorrow?" Daisy couldn't believe the hope she read in the girl's eyes. "For dinner or a quick supper?

Daisy shifted nervously. "Well, I . . . "

"We'd love for you to join us." Rebecca took a step closer as if to emphasize her point.

"Well, maybe later . . . sometime."

Hannah smiled and it looked like an easy, sincere smile. "Anytime. You're welcome here anytime."

The compassion in the girl's voice warmed Daisy's lonely heart.

During her shift at work, as men pawed at her, or did worse, Daisy kept the sisters in the forefront of her mind. They knew who she was and what she did for a living and yet they had responded to her with kindness and respect. They had made her feel that if there had been a pastor's wife or school teacher in the room, she still would have been treated the same. Feeling valued again was not something she had expected–

A drunken, smelly, and barely-still-vertical miner practically fell on her as she approached the bar with her empty tray. A toothless grin filled his face and dried mud caked his beard. Fondling and grinding on her with no shame, he waved two sizable gold nuggets at her.

"Wan' some of this, don' ya, girlie," he mumbled in her face, breathing whiskey and rotten vegetables all over her. Daisy's stomach nearly rolled over as she grimaced and pulled away. "This'd buy you s' perty dresses," he slurred heavily as his hand claimed her bottom, stopping her retreat.

Setting the tray on the counter, Daisy gritted her teeth and turned her head away to seek fresh air before his reeking breath brought up her lunch. "I don't know, Jed. I think you've had too much to drink to manage a poke."

"Oh, I'll manage!" Wildly waving his one free arm, he

held on to Daisy firmly with the other and started dragging her to the steps. "Just get me up these stairs, Daisy, girl, and I'll do the rest."

The men drinking nearby pointed and laughed. "Don't rob him blind, Daisy," one yelled and the others hee-hawed in drunken hysteria over the irony. Daisy was known for her honesty; she never went through her customers' trousers.

She could only hope that this foul smelling body of debauchery would pass out the moment he touched her bed. She would happily sleep on the floor to avoid a roll in the hay with him.

Helping the unbalanced, unwieldy miner up the stairs, Daisy caught sight of Rose leaning on the bar. Her eyes glittered like a snake's and a cold, satisfied sneer spread slowly across her face. Daisy stopped for an instant, jolted by the gratification in the look…and the promise of more torment.

~~~

Like red silk rolling off a cloth bolt, Rose poured herself into the lap of a handsome, dark-haired youth and bestowed a passionate, bewitching kiss on him. The boy beamed drunkenly, dreamy-eyed over the promises Rose's sparkling, cleavage-baring dress was making. The men at his table cheered and slapped him on the back. Rose had chosen young, dark and handsome Hank carefully because she thought he would work to perfection. She led the hypnotized boy upstairs to her room then threw him on her bed. As he struggled with fumbling, drunken hands to undo his shirt buttons, she hiked her dress up and straddled him.

Wiggling suggestively, she stretched out over him ever so slowly and tasted the salt on his neck and throat. She heard him gasp as the curves of her flesh seared his pathetic, little brain. He ran his hands up and down her, touching her fiery flesh quickly, over and over as if she were as hot as a buck stove. Knowing she had him in her power, Rose whispered, "I need you to do something for me, Hank."

~~~

## Fourteen

Daisy assumed that Lily and Iris did not consider themselves mischievous by nature, but by virtue of boredom. The three girls stood in the mercantile's middle aisle, perusing bath water scents stocked specifically for the sporting gals in town, but looked up when the door opened.

Evil glee glittered in her co-workers' eyes instantly when Naomi came in to shop. They kept their heads lowered as Naomi approached the counter. Smacking her chewing gum, Lily ribbed Iris as a fiendish idea dawned in her black eyes.

Dreading the trouble coming down the pike, Daisy quietly slipped down to the wall stacked with bolts of cloth, distancing herself from the two troublemakers. Naomi handed Mr. Boot a list and he smoothed it out on the counter so the two could study it carefully.

Lily removed the grey wad of chewing gum she'd been enjoying and grinned at Iris. The two girls had to slap their hands over their mouths to suppress their giggles. Iris nodded and nonchalantly meandered up to the candy at the counter. She pretended to study all the jars intently as if she just couldn't make up her mind which item appealed to her sweet tooth. She and Naomi exchanged tense nods then Naomi went quickly back to her business.

Iris frowned. "I'm Iris. You remember me?"

Naomi did not look at her again, but nodded. "Yes."

Iris stuck her chin out. "I don't reckon it would kill you to exchange a pleasant howdy."

Boot straightened up, as if preparing to move away from a fight. Naomi raised her head, but still didn't look at Iris. "I wasn't trying to be rude." But she sounded fed up.

As the tension between Naomi and Iris increased, Lily slithered up behind Naomi and studied that long cascade of flowing, golden hair. It wasn't braided and she exchanged a pleased glance with Iris. Deciding on the best way to handle this attack, Lily flattened the gum in her hand then slapped Naomi right in the middle of her back in a friendly, but forceful, greeting.

"Mrs. Miller, isn't it? How nice to see you again."

Naomi spun on the Negro girl like a badger ready for a fight. Lily raised her hands in mock surrender. "I'm sorry, I didn't mean to startle you." She started backing away towards the door, and tugged on Iris's sleeve. "Tell your sisters we said hello. Especially the one with the bun in the oven." Collapsing into a fit of laughter, the two prostitutes ran from the store, delighted with their evil prank.

Naomi stared after them, daggers fairly flying from her eyes. Feeling like a coward, Daisy dropped her gaze to a shelf stocked with sewing kits. The joke the two girls had played made her sick to her stomach. Weren't their lives bad enough? Why did they have to go around spreading more misery? Ashamed of them, and herself for not saying anything to Naomi, Daisy sneaked out of the store like a beaten dog avoiding its master.


Naomi did not discover the sabotage until a few hours later, when she wandered out back to the stoop to braid her hair in the last few minutes of twilight. Rebecca stumbled across her there, working in vain to peel and strip the hairs, one by one, out of the sticky mess.

Her older sister grimaced at the disaster. "What is that?"

Naomi glanced up, well aware that her expression could singe the hair off Satan's tail. "If I'm not mistaken, it's chewing gum."

"How in the world . . .?"

"I took a little trip to the mercantile today and two of our neighborly saloon girls were in there. The black one slapped me on the back by way of a *greeting*. I suspect that's when she left me this little gift."

Shaking her head with obvious dismay, Rebecca grabbed the nest of gum and examined it more closely. The confection was matted and tangled in Naomi's locks as stubbornly as manure in a sheep's coat. "Sister, I think I'd better get my scissors."

Naomi felt her stomach drop. If there was one single thing over which she had ever allowed herself some vanity, it was her rich, thick golden head of hair. Oh, how John had loved to run his hands through it.

Rebecca tried to look at the brighter side. "I'll have to take off about four inches, but it's not a disaster. It will still be plenty long."

Naomi had worked for years at getting her hair down past her waist. Now that was to be stripped away too. Deciding, however, with a tenacious resolve not to give those *girls* the satisfaction of the small triumph, she straightened. "Take what you have to. It's only hair."

Rebecca brought an empty box outside and Naomi dropped down on it. Arms crossed tightly across her chest, she sat scowling in silence as her big sister carefully and gingerly cut her shimmering tresses. The hair fell in heaps around their feet.

"I know this is the kind of thing that makes you see red, Naomi, but before you get too mad and go claw out their eyes, I was wondering if you might consider what would prompt these girls to do this."

"Meanness? Vindictiveness? Pure evil?"

"Self-loathing?" Rebecca spoke softly and patiently. "Hopelessness…maybe even jealousy?"

Naomi considered that. No doubt, their lives were probably something less than pleasant.

Rebecca stroked her sister's head. "I just think that turning the other cheek is far more important than it's ever been. We're in a different place now, Naomi, and I'm not talking about geography."

"That's easy for you to say. You're not having licorice chewing gum cut out of your hair." When Rebecca didn't respond, Naomi relented and dropped her chin. "I know, Rebecca. I know. I'll try to turn the other cheek." She pivoted on the box and raised her chin. "But I've only got two and they're both stinging."

~~~

McIntyre was distracted, a problem that had been growing in intensity since that night he caught Naomi praying. And the more distracted he grew, the more irritable he got. His card playing skills, however, had not been affected and he walked away tonight with several hundred dollars in gold dust. It had tired him, though, staring into the inebriated, hopeless eyes of miners and prospectors. Their lack of passion had taken the challenge out of the game. Or was the lack his?

He was even getting bored with Rose. She dutifully came when called, shared her passion, ignited his, but afterwards, lying with her in the dark, he could barely stand to touch her. He wondered if that was how his Flowers felt after each and every customer.

He shook his head. From where was this creeping dissatisfaction with life coming? And why, when it tried to rear its ugly head, did he repeatedly wander back to that moment when he had found Naomi praying? Why did that haunt him so?

Desperate for a break, but determined to avoid the stream, he excused himself from the pointless game, tossed Brannagh the bag of winnings for safekeeping, and snatched his hat off the table. Stretching, he ventured instead to the boardwalk. The chilly temperature bothered his leg and begged to make his limp more pronounced, but he wouldn't give in to his reminder from Chickamauga.

Enjoying the crisp, clean mountain air, he lit his ever-present cheroot. Seconds later, Ian joined him. The two men stood in silence, their breath and the cigar smoke curling and dancing around their heads like specters.

Ian looked up at the distant mountain silhouette. "I believe winter is comin' early this year. I was thinking it would be no problem to be done here by the end of September, but *now* I'm thinkin' Defiance has become a wee bit more interestin'. Wouldn't ye say?" He quirked an eyebrow at his friend and offered the smallest hint of a smile.

McIntyre shrugged noncommittally as he watched the men and horses flow by. Saturday was always busy. Miners wandered, either on foot or horseback, drunk and sober, back and forth between the Iron Horse and the tent saloons in the other part of town. Faintly, in the distance, they heard the popping sound of small caliber gunfire. Probably a Derringer going off over at the Wolf's Head.

Ian shoved his hands in his pockets and tapped his foot in time with *Buffalo Gals* floating out from the Iron Horse. "Are ye serious about cleanin' up Defiance?"

McIntyre inhaled. There was a change in the air tonight, more of a bite to it. Winter *was* coming. His favorite season, it was extremely unforgiving in Defiance. "You know I am. We'll never get the railroad in here if we don't."

"Then I'm thinkin' ye need to start with that marshal. Does he actually know how to do anything other than take orders from ye?"

"Well, that is why I hired him. He's one of my best employees. Wade is loyal to a fault."

"Precisely. He won't arrest anyone or enforce a law unless he checks with ye first. Defiance can't keep being this wild-and-wooly Donnybrook if ye want respectability. Ye need laws and ye need a lawman who can enforce them."

McIntyre raised an eyebrow and looked up at his friend. "Why, Ian, you sound as if you think I'm dragging my feet. I thought we were going to start working on that again in the spring. Is there a reason to hurry now? "

"I started thinkin' maybe I have more reason to stay in Defiance than half-ownership of a mine."

McIntyre rolled the cheroot around in his mouth. "It's the black-haired one you're fond of. What makes her so special? Other than business meetings, you've hardly talked to the woman."

Ian grinned like a schoolboy. "Aye, and I'd like to talk to her some more to see if I want to talk to her some more."

The mischievous expression on his friend's weathered face made McIntyre laugh. "I think the lot of them maybe more trouble than they're worth." He tapped Ian lightly in the gut. "But it is good to see you taking an interest in something. I swear I believe you're even looking younger."

Before Ian could reply, gunfire erupted again, but much closer this time. The boom was thunderous and came from a definite location. The two men froze.

"That sounded like a sho'gun—" Ian noted with concern.

Before he could finish, McIntyre had tossed aside his cheroot and was running like a man on fire toward the other end of town, leaving his hat in the dust.

~~~

## Fifteen

McIntyre ran as if he was racing the devil. He bounded down the boardwalks then on to the hotel's porch. The front door was open and he could hear a commotion of some kind upstairs. Drawing his gun, he bolted up the stairs.

"Mrs. Miller, ladies, are you all right?"

He turned the corner and paused to get his bearings. The second floor was no longer one, large open space. Fifteen rooms had been roughed in and he now found himself staring down a darkened hall. Light was coming from the last doorway on the right and he could hear several frantic voices, yelling and screaming all at once.

"Mrs. Miller," he yelled again, bolting down the hallway. He leaped into the room, gun pointed at—

*Hank Barrows?*

The young man was kneeling on the floor, hands laced behind his head, and he was peppered with bloody wounds down a good portion of the left side of his body. His shirt hung from him in shreds. Still wearing her faded, blue day dress, Naomi was holding a shotgun on him, smoke whisping from its barrel. Rebecca and Hannah, in their nightclothes, were cowering behind her. When they saw McIntyre, all of them started talking at once to him, but Naomi kept the gun trained on Hank.

"He broke in here—"

"I only meant to scare'em!"

"Started yelling crazy stuff—"

"Said he was going to rip off our clothes—"

"I wasn't gonna hurt anybody!"

"QUIET!" McIntyre yelled. The room fell silent. "Put that gun away, Mrs. Miller, before you shoot me. I can see the barrel shaking from here." Slowly, Naomi lowered the gun. Hank started to lower his hands, but McIntyre waved his gun at him. "Keep them up until you tell me what happened…or you bleed to death."

The boy started shaking his head back and forth as if he couldn't stand his pain. "I swear I wasn't gonna hurt'em! Rose said she'd let me have a poke for free if I'd just scare these girls. That's all. I wasn't even gonna touch'em!'"

"Then what were you doing leaning over the bed?" Rebecca's voice and eyes were wild with fear.

The sound of boots tromping up the stairs stopped her hysterics and, a moment later, Ian appeared. He assessed the situation quickly. "Are you all right, ladies?" When they nodded, he went to Hank. Helping him to his feet, he assessed the boy's condition. "Ye're fortunate her aim was off. Ye're peppered up good, but you willna die. A wee touch more to the right and ye'd be without your worthless head, though."

Naomi raised her gun again. "I was trying to miss. I only wanted to scare *him*."

The marshal entered at that moment, gun drawn, and, after taking in the scene, turned to McIntyre for instruction.

"Take him to the jail, Wade." Disgusted with all this unnecessary high drama, McIntyre grabbed Hank's shoulder and shoved him towards the marshal. "I'll be by shortly to have a talk with him. Get one of the Flowers to come over and clean him up."

Without hesitating, the marshal grabbed the whimpering sot by the arm and led him out of the room as McIntyre dropped the hammer on his gun. Clear out to the street they could hear Hank bewailing the misunderstanding. "I was only gonna scare'em. I wouldn't have hurt'em. Just scare'em; that's all. Am I dying…?"

As his voice faded, Naomi let the hammer down on her shotgun and breathed. McIntyre dropped his gun back into its holster and took a step toward her. "Tell me what happened." The gentleness with which he'd asked the question surprised even him.

"Here, ladies . . . " Ian went to Rebecca and Hannah. "Why don't ye come with me? We'll have a spo' of warm tea to calm our nerves." With his hand on their backs, he gently led them out of the room.

Naomi leaned the gun in the corner and sat down on the bed. "Our rooms are almost finished. One more night and Hannah would have been in here alone."

McIntyre found her dull stare disconcerting and her deadpan voice even more so. He approached the bed and leaned on a post. She looked weary both in body and spirit. He thought again of that night he had caught her praying and wondered if she was praying right now.

Her eyes began to glisten and she wiped the unwanted tears away angrily. He had the sudden urge to hold her, to comfort her, to feel the warmth of her head on his shoulder. The desire startled him to the point that he actually backed away a step.

"I came in from the backyard and the hotel was so quiet, but then I heard the stairs creak. They hadn't done that before, not that I'd noticed." She turned her head and stared at the wall behind him. He followed her gaze to the paneling, ripped and splintered from buckshot. "I just knew something was wrong and we keep the gun behind the door. I heard a voice whispering but it wasn't Rebecca or Hannah." She shook her and frowned. "I tried to be so quiet…When I crept into the room, I saw him standing at the end of the bed…staring at them."

Naomi looked at him then and the depth of pain and confusion in her face drew him back to the end of the bed, but no closer.

"I warned him. I tried to get him to leave." She swallowed. "What if I'd killed him? I nearly did." She wasn't asking about the legal ramifications, he knew, but the deeper meaning of taking a life. "A kind of blind fear came over me, but I was blind with rage at the same time. How can that be?"

He didn't know the answer to that, but he did know her experience wasn't unique. He had been introduced to that strange mix of fear and fury during the war. Right beside him, a dear friend's head had exploded when hit with a cannon ball; yet, he had kept firing at a sea of Yankees spilling over the ridge.

Turning from the bloody memories, he offered encouragement. "You didn't kill him...and I dare say once word of your shotgun gets out, you won't have any more unwanted visitors."

"He said Rose put him up to it. Why does she hate us so?" Naomi's chin quivered and he heard tears in her voice. He knew, though, that she wouldn't cry in front of him. No matter what it took, she wouldn't do that. He understood the need to hide weakness and vulnerability.

"I suspect she wants you to leave. You needn't concern yourself with her now. Rose will not plague you again. I'll see to it personally."

"I appreciate you coming by. Please let us know if we can press charges . . . if it even goes that far."

He detected cynicism in the comment. She didn't trust that anything would happen to the boy. "I'll stop by the jail and tell Wade to start the proceedings. He'll be punished." He hoped the promise would reassure her.

She offered nothing more and stared down at her hands in her lap. He realized he was dismissed. Wishing for something more to say, he motioned as if tipping his hat "Until tomorrow then, Mrs. Miller."


Defiant against any emotions that might make her tolerate the man, much less like him, Naomi stood, straight and tall as she could manage. She hoped she looked regal and collected. She wanted him to know she was strong and didn't need him to lean on...unlike Daisy or any of those other women in his employ.

Yet, in spite of herself, Naomi felt a slight kindness towards Mr. McIntyre. She assumed his gentle voice and attempted heroism were lulling her into a false sense of trust. He was a cad, a man who led women into prostitution; a dishonest, disreputable business man not worth her time. He was here now out of a need to protect his investment and nothing else. But she was so tired of fighting this town, the men, these evil women and their plots—

She waited till she heard his boots on the stairs and then fell backward across the bed. She was too stunned and too tired to cry. She merely wanted to get away from this abhorrent place, to go somewhere people weren't constantly trying to insult, injure, or leer at them. She wanted to lie down and feel John's arms around her. Hoping her mind would stay numb, she rolled over and curled up into a tight little ball, like a child awaiting the safe haven of sleep.

~~~

Rebecca and Hannah sat in silence while Ian bustled confidently about the kitchen, making tea. "I'm quite pleased," he muttered as he ran his hands over the new stove. He looked around at the newly renovated kitchen. "They've done a wonderful job. This is a much more functional kitchen for a commercial venture."

Neither of the sisters replied. Suddenly aware that she and Rebecca were in their night things, Hannah pulled her gown closer and hunched beneath the table, trying to make herself insignificant.

Rebecca slid her hand over and clutched Hannah's. "Are you all right?"

Hannah half-nodded, half shook her head. "I don't know. I guess so. I'm not sure really what I think. I don't know if I'm more shaken by that man coming in our room or by Naomi trying to shoot him."

"She tried to miss. A scatter gun has a wide pattern."

"She pulled the trigger."

"She had the *guts* to pull the trigger. That's not an easy burden to carry. To have a temper like that must be frightening."

Hannah bit her lip, willing to ponder that point. If not for what Rebecca had said, Hannah wouldn't have thought of it in that way. And maybe because Naomi was willing to use a gun, whether out of courage or anger, there would be no more trouble. She prayed it was so. She was scared enough as it was. Glancing down at her ever-growing midsection, she tried not to fear the future.

Ian set cups on the table then returned with a kettle of hot water. Rebecca assisted by putting the tea and strainers in each cup. He poured the water, returned the kettle to the stove then sat down with them.

Dunking the strainer, he studied the girls. "Ye've been through a lo' since ye departed yer home. I think ye're holding up remarkably well. I'd be willing to bet that once words of this gets out, ye'll have no more trouble."

Hannah wasn't so sure. She had a strong suspicion that there was one woman in town who wasn't feeling too peaceable. "What about Rose? Is she going to let this go?"

"I believe Rose's time at the Iron Horse has come to an end. She has been a thorn in Mac's side for some time now. I suspect he'll be pruning her from the Garden forthwith."

Wearing a melancholy smile, Rebecca stirred a little honey into her tea. "I can't believe how far we've come from Cary and I don't mean miles. That life seems a million years in the past."

"Aye, I know what ye mean. My life as a young man in Sco'land is a vague memory now. Everywhere I've traveled, in fact, seems vague and shadowy. I regret not having put down roots somewhere but my wanderlust wouldna let me be."

He sipped his tea and thought for a moment. "I came to Defiance in March and thought to leave this fall..." The expression on his face transformed to something deeper and softer as he studied Rebecca. Hannah knew if she could see the change, surely so could her sister. "I think now I'll stay a wee bit longer. I'd like to see the hotel up and runnin'."

Rebecca paused with her tea almost at her lips. "Do you think you'll ever go back to Scotland?"

Ian shook his head. "I knew when I left I wouldna see home again. I'm more interested in lookin' forward than back. The past is done and there's no changin' it."

Rebecca nodded, her eyes aglow. Ian shifted in his seat. "We can best honor our dead by livin' well. Movin' forward dusna mean ye love them any less. It just means ye're still alive." A shadow of a memory crossed his face. "I was married for a brief time in Sco'land. After Annie died, I came close dying as well. I just thank God he dinna leave me to perish, alone with a bottle in Glasgow."

Hannah caught the reference and knew Rebecca hadn't missed it either, judging by her wide, glimmering eyes. "You're a Believer," her sister asked, sounding stunned.

"I am a man of faith, but admittedly a wayward faith. Though, somehow I feel the prodigal son is returnin' home."

Hannah knew there was a message in that statement and hoped Rebecca didn't miss it.

Indeed, Rebecca's reply was so soft her voice was barely above a whisper. "I'm glad you found your way back."

~~~

When McIntyre walked into the jail, Wade looked up from his dime novel and shrugged apologetically. "I reckon he'll live, Mr. McIntyre, but he's sleeping' it off now. Squalled like a baby all the way here, then went out like a lamp when his head hit the pillow."

Displeased that he couldn't question Hank, McIntyre strode over to the cell and checked in on the new guest, barely visible in the low light. His drunken snoring, the wet, sloppy sound of a hog rooting through thick mud, convinced McIntyre he was indeed alive.

"Lily cleaned him up some," Wade explained from behind him, "but I told her not to worry too much about him. He ain't dyin'."

McIntyre studied the boy and decided he probably hadn't meant any harm, but he would have to make an example of him. It was that or face Her Belligerent Holiness at the end of the street. "Charge him with breaking and entering and assault, keep him here fifteen days and fine him $150. When his pa comes into see him, tell him to find me."

That handled, he marched across the street to pack Rose. He was not looking forward to the scene she would cause.

These melodramas both embarrassed and infuriated him. Tonight, however, was the end of it. Middle of the night or not, Rose was going over to the Broken Spoke. Working at the nastiest cathouse in town might teach her a little humility.

He shot straight to her room and burst in unannounced. To his great annoyance, the room was empty and some of her toiletry items were missing from her dresser. He checked her closet. Nearly all of her clothes were gone. Staring at the all-but-empty clothes rod, he traced his beard thoughtfully, trying to deal with her unexpected departure.

"She's gone." Jasmine's voice was flat and devoid of any emotion.

McIntyre turned to study his new Asian acquisition. Sultry and slender, he had been immediately impressed with her in Denver and paid well for her. Now, she bored him too, even in her exotic, traditional blue silk dress. "She said you would not lay your hands on her again."

"And?"

Jasmine shrugged, her expression inscrutable. "She was raging, not making any sense, going in and out of Spanish. I did hear her say you better keep looking over your shoulder. That she'd be back."

McIntyre muttered a vile name for Rose and slammed the closet door. She couldn't have gone far; she had to be hiding somewhere in Tent Town. He would dispatch some men to turn the slum upside down if necessary, but he would find her and hand her over to Lil for . . . *softening*.

~~~

# Sixteen

When no one could find Rose by sunup, McIntyre called off the search. It troubled him that she had so easily disappeared. Feeling the lack of sleep slowing his mind, he told Wade he was going to rest for a few hours but to wake him if he heard anything. At noon, Wade did just that. McIntyre was already dressed and working on a cup of coffee when the marshal came to his room.

"Lil's downstairs and she's none too happy."

That told McIntyre the two things he wanted to know. Rose had gone to Lil for help; Lil knew better than to give her any. "Tell her I'll be right down."

Lil was behind his bar helping herself to a drink when McIntyre descended the stairs. She tipped the bottle at him and grinned, showing the space where a tooth once resided. "I didn't figure you'd mind, after what I put up with last night."

McIntyre acquiesced with a nod as he took a seat and waited for her. Lil was a stunning beauty for a woman in her thirties, until she spoke. Then her missing tooth, raspy voice and coarse talk quickly betrayed her vocation. Her delicate European features and silky, disheveled red hair, however, had led many men to think her weak and frail. A few foolish souls had tried knocking her around and quickly discovered why she was called *Diamond* Lil. A tougher, more cold-hearted and violent woman didn't exist in the new state of Colorado. If anyone could take Crazy Rose down a peg or two, Lil could. She joined him at the table, bringing her full shot glass and the bottle with her.

"I take it you have Rose then."

Lil swore and tossed back her drink, slamming the empty glass down on the table. "She came paradin' into the Spoke about 4 this morning sayin' you'd sent her." She leaned toward McIntyre for emphasis. "I don't want her! You can't use my debt to you for nothin' like this. We said it was cash, straight up, for the liquor I buy from you."

McIntyre leaned his chair back and sighed. "I didn't send her...but I was going to. I need you to break her for me."

Lil spewed a nasty name at him as a look of total disgust crossed her face. "Ain't you something. Don't want to get your hands dirty straightening her out? You know she won't be fit for the fancy-shmancy Iron Horse when I'm done with her."

"Doesn't matter. I don't want her back, but she's got to stop causing trouble. Like you and the rest of the gals in Defiance, she's got to learn her place."

A sharp V formed between Lil's brows, but she didn't address the comment. Green eyes glittered with uncertainty as she reached up and set to re-pinning runaway red curls. "She's a mighty lot of trouble, that one. Plain crazy, I think. Them's the worse kind. Can't predict'em."

McIntyre dropped his chair and slapped his hand on the table. "She thinks you'll help her, Lil, or she wouldn't have gone to you. Straighten her out. I'll throw in two cases of whiskey and a keg of beer for your trouble."

Lil pursed her lips and thought hard. "Why don't you sell me the rest of MY saloon? I don't need a partner anymore."

"Keep Rose on your side of town and I'll consider it."

Lil stuck out her hand. "Shake on it." McIntyre took the woman's hand, relieved that at least this one problem had been handled.

~~~

"Lil will teach Rose some manners or die trying. And I'll be able to keep tabs on her. If I kicked her out of town, I wouldn't be able to do that. And I do believe Rose bears watching."

Sitting on the other side of McIntyre's desk at the Sunnyside Mine office, Ian looked as if he doubted

McIntyre's plan. "I dunna agree that Rose is the source of all the trouble in Defiance."

"Well, she's the source of most of mine. A few months working in a crib under Lil's fist and she'll settle down."

"I wouldna wish that on anyone, even on Rose." Ian pinned McIntyre with a disapproving glance then shrugged. "But ye're missing my point. Hank's escapade might embolden other men. I think these women need protection and I mean more than the marshal passing by or escorting them down the street."

Leaning back in his chair amidst squeaking leather and springs, McIntyre shook his head emphatically. "Mrs. Miller's run-in with O'Banion showed everyone she's a fire-breather. Now they know she's not afraid to actually pull a trigger. That's probably more than enough to get even the worst drunks in Defiance to stand-down."

"Mac, the reality of the situation is that ye dunna control every randy miner, prospector and gambler in these parts. Three reputable women with no men around is an awfully tempting prize, gun or no gun. If ye'll not do something more, I will."

A grin leaped to McIntyre's face. He realized where this was going and decided to help his friend. "By all means, then, I think you should spend as much time as possible with them." He couldn't help but add one dash of sarcasm, though. "I for one will sleep much better at night knowing their knight in shining armor is standing guard over them."

Ian harumphed irritably at the comment, but didn't argue. And if pressed, McIntyre might admit to a twinge of jealousy. Just a twinge. He had been the first to rush into that room the other night but Naomi had acted as if the event was somehow his fault. There was no pleasing the woman. Given that she viewed him somewhere above pond scum but a step below snakes, he would simply have to try harder–

He heard the sparking, grinding scream of mental brakes.

Try harder? No, he thought with a curse. He wouldn't try at all. This was ridiculous. No woman was worth this amount of distraction. And how had he gone from planning to get her into bed to actually caring what she thought of him? When had *that* happened?

He shook his head as if to ward off this confounded confusion and barked, "I don't have time for this nonsense." Ian jumped at the unexpected tone and McIntyre softened his voice. "Feel free to take over the inn as your project. I'll come around to check the progress, but you can be there night and day if it pleases you."

~~~

Rose picked up a glass and held it to the light. Filthy. Using her skirt to wipe the nastiness out of it, she eyed her new surroundings. The Broken Spoke was just one step above a hovel. Top half worn tent billowing in the breeze, bottom half stick built; most of the seats were just chopped logs, and the tables were slabs of timber from the mill. A rusting buck stove occupied the center of the room and gave off more smoke than heat.

But she could stay here for a while. Perhaps this was even better than being at the Iron Horse. Here she would have her own tent. She would have more time to pray and practice her arts. No one would come in except customers and she could handle them. She had a reputation for dazzling men and that wouldn't change whether she worked for Lil or McIntyre. Eventually, she would be right back over at the Iron Horse, running things, tending to McIntyre, torturing the Flowers, and the three little *gringas* would be a bad memory. Content, she splashed some whiskey into the glass and raised it up in front of her.

Lil barged through the front door and strode with grim determination up to Rose. She reached across the bar and slapped the empty glass out of her hand, sending it flying across the saloon.

Trying to burn Rose with a scorching glare, Lil growled, "It's my liquor. You'll pay for every drink you toss back." Rose's jaw tightened and she straightened a little as Lil's eyes narrowed. The two wild cats stared at each other over the worn, liquor-stained slab of wood.

"This ain't the Iron Horse. Git the notion of soft beds and one or two customers a night outta your head."

Like a sudden gust of wind, Lil changed her tact, softening her tone as she turned and sashayed over to a table. She sat down in one of the few chairs in the room and laced her fingers. "You get your tent out back. All your customers come through here. They'll pay me. You git your cut in the mornin'. Keep your nose clean, stay out of trouble, and we'll git along just fine." Lil cocked her head to one side and studied Rose for a moment. "But you're not gonna to do that, are you?"

Rose didn't answer or move. She waited to hear what else this demon *gringa* had to say. Lil laughed heartily, a sound that reminded Rose of an asthmatic donkey. Muttering a curse, but still grinning, Lil drummed her fingers on the table and considered things. Finally, she stood and walked back over to the bar.

Her voice low and ominous, she laid it out for Rose. "There's no sisterhood here. I only want easy-goin', hard-workin' girls. If you're not easy goin' and hard workin', I'll *make* you easy goin' and hard workin'."

Lil twirled a long, stray red curl around her finger and smiled. Rose knew the danger glittering in her eyes and felt an uneasy nudge of fear.

"There are different ways to break fallen angels like you," Lil continued. "Some can't stand the cold so I take away their firewood. Some can't stand to go hungry." Lil shrugged. "It's just a matter of findin' your weakness."

Rose couldn't hold back a smug smile. "Then you'll be searching for a long time."

"No." Lil leaned an elbow on the bar. "The bottom line with you is power. You think your looks give you power. So cross me just one time and I'll carve your face up like a Christmas turkey…and you know I will."

Rose had the urge to dig her claws into Lil's face and rip the flesh from her skull. Instead, she breathed and forced the hate down deep inside to use later. "You are mean, *puma*, but I am meaner," she warned Lil. "Do you think I am afraid of you?"

"You don't have to be afraid, but you should be smart." With stunning swiftness, Lil reached out, grabbed Rose by the neck and slammed her face into the bar. Pain and stars exploded in her head. Using a bear-like grip to grind Rose's cheek into the rough, splintery wood, Lil whispered menacingly, "I don't play. Remember that."

She abruptly released her and Rose smacked Lil's hand the rest of the way off as she stood. Chest heaving, nose throbbing, she felt a warm trickle of blood reach her upper lip as she stared angrily at her new *patron*. Perilously close to flying over the bar and wrapping her hands around Lil's throat, she put the anger to her feet and fled the Broken Spoke. Oh, she was going to have to kill that *gringa*, sooner rather than later.

~~~

## Seventeen

Leaning over a list at the kitchen table, Rebecca and Hannah finished writing up an order for linens and then stared at each other with dread in their eyes. "I'm not going to take it to the telegraph office," Hannah told her rather loudly, "and you can't go alone."

Rebecca cringed, well away of her little sister's plan. Ian, only a few feet away supervising the pump installation, excused himself from the carpenters and offered his elbow to Rebecca. "If ye'll have me, m'lady?"

Swallowing nervously, Rebecca nodded. Hannah grinned from ear-to-ear, adding to Rebecca's butterflies. Ian grabbed his cane from the corner and came back to her with his hand extended. She commanded the heat in her face to subside, to no avail, and lightly clutched his fingers.

As the two stepped outside, she noticed his cane with the ornately carved wolf's head on top. "It's beautiful. I think it's very distinguished."

He twirled the cane around as they strolled at a comfortable, casual speed. "It belonged to my father. Alas, I fear it makes me look as ancient as Methuselah."

"Hardly. You're dapper and handsome with it." She turned away, certain she was flushed with embarrassment over the bold comment that had just leaped out of her mouth. Ian scratched his beard and grinned at her. Shocked at herself, Rebecca prayed that God would strike her dumb and stop this runaway mouth of hers.

"Ms. Rebecca, are there other siblings between ye and yer sisters? How is it that there is such a spread in yer ages?"

She shook her head, resigned to the implication that she was noticeably older than Hannah and Naomi. "No, Momma and Daddy had me and, after twelve years of no more children, thought they were done. You can imagine what a surprise Naomi was to everyone. They thought she was a small miracle, but then six years after her, Hannah was born."

"If ye don't mind me asking, where is the father of Hannah's babe?" It was the first time he had mentioned the situation.

Rebecca tugged nervously on her braid. "I don't know exactly." Rebecca had taken quite a shine to Ian, but that didn't mean she should go spouting off the family secrets. Besides, she didn't want him to think poorly of Hannah. "His father was going to send him to some Ivy League school this fall. I hope they both think it was worth abandoning her and the baby for it."

"I take it the lad dinna marry her then?" His voice was gentle and lacking any accusations. When Rebecca didn't answer immediately, he cleared his throat and apologized. "I'm sorry. That's none o' me business. Hannah seems a very sweet girl—"

"And Billy Page is a fast-talkin', quick-movin' scallywag." Rebecca was immediately sorry the unexpected gush of anger had taken control of her sense. Crossing her arms, she shook her head and sighed. "He has no idea how many hearts he's broken."

They walked in silence after that until they reached the telegraph office. Ian plucked the order from Rebecca's hand. "Allow me. It won't take a moment. Rest on the bench and enjoy these last warm rays of the sun. Winter is comin' and it comes to Defiance with a vengeance."

She thanked him and sat down. The town bustled around her like a beehive. Everyday new folks rolled in, on the stage, with mule trains, or on their own, sure they could simply pluck ten-pound nuggets from the creeks. She had heard that most prospectors, after fruitless months of panning, eventually gave up seeking their own fortunes and went to work for Ian and Mr. McIntyre at the Sunnyside Mine.

The disproportionate number of women among the men was a fact that worried Rebecca. Ian had told them there were fewer than thirty women in town and that females sparked ninety percent of the fights. She felt safe with him, though, and knew he was watching over them.

Over her?

It had been so long since a man had looked at her. Even longer since she'd wanted to look back. Ian made her feel as though he could see right past her wrinkles and seasoned age to the girl she used to be. Near as she could tell, he hadn't noticed Naomi or Hannah.

But was she getting ahead of herself? Ian clearly favored her, but in what way? Rebecca had no desire to risk a heartbreak. Maybe he favored her precisely because of her age: that she was someone safe with whom he could be friends and there wouldn't be any romantic entanglements. Besides, Rebecca wasn't so sure she was ready for anything like that. She had her silly, romantic daydreams about Ian. That would have to do for now. Illusions were safe and didn't put either of them in awkward situations.

She settled on the bench more comfortably and shut her eyes to enjoy the gentle warmth on her face. Back home, the first day of September was just as hot as the first day of July. Here, in these mountains, at this altitude, she doubted it would ever be hot enough to melt candles like Southern heat could.

The bench moved as Ian sat beside her and she opened her eyes to thank him for sending the telegraph. To her dismay, a total stranger sat beside her, grinning widely through broken teeth and a scruffy beard. Another man stood near him, leering with an unnerving hunger.

"You're one of those new girls, ain't ya?" The man sitting beside her looked her up and down lecherously. "We heard about you up at our camp. You must be the oldest one, but you're still mighty pretty." He slapped his friend on the leg and laughed. "That's all right. I like 'em seasoned. Sometimes them young'uns don't really know how to please a man—"

"Sir," Rebecca surged to her feet. "Your conversation is rude and vulgar. Please excuse me." She thought to push past the man who was standing and slip into the telegraph office, but the man on the bench leaped to his feet and grabbed her arm as the other one blocked her way.

"No streetwalker talks to Texas Jack that way—"

The raised voices brought Ian out of the office and immediately to Rebecca's defense. With stunning force, he violently heaved the man holding Rebecca into his friend, nearly bowling them both down. As they fought to regain their balance, Ian pressed the end of his cane into the man's chest. "Apologize to the lady for yer impertinence or I'll part yer skull."

His warning was clear and Rebecca knew with a heart-pounding certainty it should be heeded. The fire in the stranger's eyes fairly screamed that he had other plans. He grabbed for his sidearm, but Ian laid his cane right down the middle of the man's head with a thunderous crack. As he fell, Ian swiftly stabbed the cane into the other man's gut. The assailant doubled over and slid to his knees, clutching his midsection. Without hesitation, Ian smacked him on the head as well, and, in what seemed the blink of an eye, both men were lying on the sidewalk. Rebecca gasped, stunned by the complete efficiency with which Ian had dispatched both men.

"Our business here is concluded." Gently, he took her arm. "Let's be on our way."

"I've never seen anything like that." Rebecca was reeling from the swiftness and perfect skill of his attack. Hand at her heart, she glanced back at the men, one still lying motionless on the ground and the other alternately grabbing his head and his midsection and groaning. "Where did you learn to do that?"

"The streets of Edinburgh."

After a few minutes, she recovered from the fright of the violent tussle and played the man's words over and over in her head. With each repeating of it, she found her spirits sinking lower and lower.

*Streetwalker.* She had never in her life heard the word, but its meaning was perfectly clear.

Staring straight ahead, she broached the man's comment.

"He called me a streetwalker." She felt the muscles in his arm tense. "Is that what we've done? Just by coming into this town, we're automatically branded as..." she couldn't even say the word. "Is that what everyone really thinks of us?"

Somberly, he steered her down the alley between two buildings and led her toward the stream. "Let's take a less traveled path."

The fact that he didn't answer right away disturbed Rebecca. Did the men in this town think they were in the process of building another brothel no matter what message Mr. McIntyre had tried to disperse? No matter how well she and her sisters behaved? What did Ian think? "Oh, this is horrible!" Mortified, Rebecca collapsed on to a boulder at the water's edge. "Does everyone think we're building a brothel? Do you?"

"No, no, no," he declared, lighting beside her. "I think nothin' of the sort. Mac has gone to great pains to let folks know that ye're only opening a respectable place...but there are a lot of men in this area who don't get into town that much." He rubbed his neck as if the stress was getting the better of him. "Men will think what they want to think. Ye'll just have to prove them wrong . . . and that might take some time."

Rebecca was stunned. She realized they had all been living in this fairy tale world, thinking that if they didn't look or act like prostitutes, eventually they would convince the men of the truth. She thought of the many trips she and her sisters had made to the bank, general store and telegraph office and cringed. The whispers and the stares, the soft laughter that followed them down the boardwalk, even when the marshal was with them. Did everyone think this was a huge joke and when the inn was open, they would rush the doors seeking *entertainment* rather than a simple meal?

Gently, Ian took Rebecca's hand. She slowly raised her face to him. Serene, blue eyes calmed her soul. She had the strangest certainty that he wanted to kiss her.

"If I might offer a suggestion . . . " At first he seemed

lost for words but she waited expectantly and tried to slow her galloping heart. "Perhaps if ye were seen in the company of a respectable man more often..." Her brow furrowed, unsure of his meaning. He muttered a mild oath under his breath and sighed. "What I'm tryin' to say, very badly, is that I'd like permission to call on ye, if ye've a mind to be courted by an old goot like meself."

Her eyes saucered, but after a moment, a smile was born. "The thought of having you around more is not an unpleasant one," she answered as honestly as she could.

His face fell. "But . . . "

"But it's been a very, very long time since I—well, I'm not a teenager anymore, Ian. The idea of courting is..."

"A bit fast for ye?"

*Terrifying*, she wanted to say, but didn't. Instead, she nodded, thankful that the excuse kept her from having to discuss her wrinkles and other insecurities. Could he really want a relationship with a woman who was at the point in life of trading beauty for wisdom? Rebecca felt so weathered and dull compared to her sisters, how could he see past them to her?

"Then may I have permission to call on ye as a friend...a dear friend."

She couldn't help herself and squeezed his hand, marveling over how warm and right it felt in hers. "Yes, a very dear friend." Taking a risk, she admitted, "I'd like that more than you can imagine."

~~~~

Naomi stared at the chicken coop and sighed. Rebecca had overseen the men who had hung the cages in here and, as a result, everything was perfect for her Amazonian sister to reach, but at least a foot too high for Naomi. Gathering eggs was now her least favorite chore as it usually resulted in a pricked elbow from jagged chicken wire or an unpleasant stain on the front of her apron.

She tried not to think about their coop back home. John

had built her a perfect hen house: neat, prim, tidy, and at an easy height to steal the eggs. He had delighted in building something that pleased her so . . .

Eager to save that memory for a later time, she looked around the little lean-to. Perhaps there was something she could stand on? She spotted a few rusty tools, some nails spilled in the dirt and a pine stump about two feet tall and a foot or so around. It would be wobbly, Naomi knew, but perhaps she could steady herself long enough . . .

She set her basket atop the chicken cages and wiggled the surprisingly heavy stump over in front of them. She eyed it warily and pushed on it. The ground was uneven and it wiggled around some, but Naomi was confident of her balance. Hiking up her skirt, she stepped gingerly on the stump. Slowly, she stood up as much as the low roof would allow. So far, so good.

She reached for the basket and the motion threatened to topple her stand, but she managed to stay on top by freezing in place. Hoping she had her balance back, she reached again for the basket and opened the first cage.


From his position on the back porch, McIntyre watched Naomi set up the makeshift stool and smiled with mischievous delight. He could see disaster right around the corner and decided to help it along. Though he had vowed to avoid her, the potential for a little fun at Her Highness's expense was simply too tempting.

Quiet as an Indian, he stole behind her as she ever-so-slowly reached under the reticent hen and retrieved an egg. Oblivious to his presence, she moved to drop the egg in her basket. The change in direction caused the stump to wobble. Naomi froze, the egg still in her hand. A breathless moment passed as she waited to make sure things were under control. Her balance regained, she let out a breath and placed the egg in her basket.

McIntyre moved a step closer. "Good morning, Mrs. Miller." Naomi squeaked in fear at the unusually loud greeting, the stump wobbled, her feet went out from under her and she fell right into his arms…as planned, though he'd been forced to move a little quicker than he'd anticipated to catch this falling angel.

Feigning shock, he rolled his eyes. "Really, Mrs. Miller. Must you throw yourself at me? It is rather embarrassing."

Practically growling, she fought to get away from him, but he held fast for just a breath. Outrage percolated in her eyes, but he didn't miss the flash of something else, either. Enjoying the feel of her pressed against him, he pulled her closer and grinned like the devil.

Boiling mad and glowing a beautiful shade of pink, she punched him in the shoulder. "Put me down this instant!"

Surprised by the ferocity behind the fist, he knew better than to press his luck. Her Highness had one whale of a jab. Unceremoniously, he released her. Naomi had to claw at his lapel to keep from falling flat on her rear end. Gaining her feet, she angrily pushed away from him, brushed a stray hair from her face and checked to see if she still had an egg in her basket.

Things in their proper places, she drew back and delivered another stunning blow to McIntyre's left bicep. "What's the matter with you?" she snapped. "I could have broken my neck."

Mustering his pride, he resisted the urge to rub his thumping muscle. Instead, he pretended exaggerated emotional distress. He clutched his vest over his heart as if she had stabbed him with a real weapon. "You have wounded me, Milady. Have you no gratitude for the peasant who saved you?"

"Saved me? You nearly killed me!"

He leaned in, pressing, he knew, too close for comfort. "If I wanted you dead…"

Naomi huffed and moved back. "Then what do you want? I'm busy."

McIntyre straightened up and shrugged in a casual way. "To check on things."

She did not need to know he had surveyed the hotel on

153

his way out here. Construction had progressed quite well and he was pleased. Getting his arms around her had been a bonus. Recently widowed or not, her vehement reaction, including that heaving chest, spoke volumes about her vulnerability to him. Perhaps the two of them mixed like oil and water, but somewhere in the recipe there was also a little nitroglycerin. His ego was stroked and he'd left her with something to think about. That would have to do for now. "Well, I believe my work here is done."

Naomi sucked in a breath and her shocked face drained of its color. She took another step back, bumping into the chicken cage. McIntyre was alarmed at her sudden pastiness. "Mrs. Miller, are you all right?"

"My husband used to say that very same thing when he would tease me. How . . . " She swallowed and shook her head, looking terribly rattled by his words.

"I do apologize, Mrs. Miller, if I caused you any pain."

"No." She pulled herself together, admirably well, he thought, considering how pale she was. "No, you didn't. It just caught me off guard."

The fun of a few moments ago obscured by this curtain of grief, McIntyre thought it best to take his leave. His simple teasing had been meant to act as a diversion, pleasant or not. Instead, it had launched her straight back to thinking of her husband, someone, in truth, he would prefer she forget. Feeling a little chagrined at the backfire, he touched the brim of his hat. "Then I will bid you good day." He glanced at the stump. "Do try to be careful, won't you?"

With a quick nod, he left her and headed down toward the back trail. McIntyre did not currently feel like dealing with the bustle of the street, and the sound of the river always settled him. He rubbed his arm as he walked. He could still feel the sting of her punch, but he could also feel her gathered up against him. She was a boney package compared to the buxom Rose, and yet he had liked holding her.

Strange, she was nothing like any of the women he'd ever been attracted to. Surely the fireworks were more about lust and conquest and a bored man's desire for variety . . .

than, say, something more noble? He shivered at the thought. Deciding that avoiding Naomi *was* the safest course, he forced her to the back of his mind.

McIntyre suspected, however, the stubborn little wench wouldn't stay there.

Naomi leaned her head against a knotty cedar pole holding up the lean-to and let a few tears fall. Her meeting with Mr. McIntyre had been emotionally tumultuous, to say the least. She thought about the last time John had said those words to her, in the back yard of their home. And now, to hear them uttered fifteen hundred miles away by a scoundrel in the truest sense of the word was beyond comprehension.

She was disgusted by the whole scene, by his hypnotic, penetrating brown eyes, maddening, devious grin,, and shocking boldness. He had purposely held her far longer than necessary, affording her ample opportunity to feel the sinewy, muscular strength of his lean frame.

How could he treat her like that, a grieving widow? Had he no shame? She straightened up and wiped her eyes. She had too much to make her cry to add him to the list. Gathering her wits about her, she stepped back up on the stump and wished Mr. McIntyre would obligingly step off the edge of the earth.

~~~

Hugging herself to ward off the chilly hint of approaching fall, Hannah stood on the front porch of the hotel and waited for her sisters. Even with what had happened to Rebecca and Ian a few weeks ago, the sisters had decided they wouldn't be prisoners in the hotel. Or at least, two of them wouldn't be.

Someone, most likely Rose, had been spreading rumors about the sisters, seeding the town with doubts about their hotel and vocation. A man with a lecherous grin had actually approached Hannah in the mercantile and suggested she find some Goodyear products before she went back to work. Puzzled, she had shared the comment with her sisters. Rebecca and Naomi were horrified by the implication, as was Hannah, when they explained that he was apparently suggesting she purchase some condoms!

Knowing what they were thinking, that they were buying into Rose's lies, the continual stares of the men passing by drove Hannah to the bench. Nestled in the corner of it, feeling shrouded by the lengthening evening shadows, she thought about home...or more specifically, Billy.

It was becoming harder and harder to remember his face. Oh, she could still hear his voice, feel the touch of his hands, even taste his heart-melting kisses, but the mischievous blue eyes and dashing smile were fading from her memory...but sadly, not her heart.

Feeling a little wistful, Hannah looked up with relief when she heard her sisters. Naomi was rolling a wheelbarrow down the side of the street, loaded with several large sheaves of hay, four colossal pumpkins and at least half a dozen ears of red and black Indian corn. Her sister weaved and dipped drunkenly with the heavy load as she tried frantically, laughably, to keep from spilling the whole thing.

Rebecca was no help as her arms were full of two smaller pumpkins and more corn. Any attempt at trying to stabilize the wheelbarrow resulted in her frantically juggling her own load.

The two women were laughing and squealing, hysterical over the mock melodrama of the teetering cargo. Hannah couldn't remember how long it had been since they'd all shared some good, rich, side-splitting humor; even passers-by on the street grinned at the comical picture of the two girls trying to control the precarious cargo. The comedy of the situation was infectious and Hannah's own heart took flight.

Not about to be left out, she hurried down the steps to meet her sisters. "Those pumpkins," she marveled. "They're so bright, they look like they're on fire."

"Here, quick," Rebecca extended her load to Hannah.

"Take these and I'll help Naomi."

Rebecca tried to pass her freight off, but Hannah's rotund abdomen got in the way. The pumpkins and corn cascaded to the ground in a blur of fall colors as the two futilely scrambled to catch them. Naomi dropped the wheelbarrow and the sisters collapsed into laughing hysterics. They were off to the side of the traffic but probably wouldn't have cared if they had been in the middle of the road. Hannah held her stomach against the pain that racked her sides and purely hee-hawed till tears streamed down her cheeks. Maybe it wasn't all *that* funny, but it felt so good to let go.

Seconds later a shadow fell across them. The laughter fizzled out grudgingly as the girls realized a man on horseback had ridden up to them and sat quietly, observing their shenanigans. Shielding their eyes against the setting sun, they struggled to douse their giggles. Hannah took in the tall figure of a clean-shaven man, forty or so, dressed in a tan suit and light jacket with a derby atop his head.

With exacting aim, he spit tobacco juice squarely at her feet. "You Hannah Frink?"

His rude behavior and solemn voice sobered them like a lightning bolt. Naomi straightened up, her squared shoulders issuing a defiant warning. "Who she is is none of your business."

The man smiled but Hannah saw only darkness in his eyes. "'Fraid you're wrong."

Dismissing them, he quickly surveyed the town, spotted what he was looking for and trotted off in the direction of the Iron Horse. Speechless, the sisters watched horse and rider disappear into the flow of traffic.

~~~

# Eighteen

Trying to keep her eye on the stranger as he melted into the sea of horses and wagons, Naomi spoke to her sisters over her shoulder. "Rebecca, you and Hannah get these things on to the front porch. I'm going to see what I can find out about him."

She did not wait for a reply. Keeping low and moving quickly, Naomi darted down the street, ignoring the men who tipped their hats in mock politeness. She dared anybody to stop her now as she focused on finding out who this man was.

He pulled up in front of the marshal's office, dismounted, and flung his reins over the hitching post as he marched inside. Naomi hid behind a post and debated her next move. Before she could form a plan, he and Marshal Hayes emerged together and crossed the street to the Iron Horse. Naomi knew there was no way she could eavesdrop on the conversation from the street. She could either wait and address the man when he left the Iron Horse or she could barge in and demand an explanation.

Tapping her foot in agitation, Naomi debated the situation for several minutes. Would it be a complete scandal if she waltzed in there right now? Would the Flowers try to pick a fight with her? Would her entrance into the saloon be telegraphed all over the valley, giving credence to the rumor that their hotel was merely a brothel? She looked around at the passers-by and weighed the curious stares aimed at her as she clung, hiding, to the pole. At the moment, did she care what these people thought?

Naomi stomped down the boardwalk and barged through the saloon's swinging doors. Slowly her eyes adjusted to the deep shadows caused by the smoke, setting sun and low lights. Realizing she was announcing her presence with a trumpet by standing silhouetted in the door, she moved deeper into the saloon.

Through the smoky haze, she could see the Iron Horse was about half-full and the man she wanted was at the bar. As she took a step to move into the crowd, Mr. McIntyre came from nowhere, hooked her waist and swung her around like they were square dancing. Before Naomi realized what was happening, she was back out on the boardwalk with Mr. McIntyre's arm around her.

Angrily shoving him off her, she stepped back and attempted to stare him down. "What do you think you're doing? There's a man in there I need to see."

"I don't care if Jesus Christ himself is in there, Mrs. Miller," his eyes blazed with startling ferocity, "The last place you need to be seen is my saloon. Blast you, woman, use your head."

Naomi blinked, quite taken aback by Mr. McIntyre's ire. "That man," she pointed at the saloon, "he was asking about Hannah. I have to find out who he is."

"My bartender says he is a Pinkerton from San Francisco. Pender Beckwith. He's seen him many times."

Naomi was stunned, but only for a second. She quickly surmised there was only one person who would have sent a Pinkerton to find Hannah. Mr. McIntyre encircled Naomi again, pulling her away from the front door and down the walk several feet. Strangely discomfited by his nearness, she quickly stepped away. It bothered her greatly that each time he put an arm around her it became a little less detestable.

"Now, I have to ask, Mrs. Miller, what is a Pinkerton doing in Defiance looking for Hannah, of all people?"

"Frank Page," she muttered in disgust, taking a seat on a nearby bench. "That no-good, greedy tyrant . . . " She trailed off, certain her face betrayed her anger.

After a moment, Mr. McIntyre joined her. "Does this have anything to do with the father of Hannah's baby?"

"The grandfather," she spat. "He owns everything in Cary. He runs everything in Cary." She cut Mr. McIntyre a side-ways glance. "Much like you. He, however, has big plans, specifically for his son. Oh, yes, indeed, Billy's going to be a North Carolina senator in a few years, as soon as he's done with college. Then after that, Frank plans to run him for president." She shook her head in disgust. "His ambition knows no bounds. He made it clear that Hannah's blood wasn't blue enough for her to be the wife of a senator or a president. He whisked Billy out of town and wouldn't allow him to return until the situation was resolved."

"And by resolved I assume you mean he ran you and your family out?"

"Not exactly," Naomi huffed indignantly. "He bought our farms and John, Rebecca and I agreed not to contact Billy. We refused to make that same promise for Hannah. She decided on her own to leave but didn't explicitly promise anything. I guess Frank figures he needs to keep up with her whereabouts."

Mr. McIntyre nodded. "Yes, I can see where it would be embarrassing for Hannah to show up in a few years declaring that the junior senator from North Carolina is the father of her child. The scandal would ruin the boy's career."

"He doesn't have enough sense to know that Hannah would never do that." Naomi leaned forward and rested her head in her hands. "Now I suppose we'll have to put up with detectives checking on us every so often."

"If I was Frank, I would want regular reports."

*You would*, Naomi thought. "Great minds think alike," she confirmed, her voice rich with sarcasm.

Mr. McIntyre harumphed and rose to his feet. "This is probably the first of semi-annual reports the Pinkertons will send back. Neither Ian, Wade nor I will tell this man anything, but the rest of the town will talk . . . freely. I can't stop that."

Naomi stood as well and looked at Mr. McIntyre. "If there's any chance that he's here on Billy's behalf, and I highly doubt that, I'd appreciate you letting us know. Otherwise, I don't care what he finds out." She shrugged, at a loss for a plan of action. "I don't know anything to do other than just go on with our lives."

~~~

McIntyre poured himself a cup of coffee at his bar and took a seat at one of his tables near the window. If the Pinkerton man followed his same routine, he would be down shortly and McIntyre planned to ask what information he would be sending back to Page. Beckwith had questioned dozens of people over the last two days. Certainly, he had come to some conclusions by now.

McIntyre told himself he was only curious because everything that happened in Defiance was his business. He denied there was any noble motive involved regarding Her Highness. This was just good business.

He took a sip and looked up when he heard a door shut. Beckwith started down the steps, hesitated when he saw McIntyre, then finished his decent.

"Help yourself to some coffee, Mr. Beckwith, and if you have a moment, I would like to talk business."

Beckwith was a stern, no nonsense man with a chiseled, bony face that matched his charming disposition. Deepening his perpetual frown, he strode toward the coffee pot sitting at the end of the bar. "Have you decided, McIntyre, to fill me in on those belles down the street? Or should I write my report based on what the townsfolk speculate about them?"

McIntyre found the question annoying. He could well imagine what the established citizenry of Defiance was telling Beckwith. A town full of bored men was just as gossipy as a church full of old biddies. In his opinion, the sisters' reputations had suffered enough and though he could clear things up, it bothered him to have to do so. It bothered him because he was fighting a *compulsion* to defend Naomi—and her sisters—from the scandalous report.

Perhaps there was a less intrusive way to fix things. "Do you ever freelance, Mr. Beckwith?"

Beckwith's eyes widened for an instant as he joined McIntyre. "I have been known to pick up work on the side, but only occasionally."

"I would like someone located. If you were to bring me this information in, say, a month, you would be back in Defiance to see the sisters' hotel up and running. You might even be here for the birth of Hannah's child. I'm sure that's information your client would like to have."

Beckwith sipped his coffee and eyed McIntyre skeptically. "Sounds like you want me out of the way."

"What I want is the whereabouts of Frank Page's son Billy. A thousand dollars now and a thousand dollars when you put his address in my hand." Sure of how this man's ego worked, McIntyre added, "If you can find him."

"Oh, I can find him. However, the client was expecting a report soon. I can't explain a delay of a month or more . . . and I assume you *do* want the report delayed?"

"Two thousand dollars upon delivery of the requested information should help you think of an excuse."

Beckwith tapped his knuckles on the table. It was a generous sum, McIntyre knew, and far above what Beckwith was getting paid working for the Pinkerton agency. Whether he would accept the side job wasn't really in doubt.

"All right," the man nodded. "I'll do it. I'll have to go back east myself, though. I also assume you don't want me using agency resources."

"You assume correctly . . . by the way, weren't you a lawman before you joined the Pinkertons?"

"Cleaned up some of the meanest cow towns in Kansas and Texas."

McIntyre nodded, speculating on future possibilities.

~~~

Fall didn't creep into the Rockies, Hannah decided, it *erupted* almost overnight. Aspens, green one day, blazed orange and yellow the next, splashing the surrounding mountains with pockets of fire. The air went from warm and flirting with humidity to drier and colder, all at once.

The change in seasons made her all too aware of her rapidly expanding middle. Though she had of course noted the rounding of her stomach, without mirrors for a daily view she wasn't able to gauge the true impact of her new profile—until she caught sight of her shadow one September morning in the backyard. The alien silhouette stopped her in her tracks.

*Is that me?* she wondered in awe. *With six more weeks to go, this baby is going to be huge. I'll be as big as Sampson by the time he's born!*

Hannah pulled her skirt in beneath her stomach to accentuate the shape. She turned this way and that, stretched and leaned back. Without warning, a stabbing pain struck deep at her midsection and she doubled over with a loud, "Oooow!"

As if by magic, Rebecca was at her side, leading Hannah over to the stoop. "Here, sit down." Gingerly, she helped Hannah settle down on the back steps. "What happened? Are you all right? Has this happened before?"

Hannah laughed at her sister's concern. "It's fine. The baby just kicked me. Hard."

Rebecca nodded acceptance of this answer and dropped down beside her. The two sat in silence for a time, studying the distant peaks and considering things. Finally, Rebecca asked Hannah, "Are you scared?"

On the surface, it was a ridiculous question, but Hannah somberly shook her head. "Only a little. Every time the baby moves, unless he kicks the daylights out of me, I think that he's such a miracle. I feel so humbled that God would let something so good and beautiful come out of such a stupid mistake." She hugged her perfectly round potbelly, anxious to meet her child, and let her mind wander home to Cary. "I wonder where Billy is. I wonder if he misses me. I wonder if he'll ever meet his baby." She looked back at Rebecca and let the regret seep into her voice. "I'm beginning to forget his face, yet, I feel like I still love him. How is that possible?"

A rhetorical question, she didn't really expect an answer. She loved Billy, probably always would, but that was water under the bridge now. Instead, squaring her shoulders, Hannah moved her focus beyond herself and tried to think of the bigger picture. "I know without a doubt that everything has happened for a reason." She smiled at Rebecca, surprised at the unexpected mix of peace and trust

163

the thought gave her. "I've seen what God can do with me if I let him. I'm willing to accept his plans for me." She glanced down. "For us."

Rebecca laced her fingers and twirled her thumbs, as if mulling over Hannah's comments. "I don't think Naomi is quite there yet."

"No, she's still wrestling with God. She hasn't accepted that all of this is by design. And she still goes down to the stream every night when she thinks we're asleep. But I do think something is changing in her heart. She's a little less sullen."

"I thought I saw some changes, too, but after that episode with Hank, I don't know. She seems so..." Rebecca shook her head. "*Disappointed* in herself. The fact that she pulled the trigger on that gun haunts her. I think she thinks God won't use her if she's too . . . "

"Hot-headed? Willful?" Naomi interrupted from behind them and the two girls jumped. "Or perhaps brash and immature are the words you're looking for?"

Rebecca flinched. "I'm sorry. We shouldn't talk about you as if we're dissecting a bug."

"No, it's all right." Naomi waved away her sister's guilt and took a seat between them. She had her Bible and stared at it for a moment, then set it down behind her. "Ever since John died, I've had some pretty heated conversations with God."

Hannah pitied her sister. Naomi was so strong and so used to fighting everyone's battles. To have to give up, step back and hand God the reins...well, she couldn't imagine how hard that must be for her. Hannah had discovered, though, that was the only way to live. Letting God take over had removed so many burdens from her heart. Now, if Naomi could just do the same...

"I had the wrong person on the throne," Naomi almost whispered. "I loved John more than God." She stared at her hands in her lap, laced as if she was praying, and her chin quivered. "Accepting that scared me, but it freed me, too. Freed me to *start over* searching for the only relationship that really matters. Trying to let go of John and accept life here has been the hardest thing God's ever asked of me—"

Her voice broke as she dropped her head into her hands. When she spoke again, through her fingers, Hannah could hear the tears and the frustration. "This place is horrible. The people are cruel and selfish. But I'm trying, I'm trying so hard to care about them and…just accept things."

Hannah gently laid her hand on Naomi's back. "Maybe you just have to go one person at a time. Starting with Emilio…"

Rebecca pulled her long, black braid around and stroked her jaw thoughtfully with the end of it. "Considering the way you've been tested, Naomi, I think you've done well." Her voice was soft and re-assuring. "You didn't let John's death break you and you've tried to turn the other cheek. Tried harder than I've ever seen you."

"Never mind the fact that I nearly shot a man?"

"Well, you're not exactly known for being a pacifist, little sister. You are protective. He's all right now and I would bet he'll never bother us again." Rebecca dropped her hand on Naomi's back too and tried to smile. "Like Hannah said, maybe for you the best way to deal with Defiance is one person at a time . . . "

Movement down by the stream stole Hannah's attention. She half-heard Rebecca's voice trail off as she and her sisters caught sight of someone ambling slowly along the water. Daisy—no, it was Mollie now—picked her way thoughtfully along the bank, head down, her shawl pulled tightly around her.

"It's Mollie. I'll go invite her up." Hannah worked to get to her feet and made it with a shove from Naomi. She waddled down to the water, hailed her friend, and the two drew near. "It's good to see you, Mollie." And Hannah truly was glad. "Do you have time to come eat some lunch with us? We were going to do a quick Bible study outside then make sandwiches for the men and us." Hannah could see a deep loneliness in Daisy's eyes. "Please?"

Daisy appraised Hannah's dress, the blue gingham

jumper. "I see the clothes are fitting?"

Hannah nodded but kept what she hoped were puppy-dog eyes trained on her friend. Buckling, Daisy nodded. Hannah hooked her arm through Daisy's and walked her friend up to her sisters.

"Hello, Mollie," Rebecca greeted.

Naomi nodded at the girl. "Nice to see you again."

Daisy dipped her chin in return and smiled self-consciously at them.

Hannah squeezed her friend's arm with warm invitation. "I told Mollie we were going to do a quick study then go inside and get lunch ready for everyone. She's agreed to stay and help."

"But I want to stay in the kitchen," Daisy told them quickly. "I don't want any of the men to see me."

"Well, for our study why don't we go sit by the fire pit?" Naomi suggested as she stood up. "There are more seats."

The group moved and as they settled down on the makeshift log seats, Hannah prayed for a Scripture that might speak to Daisy. Instead, questions came to mind.

"Mollie, how long did you say you've worked for Mr. McIntyre?"

"A year and a half. Originally I thought I would stay for a year, long enough to save up stagecoach money to go home to Kansas."

The answer seemed to beg for follow-up so Hannah didn't feel too intrusive with another. "If you don't mind me asking, then why are you still there?"

Daisy sucked in an almost imperceptible breath as she stared at the cold, blackened remnants of a fire. "After a while this life," the light died in her eyes, "it makes you feel so dirty and worthless. Your spirit dies. I couldn't go home now and face my mother." She looked up then. "I just couldn't. She'd never understand how I can do what I do." Daisy shook her head. "She'd never forgive me."

At first, Hannah was taken aback by Daisy's honesty, but obviously the girl felt comfortable enough to open up. Perhaps it was because Hannah had been so forthright about her baby. Maybe here in this circle, she knew she wasn't judged.

"I felt the same way at first," Hannah said softly, reliving the memory of bitterly scornful comments from her closest *friends*. "After I, you know, was *with* Billy, I carried that sin around like a load of bricks. I felt so dirty. I couldn't tell anybody. And I couldn't talk to God about it because I just knew he hated me. I was so isolated from everyone that mattered to me."

Daisy leaned forward, listening intently.

"Then when I found out about the baby," Hannah rolled her eyes, remembering that sick feeling of fear and shame. "I knew everything I'd done was going to come out. I was sure God had turned his back on me. I'd shamed him, I'd shamed my family. Then Billy left me."

She marveled over how the admission still hurt. "He just rode off without a backward glance." She looked at Daisy, trying to communicate all her fear and shame. "I can't tell you how miserable I was, Mollie. How much of a failure I thought I was."

Daisy's face was rapt with attention. "You seem so content now. What happened? What did you do?"

Heart beating faster, Hannah took the Bible from Naomi and held it up. She prayed she could express to Daisy what it meant to her. "I started reading this as if my life depended on it. I think it did. Let me tell you one of the first things I saw." Hannah opened the Bible to John 3:16 and read it slowly, carefully, but with an emphasis on the last sentence. "'For God did not send His son into the world to condemn the world, but to *save* the world through Him.' I kept thinking, God didn't send his son to condemn me. So how can I find my way back to him? How can I make this mess right?"

Daisy picked up a stick and poked distractedly at the dead coals. "I still don't think I understand. What did you do?" She sounded like someone who wanted very specific directions and Hannah tried to oblige.

"I saw myself through God's eyes." Hannah caressed her Bible. "It says in here that he loves me, no matter what." She smiled up at Daisy. "He rejoiced over my repentance. I *matter* to him; he cares what happens to me." Tears unexpectedly slipped down Hannah's cheeks as she swallowed a knot in her throat. "There are so many places in this book, Mollie, that tell us how much God loves us and how willing He is to forgive us when we sin. I needed to hear that more than anything."

"*Senoras*," Emilio called from the stoop, jerking the girls out of this emotional moment. "Another freight wagon is here. I theenk these one has all the beds." That meant they had to leave. Slowly, Rebecca and Naomi rose to their feet, as if they regretted leaving this circle. Hannah sat wiping her eyes with her apron.

Naomi motioned for her and Daisy to stay. "You two take your time." She glanced over at Rebecca. "We'll take care of the wagon."

Feeling the moment was gone, but that seeds had been planted, Hannah sniffled and watched her sisters climb the back steps. "I'm sorry. I didn't mean to be such a cry baby. Do you mind helping with lunch? I can use the extra hands..." Hannah fell silent. Daisy was staring at the ground, lost in thought and Hannah prayed she was seriously considering everything she had just told her.

The girl blinked. "I'm sorry, you asked me—oh, about lunch. Yes, certainly, I'll help."

Hannah draped an arm around Daisy's shoulders and slowly the two stood. "I'm glad you came by today, Mollie. Truly I am."

~~~

# Nineteen

McIntyre looked up at his partially open office door in time to see Wade about to knock. Waving the marshal in, he dropped the pencil he'd been checking inventory with and settled back in his chair.

"I've got some news about Rose." Wade removed his hat and sat stiffly in the seat across from his employer.

McIntyre wasn't particularly interested in the news as long as she was still in Defiance but out of his hair. Still, to Wade's credit, it was his job to report.

"Nothin' spectacular. Lil's whipped her twice and cut her once. Rose is still tryin' to claw everybody's eyes out, but Lil thinks she'll break soon and settle down . . . or disappear."

McIntyre clasped his hands over his middle and considered the outcome of this plan. A broken, quiet Rose was ideal. A missing Rose made him vaguely uncomfortable. He'd never known a woman as spiteful as she was and he didn't take that for granted. "I prefer Rose right here where we can keep tabs on her. Tell Lil that . . . and have a drink on the house."

Wade's eyes lit up and he jumped to his feet. "Thank you Mr. McIntyre. I believe I will." Stepping outside the office, he carefully put the door back into its half-open position and turned for the bar.

McIntyre stared out at the traffic and discovered he was more than a little glad that Rose was gone. But he felt strangely . . . bored? Or was he merely restless? He noticed two large freight wagons rumbling past and knew they were headed to the hotel. Against his better judgment, he grabbed his hat off the corner of his desk and followed after them.

The first delivery a few weeks ago had brought most of the items for the sisters' kitchen. He was anxious to see if this would finish it out so they could project an opening date for the restaurant. As he walked, he enjoyed the cool of the air and the few aspen leaves that blew across his path. Fall in Georgia had been his favorite time of year as a child. The heat would break to something tolerable and slaves would harvest the crops. His mother would decorate their home with pumpkins and Indian corn all around, creating an innocent, festive air.

Fall also had heralded the start of a new school year and the excitement of going off to the various private schools he had attended. An enterprising lad always, school had provided the opportunity to hone his entrepreneurial skills. He chuckled at the thought, remembering business ventures with everything from shoe polish to cigars. In college he had upped the ante to include whisky, gambling and, right before the war, women.

Now, years later, he was the self-appointed king of a booming mining town. Ian's urging to set up a real town government and duly deputized marshal were valid suggestions if Defiance was to go to the next step of metropolitan growth. In the last ten years, McIntyre had seen mining towns spring up overnight, develop an economy based on nothing but gold or silver and when the ore played out, the town had also *died* overnight.

He did not want that to happen to Defiance. It was his responsibility to move the town forward, not just manage an ever-increasing population. With proper planning, this could be a mining town with stable alternate economies based on lumber, farming and ranching.

Since the arrival of Naomi and her sisters, he had actually entertained the thought that brothels and liquor might not be the cornerstone of his future.

McIntyre considered that mental change of direction as he watched her and Rebecca take the bill of lading from a wagon driver. It was interesting to him how he had been pondering growth for Defiance anyway. Yet, in spite of himself, something about that scrappy little princess now made him want see his plans yield fruit sooner rather than later.

He despised admitting that.

Since she took every opportunity to look down her nose at him, he had begun feeling that his accomplishments in Defiance were meaningless. Why her opinion mattered, he couldn't say. He had tried, again, to avoid her since that afternoon she had tumbled into his arms. He liked the feel of her a little too much. The line between lust and something more dangerous was blurred when he was around her. Yet, here he was walking towards her again.

Worse, as he mulled over plans and dreams for Defiance, he found himself wanting to run them by her, to *share* them with her. He didn't just want her to faint with passion—though that would be nice—it wasn't enough. He wanted her to acknowledge that *he* had built this town and had noble plans for it.

McIntyre realized with a jolt that he wanted her to admire him.

She, however, regarded him as a predator and stayed wary around him. She never let her guard down, never said anything that could be construed as friendly; she was always cold and distant. Yet, if McIntyre knew one thing, he knew women. His instincts told him there was *something* between the two of them but she fought it like the plague . . . was she riddled with guilt over being attracted to someone else after so recently being widowed . . . or could she possibly honestly dislike him? He found that scenario highly unlikely, but Naomi Miller vexed him greatly, and he approached her and her sister with the intent to study her a bit more.

"Mrs. Castleberry, Mrs. Miller." He touched his hat in greeting. They both smiled at him pleasantly enough, but he noticed *her* smile faded faster and she went back to the bill of lading more quickly than Rebecca. "What treasures have arrived today?"

Rebecca waived the bill at the wagon. "Well, it seems as if we've got everything to finish off the kitchen, and some tables for the dining room. If we can get some chairs, which may be in the second wagon," she addressed Naomi for agreement, "and start getting groceries and staples stocked, I think we *can* open the restaurant by the end of this month."

"Have you given your establishment a name yet? There is a fine sign painter in town. You need to get your moniker up there."

"Yes," Naomi gushed unexpectedly. "We decided to call it *The Trinity Inn.*"

"That has a far more sophisticated ring to it than The Elbow Inn," he quipped and Naomi almost laughed. Rebecca's furrowed brow prompted McIntyre to explain. "I had originally thought to call it that because the hotel sits where the road bends to follow the river. It doesn't quite have the sophistication of The Trinity Inn."

"Oh," she nodded, but her brow didn't smooth out immediately. "Well, lunch should be coming right along. We'll get some men to unload all this then break. Would you like to join us?"

Before he could reply, Naomi took a quick step back from them. "I'm going to chop some wood since Emilio is helping with the carpentry work." She nodded a good-bye to McIntyre and squeezed Rebecca's arm. "I'll be out back if you need me."

McIntyre had to control the urge to offer one of his men for the task. Instead, he recognized another opportunity. He nodded good-bye to Naomi then turned back to Rebecca. "I would have thought the beds would be arriving by now, too," he puzzled.

"That's what Emilio thought these were. But tables are good too." As she spoke, he noticed the new feminine touches to the front of the hotel. Pots with bunches of Columbine planted in them and a few rocking chairs created an homey feel, but he was unexpectedly moved by the bundled sheaves of hay, pumpkins, and Indian corn set out as seasonal decorations.

"Where in the world did you get those?"

Rebecca followed his gaze and smiled. "We mentioned to Mr. Boot that we'd love to have some pumpkins and Indian corn. Three days later, *voila!*"

He shook off a surprising sense of melancholy and shoved his hands into his pockets. "It is . . . inviting."

McIntyre let himself in to the hotel and quickly surveyed the new entrance. The counter and shelves were gone. A false wall had been built separating the small hotel lobby from the dining area. A large open serving window and two swinging batwings replaced the door into the kitchen. A good cleaning to remove the stray lumber and sawdust, add some tables and chairs, and this restaurant was nearly ready for customers.

Pleased with the progress, he pushed through the bat wings into the kitchen and was astonished to see Daisy deftly assisting Hannah with lunch. He didn't mind her helping so much as her presence here would cast doubts on the ladies' reputations. Guilt by association, as it were. Ian had already dealt with a misunderstanding recently; if the workers spotted her here, it would only lead to others.

"Daisy." He spoke her name carefully, trying to sound as unruffled as possible. She glanced up from a tray of unbaked biscuits then practically leaped to attention. "I thought it was your day to clean the saloon."

"No, it's Jasmine's day."

"Well," he thought quickly, trying not to sound harsh, "I would also like you to do an inventory for me this afternoon. Could you manage that?"

Frowning, Hannah spoke up. "Does she have time to help me finish? We're trying to get lunch ready for twelve men, and Mr. Donoghue and you, if you're joining us."

Ian, who had been leaning over the new pump tightening a bolt, straightened and scowled at McIntyre. McIntyre took the hint. "Very well, be quick about it." The girls nodded and went back to their chores.

McIntyre nodded at his friend and slipped out of the kitchen, headed for the back door. But he didn't move fast enough. Ian caught him just as he reached for the doorknob.

"Why are ye makin' her leave?" he whispered angrily. "It would do the girl well to make decent friends. Are ye afraid of losin' her as an employee?"

"Afraid?" McIntyre couldn't believe his friend thought that. "After rescuing Rebecca, I'm surprised you have to ask about my reasons. If Daisy is seen hanging about here, then every man in Defiance will think he was right about these women. They'll think this hotel is nothing but a front for a high-priced social club."

Ian pointed his finger at McIntyre as if to argue, but slowly dropped his hand. Scowling, he turned and marched toward the front of the hotel.

~~~

Shortly after Ian left the kitchen, the other man working on the sink went to retrieve a tool from his wagon, freeing Daisy and Hannah to chat. Daisy couldn't wait to ask at least one question. She knew she didn't have much time before she had to head on back to the Iron Horse. She sat at the table sawing off thin slices of ham with distracted skill as questions danced in her mind. "Hannah, can a person sin so much that God will never forgive them?"

"No." Hannah sounded resolute as she peeled eggs on the opposite side of the table. "The Bible says that nothing can separate us from his love." She paused, as if trying to remember something. "For I am persuaded that neither death nor life, neither angels nor principalities, nor powers, nor things present nor things to come, nor height nor depth, nor any other creature shall be able to separate us from the love of God, which is in Christ Jesus our Lord. Romans 8:38 and 39."

Daisy liked that passage, but wasn't sure it addressed her question. She had a lot of sin under her belt. "But, Hannah, you can love someone without forgiving them."

"No, I don't think that's true." Hannah stopped what she was doing to look at Daisy. "Not if you really love them and they ask. Take me for example. If Billy Page walked through that door right now and told me he was sorry that he ran off and left me to go through this all alone, I would forgive him. How could I keep loving him, but hold the sin over his head? Because God loves us, he'll never stop offering forgiveness and since his word says nothing can separate us from his love, I guess that means he'll never stop offering forgiveness." Hannah laughed, obviously aware of the circular reasoning. "In other words, there is no escape clause for God. He loves us and wants to forgive us. Period. It's not complicated."

Daisy doubted that. Everything in life—her life—had been exceptionally complicated.

"For me," Hannah added sounding sad, "It's been much harder to forgive myself. My mistake was like a pebble dropped in a pond. The ripple effect has impacted everyone I love."

Daisy saw the pain in her friend's eyes, but didn't know how to help. The awkward moment instead prompted her to change the subject. "As soon as I finish slicing this, I'd better go." The thought formed a knot in her stomach.

"All right," Hannah bobbed her head. "But when you leave, take my Bible with you." She gestured toward the book sitting at the end of the table. "You've got questions, and your answers are in there. When you come back, we'll talk about them."

Daisy didn't have much time to read, but she sure was curious. She eyed the black, leather-covered book sitting over there waiting for her and nodded.

~~~

# Twenty

From the stoop, hands in his pockets, hat tilted back on his head, McIntyre watched the industrious Naomi. She split several pieces of wood each with one single, unnerving swing.

Musing over this little princess who seemed tougher than most men he knew, McIntyre sauntered down from the stoop. "Remind me not to rile you."

Naomi stopped the ax in mid-swing and scowled. "Too late . . . What do you want?"

"A kind word. A civil tone."

She held his gaze for only a moment, then sagged and let the ax rest on her arm. She shook her head and sighed. "I'm sorry. You are a true scoundrel, but just because I don't like you is no reason to be so rude."

"And I do so want to be friends."

Frowning deeply at his sarcasm, she went back to her work. She wasn't going to get off that easy, he thought, as he ambled towards her. "The importance of the work you're doing cannot be underestimated. If you don't stock up enough firewood for the winter, you'll be burning all this new furniture for warmth by January."

"That's why I'm out here." She carefully balanced a log on the chopping stump. "We're trying to keep someone on this chore sun up to sun down."

"Well, I've come to assist."

Her eyebrows shot up and she looked at his perfectly manicured hands. "With those?"

He approached her, stepping in too close because he knew it bothered her, and took the ax. "I can chop wood. If you recall, I was one of the first white men in this valley when the closest town was over four hundred miles away."

"I'm sure you can chop wood." Naomi backed away and crossed her arms. "But judging by those pretty hands, I'd say it's been a while."

With everything he had seen and done, how could she think him such a hapless greenhorn? Determined to split the log with one swipe of the ax, he took hold of the handle and hoped, almost prayed, for a perfect split. Naomi moved away another step and tapped her foot, her posture boldly challenging him to fail. Focusing, he raised the ax over his head and slammed it into the log. It split cleanly and fell to either side of the block. McIntyre breathed a mental sigh of relief.

Naomi pursed her lips then relaxed. "All right, I'll accept your help graciously and do the stacking." She knelt and started loading her left arm. "Just quit whenever your hands get sore."

McIntyre bristled at the comment. He wouldn't give her the satisfaction. He would work until his hands bled or *she* quit. Naomi started collecting and stacking the firewood lying about on the ground. They worked in silence for a while and eventually fell into a rhythm.

After fifteen minutes or so, McIntyre was wiping sweat from his brow and had draped his coat, vest, and hat over the corral fence. Ian popped out of the hotel, looked as if he started to ask something, but apparently lost his train of thought.

"Did you need something, Ian?" McIntyre was not pleased with his friend's bemused expression.

The Scotsman chuckled. "No, I think not."

Not long after, Hannah came out to announce lunch. Both McIntyre and Naomi were red-faced and sweaty and said they would be right there. However, when Naomi kept stacking, McIntyre kept chopping, despite the fact that, yes, his hands were beginning to form blisters.

Hannah reappeared moments later with two tall pewter mugs of cold water. "Straight from our kitchen pump," she announced, alluding to the new convenience with great pride.

McIntyre and Naomi exchanged tentative glances, but when she acquiesced and reached for the drink, he set the ax down and took the other.

Looking a little bemused herself, Hannah wiped her hands on her apron. "I'll bring you something to eat . . . so why don't you both sit down before you fall down?"

Naomi walked away and took a seat on a log near their fire pit. McIntyre followed directly. She gazed off at the mountains, to avoid him he knew, but something in her face changed, softened.

She took a long sip of water then rested the mug on her knee. "I don't care for Defiance *at all*, but I love these mountains. Long about midnight, the biggest moon I've ever seen sits right on top of that peak over there. It's amazing."

"Yes, I agree. I take a walk along the stream almost every night. The sky is beautiful here, but the full moon is breathtaking."

"A nightly walk?"

"You have time for such trivial pursuits as admiring God's handiwork?"

McIntyre clucked his tongue. "There you go again, talking down to your humble subjects with such arrogance. It is unbecoming, even for a princess."

A confused, arguably hurt looked passed quickly over Naomi's face. She didn't apologize but he could see she was a tad humbled. Good enough. "A walk helps me clear my mind."

She nodded as if that was an acceptable explanation. He took a swig of the cold water and let the crispness of it cool his throat.

"It gets hot here, but nothing like the South," he mused. "Do you miss Carolina?" She glanced over at him, this time with guarded suspicion in her eyes. He waved a hand at her. "I'm just trying to make friendly conversation."

Naomi drummed her fingers on the mug then shook her head ever so slightly. "No, the truth is, I don't miss it at all. You'd think I would." She bit her lip, looking puzzled over her lack of sentimentality. "The fact is I never felt particularly attached to the country, just my family. Land is land . . . except for here." She cast her eyes back out to the distant sentinels ringing the valley.

He drained his cup and rolled it restlessly between his hands, wincing at the blisters that had, indeed, formed. "Do you mind telling me about your husband?" She swung her gaze back to him, clearly startled by the inquiry. "I'm just curious what kind of man was able to live with a wolverine like you." He had hoped to lighten the mood with his sarcasm, but he could see that the question sent her racing down memory lane.

"How do you describe the person who completes you?" she asked softly. "He was everything I'm not."

Naomi lowered her gaze to the ground and McIntyre watched in amazement at the transformation that came over her. Everything about her softened.

"He was strong and kind, loving, funny, romantic."

The memory of love created what he could only describe as a glow about her. It fascinated and mystified him. *What must a man do to touch a woman's heart like that*, he wondered.

"He was so solid in his faith," she continued wistfully. "And everything was black-and-white to John. There were no shades of gray."

"It sounds to me as if you had more in common than you think." From his perspective, he would have described her using the same words, with, perhaps, the exception of romantic. He couldn't speak to that.

"No," she shook her head. "He was far more mature. He rarely flew off the handle . . . unlike me. He called me his little wild cat because of my temper and my mouth."

"Ah, well, I have seen those demonstrated. I'd say you're equally proficient with both."

The serene expression left her, replaced by one of deep regret. "I know, I know. Unlike my sisters, I haven't achieved that meek and quiet spirit yet."

"Surely you don't see that as a failure?"

"I realize that I'm too confrontational and too quick with my tongue. Not ideal attributes for a Christian woman."

"The West, and especially Defiance, is not an ideal setting." He straightened up to make his point. "If every

179

woman who came out here was as compassionate as Hannah or as kind as Rebecca, they wouldn't last five minutes. This land requires grit and perseverance and fierce independence. Frankly, what you see as your greatest weakness, I see as your greatest strength."

Naomi gaped at McIntyre as if he had just recited the entire Bible, chapter and verse.

"Don't misunderstand," he hurried on, wondering what in the world he had just said to bring about this reaction. "I still think you could learn a thing or two from charm school—" he flashed her his most rakish grin, "but the West needs women like you."

"No one's ever—" she started, but trailed off. Looking into her eyes, McIntyre would have sworn he saw—what, cordiality? Something about her bearing changed ... relaxed.

Hesitantly, and much to his surprise, she asked him a personal question. "How—how did you come by your limp? Is it a war wound?"

He wondered if that was her idea of an olive branch and patted his right thigh. "General Braxton Bragg made sure no one, Confederate or Yankee, left Chickamauga without something to remember the battle."

"Chickamauga?"

"In the mountains of Tennessee. The terrain was so rough and rocky, it was more like unbridled mayhem than a battlefield." He paused as the thunderous cracks of rifles and agonized screams came back to him with jarring clarity. "A small group of Yankees surprised my company by popping up out of a ravine."

He cocked his head as a memory flashed by him. "I took a bullet in the leg, and it was a young man from North Carolina who dragged me to safety."

That wasn't the truth. In fact, the opposite had happened, yet he could never find a comfortable way of saying he had saved another soldier's life. McIntyre was a lot of things, but a braggart wasn't one of them.

"He was shot for his trouble," he recalled. "A wonder it didn't kill him." That, at least, was true.

"My husband was at Chickamauga. He was injured as well."

"A lot of good men died during that battle. On both sides. Your husband and I were fortunate."

He had almost missed her simple observation, lost as he was in his own musings. Then her words sunk in and a worrisome possibility iced its way through his veins. "What regiment was your husband in?"

"The 26th." She paused then asked carefully, "Why?"

"If you'll excuse me, Mrs. Miller." McIntyre surged to his feet. "I really must be going." He kicked himself for sounding too rushed.

"But wait," Naomi pleaded, following close on his heels. "What is it? Did you know my husband? Did you meet him?"

He stopped, took a breath and regained his composure. Casually he handed her the mug and gathered his clothes and hat from the corral fence. "Of course not. I'm sorry I upset you. I merely remembered I have an appointment this afternoon. That's all." Shoving his hat on his head, he tried to smile reassuringly at her. "I do have other interests, if you recall. I apologize for the abruptness of my departure, but I really must go."

She touched his arm, halting his exit. "Why do I feel like you're hiding something from me? And please don't lie."

He relaxed his shoulders and tried to ignore those pleading green eyes. Feebly, he handed her a half-truth. "It's the battle. Chickamauga is something I've tried to forget."

She looked as if she was debating the truth of the answer. He didn't rush her and after a second or two, she pulled her hand away. Without saying anything further, McIntyre strode off toward the stream, taking the back way to the Iron Horse.

Once McIntyre rounded the bend in the trail and knew he was out of Naomi's sight, he picked up his pace significantly. Skirting aspens and out buildings, he practically jogged back to the Iron Horse. His mind burning with the impossibility, he cut through the back of the saloon, skimming the edge of the lunch crowd, and shot straight up the stairs to his room.

Once inside, McIntyre tossed his clothes on his bed and snatched open his closet door. After a few minutes of digging through boxes, suitcases and shoes, he emerged with his Confederate issue haversack. Taking no time to reminisce over the bullet hole in the worn, leather flap, he summarily dumped the bag's contents on his bed. Dirt, dust, and a small dead bug tumbled out along with a rusty razor, wooden comb, a bone-handled toothbrush and a stack of letters tied with a yellowed piece of cotton twine.

McIntyre saw the letters and froze. He slowly reached for them then withdrew his hand, clenching it into a fist. But the unimaginable possibility egged him on.

~~~

## Twenty-One

Reaching again for the stack of letters, McIntyre recalled waking up in a field hospital in September '63, on his nineteenth birthday. The nauseating smell of blood and sweat assaulted him, squeezed his guts. He and the other man lay side-by-side on cots in the makeshift infirmary. McIntyre raised his head and gulped. His right pant leg was glistening with blood. The gauze pad on his fellow soldier's neck was dark red, saturated with blood as well, and leaking in rivulets.

"I'm sorry that happened," McIntyre whispered as an almost-unbearable throbbing shot up and down his leg.

The boy shrugged weakly and touched the pad at his neck. His voice was weak and raspy. "Now I know why you wanted us to bring up the rear." He smiled at his joke and took in his surroundings. "You get me here?"

McIntyre let his head down and tried to block out the pain. "Barely." And that was the truth of it. He had taken a bullet trying to save this burly Confederate. It was a miracle they weren't both lying in a pile of bodies outside.

The boy swallowed. "Thanks."

The surgeon, a grizzled old man in a grotesquely blood-spattered white coat approached McIntyre and lifted the flap of his torn pant leg. "You can wait." He moved to the boy and carefully lifted the gauze away from his neck. Blood gushed over his fingers and his eyes widened slightly. "You first." The doctor hollered over his shoulder, "Get this man ready for surgery now."

A weary voice from somewhere at the doorway of the tent grunted. "We need at least ten minutes to clean up."

"You don't have five." The surgeon replaced the bandage and moved on to the next row of cots.

McIntyre hoped that meant his wound wasn't serious, but the boy he had risked his life to save was evidently still in peril. He thought it foolish to introduce himself under these circumstances but also unacceptable not to. "I'm Charles McIntyre."

The boy focused blank hazel eyes on him. He was a large, strapping lad, sturdy like an ox and as blonde as corn silk. The size of an oak, he had been nearly impossible to drag to the rear.

"I'm John Miller. You wouldn't happen to have a pencil and some paper on you?"

McIntyre raised himself up on his elbows and looked around his cot and down his body, trying to ignore the shredded, bloody pant leg and its painful drumbeat. "My haversack." Low and behold, it was still hanging from his body. Gingerly, every movement making his leg pound worse, he pulled the sack over his head and laid it on his lap. Taking a breath, he braced for the pain and pushed himself up to a sitting position.

Sweat popped out on his brow and his leg throbbed thunderously as he fished through the sack. He found the paper easily enough, three wrinkled sheets with torn edges, and eventually the stubby pencil with a dull point. Lying back down, he passed them over to John.

Propping himself up on his left elbow, John held the paper with that hand and wrote with his right. Blood poured even faster from under his glistening bandage as he composed. The boy scribbled with determination for a few minutes, then carefully folded the one-page note and addressed the outside. With shaking hands, he passed it, and the supplies, to McIntyre. All his strength poured into the letter, he lay back exhausted.

"If I don't come back in here, will you get that to her?" His voice held the hint of the grave and McIntyre shivered.

He glanced at the letter's addressee then shoved the items back into his sack. "Surely. But you'll be fine." He hoped he sounded convincing. "It'll take more than one Yankee ball to fell a tree like you."

John sniggered softly. "I reckon." With that, he closed his eyes and drifted off to sleep. Almost immediately two soldiers arrived and lifted him onto a stretcher. McIntyre watched them take the boy out of the tent. Curious, he retrieved the letter from his sack and again read the name. A sweetheart back in this town of Cary? McIntyre hoped he wouldn't have to mail it to her.

A day later, both men lay recovering from their wounds and the letter fell forgotten to the bottom of his sack. He never thought to ask John if he wanted it back; John never asked for its return. McIntyre wondered later if he even remembered writing it as he had lost a fair amount of blood.

The letter stayed for several months at the bottom of the sack until he tied it neatly into the stack of letters from his mother and a few female acquaintances. For no logical reason, he had never felt comfortable discarding it or reading it. He simply carried it then buried it with his other war souvenirs in the back of his closet. He hadn't bothered with any of the items in at least ten years.

Now, as he went through the letters one by one, he discovered that he didn't remember any of the females who had written him. His heart reacted slightly to seeing his mother's elegant handwriting, and then the letter from the soldier stared up at him. His breath caught in his throat and he sat down hard on the bed.

After all this time, the paper had yellowed, was brittle and wrinkled, and the pencil had faded some, but the name was inarguably legible. The letter was, indeed, addressed to Ms. Naomi Frink of Cary, North Carolina.

~~~

## Twenty-Two

Daisy woke, knowing it was close to noon. She lay in her bed, a gray melancholy washing over her . . . again. For so long she had been numb to the smell of cigar smoke, whiskey and sweat that permeated her sheets. The last few weeks, however, it greeted her every morning like a slap in the face.

Clawing her way out of bed to face another day was becoming harder and harder. She'd had moments lately in which the smell of unwashed men, their nasty hands on her body, their drunken groping had made her want to run screaming into the street...or just put a gun to her head and end it.

*Why can't I deal with it anymore,* she wondered, unable to discern why the feeling of hopelessness had crept back into her life. She preferred being numb. She supposed she could handle it like the other girls—most of them drank at least half a bottle of whiskey daily. Iris said it smoothed over the rough days.

Daisy rolled over and her eyes fell on the night stand beside the bed. The Bible Hannah had given her sat in the drawer...untouched. She hadn't been back to visit, mostly because of Mr. McIntyre, but also because she felt she should at least browse the book before returning it to her friend.

Wanting something other than whiskey to smooth over the rough, she slid open the drawer and reached inside.

~~~

"All right, a little to the left," Naomi called as Charles Cody and his brother Dalton, both on ladders, straightened then hammered the last nails into the new sign. "The Trinity Inn" hung high over the entrance of their new business, announcing itself in bright gold and red letters. Beneath that, but smaller, the sign read, "Serving the Bread of Life and

Offering Rest for the Weary." She felt an unexpected sense of pride that she and her sisters had been able to accomplish the task of opening their own business.

Pushing his black Stetson back on his head, Mr. McIntyre studied the sign as he approached the sisters and Ian gathered in the street. "Clever. Elaborate but still tasteful. Do you think you'll be ready for tomorrow?"

Naomi pulled her shawl closer and raised her chin with confidence. They'd had two full deliveries of supplies since she'd last seen him, amply stocking the restaurant's cupboard. "Yes, I think everything is in place for us to open and start serving supper."

"We hope to add lunch by November," Rebecca said cautiously. "We'll just see how things go."

Though traffic was slow, Ian kept a watchful eye on an approaching wagon as he shared his thoughts on the future. "A lot of the prospectors are leavin' before the snows come, but I'd bet most of the miners who stay will prefer spendin' their evenings eating with ye ladies than in their cold tents and one-room cabins."

Mr. McIntyre shoved his hands into his pockets and hunched his shoulders against the fall chill. "We're counting on it, and I don't think it will take much to get Martha and her Kitchen to close down for the winter."

Hannah scrunched her face in disgust. "I would be pleased if she'd just start selling better food."

Ian put his arms out and gently ushered the sisters a few steps forward, giving the wagon room to pass. The movement pushed Naomi closer to Mr. McIntyre, but she didn't back away. Ever since that day he had told her a strong spirit was a strength, not a weakness, Naomi had been doing quite a bit of thinking. For the first time in her life, someone interpreted her fiery temper not as a flaw to be corrected but as a mark of beauty. Even John had tried to soften her. Was it even remotely possible that she was the way God wanted her? Not perfect of course, but more in need of wisdom than temperance? She had never entertained the possibility.

The emotional wall that Naomi used to keep Mr.

McIntyre at a safe distance had admittedly crumbled a bit since that chat. In spite of everything she knew about him, she looked at him with different perspective now. Wondering if there was more to the man than met the eye, Naomi asked casually, "Mr. McIntyre, how much does the town change in the winter? Will many people leave?"

"Our men stay because we run the mine twenty-four hours a day, seven days a week, but most of the prospector's leave.

"Consequently, around the middle of October the stage and freight wagons start coming in just once a week, less frequently than that depending on the snow. When it's deep, supplies come in by mule, if they can make it. The town's pace slows considerably, but we're still here." She almost liked the sound of it, a slower tempo, less noise.

"I'm sure your restaurant will stay busy," he added, "though you would have trouble filling rooms in the winter. Next year will be different. Ian and I have plans to build industries in town that will not be seasonal. Your inn will eventually be busy year-round. Especially once we get the railroad."

"It will be interesting to see all that unfold," Rebecca mused. "So, we will see you gentlemen this evening?" Her eyes unmistakably lingered on Ian and Naomi had to turn away to hide a grin.

"Seven sharp," Ian replied. "We're eager to be yer first customers."

"Or victims," Hannah joked.

As the laughter and banter went back and forth, Naomi suddenly felt an unmistakable chill snake its way up her spine. She turned and gazed down the street, convinced she would spot someone watching them, but was met with the normal, busy jostling of Defiance at midday. Disturbed, she continued to study the traffic, the sidewalks, the windows on the second floors. No one seemed to be paying them any attention

*Strange*, she thought. *I could have sworn—*

"Is anything wrong?" Mr. McIntyre disengaged from

the conversation and followed her stare down the street.

"No," she murmured, knowing the denial sounded weak, but then she spotted Rose through the traffic. She was standing in front of the Empire Bakery, holding a package in her arms and wearing a glare that could melt iron. Naomi noted that besides the malice in her eyes, Rose's face was leaner, more gaunt. She didn't look well but she did look furious. "It's Rose."

Mr. McIntyre stepped closer to Naomi and scanned the street for his former employee. Spying her, his body stiffened and anger lined his face. Clearly, he was none too happy to see the woman.

"I caught her watching us the other day, too," Naomi confessed.

In the next second, a wagon blocked their view and when it passed, she was gone. Naomi rubbed her arms and wondered if it was Rose's expression or Mr. McIntyre's that gave her the shivers.

~~~

As Ian and McIntyre arrived for their inaugural dinner, Naomi was lighting the last candle on the table. McIntyre nearly stumbled. All that golden hair, loose and cascading like a shimmering, magical waterfall, begged for his touch. She gazed up at him then with big, shining eyes as green as pure emeralds and he had to force himself to breathe. When she took in his appearance and smiled, without a hint of malice, he nearly dropped his hat.

*What the devil is the matter with me*, he scolded himself.

Of course, her reaction was exactly what he'd hoped for, deny it all he wanted. He and Ian had gone to great pains to impress. Freshly bathed and smelling of lilac water, they'd had their clothes pressed, shirts starched, and boots shined.

Did Naomi notice the way his still-wet black hair curled lazily over his white collar or the way his perfectly trimmed beard traced his jaw and circled his upper lip? --He'd certainly tried hard enough.

"My, my, gentleman. I am dutifully impressed. You both are very handsome." The statement was innocent enough, but McIntyre couldn't help feeling that she had somehow made a confession. He raised an eyebrow at her comment and Naomi snatched her gaze away.

"We dressed for the importance of the occasion," Ian joked, motioning McIntyre to the table. "This isna just any other night."

McIntyre agreed, dropping his hat on a nearby table. "It is an auspicious occasion."

Both men took an instant to survey the room. Red checked table cloths covered each table, along with simple centerpieces of pine branches and holly berries. In the center, a white candle glowed invitingly. Though there were lamps on the walls and one large light hanging over the center of the room, they were all turned low. Several candles burned on the hearth, as well. The setting was simple but elegant in its own rustic way.

McIntyre pulled his chair out. "You have all done a wonderful job, but it is a little too refined for Defiance."

Naomi shrugged. "I know, but tomorrow night the lights will be turned up all the way and we'll be filled to rafters with less-than-elegant customers."

Rebecca pushed her way through the batwings and nodded at their guests. "Good evening, gentlemen. Naomi, we're ready if you're ready."

"I am."

Hannah passed the first tray out with a pitcher of tea and glasses. As Rebecca and Naomi served, Ian noticed their clothes. "Will these be yer uniforms then?"

The girls stepped back from the table to model their outfits. They had sewn simple black skirts matched with white shirts, covered with white aprons. As Hannah brought the roast chicken from the kitchen, she slowly twirled in a loose black dress covered with a white pinafore.

McIntyre was more interested in the way the candlelight turned Naomi's hair the color of spun gold. It looked so silky, so touchable—catching himself staring, he blinked and made a conscious effort to keep his eyes on Ian, Rebecca, anyone but Naomi. He couldn't help himself, though, the way she moved, the grace and confidence with which she poured tea, the way the tailored shirt clung to alluring curves.

But it wasn't just the way she looked, it was the way she looked back at him: wide-eyed and honest, without malice. For the first time since meeting Naomi, McIntyre could sense a *thawing*. Encouraged, he forced away troublesome thoughts of that letter and what he should do about it. That step could always wait.

The food flowed quickly and smoothly and reached the table hot. Before long, they were all seated and enjoying a mouth-watering meal. The conversation was as appealing as the food, and McIntyre savored the way talk of the future came naturally and with optimism, even from Naomi. He found it infectious.

Now that they had a good cook stove, the sisters told their guests that vegetable canning was underway. The backyard had been transformed into a small farm, with chicken coops and a cow and, next spring, a garden. The cow had come when Naomi had offered Sampson as trade, one of the most difficult things she had done on this journey, McIntyre surmised. But a milk cow was worth two Sampsons.

And so they were fairly settled in their new home and ready to open their doors to the public . . . pending approval of the meal by himself and Ian. Based on the empty plates and the apple pie which had practically been inhaled, McIntyre was fairly certain the girls had passed muster.

Ian wiped his mouth and laid his napkin on an empty plate. "If the meals come out tha' wonderfully every night, I will be a regular customer."

"I share your sentiments," McIntyre drawled, leaning back casually in his chair and crossing his legs. "I believe you ladies have found your true calling."

"*True calling?*" Naomi cocked her head to one side and gazed at McIntyre. A half-smile played at her lips. "I have to admit I have enjoyed getting the restaurant up and running." She turned to her sisters. "I don't know if this is our true calling, but it is our business."

"And 'tis something to be proud of," Ian weighed in, grinning. "I canna think of any other women I know who could have accomplished such a task. Especially in this town."

The night waned and Naomi thought Hannah had to be done-in. When her little sister yawned, Rebecca quickly offered to do the clean-up. Naomi started to protest, but when Ian proposed his assistance, she took the hint.

"Well," Mr. McIntyre pushed back from the table and stood. "I have a few things to check on. Ladies, I can't remember when I've had a more agreeable meal." His eyes seemed to linger on Naomi, but she passed it off as her imagination. He nodded at Ian. "I'll see you in the morning?"

"Aye. The plans are finished; I'll have them with me."

Mr. McIntyre nodded a farewell, but his eyes did not fall again on Naomi.

"I guess we'll hit the hay, too," Naomi dropped a not-so-subtle hand on Hannah's shoulder. "Let's leave the grown-ups to talk." Rising, she pulled the chair out for her little sister and smiled at Ian. "Thank you for coming tonight."

Hannah giggled as she rose to her feet. "Yes, we hope you enjoyed it Now don't stay up too late, children."

Embarrassed, Rebecca threw a napkin at her. "Get yourself to bed, little sister."

Turning to leave, Naomi saw Mr. McIntyre's hat. "Oh, he forgot this." Without hesitating, she snatched it up and raced outside.

Bursting out on to the porch, she collided with him as he was lighting a cheroot, knocking it and a lit match to the ground. To keep her from tripping over him, he grabbed her shoulders. Mischief instantly flamed in his eyes. But the cocky grin faded to something more serious as he held her, then pulled her closer.

Inexplicably panicked by his boldness instead of angered by it, Naomi wiggled free of his grasp. "Oh," was all she could muster in her shock, raising his hat between them like a shield. "You forgot this." She shoved it at him, holding her arm arrow-straight. The distance between them didn't slow her racing heart or spinning mind.

"So I did." In the one weak lamp burning on the porch, Naomi thought disappointment flitted across his face, but wasn't sure. Mr. McIntyre quickly placed the Stetson on his head and retrieved his cheroot from the ground. "Good night then." Abruptly, he turned to go.

She wanted him to leave and, yet, strangely, she didn't. The *didn't* won. "I saw the ax you used." Mr. McIntyre stopped but didn't turn. "The day you helped me chop wood. I saw the ax. The handle was smeared with blood."

He had chopped wood until his hands bled, while his hands bled, in fact. She didn't know why he'd done it, but his perseverance had impressed her.

Softly, over his shoulder, he told her, "Let the ax be our secret, Princess."

~~~

## Twenty-Three

As McIntyre trekked back to the saloon, he mulled over how Naomi affected him. She'd practically fallen into his arms coming out the door and the urge to kiss her–well, it had taken an amount of self-control he hadn't exercised in years not to. But this was more than a physical attraction and that was what rattled him. At dinner, she had laughed at one of his jokes and the sound of her gaiety had washed through his veins like a fine cabernet.

He muttered a curse at the memory. All the reasons why she would never be with a man like him stung him and he cautioned himself to remember them. They weren't merely two people from different sides of the moral tracks... they were two people from different sides of the universe. Namely, Heaven and Hell–

Wade bounded up on the boardwalk from the shadows and fell into step beside his boss. The interruption was a welcome distraction and McIntyre waited for Wade's news. However, when the marshal didn't speak immediately, McIntyre grudgingly nudged him.

"What is it, Wade?"

"Doc got called over to the Broken Spoke . . . "

"And . . . " McIntyre prompted irritably.

"Lil walked in on Rose and caught her doing some of her Mayan witchcraft mess. There was a fight..." He blew a long breath into the air, clearly disturbed by what he had to say next. "Rose practically clawed her eyes out, Mr. McIntyre." McIntyre stopped short, but didn't look at Wade. His muscles tensing like drying rawhide, he simply waited for the rest. "Then she hit her with somethin', maybe a gun, but she knocked Lil clean unconscious." Glancing around to make sure no one was near, Wade added the last piece of information in a desperately hushed voice. "While Lil was out, Rose cut three crosses on her chest."

McIntyre pulled back. *Three crosses?*

"Whatcha reckon that means?" Wade wondered, his eyes round with fear.

*What did it mean?* McIntyre rubbed his neck, fighting the tension building there. What kind of a demented monster blinded someone with fingernails? Then carved crosses on the body? Was Rose sending him some kind of grisly message? "Where is Rose now?"

The marshal folded his arms and hunched his shoulders. "She's back in her tent. You want me to go arrest her?"

"Is Doc with Lil?"

"Yessir."

Inhaling on his cheroot, McIntyre glanced down the street in the direction of the inn. He wasn't sure how worried he should be. Were the crosses a message of some sort aimed at him or the sisters? Or were they merely Rose's twisted way of inflicting a little additional misery. He assumed the latter. "Leave Rose where she's at. If we arrest these gals every time they have a cat fight, we'll be running the brothels from our office."

The second the words were spoken, though, McIntyre found they'd left a bad taste in his mouth. His attitude was flippant and callous, even for him. Lil should have been able to take Rose, no contest. Now she'd been savagely attacked and it was his fault. He'd pawned his problem off on her. A move that could cost Lil her eyes.

Maybe he shouldn't keep underestimating Rose. "On second thought, lock her up." Wade shifted uncomfortably at the directive and McIntyre knew why. "You can take help, Wade. Take a dozen men if you're that afraid of her, but put her behind bars and let her sit for a few days...till I decide what to do with her."

~~~

As the sound of Hannah's and Naomi's footsteps and whispering voices faded, Ian turned his chair to Rebecca more squarely. Rubbing his beard, he studied her in the candlelight. Rebecca tried not to squirm, but his eyes drilled

195

into her. Before she could ask why the scrutiny, he cleared his throat.

"I've high hopes for yer restaurant. It'll be no time at all and ye'll be needin' to hire more help."

The suggestion brought Rebecca round to a question she'd meant to ask him a hundred times. An issue had come to the sisters' attention, but the time had not seemed right to address it. However, the days were passing so quickly now, there was no more time to wait.

"Ian, I've heard rumors of mid-wives in Tent Town, but is there a good doctor in Defiance? I haven't seen an office or heard anyone mention him…"

"Aye, there is a doctor, of sorts. A mine that employs over two hundred men must have one. His office is down near the mine entrance, just outside o' town."

"Why do you call him a doctor *of sorts?*"

"The truth is, when he's sober, he's a fine physician."

"Sober?" Rebecca couldn't hide her disappointment. "You mean he's a drunk?"

"Aye, like a lo' of the men in this town, they're here because they're not fit for decent society. Dr. Cook, I believe, has a checkered past. That dusna mean he canna deliver a baby, though."

Rebecca was very unhappy with this news. She wanted the best care possible for Hannah, especially if anything went wrong. "I assume he's our only choice."

Ian thought for a moment. "Well, on occasion I have heard that Mary Two-Horse, a Ute medicine woman, can be availed upon for such needs. I believe a few of the girls from the Iron Horse have required her assistance in, uh, well, ending a pregnancy."

Rebecca's stomach rolled. "Our choices are midwives with who-knows-what level of skill, a drunken doctor or a baby-killer."

Ian leaned over and took her hand to offer some comfort. "Hannah is young, strong, and healthy. There's no reason at all to assume the worst." Rebecca knew her eyes revealed her fear. "God dinna bring her all this way to just let the child die, either of them."

Considering what they had been through thus far, Rebecca wasn't so sure, but she appreciated his effort at comfort. In fact, for a moment, she let herself get lost in those steely gray-blue eyes that touched her soul. The powerful force that attraction can be pulled them closer. Rebecca's rational mind flew right out the window as she wondered if he might draw her even closer for a kiss. How long had it been since a man's lips had touched hers . . . ?

When he was close enough for her to feel his breath, he whispered, "Perhaps we'd best get to the dishes."

She blinked and pulled away. "Yes, yes, absolutely." Rebecca jumped up. Flummoxed, and more than a little embarrassed, she started clearing the table with jittery hands. Ian stood and assisted in a calm, measured manner as her heart galloped like a wild mustang's. Still, she didn't miss the slight smile playing around the corners of his mouth.

~~~

McIntyre waited until close to noon to go see Lil. At first he had thought he would make this call when she was back on her feet, but that timing didn't really sit right with him. The fact was he owed Lil something. What, he couldn't exactly say. How does one balance the scales for a pair of eyes? He knew "sorry" didn't cut it, but it was better than nothing.

He rapped once on Lil's door and let himself in to the Spartan, one-room cabin. Gustav Jorgensen, "Swede" as folks called him, was sitting beside Lil's bed, wiping her forehead with a towel. It surprised McIntyre to see this burly, grizzled miner tending the woman as gently as if she were made of China. Lil was propped up in bed and enormous bandages covered each eye. One was tinged with a dark red spot near the bottom. An honest-to-God shiver went through McIntyre when he thought of the hatred it would take to try to gouge out a person's eyes. They would heal, Doc said, but Lil's vision wouldn't return.

Gustav whispered something to Lil as McIntyre entered. She stirred, spat a curse then straightened up. "You owe me big time for this, McIntyre."

There wasn't the usual fire in the raspy voice and he felt humbled. Exchanging a careful glance with Gustav, he sat down at the end of Lil's bed. The Swede put the towel in the bowl next to the bed and patted her hand gently. "I step outside so you two can talk."

They waited for the door to shut then Lil chuckled. "Well, I guess if anybody's happy, it's Swede. He's been after me to marry him for ten years."

"He's a good man," McIntyre reassured her. He heard the awkwardness in his voice and loathed it.

"I always said I'd marry a good man when I was ready to settle down, and sleep with the devil in the meantime." She sighed here, accepting her fate. "Reckon it's time to settle down."

"I am sorry about all this, Lil. I've got Rose in jail. Tell me what happened and we'll press charges." It was the least he could do.

Lil stiffened and shook her head. "No, we won't. The Broken Spoke's hers. That's all you need to know."

McIntyre froze. "What?"

"She has my half. Rose is your partner now. It was a fair fight."

McIntyre was struck dumb. It took what felt like an eternity for the information to sink in. When it did, anger coursed through him like acid. Slowly, he rose to his feet. "What have you done, Lil?"

"You know as well as I do that when a madame loses a fight with one of her girls, she's not fit—*or able*—to run her house . . . that's just the way it works."

McIntyre swallowed a sinking feeling. Rose had scratched and clawed her way into being, God help him, his *partner* all because of some twisted jungle law among prostitutes?

"She's a power hungry she-devil, that one," Lil warned. "But maybe now, with a business to run, she'll be satisfied."

Staring into the bandages that covered Lil's eyes, McIntyre didn't think he would bet on it.

~~~

Opening day for the Trinity Inn's restaurant came with an explosion of small crises, wrong deliveries, shortages, overcooked food, and a packed house. Naomi had been prepared for such mishaps. What she wasn't prepared for was the unwashed, smelly, leering customers. She had foolishly thought that something about the restaurant's atmosphere would bring out their better character. She was wrong.

Table after table, she took their orders, tolerated their ogling and tried desperately to maintain a polite, professional demeanor...until Grady O'Banion sat down.

Naomi recognized him and the dirty bowler hat instantly as she approached his table. She braced herself for the comments and stares as two other men joined him. Taking a deep breath, she squared her shoulders and greeted the men. "Good evening, gentlemen. Our menu tonight is elk steak, fried potatoes, cornbr—"

"Tell me, darlin', do ye remember me?" O'Banion snatched his hat off his head and grinned menacingly. His glassy eyes were bloodshot and he reeked of whiskey. "I'll bet I was the first to welcome ye to Defiance."

"Actually, you were the fourth," Naomi told him, recalling the men playing keep-away with Hannah's bonnet. "Now, may I take your order?"

Her tone was icy and belatedly she remembered that was a provocation with the belligerent Irishman. His dander up, O'Banion turned more fully to Naomi and grinned wider. "Well, perhaps I can be yer first real customer tonight, eh, darlin'?"

O'Banion's hand snaked out and latched on to Naomi's bottom like a vice. Mortified and furious, she slapped him hard enough across the face to convince her she'd broken her hand. O'Banion jumped to his feet, flipping his chair over behind him.

Before he could lunge at her, Mr. McIntyre quickly inserted himself between the two. Eyes blazing, he pushed O'Banion back with a determined shove. The room fell silent as the customers gawked. "If you don't want to be barred from here permanently, Grady, take your friends and go."

The warning was delivered with a gravity Naomi could not recall ever having heard in a man's voice. Grady stared past Mr. McIntyre and burned her with his vicious glare. For the moment, her anger anchored her to the spot and she stared right back.

Mr. McIntyre raked the room of interested on-lookers with a hard gaze and explained, "Any ungentlemanly conduct will result in your worthless hides being tossed out onto the street. You got that?" He shoved Grady again for emphasis. "Am I clear?"

Ian and the marshal joined the group, the two of them towering over Grady. The lawman chucked a thumb over his shoulder toward the door. "Take your friends and go, Grady."

A tense moment passed as O'Banion kept Naomi in his sights. His anger actually frightened her, but she refused to show it. Perhaps understanding this was a battle he couldn't win, the man grudgingly dropped the challenge. "Aye, we'll be havin' our dinners elsewhere." O'Banion signaled for his friends to join him and the three left the dining room.

Naomi felt like her skin was on fire as the humiliation of that man's hands on her rear end seared its way into her soul. The filthy, despicable man had groped her in front of all these people. She felt so dirty, so completely debased. Desperate to run from the dining room, to escape the fascinated stares of the amused patrons, and—especially—the sympathy in Mr. McIntyre's eyes, she closed her eyes and tried to compose herself.

Rebecca hurried out from the kitchen and rested her hands on her sister's shoulders. "Naomi, I saw what happened. I think you should take a break. We can manage for a while without you."

"Aye, ye'll not have to," Ian offered quickly. "I can tie on an apron and serve meals to the likes of these buffoons."

Without waiting to debate the offer, Naomi shoved her slate at Ian and scrambled from the dining room before anyone could see her tears.

~~~

## Twenty-Four

Because it helped him think, McIntyre sat at a table bathed in morning sunlight and played a game of Solitaire. In the quiet, he pondered the women troubling him. After seeing O'Banion treat Naomi as if she was one of the Flowers, the urge to throttle the imbecile had nearly consumed him. Still aggravated by this chivalrous emotion, he flipped his cards with short, sharp movements. It would not done to play the over-zealous knight in shining armor...not at all. Her Highness would not have appreciated it, and the men in town would have seen it as a weakness. Rose would have seen it as weakness. In Defiance, any kind of vulnerability, real or perceived, could get a man killed.

Knowing there was no easy answer there, McIntyre turned to Rose. At least he had a plan for handling her. If he played his cards right maybe he could get her to focus on running the Broken Spoke and nothing else. She needed to forget about their past relationship; she needed to forget about the three women at the other end of town. Perhaps a few days in jail had humbled her to the point that she might be interested in new possibilities.

He heard the bat wings and looked up. Wade tipped his hat to his boss from the doorway. "She's on her way."

McIntyre nodded and set his cards down. Before he could lean back in his seat, Rose shoved past the marshal and sashayed into the Iron Horse wearing a confident grin and faded red silk dress. McIntyre noted immediately that she was more gaunt, hollow-eyed, and baleful. He motioned to the seat beside him. "Sit down."

Rose fairly slithered into the seat and grinned wider. "Are you happy to see me? Have you missed me?"

"Only the way one misses a toothache," he said, bored with her.

Every muscle in Rose's face hardened and her eyes glittered with a dangerous warning. Like scenery changing on a stage, the difference in her mood was stark and sudden.

"You shouldn't talk to me like that. I came to forgive you...and start over." Just as quickly, her mood changed again. Rose's eyebrow twitched, her chin quivered and tears choked her voice. She reached out and grabbed McIntyre's hand, clinging to him with an alarming desperation. "I love you. I've never stopped loving you and I'll do anything for you. I only want things to be the way they used to be...just tell me what you want." She trailed off and swallowed. A silence as heavy and cold as a spring snow settled between them.

McIntyre slowly withdrew his hand, not only stunned by her outburst, but actually revolted by it. The woman really was coming unhinged. "I'm giving you the Broken Spoke, Rose. Not as a reward and certainly not because I have any feelings for you. I'm giving it to you because I don't want anything more to do with you. Fight with the dogs in Tent Town but stay away from this side of Defiance." He leaned forward and lowered his voice. "And stay away from Naomi, Rebecca and Hannah. I don't know what you meant by what you did to Lil, but if there was a message there, then you need to know my response. Touch one hair on their pretty little heads and I'll bury you myself."

Rose's chest started to heave and her cheeks flushed. Her mouth set into a petulant, thin line and she stood up. Tapping her knuckles restlessly on the table, she shook her head. "I'm not afraid of you. I have never been afraid of you or any man. But I tell you this, Defiance will be mine . . . and I will rid it of those *gringas*."

"You're at the end of your leash, Rose. Don't do anything else foolish."

She merely gave him a crooked smile, spun on her heels and marched out of the Iron Horse. When the doors swung closed behind her, McIntyre ran a tense hand over his forehead and through his hair. The sense that he had just freed an injured she-bear wouldn't leave him. Wounded animals were dangerous . . . and unpredictable.

~~~

Naomi only half-listened to Ian read a passage of scripture as he finished up their little church service. She'd spent the last several days so distracted and this morning was no different. She couldn't stop trying to reconcile the differences in Mr. McIntyre. The night he had forgotten his hat and she'd taken it to him on the porch, the lecherous scoundrel had attempted to pull her into his arms. Yet, the night O'Banion had so disgraced her, she'd read compassion, even sympathy, in Mr. McIntyre's eyes. His actions made no sense to Naomi. Did the profiteering pirate have a heart, after all?

Ian's voice ceased and she realized the they all had their eyes pinned to the front door. It swung open and Mr. McIntyre entered. Naomi felt a strange emotion when their eyes met and upon examination of it realized...she was actually pleased to see him.

"I am sorry for the intrusion," he apologized awkwardly, twirling his hat in his hands, "but I was wondering if I might have a word with you, Mrs. Miller."

He sent Ian a knowing glance and the man nodded. Taking his cue to provide McIntyre and Naomi some privacy, Ian suggested that he, Rebecca and Emilio finish up in the kitchen.

Rebecca, apparently willing to go along, offered up an excuse to leave the room. "We need to watch that roast anyway. It should be ready in a few minutes. Mr. McIntyre, you're invited to join us if you care for pork roast."

"Thank you. It smells too wonderful to pass up."

The group filed out and he sat down opposite Naomi. She thought again of their encounter on the porch, how she had nearly wound up in his arms, and the panic that had followed. Her reaction still baffled her. She should have been furious with him, not frightened like a child. Just what exactly was she afraid of? Why did he cause her so many questions?

"Your first several days have gone well?" he asked, sounding a little unsure of himself.

"Yes. Rebecca and Hannah have turned out to be quite

good chefs and managers. I wonder every day what I'm good for."

"Now that we've rid your establishment of O'Banion, I hear you've become quite the cordial waitress."

Naomi laced her fingers in her lap and tried not to drop her gaze. Just the mention of the man's name made her nauseous. "I have to admit that I'm glad you decided to ban him. Thank you." She licked her lips and hurried past the awkwardness. "It's hard work, though—I mean the cooking. Especially on Hannah. She's tiring more easily now. We expect the baby to come sometime around October 23rd, give or take. We need to get her off her feet more." This was the first time she had broached the subject with Mr. McIntyre since that day the Pinkerton man had arrived. It felt good to be able to discuss it so openly.

"Have you had Dr. Cook come down and check on her?"

Naomi hiked her shoulder up and rotated it. The rumors of Dr. Cook's drinking made all the muscles in her neck tense. "Well, I wanted to ask you about him. Ian said he has a checkered past and he drinks to excess."

"*Ian?*" Mr. McIntyre blinked, but rushed past the question, leaving Naomi to wonder why the use of his friend's name seemed to disturb him. "Uh, yes on both counts, but he's a fine doctor. I'll have him come down, cold sober, and check on Hannah. When it's close to her time, I'll keep him sober."

"That will have to do, then," she huffed, resigned to the situation as it was. "We should have had him come sooner but we were hesitant about his credentials. Whatever you can do would of course be greatly appreciated. Like everything else, though, Hannah's health is in God's hands." She smiled, trying to lighten her mood. "So, what did you need to see me about?"

"I want you to be suspicious of anything or anyone that doesn't seem right."

Naomi didn't like the sound of that. "Why? What's the matter?"

"Perhaps you heard that Rose attacked Lil several days

ago. You may not know that she nearly clawed her eyes out and carved three crosses on her chest—"

Naomi gasped. The brutality of the attack stunned her.

Mr. McIntyre dipped his head. "I'm sorry to be so blunt. Rose is running the Broken Spoke now and staying out of trouble, but I can't let go of the three crosses." He paused and then added carefully, "Truthfully, I don't trust her yet and I think you should be watchful."

"I don't understand. Do you think what she did to Lil was some sort of threat to us?" Naomi immediately thought of her sisters and little Billy and feared for their safety. "Good Lord, what kind of a person does something like that?"

"Hell hath no fury like a woman scorned. Rose was different from the day you came into town. When I," he paused as if searching for the right words, "*Re-affirmed* the details of our working relationship, she didn't take it very well. I think it made her resentful…dangerous."

"Reaffirmed?" Naomi couldn't help but wonder what he *wasn't* telling her.

"Rose and I were," McIntyre tugged on his collar, "well, intimate for a number of months and it gave her certain ideas that she had a claim, so to speak, on some of my affairs. She was harboring under a gross misconception."

"Oooh," Naomi dragged out a long, slow nod. "That explains a lot of things; Rose was *jealous*, not just *territorial*, as you put it. She saw us as a threat."

Mr. McIntyre set his hat on the table in front of him. "I've seen a lot of whor—excuse me—prostitutes with nasty attitudes. They so often come from horrific backgrounds, as did Rose. The fact is I've always known she would be trouble, but I wasn't exactly thinking with my head . . . "

Naomi rested her elbows on the table and rubbed her arms, wishing that she didn't feel a sense of dread down to her very soul. "What do you suggest we do?" She was asking for his advice and prayed he wouldn't gloat.

He didn't. "Watch the customers carefully. Stay together, and I would urge you to have those late-night prayer sessions in the hotel instead of down by the stream."

Naomi's heart missed a beat. *Surely he hadn't seen her there?* "How did you know I go down there to pray?"

"I, well, you mentioned you take walks. I—I just assumed you prayed."

Naomi let out a breath, mostly satisfied with the explanation.

"I know you know how to use a shotgun," he continued, turning them back to the matter at hand. "Do you know how to handle a revolver? Do you even have one?"

"I have my husband's. I can handle it if I have to, I think."

"Keep it close."

"Does Ian know all this?"

"Yes, but I asked him not to say anything until I could talk to you. You need to decide what to tell your sisters. In the meantime, I have stepped up patrols of the town and have my men watching the inn and Rose."

"Thank you." All of his shenanigans aside, Naomi was grateful to Mr. McIntyre for not only sharing his concerns, but bringing them to her first. He nodded and the look in his eyes was lacking in its usual arrogance. He was worried, and now, so was she.

~~~

Rebecca watched from the doorway as Hannah stared at the calendar pinned to her bedroom wall. The blur of motion and work at the inn made the publication an inconsequential scrap of paper to everyone but her little sister. Hannah had drawn an X through each day as it ended, but October 23 was circled with a question mark drawn in the center. It was only a guess, give or take two weeks, the doctor had said. Another exhausting day of cooking behind her, Hannah carefully drew an X through October 15.

*One more down*, Rebecca thought. *How many more to go?*

Sizing up her little sister's weary appearance, she knew what she had to say was the right thing. Though they had been letting her sleep as late as she needed, it wasn't enough. "Naomi and I have been talking. You've got to get more rest. You can help us prep for dinner in the afternoons if you'd like, but we want you to take the evenings off."

Hannah rubbed her back and glanced down at her feet which had been swelling uncomfortably over the last few weeks. With enough energy left for some humor, she squared her shoulders and saluted. "Aye, aye captain."

Rebecca smiled but it faded quickly when her hand went to her pocket and she felt the note. One more thing for Hannah to worry over. But she had a right to know . . .

"Listen," Rebecca sighed, pulling the folded square of paper from her pocket. "There is something else." She held it out for her sister and Hannah started to reach for it. "It's Billy's address at Harvard." The information froze Hannah's hand in midair. "According to Ian, Mr. McIntyre went to great effort and expense to get this information. In fact, the Pinkerton man Beckwith delivered it personally." Hannah dropped her hand and turned away. Rebecca flinched and pressed the note to her chest. "Hannah, he is the father and that gives him some rights."

"Being a father is about more than bloodlines." Hannah's voice wasn't cold, exactly, but Rebecca didn't miss the edge it carried, either.

"It's up to you, little sister. Whatever you decide, Naomi and I will stand behind you. You didn't promise Frank Page anything." When Hannah didn't respond, Rebecca set the note on the bed. It looked so small and inconsequential against the background of loudly colored quilting squares.

Hannah turned, her eyes brimming with a quiet strength. "I think I've come too far to travel back down that road, Rebecca. My child is the only Page who matters to me now."

~~~

Clutching a coat and a small, beautifully wrapped box of fancy chocolates, Daisy raised her hand to knock on the hotel's back door. With the clatter of cooking noises and chatter coming from the kitchen, she realized no one would hear her and slowly pushed open the door. Stepping inside, she peered meekly over the batwings into the kitchen.

She watched for a few seconds as Rebecca, Ian and Emilio tended to the business of cooking with efficiency and organization. Ian pulled orders off the rack in the window and hung them over the stove. Rebecca and Emilio quickly discussed the orders and then flew into motion. The three hustled and bustled about the kitchen like well-trained soldiers, cutting meat, flipping steaks, stirring pots of steaming vegetables. As Rebecca pulled a roast out of the oven and turned to set it on the table, she saw Daisy.

"I–I brought these for Hannah," she stammered, quickly stepping through the doors and thrusting out her arms as if to pass off the gifts.

"Oh, thank you," Rebecca gushed, "Why don't you give them to her in person? I know Hannah would love to have some company. Really she would."

"I need more steaks." Ian came to the table and pulled a cutting board loaded with a slab of meat closer to him. "Good evenin', Daisy." He yanked the knife from the shank of beef and raised it into the air for a violent blow.

"Here, I'll do that." Rebecca took the knife from him. "Why don't you finish with those in the pan. Emilio, we're going to need more potatoes."

The boy withdrew the spoon from the stew he had been stirring and disappeared around the corner, heading to the recently-added store room. Daisy realized she was just in the way and stepped out in the hallway. To get upstairs she had to skirt the edge of the dining room which was full of customers and she wasn't supposed to be here. What if someone told Mr. McIntyre?

She decided she wanted to see Hannah badly enough to risk another talking-to by her employer. Head down, face turned away from the guests, she clung to the wall and darted up the stairs to the second floor. Apparently no one paid her any attention, and she strode quietly down the hall to Hannah's room. At least there was light coming from underneath one door only, so she assumed it was hers. Daisy knocked timidly and waited for Hannah to let her in.

"Mollie!" Hannah exclaimed when she opened the door. Exuberant, she pulled Daisy into the room. "It's so good to see you!"

Relieved by the joyous welcome, Daisy extended her gifts. "These are for you, if you want them."

Hannah took one look at the candy and clutched the box to her chest. "Where did you get these? I love chocolate!"

Daisy waved the question away, preferring to avoid the details. "A friend brings me things some times. The coat is huge on me, but I thought you could use it to tuck the baby in when you need to go somewhere."

Hannah reached out and hugged Daisy. "Thank you so much. You are such a special blessing."

Daisy hugged her back, tentatively at first, then with more confidence. It felt good to have a friend. "How is the restaurant doing?" she asked, pulling away. "The men sure have been talking about it down at the Iron Horse."

"Really?" Curiosity glowed in Hannah's eyes. "What do they say?" She took the coat and candy to her bed and gratefully plopped down on the mattress.

Daisy quickly weeded out the crass comments, especially about Hannah being with child. She had taken it upon herself to spread the rumor that Hannah had been abandoned by her husband. That was something men in a mining town could understand, since many of them had left home and hearth due to an infection of Gold Fever. Starting to believe that their newest citizens were exactly what they appeared to be, the men were finding things to respect about the sisters.

"It's funny, but they don't talk about the food as much as they do you and your sisters. I think a lot of the men are actually glad that maybe the town might be settling down some now." Daisy realized then that many of the comments lumped her in with the bad elements in town, but shared them anyway. "One man said that when a few respectable girls come into town, a church and schools won't be far behind. I overheard Matt Wilson tell Nate Ledford that even if the food tasted like cow dung he'd come just to sit and watch you pour his tea. Isn't that funny?"

Hannah laughed and shook her head. "It's almost like they want a chance to act civilized."

"Defiance is out of hand because of a few really bad folks," Daisy explained. "The worst group is among the prospectors. They're just drifters, going from gold camp to gold camp. They're the ones who start most of the trouble."

Hannah patted the bed. "Forgive my manners. Please, have a seat. Tell me, what about the men who work in the mine? Are they a rough lot? I've tried so hard to stay behind closed doors, I feel like a hermit."

"Well, the miners aren't so bad, really," Daisy sat down on the bed, almost at the opposite end. For her, it was a comfortable space. "Most of them aren't boys anymore. They've tried their hand at prospecting and would rather just have a regular paycheck. A ton of them send money back home to mothers and wives and, since Mr. McIntyre won't tolerate drunk or sloppy workers, they pretty much mind their P's and Q's."

The conversation dragged then and Daisy thought Hannah looked preoccupied. Finally, her friend asked about the Bible. "So, have you had a chance to do any reading?"

The question opened the door for Daisy to ask something that had burned in her heart since hearing Hannah's story out in the backyard. "Some. A little. It's hard for me, though." She leaned forward and asked with sincerity, "Is it wrong to have a Bible in a saloon?"

Hannah thought about the question then shook her head. "I wouldn't think so. Jesus said it's not the healthy who need a doctor but the sick. And he was accused of being a winebibber because he ate so often with known sinners. But they came to hear him speak. They wanted to be near him because he didn't judge them." Hannah took a deep breath and smiled warmly at Daisy. "Mollie, I've never been around prostitutes. I can't imagine what your life is like. But you said it makes you feel dirty and worthless. *That* I do know something about. And I know Jesus didn't die so I could stay trapped in those feelings."

Daisy's heart started racing again. The fire in Hannah's eyes captivated her soul; she found the girl's passion was contagious.

"God loves us just the way we are but he refuses to leave us that way. Think about giving him your heart, Mollie. If you can accept that he forgives you, I promise he'll change your life." Hannah scooted over and clutched Daisy's hands. "He is so willing to forgive you. In fact, his word says, if we confess our sins, he is faithful and just and will forgive us our sins and purify us from all unrighteousness."

Daisy bit her lip as she felt her eyes tearing up. Hannah believed so ardently in Jesus, she made it hard to turn away from him.

"I don't mean to push you, Mollie, and I know you probably have lots of questions. It's just that, sometimes, I feel like you're the reason we're here."

Daisy looked away, almost scared to speculate on the meaning of that.

Hannah squeezed Mollie's hand. "In my wildest dreams, I would have never thought things would turn out like this. But I'm glad we're here...and I'm glad I've gotten to know you."

Daisy blinked, sending the tears spilling, and thought about the life she was living. "Are there any women like me in the Bible?" Was there, she wanted to know, a black-and-white example of what Jesus would say to someone like her?

"Yes. And he loved them dearly."

Hannah had a pencil and several sheets of paper sitting on the trunk next to her bed. She took a sheet and the pencil and started writing, using her great, round abdomen for a desk. She quickly scribbled something down and handed the paper over to Daisy. "Once you've read these, will you come back and tell me what you think?"

Hand trembling, Daisy slowly took the paper and nodded.

When Daisy returned to the saloon that night, she tucked the sheet of paper away in her night stand with the Bible and started dressing for work. As she fastened each button in her worn, low-cut dress, her spirits sank deeper and deeper. And with each step down the staircase, the lewd laughter, choking smoke, and bawdy music assaulted her like physical blows.

A group of rowdy prospectors departing the next day for warmer climates had invaded the Iron Horse. For one more Friday night in Defiance, they brought Hell to earth... at least for her. The shame and guilt of it left her unable to even look at the Bible for days.

~~~

## Twenty-Five

The end of October was feeling fickle and decided one morning to drop an unexpected autumn snow on Defiance. A pure, undefiled blanket of white draped itself gently over the town, hiding its sins. Naomi stood on the porch, amazed at the deceptive beauty of it . . . and the silence. For an hour or so at dawn, Defiance sat still and quiet as if everyone had agreed not to disturb the picturesque scene.

As she savored the quiet, Hannah screamed from upstairs. The fear and pain in her little sister's voice jolted Naomi out of her reverie. Heart in her throat, she raced to Hannah's room, fearing unimaginable tragedy. Instead, she found Rebecca calmly helping a pasty-faced Hannah back to bed.

"The baby's coming." Rebecca sounded calm as she pulled the covers over Hannah. "She said she's been having contractions since around midnight, but they're only a few minutes apart now and more intense."

Naomi swallowed the fear that tried to tighten her throat. "What should we do?"

Just then another contraction hit Hannah. A deep groan escaped her as her face contorted into a grim mask of pain. She writhed in the bed but Rebecca held onto her hand and whispered comforting words in a soothing voice.

"I should get the doctor," Naomi whispered.

*Oh, God, please let him be sober.*

"Yes, but let's pray first," Rebecca suggested. Hannah nodded emphatically as the pain faded away and her breathing eased. Naomi rushed to the bed and knelt on the floor. She caressed her little sister's forehead then took her hand and Rebecca's. "Everything is going to be just fine…" Naomi wasn't sure who she was trying to convince with her words, but repeated them anyway. "Just fine."

Unclear on how to contact the doctor, which now struck her as a painfully stupid lack of preparation, Naomi was forced to go to the saloon. She stopped in the middle of the dark, silent room and simply shouted for Mr. McIntyre. She didn't know which room was his and she had no desire to go upstairs knocking on doors at this hour. If her yelling woke the entire building, so be it.

He came out of the first room at the top of the stairs, tugging on a robe and looking astonished to find her standing in the Iron Horse. Other doors opened and Flowers, Naomi assumed, peered down as well.

"The doctor. We need the doctor. Hannah's baby is coming."

Despite his groggy appearance, Mr. McIntyre didn't hesitate in responding. "I'll dress and fetch him immediately."

~~~

By early afternoon, Hannah had delivered a healthy, seven-pound baby boy who shared an uncanny resemblance to his father. She had known all along he would be a boy just as she had known all along his name would be William Aaron Page. The Page part, of course, was legally debatable, but no one in Defiance would ever have cause to argue it.

In bed, cuddling her little fat, pink cherub, Hannah wondered where Billy was right at that moment. Did he ever think of her? If he could see his newborn son, she had no doubt he would fall in love with the round face, blue eyes and perfect little hands. He was adorable and beautiful, and Hannah's heart overflowed into her eyes. She couldn't recall ever having cried out of sheer joy. Overcome with peace and gratitude, she kissed her precious angel on the forehead and mused over how amazingly good God had been to her.

A gentle knock on her door brought her out of her tender daydreaming. She quickly dried her face with her one free hand and smoothed her hair. "Come in."

Awkwardly, hesitantly, Emilio peered around the door. A true sense of deep friendship washed over her at the sight of him. "Emilio, I'm so glad to see you. Please come in."

Softly, he shut the door and wandered over to the bed. Hands behind his back, he leaned over to take a peek at the new arrival. Hannah moved the blanket out of the way for a better view and Emilio's face lit up. "Aah, hees so beautiful."

Hannah grinned, as much from pride as enjoyment of Emilio's company. She thought of him now as a brother and couldn't imagine life without him.

The boy straightened up and shook his head. In a matter-of-fact voice he murmured, "The father. I theenk he ees an idiot."

~~~

The restaurant was closed on Thanksgiving Day, a decision Naomi and her sisters had made with great difficulty. They wanted, however, a time to truly thank God for the fact they were still together and that Hannah's baby was just perfect and as healthy as a new foal. They insisted that Emilio join them and Ian arrived with a stunning gift of fancy candies. Hannah had invited Daisy by way of Emilio, but she had politely declined.

As Naomi set the table and listened to the easy conversation coming from the kitchen, she pondered the strange mix of people who would sit around this table today . . . and those who wouldn't. She missed John terribly, sometimes more than others, but Defiance had forced her to cope with the loss. He was gone and he wasn't coming back. It still hurt, but she tried to occupy her heart with the things she could control: taking care of Hannah, opening the restaurant, making a life here.

She had toyed with the idea of inviting Mr. McIntyre for Thanksgiving, but shied away from it in the end, puzzled she'd even thought of him. This was a gathering of friends and loved ones, she argued, setting an apple pie on the table. Not meeting her definition of either, Mr. McIntyre was something of a round peg in a square hole. She didn't know what to do with him.

The thought brought her to a halt. Why did she have to do anything at all with him? He was an acquaintance and one didn't necessarily invite acquaintances for Thanksgiving supper. Convinced she was satisfied with that reasoning, Naomi headed back to the kitchen for more food.

~~~

Thanksgiving Day for Daisy was quiet. She knew the saloon would be slow until evening. Bored, she looked out her window at the falling snow and wondered what to do with her free time. Of course, the answer nagged at her, but she was almost afraid of what she might find if she read the stories of those Bible women.

Had Jesus chastised them for living this way? Had he challenged them to do anything—sweep streets, sew clothes, beg even—before settling for this lifestyle? Or had he so touched their hearts with His forgiveness that the women had up-ended their lives to follow him, casting off everything they had become to start over fresh and changed?

She stared at the night stand. How many customers had she been with since her last visit to Hannah? A dozen? More? She didn't want to face God with the stench of sin on her, but she didn't want to face her friend not having read those stories. And she wanted to see Hannah, to see the baby, maybe hold him . . .

Sighing nervously, she walked over to the night stand. The piece of paper Hannah had given her sat on top of the book. She looked at the first scripture written on it then flipped her way over to John 8. She sat down and began to read a story that spoke to her as if she had been there herself.

She saw the woman, thrown like a worthless little pawn into the midst of the arrogant, puffed-up men. Daisy wondered if the woman's heart had beat at a breakneck pace as the men accused her, badgered Jesus, and urged Him to allow them to stone her. In her humiliation, had she wanted to crawl into a cave or had she stared defiantly at those vipers? She wondered what Jesus wrote in the sand as He knelt down, trying to ignore their complaints. Then she saw the most miraculous thing of all: He had focused on their sins, not those of the woman.

"So when they continued asking him, he lifted up himself, and said unto them, he that is without sin among you, let him first cast a stone at her. And again he stooped down, and wrote on the ground. And they which heard it, being convicted by their own conscience, went out one by one, beginning at the eldest, even unto the last: and Jesus was left alone, and the woman standing in the midst. When Jesus had lifted up himself, and saw none but the woman, he said unto her, Woman, where are those thine accusers? Hath no man condemned thee? She said, No man, Lord. And Jesus said unto her, *Neither do I condemn thee: go and sin no more."*

Daisy read the last sentence at least ten times. *Neither do I condemn thee. Go and sin no more.* It kept running through her head as she stared down at the words. He had forgiven that woman so easily; in fact, he had been more interested in making a point to the hypocrites who had paraded her out to him. He had spoken to the woman with kindness but firmness.

It amazed Daisy. This glimpse at Christ's heart toward a loose woman intrigued her; made her hunger to know more. Eagerly, she flipped to Luke 7 and read the story of a prostitute who had slipped into the Pharisees' home without a word and began humbly ministering to Jesus. She felt this woman's tears and broken heart as she desperately and with reverence washed her Lord's feet.

What did Jesus see when he looked at her? Her desperate desire to find forgiveness, to know that someone cared about her? She wasn't welcome in this home, but had come anyway, to offer up this simple act of love. Had she come expecting him to forgive her sins, or did she so love this Savior that to serve him was all that mattered?

Daisy imagined he had touched her cheek lovingly when He announced, "Wherefore I say unto thee, her sins, which are many, are forgiven; for she loved much: but to whom little is forgiven, the same loveth little. And He said unto her, Thy sins are forgiven. And He said to the woman, thy faith has saved thee; go in peace."

*Her sins, which are many, are forgiven.*

*Thy faith hath saved thee; go in peace.*

If he could forgive her, could he—would he—forgive the Flower known as Daisy? Did he know that her real name was Mollie Stewart?

Crying, she held the Bible to her chest and slipped to her knees to find out.

~~~

## Twenty-Six

"*Senoras, Senoras*! There ees someone at the door!"

Naomi's eyes flew open when she heard the panic in Emilio's voice, and the frantic banging on the front door. Leaping out of bed, Naomi threw on her robe and grabbed the shotgun. She raced down the stairs, followed by Rebecca. Hannah stopped at the landing, obviously unwilling to go too far away from little Billy.

The sisters had taken Emilio completely under their wings after clearing it with Mr. McIntyre, and moved the boy into the small room beneath the stairs, behind the hotel's new registration desk. Because of his proximity to the front, he was the first to hear the desperate knocking in the middle of the night. As if he was afraid of who might be standing on the other side at this late hour, he had lit a lamp and called up to the sisters.

Naomi heard more frenzied pounding as a female voice called from the other side of the door. "It's me, Lily. Please come quick. Daisy's been—"

Naomi jerked the door half way open, freezing Lily's hand in mid-knock. Once sure the girl was alone, she opened it wider and let her come in along with a whirl of snowflakes. The Negro girl from the Garden wasn't even wearing a coat, but was, instead, running about in a very revealing dress. Rubbing the chill and snow from her dark arms, she frantically blurted out a jumble of details.

"Woah, woah, woah!" Naomi bellowed, grabbing her shoulder. "Calm down. Now *what* about Daisy?"

The girl breathed and tried again. "She's hurt real bad. A customer knocked her around when she wouldn't go along. She asked if Hannah would come."

Hannah pressed her hand to her stomach, as if quelling butterflies.

"Get dressed, Hannah," Naomi ordered over her shoulder, but then looked up and understood the concern in her sister's eyes. "Little Billy will be all right for a while. Mollie needs you."

Rebecca walked back to the stairs and reassured her little sister. "You go with her, Hannah. I'll tend to Billy."

Naomi grabbed a coat from the rack beside the door and hung it on Lily. "We'll be right along. Tell Daisy we're coming."

The two women exchanged understanding glances then Lily sprinted out the door.


Mr. McIntyre greeted Hannah and Naomi as they climbed the stairs in the closed saloon.

Naomi stopped one step below him. She knew she was on a slow burn because whatever trouble was on the other side of that door was arguably his fault. "Have you called the doctor?" she asked.

Mr. McIntyre tugged at his collar. "She insisted on seeing Hannah first." Naomi hoped her expression showed that she did not approve of that answer. He tried to explain. "She seemed rather emphatic about it."

Gently, Hannah pushed past them both and went to the door. Opening it slowly, she looked back at Naomi and motioned for her to follow. They found Daisy asleep on the bed while an Asian Flower dabbed delicately at a bloodied and bruised cheekbone. Both sisters gasped when they saw Daisy's face, almost unrecognizable from the swelling, discoloration and drying blood.

The Asian girl, her expression inscrutable and cold, immediately passed the hand towel and bowl of water to Hannah. "She's been waiting for you."

Naomi grabbed the girl's arm as she attempted to slip past her. "Can you get us some witch hazel, liniment, and a steak?" It wasn't really a request.

Without meeting Naomi's gaze, the girl nodded and added dryly, "I think you will need bandages also. Her ribs are broken."

Naomi watched the woman leave then drew in a breath.

Hannah had already sat down next to Daisy and was tending to the cut on her cheek. Daisy's left eye was red, black and blue, and completely swollen shut. Her top lip, smeared with blood, was puffed up to twice its normal size. A trail of dried blood trickled from one nostril in her slightly askew nose and there were bruises on her throat that clearly matched the placement of fingers. As Hannah dabbed at the blood, unbridled tears ran down her face.

Naomi wanted to cry too, and scream, and beat the ever-loving daylights out of the monster that had done this. Reining in her anger for the moment, she touched Hannah on the shoulder. "I need to pull the blanket back. That girl said she's got some broken ribs. I need to check and see if there are any other injuries."

Hannah nodded and moved enough to allow the blanket to come down. Slowly, trying not to wake Daisy, Naomi pulled the cover back and flinched. The abuse her body had taken from the customer was obvious. Her ribs were turning all shades of blue, bruises were discoloring her thighs; her knees and elbows were scratched and bloodied, and her right hand was wrapped in a cold, damp towel resting on her chest.

Naomi covered her back up, but left the hand on top of the blanket. Carefully, she pulled the towel away and flinched. Three of Daisy's fingers were bent in grotesque angles. Not broken, necessarily, but badly dislocated.

Hannah regarded her sister with grief-stricken eyes and Naomi nodded. "I'll send for the doctor."

Daisy moaned as Hannah dabbed at a cut along her jaw. "It's all right, Mollie. We're here now. Everything's going to be fine."

Her one good eye fluttered open and the girl tried to smile when she recognized her friend. She attempted to talk, but Hannah shushed her. "Don't say anything. Just be quiet—"

Daisy rolled her head weakly from side to side and tried again to talk. Her voice was raspy at first but she persisted. Finally, hoarsely, she whispered, "Go and sin no more." She closed her eye and swallowed hard against the pain. "My sins are forgiven." Then she smiled as big as she could. "He told me so."

Naomi and Hannah cleaned Daisy up as much as they could and then assisted when the doctor arrived. The girls smelled whisky on his breath, but he seemed sober enough. An elderly gentleman with a short shock of tousled, gray hair and thick, silver glasses, he handled Daisy like a china doll as he wrapped her ribs.

Perhaps he was a slave to liquor, Naomi thought, but he was extremely compassionate with his patients. He had been kind and reassuring with Hannah during her labor and now treated Daisy as if she was a fragile princess. Lifting the girl and moving her caused her extreme pain but he dealt with her gingerly, speaking low and soothingly.

Naomi appreciated his bedside manner, especially when he got to the last task at hand. They had cleaned Daisy's wounds, placed a steak over her eye, bandaged her ribs… now he had to relocate her fingers.

"Daisy, girl," he rubbed her arm gently, "this is going to hurt like the devil, but when it's over, it's over. The pain will stop almost instantly, unlike those ribs of yours." He grasped her index finger and looked at her. She closed her eye and nodded.

He had to perform the procedure three times and each time Daisy cried out, writhing in pain. Hannah sat on the other side of the bed, holding her free hand and whispering calm words. When the last finger was done, Dr. Cook gave her a teaspoon of laudanum and packed up his bag. He stepped away from the bed and brought Naomi with him.

"I think she'll be all right, despite the fact that she looks as if she was run over by a freight wagon. She's mostly just going to be very sore." He handed her the bottle of laudanum. "Give her a teaspoon of this every four to six hours for two days. Start slacking off after that."

Naomi took the bottle and clutched it to her heart.

"When can we move her?"

His eyebrows shot up. "Move her? To where?"

"To our hotel. She's leaving this place and never coming back."

He thought for a moment, scratching his chin. "Well, it's not far, but those ribs of hers are going to make her wish she were dead. I suppose, though, you could move her tomorrow sometime. Give her a dose of that," he pointed at the medicine, "wait for it to take effect then do it...*carefully*. Use a stretcher."

He gave Daisy one last, sad look. "I'm getting' tired of seein' this kind of thing. It's enough to take the steam out of a man."

Naomi shut the door behind him thinking angrily, *I'd like to do just that.* The man who did this was a vile monster, but what kind of a man opened a business that traded in the flesh of women as if they were horses—no, worse—mere toys for a man's amusement? It was sick and disgusting. It was the height of selfishness and arrogance. Naomi felt a painful new level of loathing for Mr. McIntyre, though she didn't exactly understand why it should grieve her so to feel this way about him.

Daisy slept quietly now and Hannah fidgeted as she stared uncertainly at her sister. "I need to go, Naomi. I've been gone too long."

Lost in her roiling thoughts, it took a moment for Hannah's voice to intrude. "What? Oh, I'm sorry. Yes, yes, of course you must go. Send Rebecca down when it's light."

Hannah patted her friend's hand one more time then started for the door. Something stopped her, though. Gazing over her shoulder at her sister she warned, "Hate and anger just give Satan a foothold in our lives, Naomi. I know you're seething; so am I, but we can't hate the people responsible for this."

Naomi clamped her jaws shut and offered no reply. Nothing she could say at this moment would sound very Christian.

When Naomi didn't reply, Hannah opened the door only

to find Mr. McIntyre about to knock. "I was just coming to check on the patient."

"Certainly." Hannah stepped aside for him. "I'll see you in a while, Naomi. Mr. McIntyre." With that, she slipped out the door.

Naomi stepped closer to the bed to avoid being near Mr. McIntyre and reported on Daisy's condition with her back to him. "Dr. Cook says she'll recover. Cuts and bruises. Broken ribs."

She shook her head, so livid she wasn't sure she could stop the tears. Her chin quivered as she fought for control. Swallowing, she turned on Mr. McIntyre.

~~~

## Twenty-Seven

Naomi's eyes hid nothing of her heart. McIntyre recognized instantly that where once a friendship had started blossoming, now there were only ashes. She blamed him for Daisy's injuries and, he supposed, in a roundabout way, it was his fault.

"Where's the man who did this to her?"

"In jail."

"What will he be charged with?"

He sensed no answer would be the right one, but he told the truth nonetheless. "Assault and battery. He'll get thirty days in jail and a $75 fine."

"And you? Will he compensate you for lost revenue?"

The disgusted, embittered look in her eyes affected him, though he couldn't say how exactly. He had almost seen a spark of happiness in her eyes lately when she looked at him; not now. The passion he saw burning there at the moment was not the kind he ever wanted to see again. She hated him, even loathed him. It left him speechless—the heat of it, the disappointment of it.

"What kind of a man are you? How can you live with yourself? These women are human beings, not horses to hook up to a freight wagon. In fact, you probably treat your horses better." Shuffling sounds behind him drew her eyes to the hallway. He knew his Flowers had gathered in the shadows to listen-in.

Naomi raised her chin. "We're moving Mollie out of here tomorrow. She has a room at our hotel as long as she wants it." She shifted her attention to the audience in the hallway. "*None* of you have to live like this." Her voice was choked with anger, but she was pleading as well. "You are beautiful, valuable children of God and he loves you. He doesn't want to see you living in this filth. Mollie discovered that, which is why she said 'no more.'"

McIntyre heard Iris's cynical cackle. "Yea, and look

where that got her."

"Heaven," Naomi fired back. "And eternity with the King. Until then, a home with us."

Out of the corner of his eye, he watched the shadowy figures shift under the weight of Naomi's pleading gaze. She moved to the door and spoke in a softer, kinder voice. "We have room for you. Any time you want to leave this place, this life, knock on our door."

A strange, tense silence hung in the air; no one breathed, no one moved. Finished, Naomi stepped back and gestured toward the door. "Mr. McIntyre, please . . . "

He studied her for a moment, searching for even the most ghostly hint of compassion towards him. There was only a chill in her eyes so brutal it burned him and his heart was inexplicably heavy.

He walked toward the door and stopped just before the threshold. Without looking at her, he straightened a bit and whispered a painful confession. "I am what I am, Mrs. Miller . . . but for the first time in my life, I'm sorry for it."

"Then choose to be a better man."

He wondered if he had imagined the slightly desperate plea in her voice. It didn't matter. He had made such choices long ago. Focused on the darkness, he left the room.

~~~

Doris, a toothless, two-hundred pound hag who had wisely aligned herself with the Broken Spoke's new management, leaned into Rose's ear. "Emilio is out back. Says he needs to see you."

Rose poured a glass of whiskey and shoved it across the grayed, rough-sawed plank to the waiting miner. "Take over here for me."

She handed the bottle to Doris and exited by the back door. Emilio was waiting in the snowy shadows next to the wood pile, coat pulled up around his jaws, hands in his pockets. Hiding and cowering. She hated the sight of him, but he had at least proven to be a useful, if not grudging, spy.

In the faint glow from the saloon, she could see he looked especially nervous tonight.

"You must have something interesting to tell me."

The boy glared at her as he took a deep breath and straightened up. "Daisy was beaten so bad a few days ago that the seesters took her to the hotel."

Rose grinned, delighted with the news and the pain she heard in her little brother's voice. This particular plan had yielded even better results than she'd hoped for. "Tell me she's going to die and my joy will be complete."

Enraged, Emilio cried out and lunged at Rose, shoving her back against the saloon door. She was startled, but only for an instant, then pushed him off her.

"Be careful little, brother. I can send a friend to visit you, too."

He tossed his head side to side, as if in agony, and she could hear the tears in his voice. "I swear to God, Rose..." He swallowed hard then whipped out a knife from inside his jacket. Brandishing it at her, he screamed, "I HATE YOU! I HATE YOU!" Eyes wide and glowing with outrage, lips peeled back in a snarl, he raised the knife. "I swear, if you touch any of them, I'll kill you!"

Weary of this, she purposefully turned her back on him and grabbed the door knob. "If you could, you would have already." She knew the condescension in her voice was unmistakable. "I tell you this, little brother. You better sleep with one eye open."

~~~

McIntyre read over the mining report but couldn't take in the staggering numbers. His vein of quartz was making him and Ian wealthy beyond imagination, yet that wasn't the reason the numbers wouldn't make sense. He kept seeing Daisy's bloodied and battered face . . . and that frigid look in Naomi's eyes.

He felt the burst of cold air that accompanied his front door opening, but didn't look up. Ian paused at the door and cleared his throat to get McIntyre's attention. "Good afternoon, Mac." Peeling off his coat, the Scotsman hung it on the hook just inside the entrance and slid into a seat in front of the desk. "How is the mining business today?"

McIntyre tried to pretend he had actually read the report he'd been staring at for the last ten minutes. "A sixty-foot thick vein of quartz that stretches from here to Animas Forks, partner. I would say we'll be in business for quite some time to come."

Ian crossed his legs and nodded at the observation.

"How is Daisy?" McIntyre shuffled the papers nonchalantly. "Is she settled?"

"Aye, and I believe I've seen improvements already. Gettin' out of that hole you call a saloon was the best thing that could've happened to her. I'm only sorry I never said anything to ye about her . . . or any of them for that matter."

McIntyre leaned back in his chair. "Have you come to preach to me, Ian? I warn you, I've had enough chastising."

To his frustration, Ian chuckled. "I heard. I went back to the saloon to pick up a few more of Daisy's belongings and your Flowers told me what Naomi said to ye. Burnt your ears, dinna she, lad?"

McIntyre clenched and unclenched his fists but kept silent. He'd never wanted to hit his friend this badly.

"Dunna look at me like that. If ye want Defiance to be a respectable town, if you want to be a respectable businessman—nay," Ian pointed his index finger at him for emphasis, "if ye want to be a respectable *man*, then ye should shut down yer Garden, if not the whole saloon."

McIntyre reached up and rubbed the tense muscles in his neck. He had gambled, sold whiskey, and run prostitutes since before the war. It was a setup with which he was comfortable. If the mine shut down, if the price of timber dropped, if cattle bottomed out, he could always sell whiskey and women. No, it wasn't a pretty way to make a living but it had always kept him up in style. Usually, the girls were manageable, unlike Rose, and the violence was minor, unlike Daisy's beating.

"I guess I'm just not ready to be that respectable yet."

Casually, Ian settled more comfortably in his chair and put his feet up on McIntyre's desk. "The winters in Defiance are long and cold. Now me, I am enjoyin' the company of fine, sweet sisters such as they are. Their inn is filled with laughter and warmth, the scent of baking bread and roast meat. The fact that they've taken in misfits such as meself and Emilio and now Daisy, well, we're like one odd but happy family.

"At fifty years of age, I saw nothin' in my future but roamin' aimlessly across this country, wrestling with God every day and slowly killing meself with whiskey every night. Now I have new plans for my twilight years and I'm as excited about them as a child on Christmas morn. Bein' respectable, in my humble opinion, is quite underappreciated."

"You plan to marry that girl, then? Rebecca?"

"I've become very fond of all of them, but especially Rebecca. If she willna marry me then I'll just have to stay on as a cook."

McIntyre considered the change in Ian and wondered if it was caused by more than the sisters' arrival. "You never talked much about your faith before they showed up."

Ian chewed on the comment for a minute and shrugged. "We're in the middle of nowhere and three beautiful, decent, God-fearin' women fall into our laps. If ye dunna see the hand of God in that, mon, you're blind *and* stupid. Their comin' here was no accident and as far I'm concerned, they've saved my life. Ye'd do well yerself to give the Lord a word of thanks."

It was McIntyre's turn to chuckle. "I'll thank him when I'm convinced they're a blessing and not a curse. Given a choice, I think they'd run me out of town on a rail for being such an unrepentant sinner."

A wide grin illuminated Ian's face. "Well, you know what they say: if you canna beat'em, join'em."

Long after Ian departed, McIntyre was still rolling the idea of Divine Intervention around and around in his head. Had the Almighty literally manipulated things so these women would wind up in this gritty hell-hole at this precise time? Had he saved John Miller's life all those years ago just so the man could bring his wife to within spitting distance of Defiance before conveniently dying? Why? To what end? Did God really care so much he would engineer a grand plan for one remote town . . . one selfish man?

As if answering the questions, McIntyre heard his mother's voice from long ago reading a familiar scripture.

*For the Son of man is come to seek and to save that which was lost.*

~~~

## Twenty-Eight

Daisy didn't know if she could be any happier. Defiance had dragged her to the bottom of a deep, murky well, but because of Jesus, she had burst forth from the depths and was drinking from the fountain of living water! She lay in bed recovering from her wounds and had moments when she wanted to run and shout praises to God, her heart was so full of gratitude. She blessed the name of Jesus and thanked him every day for her release from captivity. She might wind up on the street tomorrow, but she knew she'd never have to go back to that life.

As she pondered the blessings of finding Jesus, Naomi entered carrying her breakfast.

"Good morning, Mollie."

As she set the tray on her lap, Daisy clutched the woman's hand and looked her in the eye. "If you hadn't come here, most likely no one would have ever told me about Jesus and I think I would have died in that saloon. I'm so sorry you lost your man along the way, but I pray that someday you'll think it was worth it . . . that *I* was worth it."

Naomi smiled and sat down on the bed. "You know, Hannah asked me months ago if God would have sent us here on behalf of one person. Initially, I told her no, but now, after seeing you freed from that life," she nodded contentedly, "I think it has been worth it."

"Oh, but there will be more!" Daisy squeezed Naomi's arm with fervor. "If God can pour out this much mercy on me, think what He can do in this town."

~~~

As Naomi finished making her bed, she thought about what she had told Daisy and knew it was the truth. Finally, she could accept that God would not let John's death be a pointless and inexplicable event. Something good had come from it. The realization gave Naomi some peace and she wondered if there would, indeed, be more souls saved in this town.

She wandered to her bedroom window and moved the curtain aside. Snow was falling–again–with sincere determination

In the weeks before Christmas, Defiance had been perpetually engulfed by a fluffy, gray sky. And when the sky wasn't spitting snow, it fell in great, overwhelming quantities, like now. Consequently, the town had racked up over twenty inches.

The odd little family at the Trinity Inn hadn't minded the weather, though; in fact they reveled in it and the Christmas spirit. Together they had decorated the hotel from one end to the other with garlands made of pine boughs, popcorn and red gingham bows. Candles sat in every window, burned at every table amidst more pine boughs and holly berries.

The girls went about their chores humming Christmas carols, Ian sang *Jingle Bells* to little Billy at least once a day while holding him close, and they all had quietly tucked Christmas packages for each other in the corner where the Christmas tree would go. It was going to be a fine Christmas, Naomi thought. Different, poignant, but filled with cheer, warmth and love. She could hardly stand to wait twelve more days.

If it wasn't for a nagging sense of loss related to Mr. McIntyre, she would actually be quite content today. She felt completely justified in her anger towards him, but she was also a little disappointed in the loss of his friendship–not that they were friends . . . not that she wanted to be friends. She couldn't really explain what she thought she'd lost. Frustrated by these nonsensical musings about a man she barely knew, she dropped the curtain and turned away.

A commotion in the backyard below drew her back to the window. Daisy, Hannah and Emilio spilled out into the snow and within seconds the snowballs were flying and the girls had teamed up on the boy.

Naomi shifted for a better view and watched Daisy. After a few weeks of rest and short, stiff walks around the inn, the girl had begged them to let her join in and be useful. She had taken it easy at first, folding napkins and washing the silverware, but it wasn't long before the bruises had faded and most of her strength had returned. Daisy boldly credited the renewed energy she felt to the desire to live a new life full of Jesus. Her face was always aglow with a smile, and there was a noticeable spring in her still-weak step.

Watching her now, gingerly tossing snowballs, Naomi knew the girl's future was bright. There was an abundance of heartbreak in Defiance, but even here there was also the joy of the Lord. Naomi smiled at the battle scene below and decided Emilio could use reinforcements.


As Naomi pulled her coat from the tree downstairs, she absently noted in the back of her mind what sounded like a soft, distant rolling clap of thunder. However, the sound increased and she stopped to listen. Strange, thunder didn't happen in December.

Instinctive fear blossomed in her stomach. A rumbling, growling noise, she could actually *feel* it now, vibrating up from the ground. The volume increased exponentially with each beat of her heart.

The back door flew open and Emilio streaked through the hotel, his eyes wide and his face ashen. "Avalanche!" the boy screamed, racing to the front door. "Sounds like eet ees near the mine!"

He flung the front door open and skidded out on to porch. Naomi hurried to the door in time to see him leap into the street and tear off towards the Iron Horse. Terrified and confused by this growing roar, Naomi turned back at Daisy and Hannah. Her sister was taking the stairs two at a time to get to Billy and Daisy was racing toward Naomi with outstretched arms. The clamor was deafening and the whole earth seemed to be shaking. Naomi and Daisy clutched each other's hands. After several seconds, the din started diminishing then stopped, like a train grinding to a halt. The ground ceased its humming and a silence like a death shroud fell over the town.

The girls stood frozen; Daisy had Naomi's hand in a death grip and Hannah stopped, nearly at the stop of the stairs. The quiet was so pristine Naomi could hear her heart pounding in her chest. Afraid of moving, their eyes roamed the hotel. Naomi could imagine a great explosion of snow crashing through the walls any second.

Rebecca appeared at the top of the stairs holding Billy; Hannah stumbled as if her knees nearly buckled with relief. She took the baby in her arms and squeezed him tight. Rebecca switched her gaze to Naomi, terror in her eyes. "What in the Sam Hill was that?"

"Emilio said it was an avalanche." Naomi could hardly believe she had just uttered those words.

Daisy shook her head and sighed. "Twenty-two people died last season."

"Died?" Naomi squeezed the girl's hand, countering her desperate grip. "Season? How often does this happen?" Her immediate concern was for her sisters and the baby in Hannah's arms. "Are we safe here?"

Daisy shrugged apologetically. "Mostly, I think. The folks up near the mine entrance have it the roughest. It's really steep up there."

Before Naomi could reply, they heard a chorus of townsfolk yelling in panicked voices from the street. The girls scrambled outside and watched as a crowd of men ran hell-bent-for-leather down the street, past the Iron Horse and out of town. Some were carrying shovels, others pick axes.

A somber Daisy inched forward and watched the panicked throng. "This is awfully early. I guess it's gonna be a bad winter." Naomi heard the doom in the girl's voice and rubbed her arms against the chilling prophecy.

The sound of a whip cracking and graphic curses drew their attention to a driver trying impatiently to navigate his wagon through the snaking sea of men. Breaking free, he cracked the whip again and the horses lunged in the direction of the inn. Mr. McIntyre pushed the team of horses hard the last several yards then brought them to a sliding halt in the snow right in front of her.

"I've an injured man here and there will be more coming." He set a firm gaze on Naomi, as if daring her to deny him help. "We need beds for them. May we use the hotel?"

Naomi blinked. "Of course . . . absolutely."

McIntyre leaped down from his seat. "They're digging for survivors now."

As he dropped the gate at the back of the wagon, Rebecca stepped forward. "What can we do to get ready, Mr. McIntyre?"

He grabbed something and started pulling. "First, help me get him inside." Naomi rushed over to offer assistance and realized Mr. McIntyre was trying to pull a man from the wagon. Her shoulders sagged when she realized the patient was Grady O'Banion.

"He's badly injured." Mr. McIntyre's tone was solemn. "Doc Cook said he's pretty broken up."

Naomi swallowed, recalling her last encounter with O'Banion, but this was certainly no time to dwell on grudges—she glanced up at Mr. McIntyre—grudges of any kind. Sucking in a resolute breath, she nodded. "All right, give me his legs. You take his shoulders."

As they worked to get O'Banion out of the wagon, McIntyre shouted orders at Rebecca and Daisy. "We need to turn the dining room into an infirmary. We need blankets, bandages, anything else Doc Cook tells you to get. He'll be along momentarily." He looked again at Naomi. "Let's put him in front of the fireplace."

"I'll move the tables out of the way," Rebecca told them, pulling Daisy along as she hurried back inside. "Daisy will get some blankets for him."

~~~

By midnight, a sixth victim had been brought to the hotel's make-shift infirmary. Four men were still missing. The casualties ranged from compound fractures to concussions to O'Banion's massive internal injuries.

As Naomi wiped the brow of a sleeping miner, Hannah slipped up quietly beside her. "You wouldn't believe who one of these patients is," she half-whispered.

Naomi stared into the sleeping face of her own patient, bloodied, bruised and swollen, and turned her head a little, just to let Hannah know she was listening.

"It's that Pinkerton man."

Naomi stiffened and met her sister's gaze. "What's he doing here?"

"I asked Mr. McIntyre that. He said he was going to make him our new marshal."

Naomi frowned and put her towel back in the water bowl on her lap. "The Pinkerton man?"

"Maybe he wants a tough law man to calm things down. But really I came to tell you that I'm going to go check on Billy. I'll be back quick as I can."

Naomi nodded. Out of the corner of her eye, she saw Dr. Cook step away from O'Banion and lightly clutch Mr. McIntyre's arm. The two leaned into each other, as if sharing secrets. Unintentionally, she overheard the doctor's sad diagnosis. "Broken to bits…bread crumbs . . . won't make it till morning."

They broke apart and Dr. Cook went back to checking on other patients. Mr. McIntyre left, presumably to determine the status of the search. Actively involved in the recovery effort, he had shown, to Naomi's surprise, great concern for the victims as they came in. Why was it, she wondered, that he cared so much for these men but had so little regard for his Flowers?

The thought struck Naomi as hypocritical and a heavy guilt washed over her. She glanced around the dim, fire lit room as Rebecca and Daisy tended to the miners, touched them reassuringly, held their hands, whispered comforting words in their ears. She herself had barely muttered two words to these men. Her gaze swung back to O'Banion, resting on a pallet less than two feet from the fireplace. Would he die there?

Silhouetted by the fire, she could see his chest rising and falling in labored, irregular movements. She didn't want him to die. No matter how much she disliked him, she didn't wish that on him, to pass away here, alone, most likely lost, with no one to mourn him.

Abruptly, Naomi took her bowl and rag, crossed the room and knelt beside O'Banion. She gently touched his brow with the cool, damp rag and wondered if she could bring herself to pray for him. His eyes opened and at first he merely stared off into space. Momentarily, though, his expression cleared and he looked at Naomi with gratitude in his eyes.

"Thank ye, ma'am," he whispered. "I'm no' worthy of yer attentions this night. Leave me to die. 'Tis what I deserve."

"Nonsense, Mr. O'Banion. You're a little banged up, but I'm sure you'll be fit as a fiddle soon."

The Irishman shook his head and grimaced at the pain the movement caused him. "No, ma'am. It's time to pay the fiddler."

Her hand froze as she realized he was speaking of all the sins in his life not discharged. "Mr. O'Banion, you needn't fear death." Afraid she sounded cavalier, she lowered her voice and spoke with sincere compassion. "There is one who has paid the debts for you, if you'll only accept him. May I . . . " A lump tightened Naomi's throat and she swallowed to force it away. "May I pray with you?"

Afraid she might do this wrong, Naomi didn't wait for a reply but timidly took Mr. O'Banion's hand and held it to her chest. She spoke tenderly to him, telling him of the love of a Savior and the debt he came to pay. O'Banion listened quietly but attentively and nodded in understanding at the end.

As Naomi bent her head to pray for him, she watched a single tear, glistening in the firelight, slide from the corner of his eye. Before it reached his sideburn, Mr. O'Banion took his last breath. His eyes glazed over and she knew he was gone. Fighting a sob that threatened to rip lose from her, Naomi squeezed his hand tighter and prayed anyway.

~~~

## Twenty-Nine

The avalanche had been an early one. It didn't bode well for the rest of the season, McIntyre thought as he watched Willie Sackett toss another shovel of dirt out of the grave and splatter it across the snow. Any later in the year, and the ground would have been too frozen for O'Banion's body. That was one of the drawbacks to spring in the Rockies: it often started out with funerals.

"I think that's got it, Mr. McIntyre," Sackett announced, clawing his way out of the grave.

"Yes, that's fine. Go down and tell Doc we're ready."

As a frigid wind whipped his coat and reached its icy hand around his neck, McIntyre wondered again what Naomi had said to O'Banion. He'd watched them for a few minutes from the doorway and had decided Naomi wasn't reading him the riot act.

Instead, it had looked as if she was speaking kindly to him. O'Banion's breathing had smoothed out and he had seemed almost *peaceful*. Then, to McIntyre's amazement, she had slumped over the man and sobbed for him as if her own father had passed away. Admittedly more than a little curious, he had thought to ask her about the conversation. However, the look in her eyes when he had approached her made this December wind feel absolutely balmy and he had backed off.

McIntyre heard a noise behind him and turned. He was astounded to see Naomi making her way up the hill to the cemetery, scrambling clumsily through the deep snow. Knowing he was a glutton for punishment, he met her half way and offered his hand. "Allow me. It is exceedingly deep up here."

A flash of disdain crossed her face, almost instantly replaced by a mere stony expression. "Thank you."

As the two worked their way through the knee-deep snow, McIntyre felt he had to try again. He needed to understand how she could go from a complete contempt for O'Banion to mourning the man's death. "I was wondering, Mrs. Miller, about your last conversation with our Mr. O'Banion. . ."

"What about it?" She sounded weary, or worse, indifferent to him.

"Well, I would be lying if I said I wasn't astonished to see you here. And I saw you crying over him last night."

They trudged on in silence for another minute, but he could see she was working on an answer. Finally, she said, "I didn't want to be a hypocrite . . . " Somehow, he knew that was aimed at him. "But even more," she continued softly, "I didn't want him to die lost and alone."

Done with him, she pushed away and found a spot at the edge of the grave. He wanted to ponder her response, but the sound of voices in a small funeral procession drew his attention to the bottom of the hill. Four miners carried one lone pine coffin over a narrow, hurriedly cleared path. Dr. Cook and Wade trailed behind, coats and scarves flapping in the biting wind.

In a town of over seven hundred and fifty people, only four neighbors had shown up to send O'Banion off. Today, he would be buried and forgotten—McIntyre looked over at Naomi, staring into the empty grave—except by her. Unbidden, a cold melancholy settled into his bones. Was this to be his legacy as well? A handful of mourners? A lonely grave site on the side of a windswept mountain?

His heart started racing as he realized, like Ebenezer Scrooge, he was actually seeing a foreshadowing of his own death. And to know that Naomi might *not* weep for him troubled him deeply. He resolved at that moment to somehow change his future...

~~~

On Christmas Day, as the girls, along with Ian and Emilio, had opened presents, then sat down to a feast fit for a king, Naomi pondered the direction her mind kept wandering. She slipped so effortlessly from reminiscing about John and remembering last Christmas to wondering what Mr. McIntyre might be doing with this most special of days. Since none of the Flowers had accepted Daisy's invitation to join them, she wondered if they were keeping him company? Were they exchanging gifts of some sort? What exactly did saloon girls do with a day off ? Would he do anything special for them?

Irritated at how she kept coming back to him, she turned her mind to wondering about the avalanche and its victims. After O'Banion's death, the patients in the makeshift infirmary had only stayed another few days. Those feeling better and able to walk had recruited comrades to help them dig their cabins out of the snow. One patient, a Silas Biggs, had been moved to Doc's cabin for tending of a viciously snapped femur.

Though these men had all gone in separate directions, the one thing they had in common was the simple fact that they were happy to be alive. On their departure, they had each thanked the girls profusely for the nursing and wished them a Merry Christmas. Even the Pinkerton-agent-turned-marshal Pender Beckwith had said a curt thank you as he limped out, arm in a sling, headed off to a cabin given him by Mr. McIntyre. These men had left Naomi with the sense that she had turned a corner with the citizens of Defiance.

In light of that, she couldn't help but wonder if her argument to *not* invite Mr. McIntyre for Christmas had been a mistake. Because of Naomi's passionate argument, everyone had acquiesced, though Ian had said he would visit him for a spell. Besides, if the Flowers did come, having Mr. McIntyre here would make it an awkward Christmas. Or so she had reasoned, but Naomi wondered if she was still being a hypocrite.

Confused and waffling between anger and compassion, Naomi was haunted by his last words to her in Daisy's room. He had said he was sorry for the kind of man he was. If he had been invited, would he have come? And if he had, would the Flowers have also joined them? Had he kept them from coming or were they just too uncomfortable to celebrate Christmas with the sisters?

Frustrated by her jumbled thoughts, Naomi let out a long sigh and Daisy, sitting closest to her, touched her on the shoulder. "The Flowers still might show. I told them anytime around–"

At exactly that moment, the front door opened slowly and Lily, Iris, and Jasmine tentatively filed in to the lobby of the hotel.


Daisy couldn't believe the Flowers from the Iron Horse had come for Christmas dinner. For an instant, everyone at the table was too stunned to react. Then, in one accord, they jumped to their feet like a fire brigade and all but ran to the women. They greeted them at the door with handshakes and a flurry of "Thank you for coming," "It's so nice to see you," and "Merry Christmas." Daisy gave them all hugs, evoking shocked looks from the guests.

Then Ian, ever the gentleman, offered to take their coats. Apprehensive glances fluttered among Lily, Iris and Jasmine. Reluctantly, Lily slowly removed her cape and handed it to him. She was wearing a low-cut plum dress, a bit tattered and faded, but Daisy knew it was the best–and most modest–in her collection.

Seeing her embarrassment, Naomi responded a little too eagerly. "That's a lovely dress."

Lily didn't thank her for the compliment; she merely nodded. That broke the tension at least and Iris and Jasmine then slid out of their coats, handing them to Ian. Their dresses were no more modest but the perceived judgment of their fashion choices had been removed.

"Rebecca . . . " Naomi pulled her sister away from the group. "Why don't you and I bus the table to make room for our guests?"

Rebecca called over her shoulder to the Flowers, "We'll be ready in just a moment."

With their departure, the conversation lagged a bit in the

lobby as the girls took in their surroundings. Daisy garnered especially long, studious looks. She beamed at them, feeling as though she could walk on air. Fresh-faced and wearing a buttoned-up-to-her chin red plaid dress courtesy of Hannah, she knew she bore very little resemblance to the battered and bruised girl they had seen carried from the saloon. Nor was she the frail, tortured soul Rose used to verbally abuse for sheer amusement. Daisy had been re-born and knew her hope shined forth.

"You look, um . . . " Lily struggled for the right word, but settled on, "well. Very well."

"I am restored," Daisy gushed, delighted that they had come.

A baby's hungry cry from upstairs interrupted her and Hannah apologized. "Oh, I'm sorry, there's my little one and he's looking for supper. Please excuse me. We'll be down as soon as we can."

"We really are glad that you're here." She left the group and dashed up the stairs.

Ian excused himself as well. "Let me see what I can do help clear the table. Pardon me, ladies."

When he was out of earshot, Iris stepped closer to Daisy. "Why do you want us here? We haven't been nice to you or them."

"We invited you because we all want you to see how different your lives can be. You're not trapped in the Iron Horse. I'll help you. They'll help you."

Lily looked highly skeptical of that statement. "Why would they care about us?"

Daisy knew the question was easy to answer with her heart, but more difficult to nail down with words. "Will you come and eat with us? Enjoy the day then I'll try to answer that."

She seated the Flowers at the table, Ian pulling chairs out for each of them as if they were eating at Delmonico's in New York. Rebecca and Naomi reheated the food and served everything as warm and fresh as possible. They waited on the girls hand and foot, anticipating their needs and treating them like royalty.

Once settled, the sisters joined them, delicately inquiring about their histories, asking how long each girl had been in Defiance, where their hometowns were, did they have family somewhere? Gradually, the conversation thawed the icy atmosphere. When Hannah rejoined them with little Billy, there were plenty of maternal oohs and aaahs, and Iris even asked if she could hold him. The baby, dressed in a festive red velvet suit like a little elf, liked her immediately. Smiling and cooing innocently, he delighted in tangling his hands through those inviting strands of red curls. Iris held him close, talking sweetly and indulgently.

Daisy watched the interaction between Flower and baby and was amazed at this tender side of the ornery redhead. Iris studied the baby's face longingly, stroked his little pug nose, softly blew air in his face and grinned at the startled but curious reaction. After a moment, the peaceful look on the prostitute's face changed to a more melancholy one. "Did Rose guess right? Is this boy a bast—illegitimate?"

The question froze everyone like an arctic wind.

"Left me high and dry," Hannah half-joked, her humor not quite masking the pain. "Promised me the moon, then took off like a shot when I gave him the news." There was no bitterness in her voice, just the sound of acceptance.

"That's just like a man." Lily stabbed her turkey a little too hard and her fork clinked on her plate. "Do most of their thinkin' with everything but their brains."

"Now ladies," Ian held up his hands, surrendering to their superior numbers, "in defense of my fellow twits, I must point out that we're no' all like that."

"Most of you are, though," Jasmine argued in her stoic, Asian way. "I will agree you are the most gentlemanly gentleman I have ever met, but you, Mr. Donoghue, are the exception. Generally speaking, men are the same brand the world over."

"Aye, that may be true, but there are a few pearls amongst the swine. Nothin' says ye must choose the rule. Instead, find the exception."

Daisy knew the unspoken thought that went through the Flowers' minds was that based on their profession, they could not expect better. She begged to differ. "You asked me why we care about you. I'll tell you. We know a man who loves us for our souls, not our bodies. He is a king and we are his daughters. When I read how willing he was to forgive me and then what he did to prove how much he loved me, it changed everything: the way I saw myself, the way I saw the future, the way I wanted to live every day. I'll never go back to any place like the Iron Horse Saloon. I have the faith to know I don't have to."

~~~

While his Flowers were, he was sure, having the gospel preached to them, McIntyre passed the holiday engaged in business. Defiance was going to change. For better or worse, it was going to change. To that end, he had spent the day in his room writing several letters and telegrams to friends and acquaintances. There was too much gold, too much timber, too much opportunity for a man in search of a vision not to see the potential in Defiance.

While this had been his plan all along, now there was an added sense of urgency to his goal. As he composed, he thought about the money he stood to make, but he had now come to appreciate the legacy of it. He wanted to build Defiance into a sophisticated, successful municipality and have his name remembered with respect and dignity, especially by certain parties.

Of course, this business plan meant the women and the whiskey had to go. It would be a leap of faith. What if he failed and Defiance turned out to be nothing but another dirty, seedy, mining eyesore? Or worse, a ghost town?

It didn't matter. He had a gift. He could lose everything today, start over tomorrow and be rich again in less than a year.

*While Ian becomes the beloved patriarch of three beautiful, loving, tight-knit sisters,* he thought sourly.

Frustrated, he poured himself a shot of brandy and went to his window. The snow was coming down at a lazy pace and Defiance could have passed for a Courier and Ives Christmas card. He could see the inn at the end of town, the windows casting a warm, amber glow on the empty street. Taking a sip, he wondered what they were doing in there. Were all his Flowers going to come back dressed in white with halos floating above their heads? Perhaps he should convert the saloon into a church and keep the Flowers just to pass the collection plate.

The thought made him smile wryly, but the truth was, shutting it down would show the Denver and Rio Grande he was serious about taking the town in a new direction. It would make her Highness happy as well. Not that he cared. Besides, he doubted anything would get him back into her good graces. That was most likely moral high ground he would never see.

More light spilled on to the street and his girls drifted out of the inn and headed up the boardwalk. They walked slowly, somberly, not as if they were unhappy, but more like they were lost in thought. He could see they were carrying items, gifts perhaps.

Gifts? Well, the little missionaries had thought of everything.

To his surprise, when the girls entered the saloon, they came straight to his room and delivered leftovers to him. "From the sisters." Lily held a lunch pail out to him. In her other arm, she clutched a small package.

He took the bucket and Iris and Jasmine set theirs down on his desk. They hesitated, as if they wanted to say something, but apparently couldn't find their voice or nerves. After an awkward moment, they nodded to him and left.

As Iris shut the door, she wished him a Merry Christmas.

Something in the tone of her voice left him staring at the closed door. She had sounded . . . well, sincere. McIntyre did not recall that one of his girls had ever wished him so much as a happy birthday, much less Merry Christmas. What had happened down at that hotel?

Curiosity getting the better of him, he set his drink down and stole down the hallway to stand outside Iris' room. As he had supposed, the Flowers had gathered there. He heard the chink of glasses and the sloshing sound of liquor being poured then bed springs creaking as Iris, most likely, took her seat.

"That was nice of them to give us those sachets," she observed. "They sure smell sweet."

"I'll tell you what smelled sweet..." McIntyre heard pure awe in Lily's voice. "That hotel. It smelled like my Mama's house back in Ohio, all filled up with the scent of cinnamon and nutmeg and a Christmas tree."

"I know, the Christmas tree was somethin'," Iris agreed.

"The Chinese don't celebrate Christmas." That was Jasmine. "I thought it was nice, though. Pleasant. We Asians pour so much formal ceremony into everything."

"Daisy sure looked different. Makes you wonder . . . " Lily faded off then added, "Oh, well, she never really belonged here anyway, but then, maybe none of us do."

"Then why are we still here?" Iris asked sounding irate.

"Because we have no place else to go." Jasmine, as usual, was the voice of jaded reality.

But Iris countered, "Maybe we do."

"Do you think they meant it?" Lily asked. "That we could stay there until . . . "

"Until what?" Jasmine sounded as if she was talking to starry-eyed children deserving of pity. "We learn to cook or sew? Pick up some new skill? Open a Chinese laundry?"

"It would be a start." Iris must have shifted as the bed springs squeaked again. "If we worked in a hotel or a kitchen, it would be a way to distance ourselves from what we're doing now."

"And just what do you think Mr. McIntyre would do?" Jasmine seemed to love playing the spoiler. "Smile and wave as we walk out the door?"

"Frankly, I don't think he'd notice." Lily observed casually. "He aint' been the same since the belles rolled into town. Somethins' caught in his craw about'em."

"I think it is the middle one—Naomi," Jasmine ventured, sounding confident with her guess. "From what I gather, she looks down her nose at him and I don't think Mr. McIntyre likes it."

Iris giggled. "Maybe 'cause he likes her."

"I don't know, could be I guess." Lily agreed thoughtfully. "He sure put tracks up Rose's backside for messin' with 'em. And he has seemed sort of bored with things here lately. Be just like a man to go sniffin' after a woman who wouldn't give him the time of day . . . but she didn't act like that towards us and she must know we were the ones who put the gum in her hair."

"She did treat us well," Iris agreed, sounding surprised. "It was the first purely sociable meal I've had in years. They never once treated us like sportin' gals."

"Maybe Daisy, uh—" Lily corrected the name, "I mean, Mollie. Maybe Mollie is right about how we see ourselves. She kept tellin' us that Jesus sees us as daughters of the King. Maybe we count for more than we think. Maybe we do matter to someone."

"Just because folks say our kind is trash doesn't mean it's so," Iris agreed. "There are a lot of losers in Defiance, who says we have to be part of 'em?

"If God thinks we're beautiful," Lily pondered, "maybe we are?"

McIntyre took a step away from the door, deciding he had heard enough. He wasn't sure what he had learned, exactly, other than perhaps the seeds of discontent and hope had been planted in the remaining Flowers' hearts. He wouldn't be surprised if tomorrow Naomi showed up at his door holding a staff and yelling, "Let my people go!" He almost chuckled at the image but didn't because it was entirely possible.

Yearning for something to fill an unexpected sense of loneliness—even emptiness—plaguing him, he decided a walk down the snowy street might lift his mood. Change was coming to Defiance, he could feel it. In the Christmas dusk, he sensed it.

She had asked him to choose a better life.

Kicking at snow as he ambled down the boardwalk, he wondered what it would take to change that distant look in her eyes to something better . . . to say, love? If he cleaned up the town, if he cleaned up his own life, would that melt the ice in her heart? And when the time came, would she weep for him at his funeral?

~~~

## Thirty

During the first week of February, a mule train managed to make it the rest of the way up from Animas City, the first in nearly five weeks. The men from the mule train were the first official guests of the Trinity Inn. It had taken them eight days to make the fifty-mile trek from Silverton. Averaging only about seven and-a-half miles a day in good weather but deep snow, the effort had sucked the life out of them. The six men were bone-tired, cold and hungry. Though the hotel was weeks away from opening, there was not a chance the sisters would have turned them away.

As Hannah checked them in at the hotel desk, little Billy wiggling on her hip, Naomi stood at the top of the stairs and marveled over the human peculiarity of perseverance. Life in Defiance was hard, the weather unforgiving and the people lawless.

But this place proved a person's mettle.

Everyone from gritty, weathered mountain men to gentle, petite mothers like Hannah discovered an inner strength folks back in Cary would never know. Naomi was astonished to realize she felt a little pride over the hardy souls surviving here, herself included.

And without Mr. McIntyre, the town might not have been settled at all. Perhaps he was the hardiest soul of all. He had certainly proven one thing: he did not need the sisters or their food. The man hadn't set foot in the place since Naomi had raked him over the coals and she hadn't seen him since O'Banion's funeral. Her suggestion that he look for a better life had apparently fallen on deaf ears. Plainly, Mr. McIntyre didn't need or want her friendship.

Fine. Besides, according to Ian, he was working on something important and that was filling his days. Whether he was truly busy and/or avoiding her, so be it. That meant she didn't have to worry about bumping into him at the store or waiting on him in the restaurant. She didn't need his irreverent talk. She didn't need to hear "your ladyship," or "your highness." She certainly didn't miss that arrogant grin of his. Naomi was just fine without him. Absolutely, perfectly fine.

~~~

Hannah cooed and snuggled little Billy as she slowly descended the stairs. She was making the turn on the landing when Lily, Jasmine and Iris sauntered in for dinner. Dressed in feathers and finery, this was the first time since Christmas that the Flowers had come by.

"Ladies, what a pleasant surprise."

"We're here to celebrate, Miss Hannah," Iris told her shrugging off her coat. Nodding at Hannah and the baby, the other girls excitedly followed suit.

Readjusting Billy to her other hip, Hannah motioned toward the dining area. "Well then, let me give you our finest table. I can't wait to hear your news…if you'll be sharing it?"

Heads high, shoulders squared, the girls giggled and sniggered and followed Hannah over to a table. The men at the surrounding tables, including those from the mule train, stopped in mid-bite, holding forks in the air as the girls strolled on by.

Naomi and Daisy acknowledged the Flowers with obvious delight as they delivered food to the waiting, staring customers. "I'll be right with you girls," Naomi told them, setting down food for some gentlemen.

Hannah stopped at the table closest to the kitchen and leaned toward the group. "Do you girls mind if I join you for dinner? I need to feed Billy."

"Oh, do you mind if I do it?" Iris reached for the boy. "I haven't fed a baby in years."

Hannah caught the quick flash of sadness in the woman's face and wondered about Iris' past. "Of course. He just started on cereal so he's pretty messy, but I would appreciate the break."

Finally, after several minutes of watching these surprising patrons settle in, moon over the baby, and order their food, one man sitting nearby attempted to investigate. Wiping catsup out of his beard, he leaned back in his chair. "What's the occasion, girls? Are you settin' up shop here at the inn?"

"Can we get better rates than at the Iron Horse?" another asked laughing.

"The beds are softer here anyway," a man from the mule train chimed in, drawing a furious stare from Naomi.

"And all this time those belles have been slappin' our hands if we reached for the bread too fast." The first man cut his eyes over to Daisy. "I guess Defiance must've brought'em round to our way of thinkin'."

Naomi, approaching the table with a tray of glasses and a pitcher of tea, sucked in a breath to set the record straight, but Iris beat her to it. "For your information, Harvey Cramer, you dirty, worthless, walking clump of cow dung, we're celebratin' quittin' the business altogether. Mr. McIntyre's closin' the saloon."

Harvey dropped his jaw and his fork, as did most of the men, and Naomi looked like she almost dropped the tray she was carrying.

"You're joking," Hannah squeaked in shock.

Hands a little unsteady, Naomi placed the glasses and tea on the Flowers' table. "What brought all this about? Is Mr. McIntyre leaving town?"

Hannah was struck by the expression on her sister's face. Naomi was shocked, but there was something else there as well. Dread? Fear?

Iris, still holding Billy, took a swig of tea before explaining, "No. He said he is moving past selling whiskey and women. He wants to be *respectable*."

"And," Jasmine stuck her nose in the air in mock snobbery, "he's making rich women of us." Abruptly, she lowered her voice so only Hannah and Naomi and the other girls at the table could hear. "He's giving us *one thousand* dollars to start over with."

"He's going to give Daisy, I mean Mollie, a thousand dollars, too," Iris added softly, sliding a spoonful of porridge into Little Billy's gaping mouth. "It's almost like he's turned over a new leaf. I wouldn't have believed if it hadn't happened to me."

Hannah had to fight back tears at the news. Crying with joy was becoming a habit in Defiance. "Does Mollie know?" she asked awestruck.

"Nope." Lily shook her head from side to side, looking pleased with their secret. "We wanted to surprise her."

Hannah locked eyes with Naomi and grinned. She wanted to say something, but there were just no words to express her joy over this miracle. And to think God had used her and her sisters in some small way to bring these things about.

Naomi grinned, too. "Mollie's not your server, but I'll switch with her. Congratulations, girls."


*One thousand dollars?* Daisy blinked and said it out loud. "One thousand dollars?"

Lily quickly snatched a chair from the adjacent table just in time to catch Daisy as she collapsed into it.

Every woman at the table pressed fingers to their lips and heartily shushed her. "We do not think the entire town needs to know about that," Jasmine scolded.

Little Billy began to fuss and Hannah took him from Iris, thanking her for feeding him. "He was so good for you." She sat back down and bounced him gently on her knee, trying to work a burp out of the child. "Do you have plans, any of you? Do you know where you want to go?"

Dreamy expressions settled on the Flowers' faces. "We are going to stay until the first spring stage," Jasmine explained, "but just to serve and run the games. Then I am going to go to San Francisco. I think I will buy a house and a business of some sort. I might even buy stock in the railroad."

Impressed nods greeted her apparently well-thought out

plans.

"I used to could sew when I was about twelve or thereabouts," Iris volunteered. "I'd like to pick that up again and maybe open a nice, proper dress shop, somewhere in Texas. It's a big state; I think I could reinvent myself there."

"I just want to go home." Lily plopped her elbows on the table and rested her chin in her hands. "My momma had a farm just outside Dayton. I haven't written her in years, I don't even know if she's still alive. But that's where I'm gonna start."

Daisy had never heard such longing in anyone's voice and she nodded, feeling that pain, that emptiness. "Me too. I want to see my momma even if she doesn't want to see me. I just want to know she's all right."

Hannah clutched Daisy's hand. "Well, you've all been given a second chance, praise God. I pray you'll use it wisely and be abundantly blessed."

~~~

For days after the news of the saloon closing, Naomi wrestled with why she couldn't get Mr. McIntyre out of her head. Guilt-ridden, she acknowledged that with each passing day she was thinking less and less about John and more and more about the saloon owner. The confession flustered her and she angrily tossed a pillow to the head of the bed she was making.

He was the last man on earth she should give any thought to. Besides, it had been over *two months* since she'd seen him. A person had to work pretty hard to avoid another person in a town this size. Clearly, he was done with the sisters...with her. She snatched the coverlet tight and smacked at a rebellious wrinkle. Huffing with frustration, she whipped a rag from her apron as if she was unsheathing a sword and attacked the dust on the posts.

"Naomi, what is wrong with you?" Rebecca's voice from the doorway startled her. "You're not cleaning, you're doing battle."

Naomi froze, suddenly aware she *had* been working with a vengeance. Embarrassed, she laughed nervously and shook her head. "I just have some things on my mind."

The sympathetic look in Rebecca's eyes urged her to share her thoughts. Overwhelmed, Naomi gave in to the need to talk to someone and hung her head. "After Mollie was beaten up, I had some harsh words with Mr. McIntyre, Rebecca. I blamed him for that and everything that's wrong in this town. Now he's gone and shut down the saloon. Why would he do that?" Her shoulders slumped, misery and confusion weighing her down. "I've said awful things and acted so coldly to him." She looked up then, ashamed of herself. "He spent Christmas alone. No one should be alone on Christmas." She twisted her head from side to side in frustration. "I'm all jumbled up inside. I wrestle with why I don't think of John as much anymore. But Mr. McIntyre . . . it seems I think of him too much."

Rebecca folded her arms slowly, evaluating things. "You have always been so hard on yourself, Naomi. You think you haven't grieved long enough for John; that's part of this, isn't it? I think you think if you have any compassion for Mr. McIntyre that you're somehow betraying John and that's just not true." Rebecca leaned on the doorpost and sighed. "Time is passing and you are healing. You'll never forget John...but focus on the love and not his absence. Life goes on.

"As for Mr. McIntyre, he's a very likable fellow in spite of his misguided morals. I agree that you've shown him a lot of anger but very little grace." She shrugged. "Being haughty isn't very Christian."

Chaffing under Rebecca's gentle, but honest, scrutiny, Naomi rubbed her neck and sat down on the bed. Why were she and Mr. McIntyre as compatible as oil and water? Naomi wondered if she was afraid of making friends with him because it stepped on the relationship she'd had with John. Or was Rebecca right and she just thought she was too good to share the love of God with such an accomplished sinner? Was it all of the above or was there something else here entirely?

"Look, Naomi," Rebecca moved to sit beside her on the bed, "God loves Mr. McIntyre just like he loves the rest of us. Showing him some compassion, some kindness doesn't make you unfaithful to John." Rebecca draped her arm over Naomi's shoulders. "And it doesn't mean you approve of Mr. McIntyre's lifestyle. He is lost and I think he is hurting, but I also think God is moving in his life; otherwise he wouldn't be shutting down the saloon." She hugged her sister for encouragement then squeezed her shoulder affectionately. "Pray about it…about him."

After Rebecca left, Naomi sat on the bed a long while pondering her sister's sage advice and wondering just why it was that she had such turmoil in her heart. She knelt right there beside the bed and prayed for clarity.

By and by what came through was that she did owe Mr. McIntyre an apology. Oh, she had to wrestle with God over that. After all, she argued, it was Mr. McIntyre who employed the prostitutes like Daisy, supplied the liquor to the customers, and then paraded the girls in front of them. But it was also true that Mollie and her customer had made their own choices.

As a sinner, Mr. McIntyre was just as in need of seeing the extended hand of Jesus as the Flowers or anyone else in this town. Salvation, the Lord reminded her, was not about giving a man what he deserved. It was about the grace of God. She had availed herself of that grace many times. Why was Mr. McIntyre less worthy?

He wasn't, she acknowledged. And she determined to apologize at the earliest opportunity, though her stomach felt queasy at the thought. Seeking forgiveness had never been Naomi's strength and she doubted he would be gracious.

But there was still something between her and God. Left unspoken but there and hiding, like a secret sitting at the bottom of a dark pond. Finally, in a painful moment of surrender, she dredged it up.

It was her wayward heart.

*God, how can I have even the slightest feelings for Mr.*

*McIntyre when my husband has been gone so short a time? Please guard my heart from him. I am . . . drawn to him and it grieves me. I can't love him—not him. Especially not him. Oh, Lord,* she begged, *especially not him . . .*

*I know that Satan is just using him somehow to divert my attention from you. I'm grieving and I'm lonely, that's all.*

Naomi grabbed on to the idea as if it were a lifeline. *Satan is just toying with my heart because I am vulnerable. That's it; she was sure of it.* The idea, accepted as fact, helped her regain some focus.

*Mr. McIntyre is a lost soul in need of salvation, just like Mollie, just like anyone in this town who doesn't know you. Use me to reach him, Lord, but help me keep my heart out of it.*

Much to Naomi's dismay, a Scripture leaped to mind: *If I speak in the tongues of men and of angels, but have not love, I am only a resounding gong or a clanging cymbal.*

The message was clear; guarding her heart would prevent God from using her. It was all or nothing.

*Father, Your word says you are a husband to the husbandless. Please help me keep my eyes, and my heart, focused on you and I'll do the best I can to show Mr. McIntyre Jesus in me. Just don't let me fall . . . please don't let me fall.*

~~~

Sunday morning, the cobbled-together family gathered for their makeshift church service. Naomi stood at the serving counter and poured cups full of coffee as Ian and Emilio pulled chairs together near the dining room's fireplace. Hannah gingerly tucked a sleeping baby into his crib, picked up a cup of the fragrant coffee and took a seat next to her boy. Lately, Ian had been playing a more active part in leading the discussion and they were all impressed at his knowledge of the scriptures. The more they studied, though, the more they agreed on how much of a blessing a true pastor would be.

Naomi settled in between her sisters and laid her Bible in her lap. As Ian was about to lead them in prayer, the front door slowly squeaked open and the Flowers furtively drifted in like lost snowflakes. Overjoyed to see them, Naomi had to force what felt like a huge grin from her face so as not to embarrass their guests.

By way of explanation to the pleasantly shocked little congregation, Lily told them, "Ever since you got here, things have started changing for us. Rose is out of our hair. Dais—er, Mollie's got Jesus." She and Iris and Jasmine crept closer, clutching their coats. "We're rich women now with a future in front of us. Even Mr. McIntyre is different." She shrugged in surrender. "We started thinking maybe there could be something to your Jesus stories."

"Besides," Iris kicked in lightheartedly, "Dais—er, Mollie has been buggin' the stuffin' out of us to come one Sunday."

Laughing, and caught somewhere between shock and awe, the group stood. Daisy picked up her Bible and walked over to her friends. "I read something this morning and it made me think of you. From Psalms," she flipped to Psalm 126 and read with joy in her voice:

*"Our mouths were filled with laughter, our tongues with songs of joy. Then it was said among the nations, " 'the Lord has done great things for them.'"* She smiled up at her friends. "Great things, indeed."

~~~

## Thirty-One

Naomi tossed a log onto the fire, shoved it further in with the poker then sat down to absorb some of the heat. She had been warned repeatedly about the winters in Defiance, but the cold only bothered her when she stopped to think about it. Compared to everything they had been through thus far, the mean temperatures were only an annoyance, one that would not get the better of her. There were too many other things to occupy her mind.

Laughter from the kitchen interrupted her thoughts and she reexamined the stunning fact that they had just shared a church service with four former prostitutes. Prostitutes who were now helping fix Sunday dinner. If she and her sisters had stayed in Cary, in their nice comfortable little world, none of this would have happened. Naomi found it mind-boggling and quite humbling what God could do if you let him. That was the trick, though, you had to let him. Like now, for example. She could sit here, watching the pine burn down to coals, or she could put one foot in front of the other and go see Mr. McIntyre.

Naomi trekked quickly down the empty boardwalk, feeling a little bit nervous and a little bit nauseous. She wasn't actually sure if the Iron Horse itself was closed yet, but she assumed it was not open for business on Sundays. She needed to see him and offer this apology, but the gap between thinking about a thing and actually doing it was like stepping off a cliff. There was a moment of no return and she was in the middle of it.

*One foot in front of the other*, she told herself.

The "closed" sign was hanging in the door. Tentatively, she tried the knob. It turned freely and she entered the saloon. The quiet was tomb-like and astonishing, the same as that morning she had come to find the doctor. She listened for a moment and heard the rustle of paper coming from Mr. McIntyre's office. Taking a deep breath, she approached his door. It was cracked and she could see his right shoulder moving as if he was writing.

Gently, she rapped on the door then hesitantly pushed it open. When he saw her, he jumped to his feet obviously out of shock as much as etiquette. "Mrs. Miller, what a pleasant surprise."

She fidgeted nervously and didn't answer right away. She noticed he was dressed simply, wearing only a white silk shirt and brown pants, no fancy vest today, no perfectly tailored jacket, nor had he shaved and his beard was scruffy. He was the most casual looking she'd seen yet. Admittedly, she found him more appealing, less pretentious, this way.

"May I take your coat?" he asked.

"No, no thank you," she muttered, looking around the office.

Mr. McIntyre cocked his head to one side, a perplexed expression on his face. "Is everything all right? You seem rather nervous?"

*Rather* wasn't the word for it. His stare making her chafe, she darted glances at him. "We just finished with church. Lily, Jasmine and Iris came. It was nice."

"Yes, they told me they were going today." He motioned to the chair beside her as he sat down again. She did sit but on the edge of the chair so she could sprint for the door if the need arose.

"I had some very harsh words for you when Mollie was beaten." She stared at her hands in her lap and forced herself to keep talking. "I blamed you for what happened to her."

"To some extent I was to blame."

"But not completely, yet I chose to make you the target of my anger. I saw Mollie too much as an innocent victim and she wasn't. The man who did that to her I've hardly given any thought."

Acknowledging that she was meandering around the point, she swallowed, and looked him in the eye. "Look, it's the hardest thing in the world for me to apologize to someone. I suppose I'm not good at admitting when I'm wrong." She tried to read his face, but he hadn't moved a muscle. "I've let anger keep me from reaching out to you as a Christian should. I'm sorry for that." When he didn't offer a comment or change in his expression, she tried to explain further. "You should be just as welcome at our table as Mollie or the Flowers or anyone else in this town. I just find it more difficult to deal with you."

His eyebrows rose and he leaned slightly forward. "Why do you think that is?" He sounded honestly baffled by her observation.

His dark brown eyes boring into her, she dropped her gaze and fidgeted absently with her thumbnail. "I suppose it's mostly that my husband hasn't been gone long and I, I don't know, you're so different from him. You're so full of bravado and selfishness and he was such a good man–"

"And it's unfair that he's dead and I'm alive."

"No, that's not what I meant." Her retort was curt and she breathed to find her focus again. "I think I just need to care about you the way you are and–"

"Care about me," he mocked with a single raised brow.

"In a *Christian* way. You're not making this any easier."

"I'm not sure what *this* is."

"I just wanted to tell you that I'm sorry I'm so hard on you," she fumed, the pitch of her voice rising. "It just frustrates me to see the way you treat people and the way you're squandering your life away in this place. You're a born leader, you're smart, you're tough, you're handsome but you don't care about anyone but yourself."

A crooked smile worked its way across his lips. "I think I heard a few back-handed compliments in there somewhere."

Growling with frustration, she stood up and he stood with her. Well, this had gone exactly as she knew it would. The man didn't know how to be gracious. Still, she had to say her piece.

She took a calming breath and tried to finish. "If you were staying away because of the things I've said," she sighed heavily, miserably, "then don't, please. I told you once that we felt God led us here. I fear that when it comes to you I've been a poor witness." Finally, she risked a glance at him. Wetting her lips, she finished. "I'd like to start over. Obviously there is *some* good in you based on your recent actions." He smiled smugly at that, but she kept on explaining. "It's not up to me to pick and choose who I deign to share the gospel with. It shouldn't be like that . . . " His smile broadened, but there was no warmth in it. It made her feel stupid, as if she was missing something obvious. "Why are you looking at me that way?"

"Do you feel better? Have you eased your conscience?" he asked, rapping his knuckles on his desk.

Naomi's spine stiffened. "I don't understand."

"Your coming here today. You've confessed your sin of arrogance at not wanting to associate with a reprobate such as myself, but you're just going through the motions—like taking food to a sick man or visiting a lonely shut-in. It is the right thing to do but your heart is not in it. You don't really have any compassion for me. Or forgiveness."

"I didn't hear you ask for it," she shot back, unwilling to be chastised by the likes of him.

"I shouldn't have to, not if you truly understand the god you say you represent. Are you familiar with the scripture, *'If I speak in the tongues of men and of angels, but have not love I am only a resounding gong or a clanging cymbal'*?" Naomi felt her stomach roll and she swallowed nervously. "I'll take that as a yes," he dead-panned. "You can forgive prostitutes, your little sisters' indiscretion, Grady O'Banion, even God for taking your husband, but you can't find it in your heart to forgive me."

"Because you sin with such pride and boldness." She pointed an accusing finger at him. "You know exactly what you're doing. I've never seen a man use people with such calculated deliberation."

"And that makes me less worthy of forgiveness?"

After staring back at him defiantly for several seconds, she finally softened a bit, out of pure fatigue. Shaking her head, she looked up at the ceiling. "Back home, it was so much easier. Go to church on Sundays, say 'Amen' in the right places, and then have company for Sunday dinner. It was easy being a Believer when we didn't have to put our faith to the test day in and day out . . . " She met his gaze again. "Here it's a challenge every second to live what we believe. I feel like all I do is make mistakes." Her shoulders sagged with the admission. "Is that what you wanted hear?"

Slowly, Mr. McIntyre walked around his desk and stood before her, pushing through all her personal barriers to stand too close. Naomi had the irrational desire to run but her feet wouldn't move. His eyes pinned her to the spot. He raised his hands as if to touch her face, but dropped them to his sides.

"I'm closing the saloon. I retired the Flowers." He stepped even closer and his nearness made her feel astonishingly light-headed. "Ian and I are setting up a town government. I've invited investors to come look the area over for opportunities in mining, timber and ranching."

Fighting the sensation that she was drowning, Naomi managed an unsteady step backward. Gently, he grasped her hand and while he didn't draw her forward, she knew he wouldn't let her retreat further.

"I truly am endeavoring to make an honest living . . . to be a better man."

She tried to swallow the white-hot fear that had risen in her throat, tried to pull her hand away but her muscles wouldn't obey. Her heart was beating so fast, she was sure the pounding was audible.

"I haven't waited for a girl since I was fifteen. And then I only waited a week before I kissed her."

Naomi's eyes widened in terror at the mention of a kiss.

"Because of you I find myself revisiting assumptions I've made about my life, God . . . women. You have had an undeniable influence on Defiance." He caressed her hand gently with his thumb. "On me. I know your husband hasn't been gone even a year. I know that you and I seem to get along about as well as Lee and Sherman . . . but I was wondering," he lowered his voice and asked carefully, "if it's all an act. Is there the smallest possibility that you're afraid of me because you might actually . . . have feelings for me?"

Naomi was sure her heart had stopped. Everything else had. Her blood. Her brain. Time. All she could see were those mesmerizing brown eyes; all she could feel was the warmth of his hand covering hers.

But like a stick of dynamite, the reality of who he was, the kind of man he was, and the memory of her husband, it all blew up in her face. "No," she croaked, awed by how difficult it was to move away from him. Pure panic filled her veins. "No." It came out as a whimper, and she pulled her hand away. Shaking her head, she stepped back, unable to express anything other than a denial of his feelings . . . and hers. "I don't," and like a panicked rabbit, she bolted. She turned and ran from the saloon as if her life depended on getting out of there.

Only, the moment the door slammed shut behind her and the snow was crunching beneath her feet, she knew she had lied to him.

~~~

## Thirty-Two

Naomi raced back to the hotel, but then stood on the porch for a full five minutes trying to regain control of her emotions. She couldn't go in there with her cheeks blazing and her chest heaving. They would think she'd seen a ghost.

If only she could. The ghost of her dead husband, the memory of him, wasn't enough to keep her from losing her heart to a man who—well, it just made no sense, she fumed. How could she possibly love him!? A man who wouldn't give God the time of day if the Almighty walked right up and asked for it.

*Oh, Lord*, she cried out. *Please help me resist this foolish attraction. It makes no sense. No good can come of it. It's you and only you I want—*

"Naomi, what are you doing out here?" Hannah peeked through the cracked door.

Naomi quickly turned her face away, wiped off the embarrassing tears and tried to calm her racing heart. Her lack of a response, though, did not dissuade her little sister. Naomi heard the front door shut and Hannah persisted in her probing. "Talk to me. Maybe I can help."

Actually, Hannah was the last person Naomi wanted to confide in about man troubles. She was too young to understand her guilt and Naomi hadn't ever had kind words for Billy. Now here she was, attracted to basically the same kind of man. That was justice for you.

"I'd really rather not talk about it just yet, Hannah."

Hannah mulled that over for a minute then asked, "Is it something to do with Mr. McIntyre?" Naomi snapped her head around. Hannah nodded. "I noticed you disappeared after dinner today. Did you go see him?"

"I went to apologize for being so unforgiving of him." She shook her head in astonishment. "It just didn't turn out the way I thought it would."

"I've known there was something between you two ever

since that day you chopped wood out back. I didn't know what that something was, but it was there."

Miserable and getting cold, Naomi flopped down on a bench and hugged herself for warmth. "It's like he's quicksand or something. The harder I try to get away from him, the deeper I sink."

Hannah sat down beside her. "What happened?"

"He—he held my hand." Naomi swallowed hard. She would have sworn she could still feel the heat there. "Then he asked if I possibly had feelings for him."

Hannah's eyes saucered. "Good gravy, I guess that did take you by surprise. Although . . . " She faded off, piquing Naomi's curiosity.

"What?"

"I've heard things, especially from Mollie. In retrospect, I guess a definite pattern developed but no one was looking for it." She shook her head, as if trying to regroup her thoughts. "Not that long after we got here, he ended his relationship with Rose. He didn't fill the gap by visiting any of the other Flowers, either. In fact, they said he seemed rather bored with the whole saloon business. I know I'm young, Naomi, but if a man turns his world upside down for a woman, surely that means he loves her."

"He's not a Believer, Hannah," Naomi whispered mournfully. "How can I even consider him? Never mind the fact that I'm riddled with guilt for even thinking of another man." Naomi hung her head in despair. "I loved John with every breath I took. He was the best thing that ever happened to me in this life."

Hannah lowered her voice and framed her next question tenderly. "Have you considered the possibility that he was the second-best thing?"

"You mean after God." Naomi nodded, acknowledging the correction.

"No. I mean that you still have your whole life ahead of you. If Mr. McIntyre was to become a Christian, he could be an amazing man. And the two of you are so much alike."

"We're nothing alike."

"Says you," quipped Hannah. She snuggled up to her sister for warmth. "I let a man lead me astray instead of me leading him to the Lord–"

"You were young and immature in your faith."

"Exactly. And you're not. Especially after everything you've been through. If you were the tool God would use to lead Mr. McIntyre to Christ, would you surrender your heart?"

"That's not a fair question. I don't have to love him like that to lead him to the Lord."

"What if that *was* the sacrifice God required? You're holding back from God and holding back from Mr. McIntyre. You're making God qualify what he can and can't have of you. If Abraham didn't hold back his son, can you hold back your heart?"

Naomi searched Hannah's face for clarity. "What are you telling me to do? Pursue a relationship with a man who is not a Believer?"

"I don't think God brought you fifteen hundred miles so you could run from him."

Exasperation fogged Naomi's weary mind. She pressed the space between her eyes, warding off a headache, and prayed that Hannah would stop talking.

"Well, for what it's worth, Naomi, I'll tell you what I think." Hannah burrowed in even closer to her sister for warmth. "I think that God is going to use you to reach Mr. McIntyre. I think that Mr. McIntyre has the words 'Naomi's Destiny' stamped across his forehead. I can't explain why God didn't give you a socially respectable time to morn. Having all the answers isn't my job."

"No, apparently just having some of them is," Naomi quipped. "I hope you marry a pastor, Hannah. That way the pulpit will be in good hands when your husband is out of town."

~~~

McIntyre tore a biscuit in half and perused a month-old copy of the Rocky Mountain News. At his desk in the saloon, he was trying to focus on the news and a breakfast of semi-cold ham and eggs. While his eyes saw the words on the page, his mind wouldn't stop showing the image of Naomi fleeing from his office. The urge to chase after her, spin her around and take her in his arms had been maddeningly strong, but he had resisted. She had rejected him outright, but the battle he had witnessed behind her eyes gave him the audacity to hope. He reasoned that if it had been easy for her to say no, she wouldn't have bolted and he was oddly encouraged.

McIntyre questioned, though, how much more time this was going to take. He wasn't exactly used to being a monk and having such pure thoughts about a woman, such *honorable* thoughts. This was all strikingly new territory for him. He ran his hand through his hair and sighed deeply.

*Time*, he thought. *Just give her more time.* But it had been two weeks and neither of them had made a move–

Ian strolled in, tossed his hat on to a side table, sat down and waited. Without looking up from his newspaper, McIntyre commented blandly, "I believe you're putting on weight."

Grinning, Ian patted his small but arguably increasing belly. "Family life agrees with me."

While McIntyre was grateful for the interruption, he wasn't in the mood for his friend's annoyingly sunshiny attitude. The Scotsman had become downright exuberant since those women had hit town.

"Naomi told me she came by a few weeks ago and invited ye back in to our fold. Said she was sorry for treatin' ye so cruelly. A prideful woman, it's no' an easy thing for her to apologize, especially to a man like ye."

McIntyre slapped the newspaper, frustrated over what he wasn't exactly sure. "Just what does that mean? Why is it that your little family can accept unwed mothers, prostitutes and orphans but it is such a tall order to associate with me?"

Ian's eyes widened in response to the outburst. "It's no' that any of us think we shouldn't associate with ye, my friend." He softened his voice to a conciliatory tone. "And I apologize if I've played a part in givin' ye that impression. Unlike the others, though, ye've built an empire in defiance of God, if ye'll pardon the pun. By givin' yer life to God, ye stand to lose, and gain, the most. That makes ye harder to approach."

McIntyre mulled that over. "Just because I'd like to be included in your little circle doesn't mean that I'm suddenly going to start preaching salvation and feeding the poor."

"Aye, that's exactly what I'm sayin'." Ian moved to the edge of his seat. "Ye're the most resistant because ye don't think ye need God. Lily, Iris and Jasmine—little Chinese Jasmine who is completely unfamiliar with the concept of a Christian god—will come to know the Lord before ye do." While McIntyre considered that, Ian asked, "Tell me this, why now? Ye've wanted all along to make Defiance a better place to live but ye've dragged yer feet. What's put the fire in ye to get the wheels turnin' now?"

"Her." There. He had said it. Saying it aloud didn't make him feel any better but he hoped his friend might have something encouraging to say that would lessen the blow of her rejection. "I want to be a respectable man because I know that's the only way a woman like her would ever consider a man like me. Before, I wanted to build the town up into something so it could serve my interests. Now, I want Defiance to be something I give a part of myself to. She's the reason."

"The changes yer makin' are fine, noble ones, but they willna be enough for her. There's always goin' to be a man between ye."

"Yes, I know the husband. But with time—"

"No' the husband" Ian shook his head and gave McIntyre a look to be heeded. "Jesus Christ. From what I've learned about these girls, and Naomi in particular, they were close to Him before coming to Defiance, but now they're more dedicated than ever. Until ye at least try to understand her relationship with God, she'll keep her heart away from ye."

McIntyre laced his fingers together and rested his chin on his hands. "Why should that be an issue? If she came to know me—"

"She has the conviction of her faith, mon. She knows the Scriptures. A believer is no' to be wed to an unbeliever. It could corrupt, or weaken, her faith. To find your way to her heart, I suspect ye'll find the path goes through God first." As if he was suddenly in a hurry, Ian stood. "Put that in yer pipe and smoke it. And join us for dinner tomorrow night. We've not seen much of ye lately." As he turned to leave, however, he apparently felt impressed to offer one final thought. "Ye know, ye may think ye've made all these changes and are pursuing this path of yer own volition. I'm inclined to think, though, tha' the Lord has directed your steps. Ye don't need to believe in him for him to believe in ye."

~~~

# Thirty-Three

March first stunned everyone in Defiance by dawning like a fireball. The weather did a complete, but welcome, turnabout from the snow and ice of February. The sun burned away clouds and the temperature rocketed into the forties, melting ice and snow in a torrent of rivulets. The vast, empty blue sky shocked Naomi with its brilliance as she stepped outside to sweep the front porch. She was tempted to believe spring was just around the corner, but knew not to bet on it.

Soon the false spring would be a real one and wagon trains would trudge into Defiance with more regularity than the sporadic mule trains. In fact, she had just heard from a customer that the first stagecoach would attempt to make the Defiance and Silverton route by the first week in April. With its arrival, Lily, Jasmine and Iris would be saying good-bye to Defiance. She prayed the good-bye would be figurative as well as literal.

Working hard to sweep the stubborn snow and mud off the steps, Naomi guessed Daisy would go soon as well. She had told the sisters she was satisfied to stay here through the summer since they were paying her now. Naomi doubted, however, that she would make it that long. The pull to see her family was something she mentioned on a daily basis.

Naomi wondered about her own desire to see Mr. McIntyre. Straight out, undeniably, all guilt aside, she missed him.

Oh, it was not an easy thing to admit, but the truth stared at her as boldly as her reflection in a mirror. She wanted to see him, talk to him, fuss with him. She missed his arrogance and the way he called her Princess. She had apologized for her own arrogance, invited him to start coming around again...and then rejected him by running from his office like a frightened, petulant child. No wonder he hadn't shown his face at the inn.

Her humiliation driving her to desperation, Naomi had

discussed things with Ian. As she'd hoped, he had gone to see Mr. McIntyre and urged him to come to dinner. Would he, though? Had her reaction put an insurmountable wall between them? What if he did show up for dinner? What then?

She happened to glance up at that moment and was stunned to discover Rose watching her from across the street. Standing in front of the pharmacy, the woman glared at her with a palpable hate. The wind blew her ragged, red cloak open revealing a frightfully haggard and bony frame. Rose's face was gaunt and her skin pasty, but her sunken eyes carried an undeniable message. Clearly, the managerial role at the Broken Spoke was sucking the life out of her...but not the venom. Oddly, Naomi felt a flash of pity, but it was instantly replaced by a shot of fear. There was something more menacing in Rose's stare causing Naomi to back up a step.

She heard a voice whisper with great urgency, "Pray now." So strong was the feeling that she tightened her grip on the broom and murmured, "Lord, in the name of Jesus I just ask your protection on our home . . . " Staring into Rose's hate-filled face, she spoke louder. "My loved ones . . . and our friends. Keep us safe, Lord, please..." A group of several men on horseback trotted between her and Rose. When they passed, the woman was gone.

The incident chilled Naomi to the bone. She thought of Mr. McIntyre telling her to keep her gun close, but over the months she had let herself be lulled into a false sense of security. Haunted by the look in Rose's eyes, she took one last swipe at the porch and marched back inside. She followed voices to the kitchen and found Daisy and Hannah prepping food for dinner that night. Little Billy was sitting on the floor on a blanket, pillows tucked all around him.

"Well, look at you," Naomi squealed, dropping to her knees in front of him. "What a big boy, sitting up all by yourself!" Unable to resist his smiles and coos, she picked him up and hugged him, then peppered him with kisses. A determined protectiveness reared up in Naomi and she hugged Billy tighter. "Aunt Naomi sure loves her little man."

Rising to her feet, she danced and swayed with the babe over to the table where Hannah was slicing potatoes. "Have you seen Ian?" she asked her little sister. Naomi really wanted to discuss Rose with Mr. McIntyre, but Ian was the more comfortable choice.

Hannah shook her head. "Not in the last little bit."

"I heard him say he had to go see Mr. McIntyre," Daisy told her as she slid sliced carrots into a pot of boiling water. "Rebecca showed him a letter or a postcard that seemed to upset him."

Again, Naomi felt the flutter of fear. "Where is Rebecca?"

Hannah rolled her eyes innocently. "In her room, mooning over Ian—oh, I mean, writing in her journal."

Daisy chuckled. "She writes a lot these days."

"Yes." Naomi nodded, but she wasn't listening to the teasing. Absently shoving little Billy into his mother's arms, garnering a perplexed look from Hannah, she headed upstairs.


Rebecca was sitting at her desk, a half-written page in front of her, but obviously her mind had wandered. Naomi found her staring blankly at the page, pen poised to write but frozen in midair.

"Did we get some mail that upset Ian?"

Rebecca jumped at the interruption, clutching her chest in fear. "Goodness, you gave me a start." She shrugged then answered the question hesitantly. "Well, we got a note; it was with our mail. It did seem to disturb him, but he said he didn't want to explain why just yet."

"What did it say?"

"Here," she rifled through a mess of letters and statements on her desk and produced the note. "It's addressed to you but Ian said I should wait before I gave it to you. He wanted to talk to Mr. McIntyre first. He wouldn't tell me why." She handed her sister the note. "Perhaps I shouldn't have kept it from you, but Ian was emphatic. What's going on? Why would someone send you a note with nothing on it but three crosses?"

In sloppy, rushed handwriting, someone had written Naomi Miller on the outside of the note. Naomi opened it and stared at three crudely scribbled crosses. There was nothing else on the page or on the back of it. Naomi had told her sisters about Rose attacking Diamond Lil, but not what she had done to her. The omission had been a mistake.

"When Rose attacked Lil . . . she also carved three crosses on her chest."

Rebecca cringed. "You think that's from Rose? Are you in danger?"

Naomi was far less worried about herself than the others, especially little Billy. "I think she's just trying to rattle us... but I also think it wouldn't hurt to gather for prayer tonight."

~~~

Mr. McIntyre came for dinner near closing time when the restaurant was down to a handful of quiet customers. Naomi was bussing a table when he wandered in and settled at a corner table. Her heart leaped at the sight of him. Handsome as ever, he wore a dapper black suit and red silk vest. His raven hair was still wet and the ends curled up slightly over his collar. She knew he would smell of sweet tobacco and lilac water. Watching him made all those dark thoughts about Rose fly away.

She had been praying about him since their startling *talk* and Hannah's lecture. From her reaction to Mr. McIntyre now, Naomi knew it was time to step off this cliff. She prayed for wisdom, then left the tray on the table and approached him.

"It's good to see you, Mr. McIntyre." She clasped her hands in front of her, trying to show a humble and repentant attitude.

"Is it?" He leaned back in his chair and shared a smug look with her. "Are you sure you wouldn't rather run out the back door?"

He had a right to be sarcastic after her panicked departure last time. Knowing he was protecting a bruised ego, she straightened her shoulders and eyed him defiantly. "I'm through running."

~~~

McIntyre watched Naomi walk away as he held his face perfectly still. When she disappeared into the kitchen, he let out a breath. *I'm through running?* Could her meaning be as clear as it seemed? The turnabout was unexpected and almost alarming.

Ian joined McIntyre, warmly slapping him on the back. "It's good to see ye, lad." He settled across from him and grinned. "We've missed yer rapier wit."

Before the two even had their napkins in their laps, Naomi delivered the meals to the table. She smiled at both of them, but held McIntyre's gaze the longest. Both men noticed, but neither understood it.

When she was gone, Ian scratched his head, clearly puzzled. "I've this feelin' the two of ye have turned a corner somehow. It does my spirit good."

"Something has changed." And he was dying to find out what.

He and Ian ate the food while it was hot and enjoyed the lofty discussion of building the future Defiance. Eventually, however, McIntyre pulled a note from his breast pocket. "So, have you told her about mine?"

"As we discussed, I started to. But then I wasna sure what purpose it would serve."

McIntyre had suggested Ian tell Naomi so she wouldn't think Rose was after only her and her sisters. If the notes were a threat, it seemed to be aimed at all of them. But perhaps Ian was right. If there wasn't a compelling reason to tell her—

"Did you get one, too?" Naomi spied the note as she approached their table. She took it from McIntyre and studied the drawing. The art was virtually the same. "Do you think it's from Rose?"

"Yes. She may not mean anything by it, but be watchful." A picture of Diamond Lil with bandages over her eyes flashed through his mind. The thought of something like that happening to Naomi twisted his guts and he berated himself for the hundredth time for having let Rose stay around.

Naomi handed the note back to him. "We're going to have prayer tonight when the restaurant closes. If you could stay, I'd like to talk to you afterwards."

"I'll either stay or come back." He was curious about her invitation but not enough to sit through a prayer meeting.

She nodded. "Can I get you gentlemen anything else?"

They were fine. Perfect, in fact, McIntyre thought, pleased that at least there was something happening in this strange, strained relationship.

~~~

After the restaurant closed, and the cleaning was finished, the sisters, Daisy, Emilio and Ian gathered in a tight circle in the kitchen. Mr. McIntyre had made his excuses, but said he would return. In a way, Naomi was relieved. His absence left her free to focus on her worries over Rose. As they reached for each other's hands, Naomi looked into the eyes of her family.

"When Rose left the Iron Horse, I was initially under the impression she had settled things with us, so to speak. I didn't tell all of you that she nearly clawed Lil's eyes out, but she also carved three crosses on her chest."

Puzzled and frightened looks made their way around the circle, though Ian appeared the most somber. Emilio's jaw tightened with the announcement.

"Today I received a note with three crosses drawn on it," Naomi continued. "Nothing else. No message. No signature. I learned this evening that Mr. McIntyre also received one. He's convinced these notes are from Rose. I think he also believes they're veiled threats."

Emilio hung his head and groaned. "I'm sorry," he

whispered. "I'm so sorry. I knew she would not leave us alone. I should've killed her when I had the chance."

Hannah and Daisy, flanking the boy, quickly moved to comfort him. Daisy squeezed his hand and Hannah shook her head in disagreement. "No, no." She put her arm around him. "Don't say things like that. We'll be all right. Rose can't do anything to us."

Clutching Naomi's hand with her left and Ian's with her right, Rebecca raised their hands. "We're going to pray, Emilio. Our God is more powerful than the darkness surrounding your sister. She's not going to hurt anyone here."

"She's not going to hurt *anyone* we care about," Naomi added, thinking of someone who wasn't in the room, but needed these prayers just the same. They bowed their heads and Naomi, ever ready for a fight, lifted up the first battle cry. "Father, we know that you are King of Kings and Lord of Lords. We know that your word says that we battle not with flesh and blood, but principalities and powers of the air. You have given us power and authority over the enemies of your kingdom and we claim, in the name of Jesus, that no one here will be harmed by Rose. We put on the full armor of God, Lord, so that we may stand against evil."

Her voice grew stronger as a feeling of protection settled over them. "In the name of Jesus, we bind the demons who would come against this family and remind you that you have no power here. We lift up our shield of faith and extinguish the flaming arrows of the enemy. In the name of Jesus, in the name of Jesus, you will not prevail against the children of the Most High God!"

~~~

From across the street, hidden deep in the shadows, Rose watched the hotel. For at least half an hour, her breath had swirled in the chilly night air and her hatred had grown exponentially. When McIntyre walked down the street and entered into that awful place of light, her head had nearly exploded with fury, but the voices bid her wait. And so she settled deeper into the darkness, pulling her cloak closer, listening to the sound of melting snow all around her.

The voices would tell her when the time was right. They promised her the children of the Holy One would die tonight and the Most High God would stand by silently as their blood ran. She need only be patient. Warmed by her hatred, she waited.

~~~

Feeling totally out of place at the thought of extemporaneous prayer and spiritual warfare, McIntyre had made his departure with the promise to return in an hour or so. A gentle, no, *peaceful* look in Naomi's eyes had brought him peace as well. He didn't know what she wanted to talk about, but he was eager to hear it. Of course, for all he knew, she may be preparing to tell him she was going to a convent.

Stepping out into the cold, a sudden feeling of unease wrapped its tentacles around him. Pretending to shake it off, he pulled his coat tighter and headed back to the saloon, thinking a drink might make the time pass a little faster . . . and ward off this sudden apprehension.

It was time to tell her about the letter.

The conviction came upon him strong and insistent. He dreaded it and knew whatever kind words she might have for him, they would dissipate like smoke with this news. Handing a woman a letter from her dead husband would certainly have to cause a reexamination of whatever future plans she was making. McIntyre was inexplicably and suddenly committed, however, and could only let the chips fall where they may.

~~~

Rose cursed under her breath, disappointed McIntyre was marching away from the hotel. She had hoped he could see the *gringas* die.

When he left her field of vision, she listened to his fading steps. She could not see the Iron Horse from her hiding place but knew that within seconds he would be inside. She was eager to cross the street and anxiously caressed the Colt .45 in her hand.

The dining room went dim and she smiled. Another half hour or so passed and lights flickered out one by one on the second floor as, she assumed, the sisters and their guests turned in for the night. Rose hugged the gun to her chest as she thought of the *gringas*, smugly content that they were warm and safe against the beast lurking outside. If Ian and the black-haired girl followed their pattern, they would be in the kitchen for a while yet. Rose would sneak upstairs, find the wiry sister and shoot her first, then the young girl and the baby, and then whoever else came across her path.

*Now*, the voices whispered urgently. *Now!*

Rose moved, started to slither out of her darkness, when she heard the hollow footsteps of boots. Whispering a curse, she drew back and saw McIntyre strolling his way back to the hotel. He went to the door, paused, then quietly slipped inside.

Blood pumping, heart pounding, the voices screamed at Rose to go. Peering out of the darkness again, she hurried across the street. Slogging through the deep spring mud, she stepped up onto the porch and peered through a window. McIntyre gazed over the batwing doors into the kitchen, hands clasped behind his back. What was he looking at?

The voices egged her on. Now was the time, they told her. *Go!*

Obediently, she cocked the six-shooter in her hand.


McIntyre stood quietly, mesmerized by the divine authority in the voices and the expressions of strength in their faces. It was a power he recognized instantly as holy and pure and all-mighty. Something was happening here, something with life and death implications. Instinct rose up in him.

They were preparing for battle.

"Hello, Mac," Rose whispered in his ear. The cold steel of a gun barrel pressed into the back of his head and he cursed himself for not having heard the door. "Let's go see your friends." He raised his hands and they took a step forward, but Rose grabbed his shoulder, stopping him. She listened intently to the prayers coming out of the kitchen in commanding tones. For a moment, he thought her resolve might be wavering. "What are they doing in there?"

McIntyre smiled grimly. "Praying."

And he offered up his own, hoping desperately God would hear the plea of a selfish, arrogant man. Rose shoved him forward, brutally ramming the barrel into his skull, and the two burst through the bat wing doors. The prayers died in astonishment when the group realized McIntyre was not alone. Their circle opened up so they could face Rose, Naomi moving to one end, Ian to the other. Rose propelled McIntyre towards Ian with another vicious nudge from the gun barrel and eyed the group triumphantly.

~~~

## Thirty-four

Naomi felt her body turn to glass, as if one move would shatter her. Rose had managed to trap them all together. She couldn't believe the horror of it. Shock threatened to seize up the wheels in her mind.

Rose waved her gun at Mr. McIntyre. "Slowly, my love, take your gun out…" Rage filled his eyes, but his face was expressionless. He eased his revolver out of its holster and held it up by two fingers, awaiting further instructions. "Very good. Put it on the ground and kick it over to me."

He hesitated then did as she asked. It slid across the floor stopping an equal distance between her and Naomi.

Rose's eyes quickly followed the gun's path then traveled on to Naomi. "Did you get my love note, little gringa?" Before Naomi could answer, Rose spotted Emilio. She flamed with outrage. "I heard you moved in with these witches? I should shoot you first!"

"No," Hannah cried, putting an arm in front of the boy.

A wicked smile burned across Rose's face. "Ah, maybe I should shoot you first and let him watch you die—"

"Rose," Mr. McIntyre barked, drawing her attention. "What do you want?"

Rose looked taken aback, as if she couldn't believe the stupidity of the question. "I want you to die. I might have let you live if you hadn't come back here tonight, but that was your choice." She shrugged. "So be it."

"Rose, there are eight of us." Naomi spoke, white-hot fear practically choking her. "There's no way you can kill us all."

"She's right." Mr. McIntyre pointed at the gun in Rose's hand. "Pull that trigger and the rest of us will take you down."

"Not before I take a few of you with me." She waved the gun over them, back and forth, meeting their eyes, tormenting them. "Little Daisy, you've made such good friends. Too bad they'll be the last ones you ever have." Her gaze shifted to Ian. "I am sorry that you're here, Mr. Donoghue. I always liked you. You were kind, all the time, kind."

"Why are ye doin' this, Rose?" Naomi heard desperation in Ian's voice. "These girls have done nothing' to ye."

"They changed everything!" Rose screamed, making the group jump. "It was finally perfect. Money, power, this town. I had it all just the way I wanted it here and Mac was so good to me." She looked at Mr. McIntyre and her face changed, softened. Then her eyes traveled back to Naomi and the sinister darkness returned. "They told me you *gringas* would come, but that my power was stronger than your god. Now look where we are. You're about to die and I will have Defiance."

"Rose, it's me you want." Attempting to bargain, Mr. McIntyre took a step forward. "Leave the others alone. Defiance is yours. If the Broken Spoke isn't enough, I'll give you the Iron Horse, the mine, everything. Just step in take over."

She waved the gun, forcing him back in line. "Oh, that's what I will do. I had hoped to have you by my side, darling, but it appears that will not be the case."

Naomi felt a vicious fear gnawing at her as Rose eyed them each one by one. A tear roll down Hannah's cheek and she knew she was thinking of her angel upstairs. Emilio, ever-so-subtly, reached out and squeezed her hand. Rebecca glanced across the half circle at Ian and he winked bravely at her. She smiled in a pained way. Daisy had eyes closed and was praying silently.

Trying to draw strength from the unspoken words, Naomi looked at Mr. McIntyre. He was waiting to meet her gaze. Time stopped and she would have sworn she felt God rest His hand reassuringly on her shoulder. Divine love formed a bond between her and Mr. McIntyre, establishing a path, cementing a plan. She understood the unmistakable message in his eyes when he glanced quickly at the gun on the floor. She felt the peace of this course in her soul. Mr. McIntyre gave her an almost imperceptible nod and it spoke more loudly than words…he would take the greatest risk of all.

In her mind, the room went absolutely silent and time slowed. Washed in the amber glow of the kitchen lamp, Mr. McIntyre lunged for the gun in Rose's hand. Naomi simultaneously dove for the gun on the floor. Before her body hit the wood, Rose squeezed the trigger.

Naomi heard the shot, heard her sisters scream. She wrapped her fingers around the ivory handle of the Colt and in one lightning swift move, raised the gun and fired. Rose shrieked like a demon in pain as the gun jumped out of her hand. It flew over their heads, landed on the kitchen table and skittered across it as Mr. McIntyre collapsed to the floor, clutching his chest.

Like hungry lions, Ian and Emilio leaped on Rose as Naomi scrambled over to Mr. McIntyre and gathered him into her arms. She could hear the two men scuffling with Rose as the woman cursed and raged vilely against heaven.

Naomi gently rolled Mr. McIntyre over and gasped over the spreading stain in his shirt. Stunned, she looked up at Rebecca.

"I'll get the doctor!" Her sister spun, already sprinting for the door.

Naomi cradled Mr. McIntyre in her lap and started praying, though she couldn't help thinking of the last time she'd held John. *Not him, too, Lord,* she begged, *surely not him too.*

Hannah and Daisy knelt beside Mr. McIntyre, laid their hands on him and commenced praying in soft whispers with the determination of well-trained soldiers. From behind them, Naomi heard a sharp smack and Rose's tirade ended abruptly. One of Naomi's tears fell on Mr. McIntyre's cheek and his eyes fluttered open. He looked into her face and smiled weakly.

"The gun . . . knew you could take her. I . . . prayed." His voice was barely a whisper and he struggled to speak, grimacing in pain with each word. He swallowed and tried to smile. "I . . . I told you . . . the West needs women . . . like you."

Tracing the thin line of that painfully perfect beard, she stared into his unfathomable, brown eyes and tried to smile. "You have no idea how miraculous a shot that was."

Flinching, he covered her hand with his and murmured weakly, "Made a Believer . . . out of me."

His meaning sank in and Naomi nearly fainted. Overcome with joy and relief and, finally, the freedom to love, she leaned down and kissed him softly. "Don't you dare die on me," she commanded gently.

Letting his eyes close, he shook his head weakly side to side. "If I do, the letter . . . my pocket . . . " His voice was growing faint and Naomi couldn't understand his disjointed sentence.

"What? What letter?"

"Was going to tell you . . . "

~~~

Naomi sat and waited by Mr. McIntyre for three days. He'd lost quite a bit of blood before Doc Cook was able to stop the bleeding then he'd had to operate to retrieve the bullet. A hair more to the left and it would have hit a lung. Mr. McIntyre survived the exquisitely dangerous operation only to have a fight with infection. They had all gathered and prayed over him daily; Naomi had wiped his brow, changed his bandage and whispered desperate pleas. She couldn't believe God might take him, too, but he was so pale, so ghostly, she feared he might slip away any second.

Finally, after three days, the danger passed. Naomi was with Mr. McIntyre when he awoke. He took in the unfamiliar surroundings of her room with a vexed expression. His eyes widened even more when he saw her. He tried to rise from his pillow and winced from pain. Moving more slowly, he eased back, touching the bandage across his chest. "Rose? Where is she?" His throat was dry and it came out as little more than a rasp.

"In jail." Beyond that simple answer she wasn't sure what she was going to say when he remembered something else.

He considered Rose for a second, then his eyes widened again. He looked at her with astonishment and his voice strengthened. "You kissed me." His expression fell. ". . . Or did I dream that?"

Naomi cheek's burned and that made her feel ridiculous. It also made it impossible to lie. He grinned with as much satisfaction as he could muster in his weakened state. His coal black beard against his pale skin did nothing to make the smile less devilish. "I've never kissed a woman with whom I wasn't on a first-name basis."

"I've never kissed a man I didn't marry," she shot back.

Mr. McIntyre cleared his throat nervously and tried to pull himself up in the bed. She fluffed the pillow behind him and quickly sat back down again, all too aware of the fact that he was bare from the waist up. Naomi had touched his chest and face often while he was unconscious, marveling over how different he was from John.

Yet, Mr. McIntyre was just as strong, in a lean, more lithesome way. She wanted to feel his arms around her again without the burden of fighting the attraction. Now that he was awake and staring at her, though, such thoughts set her butterflies to fluttering. Naomi loved John, but now she could admit she loved this man, too. If only he'd given her that letter sooner . . .

Mr. McIntyre laid his left hand over the bandage on his chest and gathered in a deep breath. "You can take it back—the kiss—and whatever was behind it. If there was anything behind it."

Hiding a smile, she poured him a glass of water from the pitcher next to his bed and held it out for him. "You think I go around just kissing whatever wounded man falls into my lap?" He didn't answer, but instead held her gaze. He took the glass from her and their fingers touched. They both felt the weight of this moment.

"I've never known a woman like you."

"I've never known a man like you." She moved to the bed. "Tell me, what happened that night. Between you and God. I have to know. You said you were a Believer and I took it to mean that you . . ."

He nodded. "We . . . came to an understanding." He took a sip of the water then handed it back to her. "I realized I would die to save you and in that moment, I understood what he did for us . . . and why." He shook his head, clearly bewildered by it all. "Love is an astonishing thing. It can drive a man to amazingly selfless acts."

Relieved, Naomi set the water down and took hold of his hand with both of hers. "It seems you've made a habit of saving my family." Mr. McIntyre frowned as if he had no clue about her reference. Naomi was shocked. "You had that letter for twelve years and never read it?"

"It wasn't addressed to me."

"Not even after you knew it was for me, you still didn't read it?"

"I could well imagine what his last words were to his sweetheart. I didn't need to read it."

Mr. McIntyre's level of respect for a fellow soldier moved her. This man held so much promise; if only she had seen it sooner. Based on where things now stood, Naomi felt it was appropriate to share the letter and she pulled it from her pocket. "I'd like to read it to you now." She unfolded it and glanced over the faint, shaky handwriting. She missed John so, but this letter was a sign clearly pointing the way to the future.

"My dearest Naomi," she read softly, "This war has claimed my body and heaven now claims my soul, but you will always own my heart.

"I thank God for the precious little time we had together, but I urge you to go on with your life. Do not pine for me, my love. Live the rest of your life with joy and laughter and keep your eyes lifted up to Heaven.

"A man named Charles McIntyre risked his life today to save mine," she glanced up quickly then to let him know she remembered his lie, "apparently in vain. I asked him to pass this along to you should the situation warrant. His selflessness was determined and heroic. He has my eternal gratitude and I didn't want him left an unsung hero." From the corner of her eye, Naomi could see Mr. McIntyre's expression was deeply somber. "Never forget me, Naomi, but live looking forward. I love you with all my heart and will see you again. Eternally yours, John."

Naomi carefully refolded the letter and slipped it back into her apron. "When I think of all the things that had to happen, that God allowed and then used to bring us to this moment, I am left speechless . . . and humbled." She swallowed, pushing forward with her confession. "I am so sorry for the time I wasted, judging you, holding you at bay." This time, her apology was real and came from deep within her heart. "Can you forgive me for being so proud and self-righteous? You are a far better man than I gave you credit for."

Mr. McIntyre held his breath and pushed himself up straighter in the bed. Then, leaning forward so that Naomi's world was filled with nothing but his gentle gaze, he drawled casually, "I agree that God went to a lot of trouble to bring you to me. I wouldn't want to disappoint him by throwing you back, Your Ladyship." They both grinned. A mischievous twinkle danced in his eyes. "Embrace your future, Naomi."

Biting her lip, she whispered humbly, "Yes, Charles." Amazed at how his name sounded like a prayer on her lips, she said it again. "Charles."

He stroked her cheek and searched her eyes. "I want you with me always, Naomi. Always."

"Always," she breathed, her heart galloping in her chest as he drew closer.

Their breath mingled and their lips touched. Her mind did not race back to John for comparison. Instead, it flew forward and she saw the promise of an unmapped, unforeseeable future designed by God—one without any arguments from her. As Charles pulled her into a long-awaited embrace and literally stole her breath, she knew God's plans for her were truly far better than anything she could ever create.

~~~~~~~

If you liked *A Lady in Defiance*, your review would be very much appreciated! Authors on Amazon live and die by those things! But more importantly, there is a crucial message in this book. Please share it, and His love, whenever you can.

And be sure to check out *In Time for Christmas – a Novella* if you would like to learn a little more about what happens to Naomi, Rebecca, and Hannah.

*Hearts in Defiance*, the sequel to *A Lady in Defiance* will be released in 2014. To be among the first to know, I hope you'll join me on my Facebook reader page. (And **DON'T MISS THE *SNEAK PEAK*** at the end of this book)! Come on over to http://www. facebook.com/#!/heatherfreyblanton. I Twitter, too! @ heatherfblanton! If you'd like to learn more about real-life feisty American women, then please join me on my blog: http://ladiesindefiance.com//.

And I really enjoy Skyping with book clubs, homeschool groups and Bible study groups. Email me directly at livingindefiance@yahoo.com to set up a chat! Thanks for reading! Blessings!

About the Author—

Heather started writing when she was five; her first tale was a ghost story that her mom typed up for her on a Brother typewriter. Over the years, she has worked as a journalist for newspapers, magazines, and blogs. She has also spent decades in the corporate communications field, marketing everything from software to motorcycles. (Did she really just say "decades"?)

*A Lady in Defiance* is inspired by true events and is set amongst what are now the ghost towns of the San Juan Mountains in Colorado. Back in '92, Heather spent a summer there camping, hiking and listening. The former residents whispered their stories to her across pine-scented valleys and crackling campfires and she has yet to forget them. Everyone should spend at least one night in a ghost town. .

Heather grew up on a steady diet of Bonanza, Gunsmoke, and John Wayne Westerns. Her most fond memories are of sitting next to her dad, munching on popcorn, and watching Lucas McCain unload that Winchester! She loves exploring out West and would happily spend all her time researching and combing through ghost towns till the cows come home.

Heather has two sisters whom she loves dearly. One is still with us. The other went home to be with Lord in 1999 and it is she who inspired the character of Hannah. Heather lives with her husband and two adventurous boys on a farm outside Raleigh, NC.

~~~~~~~~~

# MEN MAKE MISTAKES.
# GOD WILL FORGIVE THEM.
# WILL THEIR WOMEN?

Charles McIntyre built the lawless, godless mining town of Defiance practically with his bare hands ... and without any remorse for the lives he destroyed along the way. Then a glimpse of true love, both earthly and heavenly, changed him. The question is, how much? Naomi Miller is a beautiful, decent woman. She says she loves McIntyre, that God does, too, and the past is behind them. McIntyre struggles, though, to believe a man like he is can be redeemed. And the temptations in Defiance only reinforce his doubts.

Billy Page was a coward. He abandoned Hannah Frink when he discovered she was going to have his baby ... and now he can't live with himself. Or without her. Determined to prove his love, he leaves his family and fortune behind and makes his way to Defiance. Will Hannah take him back? Or is he one man too late?

HEATHER BLANTON

Men make mistakes.
God will forgive them.
Will their women?

HEARTS
IN
DEFIANCE

ROMANCE IN THE ROCKIES: BOOK TWO

One man needs to accept
God's forgiveness,
the other needs to find it.
But in Defiance, the past
doesn't go down
without a fight.

# One

Charles McIntyre sat down at his desk in his *saloon* and stared at his *Bible*.

He almost laughed out loud but in the silence, the sound would have been deafening. He knew plenty of people who would laugh. A former pimp, saloon owner, and gunman reading the Bible.

*Do you really think you're worthy to come before Him?*

The subtle rebuke pricked his soul. But he was determined and reached for the book. Naomi had said several times during his convalescence that all the answers to his questions would be found there. Rolling mental dice, since he didn't know exactly how to start, he opened the book and read the first words his eyes fell upon:

*Let thy fountain be blessed: and rejoice with the wife of thy youth.*

*Let her be as the loving hind and pleasant roe; let her breasts satisfy thee at all times.*

McIntyre's eyebrows shot up. That wasn't what he was expecting.

Intrigued, he read on.

*And be thou ravished always with her love.*

*And why wilt thou, my son, be ravished with a strange woman, and embrace the bosom of a stranger?*

He sat back and pondered the Scripture, chastised by it. He had spent a shameful number of nights embracing the bosoms of strangers, and it had never led to anything like what he felt for Naomi. Perhaps this was what God was trying to tell him. There would never be anything as passionate and pure in a man's life as loving and honoring the one woman whom God chooses for him.

That acknowledgement led him, unfortunately, to face a bigger issue.

*God, what is the matter with me? Why can't I give You my life as willingly as I gave Naomi my heart?*

He shifted in his seat, uncomfortable with the question. A man who had once preferred to rule in hell rather than serve in heaven, McIntyre admitted that making Jesus Lord of his *life*—well, that stirred up resistance in him.

Through his half-open door, he could see the length of his bar. Once full of rowdy, dirty, jostling miners, the place now was as empty and silent as Christ's tomb. No bawdy tunes pounded forth from the player piano. No siren call of female laughter tempted men into sin. No shady deals simmered in his brain, and he hadn't meted out any frontier *justice* in months. All of that was behind him. He was glad too.

But something was still missing.

Footfalls and a soft tap at his office door drew him back to the moment. Ian Donoghue slipped in, saluting him with his cane.

"Good morning, lad." The Scotsman tugged off his Balmoral bonnet, revealing a shock of unruly silver hair, and claimed the seat in front of McIntyre's desk. His deep blue eyes shone with amusement when he saw the book open before Charles. "Well, looks as though ye're starting your day off with the right priorities. I'm heartened to see it."

"It is ..." *Shocking? Unbelievable?*

"Aboot time." Ian chuckled and laid the cane and hat across his ever-growing midsection.

McIntyre smiled at his friend's burr and its contrast to his own Southern drawl.

"Of course, I knew all along ye'd come to your senses. No God," he shook his head, "no path to Naomi."

Almost offended, McIntyre picked up the black leatherbound book. "Do you think I'm doing this just for her?"

"No, no." Ian patted the air with his hands, defusing the tension. "That's not what I mean at all. Having that crazy Mexican wench blow a hole in yer shoulder would give any man his come-to-Jesus moment." He smiled at McIntyre like a father approving his son's behavior. "It was the way ye stepped in front of the bullet—for her, for love. I knew ye had it in ye."

293

McIntyre touched his aching shoulder, the sling still in place. "Don't remind me."

"Aye, lad, ye'd run from God a long time, but I saw ye slowing down. Naomi was yer—"

"Salvation." The word leapt out of its own accord, but it felt right. One glance at the grieving widow last July *had* started McIntyre down this path to becoming a better man. He'd closed the Iron Horse Saloon and Garden, retired all his lovely *Flowers*, and made an effort to recruit legitimate businesses for Defiance. He'd even hired a marshal. All in a vain attempt to get Naomi Miller to love him. Nothing had convinced her Charles McIntyre might be the man for her until Rose pulled the trigger on the .44.

He'd taken the bullet to save Naomi, not because he was a hero or because he was a noble man, but because he *loved* her. And for an instant, he'd seen the heart of God and understood that no sacrifice was too great to save the ones you love.

McIntyre's sacrifice had finally brought Naomi around. But it had also brought his wretched past into brutal clarity. "Ian, I have to tell her things about myself." His friend's face clouded with concern. "She has to know. I suppose, in reality, I never thought I'd actually win her. These past two weeks I've spent with her," Charles laid the Bible back down on the desk and evaluated their time together. "She nursed me, body and soul. She's tried to make me understand grace and forgiveness."

With infectious passion, she had attempted to make him believe his sins were washed away, that he was a new man, and the past was in the past.

Only it wasn't.

He blinked and returned his attention to Ian. "My past only weighs heavier upon me. She deserves more than me, Ian, and she deserves to know who I was."

Ian leaned forward. "Exactly. *Was*. Ye're not the man ye were." He spoke with firmness and conviction. "I saw ye changing the moment Naomi and her sisters rode into town.

I see no argument for parading all the skeletons from yer closet. They dinna matter anymore."

The skeletons that still had flesh on them might matter quite a bit. "There are *some* things I have to tell her. The passes are open, and the stages will start up again soon. I won't have her ambushed by the truth."

Understanding and regret dawned on Ian's face, and he nodded. "Aye, I suppose 'tis not so grand to be the cock o' the walk now, is it?"

~~~

Ghost towns, trains, historic sights, wonderful shopping, and the doorways to infinite adventures. In no particular order, here are some of my favorite places to visit when I'm in Colorado!

You've seen this train in countless Westerns. Now, come take a ride and see some of the most breath-taking scenery in Colorado! An awesome trek from Durango to Silverton!

And this is a fabuluous bookstore in Durango with lots of personality!

A great little bookstore in Telluride! And they have coffee!

I mention a few ghost towns in my books. See them for yourself with these guys!

There is more history in this area than you can shake a stick at. The San Juan Mountain Range and all these wonderful places to stop, shop, and hang out will make you fall in love with Colorado just like I did so many years ago. If you go, don't skip the ghost town tours, a must for any true Western fan.

17042473R00178

Made in the USA
San Bernardino, CA
28 November 2014